Broc pulled her onto his lap, fingers tangled through her hair, drawing her head back. She searched his face with an intensity that burned his flesh.

Her eyes, beautiful, golden, trusting, would haunt him for the rest of his days. "Lizbeth," he whispered, and intended to say more, but her fingers slipped between them to still his lips.

She couldn't know that her simple caress stole the last of his resistance.

He lowered his head and pressed his lips to hers, knowing he would never leave her behind.

BOOK YOUR PLACE ON OUR WEBSITE AND MAKE THE READING CONNECTION!

We've created a customized website just for our very special readers, where you can get the inside scoop on everything that's going on with Zebra, Pinnacle and Kensington books.

When you come online, you'll have the exciting opportunity to:

- View covers of upcoming books
- Read sample chapters
- Learn about our future publishing schedule (listed by publication month *and author*)
- Find out when your favorite authors will be visiting a city near you
- Search for and order backlist books from our online catalog
- Check out author bios and background information
- Send e-mail to your favorite authors
- Meet the Kensington staff online
- Join us in weekly chats with authors, readers and other guests
- Get writing guidelines
- AND MUCH MORE!

**Visit our website at
http://www.kensingtonbooks.com**

Her One Desire

Kimberly Killion

Enjoy
the Magic :)!
Kimberly
Killion

ZEBRA BOOKS
Kensington Publishing Corp.
www.kensingtonbooks.com

ZEBRA BOOKS are published by

Kensington Publishing Corp.
850 Third Avenue
New York, NY 10022

All Kensington titles, imprints, and distributed lines are available at special quantity discounts for bulk purchases for sales promotion, premiums, fund-raising, educational, or institutional use.

Special book excerpts or customized printings can also be created to fit specific needs. For details, write or phone the office of the Kensington Special Sales Manager: Attn. Special Sales Department. Kensington Publishing Corp., 850 Third Avenue, New York, NY 10022. Phone: 1-800-221-2647.

Zebra and the Z logo Reg. U.S. Pat. & TM Off.

ISBN-13: 978-1-4201-0442-4
ISBN-10: 1-4201-0442-X

First Printing: July 2008
10 9 8 7 6 5 4 3 2 1

Printed in the United States of America

For Tim:
You will always be the ace of hearts in my royal flush

Acknowledgments

As this is my first book, there are several people
I would like to thank:

For the ladies of MORWA, especially
Peggy, Judy, Julie, Melinda, Regan, Wendy, and Carol.
GO CORE!

Nancy Litzau, critique partner extraordinaire,
I'm glad your prediction came true.

The very informative ladies at
Hearts through History,
your support makes research enjoyable.

Chapter 1

London, Eastertide, 1483

Father must protect me or I am dead.

Lizbeth Ives stumbled off the last step of the stairwell in her haste and landed hard on her knees. The guards' footsteps echoed in the distance. She glanced over her shoulder. Dancing shadows brought the torch-lit stone walls to life and sent her already pounding heart into a frenzy.

Scrambling to her feet, Lizzy clutched the neck of her mantle, safeguarding the document hidden in the bodice of her gown, already envisioning her head atop the chopping block. Her throat burned with every step. The passageway seemed longer, narrower, darker than it had when she was a child. She rounded the corner, and a bout of dizziness set her off balance. Her eyelids pinched shut, if only for a moment, to ease her escalating fear. She swallowed hard, then inhaled the sour stench of the dungeon, a smell she would never grow accustomed to regardless of the years she'd spent in the Tower.

Two men, who'd guarded the dungeon since her childhood, straightened in front of the arched doorway as she approached. She forced her steps to a calm, even clip.

"Good den, Lady Ives." One guard dipped his head in greeting.

"Sirs." She acknowledged them with a quick bow. "I have need to speak with my father."

"He is at work," the taller replied. "Lord Ives will not be pleased with your interruption, m'lady."

"Then I will suffer his fury of my own will. Now step aside, and allow me entrance." The authority in her voice shocked her, but she had no time for niceties. Lord Hollister's blackguards would be upon her any moment.

"As ye wish." Each guard slid sideways, granting her access.

She entered the antechamber and set the bolt in place. A single rushlight illuminated the short passage before her.

Only ten more steps.

She clutched Mother's rosary, sliding her fingers over the glass beads to count her steps, until she reached the chamber door.

Crack.

The sound of Father's whip snapped in her ears and jarred her insides. Her fingers stilled over the door lever. She cursed her lack of bravery and wished for the thousandth time she'd been born to the smith or the miller. She wrapped her rosary around her wrist, shook out her hands, and then fisted them to cease their trembling.

Father would not pity a coward.

She summoned the courage to push open the heavy door. The sharp odor of burnt flesh singed her nostrils, sending her hand immediately to her face. She set the iron bar in its catch, then turned toward her father.

Her presence went without notice. Father wouldn't hear a tree if it fell behind him.

Crack.

He wielded his whip, delivering a blow that sliced into a man's back in a slash of crimson. "Confess and pledge fealty to the sovereign liege of England or die as a result of your obstinacy," Father demanded, his tone heinous, cold, cruel. She hated the person he portrayed beneath the black cloak.

"I confess naught." The prisoner's white-knuckled fists gripped the iron rings binding his shackles to the stone wall. Thick blue veins laced through his forearms, matching the color of an ancient symbol inked around his muscular arm above his elbow. Black hair clung to his nape by the sweat of his suffering. He did not cry out or plead for mercy, though the bold red lines painting his bronze skin told her he'd been in Father's company long enough to yield. Still, the fool held tight to his tongue.

She turned her head away from the scene only to fall upon a blood-soaked man crumpled in the corner. He bore a similar mark around his arm, indicating an affiliation between the two prisoners. Father's methods had obviously been more than he could withstand. The pallid color of his skin told her his blood had failed to flow some time ago.

The scrape of metal knifed up her spine as Father released the prisoner's manacles from the hooks in the wall. The large breath of relief he blew as he fell into a puddle at Father's boots came prematurely. She knew Father's routine—whipping preceded the burning. The man's crime would determine what followed.

She squared her shoulders. "Lord Ives." Her voice sounded small, weak, and she abhorred herself for fearing her father. She cleared her throat and clutched the tails of her sleeves, now a tangled mass in her hands. "Lord Ives," she called out louder. "I have need to speak with you."

Father whirled, his amber eyes filled with the light of madness. "Begone!"

He raised his whip to her, and she searched for a glimpse of the gentle man she once knew. Her heart jumped. She pushed the hood of her mantle back. "Nay, Father! 'Tis I, Lizzy." Holding her arm in front of her face, she braced herself for the biting sting, all the while praying he would not deliver the blow.

His grip on the knout eased the same time a raspy howl filled the chamber.

The prisoner reared up from the floor, all flesh and rigid muscles. With his fingers clasped into a giant fist, he drove the iron cuffs into Father's temple, knocking him sideways into a trestle table. Wood splintered like miniature arrows. Metal instruments clanked onto the floor. Father faltered but retained his footing.

"Nay!" She vaulted across the chamber and clung to the prisoner's forearm as his powerful fist caught Father in the nose. Osborn Ives was a big man indeed, but the force behind that blow knocked him off his feet and into the wall.

The impact sent a jolt through her breast.

Father staggered. The black whip slipped from his gloved hand and coiled into a ring like a dead serpent. The lump sliding down her throat mimicked her father's body withering to the floor along with her hope for protection. Desperation, hopelessness, and anger surged.

"Get away from him." She shoved the prisoner hard.

He grunted, but remained steadfast to his position. His fingers curled around her forearm. "Scream, and ye will cease to breathe."

"I will not. I vow it upon my soul." She struggled to break free of his bruising grip, her eyes fixed on the only person she had left in the world. "Please, he is my father."

The brute released her and made only a slight hesitation before going to the other prisoner. She dropped to her knees alongside her father and checked his breathing. The pulse in his neck flittered, but he remained unmoving. She feared Lord Hollister would see her head in the basket before Father awoke. In truth, that act would be preferred to the fate Lord Hollister planned for her. She would be no man's concubine. As the chief warder he might hold favor with the king's coun-

cil now, but once she exposed his association with the man
conspiring against the crown, she and Father would finally
be free of Lord Hollister's personal vendetta.

". . . May God sustain you, and the company of Heaven
enfold you, my brother," the prisoner whispered in Latin.

*In communion with all the faithful, may you dwell this day
in peace.* She couldn't prevent her mind from finishing the
familiar chant. She looked up. The prisoner reflected her
pose. His large hands cupped the dead man's face. Try as she
might to quell her sympathy, she knew the pain of losing
someone close and her heart ached for him.

A crash blasted and nearly sent her heart through her ribs.
Only seconds later, the chamber door shook within its frame.

"Open, by order of Lord Hollister." A shuffling of feet
accompanied the guard's order.

Her breath caught. She shook Father's shoulders. "Please
wake. You must help me." Tears she'd held back for years
dripped from her chin and splashed over his cheek.

The prisoner stood and swayed. His weight fell against the
wall. Hugging his midsection, he drew a deep breath, then
turned toward her. Piercing ice-blue eyes held her paralyzed.
No words passed between them, but the dire consequences
of their situation grew in volume.

Another bang at the door set them into motion.

She sprang to her feet.

The prisoner collected two daggers from the floor and
tucked them into the waistband of light-colored trews. He hesitated only long enough to snarl at her. "Where are the keys?"

She scoffed internally. The man was a fool if he thought
she would release his shackles and give him an advantage
over her. She had enough trouble of her own. She knew too
much and had to find protection. Lord Hollister was an adversary she could not fight alone.

"The keys, lass." The prisoner held out lightly fisted hands.

"You are a prisoner of the crown. I cannot help you."

His response came in the form of a glare and a snort, both of which she ignored. She rushed across the chamber and frantically dug her fingertips along the wall's seam. The secret door ground open, her passage into the darkened maze beneath the city. A burst of musty air brushed her face. The blackness promised freedom, but curse her coward's heart, she was terrified to enter. Three and twenty was far too old to fear the dark, yet she couldn't prevent the panic taking over her mind and body. Her breath came in tight gulps.

She reached for the wall torch as another crash splintered the door behind her.

"Go!" The prisoner pushed her into the narrow tunnel.

Her fingers fell short of retrieving the torch. The thick stone door sealed shut behind them, blinding her instantly. Her eyes widened, searching the pitch for the smallest existence of light. A pinhole. A slit. But the only source she found was the bright white explosion of terror behind her eyes.

Arms bent, she steadied herself between the walls closing in around her. In one sweeping motion, she was hauled up against the prisoner's chest. She sucked in an audible breath. A strong hand covered her mouth and trapped the scream inside her. Raising high up on her toes, she clawed at the forearm imprisoning her. *Oh, God, protect me.*

She had to get back on the other side of the wall.

Back to the light.

She couldn't breathe. Her legs wilted beneath her. A palm pressed flat against her stomach. The chain binding his manacles draped between her heaving breasts and pressed against the document that had brought her here—a document promising to endanger the crown, and now, her only hope of freedom.

"Cease your struggles." Broderick Maxwell held firm to the woman shaking like a freshly sheared sheep in the Highlands. She'd attacked him with a strong enough resolve in her efforts to protect the heinous man flogging him to death, but had since turned craven in his arms.

After a sennight in this louse-ridden dungeon, escape was finally within his reach. No mere slip of a woman would prevent him from returning to the borderlands. Unfortunately, he would return a failure. Damn! He and his brother had been so close to uncovering the leader of the rebellion plotting to seize England's crown. He could name a dozen nobles involved in that conspiracy, but had no proof of any of it for his king.

The wench dug her nails into his forearm. The action, at the very least, should have felt like thistle pricks, but like the rest of his flesh, he only registered a dull pressure. Broc leaned close to her ear. "If ye call out, I'll snap your wee neck. Do ye understand?"

She nodded beneath his hand.

"Do the guards have knowledge of this tunnel?"

Her head moved side to side against his chest and released a foreign scent that attacked his nose. Heady. Exotic. Unmistakably female. No doubt, she was the seraph the prisoners buzzed about. The one they called "the Angel of Fire." He'd thought them wowf. Mayhap plagued by fever as a result of torture. He wouldn't have given pause to the existence of such a creature until he'd witnessed the firelight dance in her golden eyes. He doubted they would weep for her if they knew their angel was Lady Ives, kin to the Lord High Executioner.

Turning his head, he tried to distance his nose from her hair. His efforts failed. Shifting his weight in the narrow space, he tuned his ear to the ruckus in the chamber. Deep voices droned behind the thick stone. Part of him wanted to retrieve Aiden's body for burial—the part seeking his mother's affection—but the warrior in him cast the fool's quest aside. As the oldest living son to the laird of Clan Maxwell, Broc's responsibilities now included keeping himself alive. The guilt he bore for desiring his brother's title now weighed as heavily on his conscience as his sisters' deaths.

The English minx swatted haphazardly at his head. He gave her a little shake to let her know he was in control. "Do ye know the way out?" Cautiously, he removed his hand from Lady Ives's mouth, fully prepared to stifle any sound that might arise from her.

"Eight steps forward, twenty-six to the right, seventeen around the—"

"Where does it lead?"

"To a door hidden behind the goldsmith, north of Cheapside," she whispered against his palm, sending a frisson of heat up his arm. His body hummed. What was wrong with him? Though confident Lady Ives was no angel, Broc remained neutral to the possibility of her being a sorceress.

"Lead the way." He gave her a nudge of encouragement, but her feet seemed fixed to the floor.

"I cannot. I must go back."

"I cannae allow ye to do that." He gave her another shove, after which she spun around in his arms, knocking his elbows against the sides of the tunnel. Her icy palms flattened against his bare chest. Another unusual tingle raised gooseflesh over his skin. She was definitely a witch.

"We must wait until they leave and then retrieve the torch."

Paying no heed to her suggestion, Broc moved forward. She stepped up on his toes and clung even tighter to his bruised ribs. "Ach, lassie! Think ye could ease your grip?" Only then did it occur to him that her fear didn't lie with him. She'd been as eager as he to rid herself from the chamber. Yet, now she seemed afflicted with a greater problem.

"I cannot make it through the tunnel," she insisted. Obvious panic altered her words in high and low pitches.

The woman pressed so tight against his chest he was certain she intended to walk through him to get back into the chamber. He raised his gaze over her head, but the abyss was as black as the devil's heart. "Are ye afraid of the dark?"

She nodded beneath his chin, and her alluring scent again assaulted him. *God's hooks!* As if he had the time to play protector to a cowering angel who smelled like a valley of flowers dipped in honey. A moment of weariness sent him swaying. A trickle of sweat rolled down his neck. He shivered.

She stilled in his arms, then inched back. A small hand pressed against his neck, then his jaw, his cheek. "You have little time. You must go before your body fails you."

Broc worried over her swift change in demeanor, and even more so over his body's reaction to her simple caress. "Explain."

"The whip was coated with a numbing tonic, so your flesh can bear the elements of torture."

"'Tis poison?"

"Nay. A product of mercy."

Broc snorted. "The executioner delivered twenty lashes upon my brother's back, then burned the flesh from his hands and feet without any regard for mercy. Think me a fool to believe he cares a nit about those he persecutes?"

"My father did not coat the whip. I did." Her head fell beneath his chin. "You will not feel the pain of your lashes until the moon is high, but within an hour's time your legs will struggle to carry your weight."

Broc had not spent the last six months befriending the damned English only to die and rot in the veins of London. "Then we have less time than I predicted." Raising his shackled hands over her head, he turned Lady Ives around and attempted to push her into the tunnel. Her velvet skirts brushed against his knees, and another wisp of her troublesome fragrance tickled his nose. She crawled between the space of his arm and side, and then clung sweetly to his backside.

He might not be able to feel his fingertips or the gashes in his back, but he definitely felt the executioner's daughter curved around his arse. He'd yearned for only one woman in all his twenty-nine years, but this English angel seemed to heat his blood with her scent alone.

It must be the poison.

Clearing the unwanted lust from his head with a shake, Broc began counting the initial eight steps. His toe jammed against a stone wall when he reached four. "Ach! I thought ye said eight steps forward."

"Eight small steps. I was a child when last I tallied."

A scuffling of claws plucked out to his right. He followed, stumbling through the pitch. He was certain to have more success following the vermin than placing trust in Lady Ives's directions.

"Fourteen, fifteen, sixteen . . ." Numbers rolled off her lips in whispered chaos. "Eight, nine, ten . . ." They came in sets of three, and no longer followed the count of her steps. Broc wondered briefly if she even knew how to count.

The tunnel came to a tee. The floor disappeared under his toe. "Which way?"

"To the right and down. You must walk through seepage before you go back up the other side. We are beneath the moat."

He started down slick steps and stopped. She was there. He could hear her breathing, but she was no longer attached to him. "Lady Ives, you are either going to lead or follow. Choose."

Soft footsteps walked slowly toward him. Her fingertips touched his elbow; then her arms curled around his with formidable strength. He dragged her into calf-deep water, her face buried in his shoulder. He continued forward, not knowing if her feet even aided her cause, and fumbled over the wet stone cautiously, searching for the way.

"'Tis a straightaway. At least thirty more steps. Make haste before I am ill."

He rolled his eyes in the darkness. That comment ruined

the image of a naked angel he'd been forming in his head. 'Twas for the best. He had no business picturing her naked anyway.

With one hand extended in front of him and one arm wrapped around her waist, Broc trudged through the seepage until he met an incline. Three steps led him out of the water. Lady Ives seemed to gather enough courage to stand, but didn't release his arm as they purged onward. He lost count of his steps, focused as he was on the sound of her erratic breathing. The lass was certain to swoon before they reached an exit. He might have offered her an encouraging word, if he thought it would have helped. Another damned wall stopped him. A muffled drumming beat in his ear. Mayhap his pulse? Mayhap hers? Then came a lute and viols. The sounds of festival broke through the hollowed silence.

"This way." A tug on his arm pulled him left.

Several more blind steps brought them to another barricade. He heard her pat the wall, searching for what he hoped might be the exit. Her numbers were replaced with whimpers, moans, and heavy breathing. All of which made his body tighten. Then the sound of grating stone filled his vision with speckled light. Tiny rays of gold filtered through a web of vines covering the opening, making him squint.

Lady Ives punched a fist through the greenery. Merriment exploded into their silence. Broc caught her arm before she dove through to the other side. "Wait. The city celebrates Eastertide. We will not go unnoticed. Lend me your mantle." He twisted her around to face him.

Her enchanting eyes studied him from beneath the ermine fir–trimmed hood. "You place my life in danger by asking for my assistance."

"I suspect your life is already in danger, Lady Ives. And I am not asking for your assistance, simply for an article of your clothing." He couldn't blend into the celebration half naked and beaten. He and Aiden had mingled with the aristocrats and the drunkards. Recognition was inevitable.

Lady Ives's head tilted, fine thin brows pinched together in thought. "If I am to aid you, I would know your crime first."

He could hardly tell her he was a spy seeking information to convince the King of Scotland to align with France. She waited for his answer, no doubt expecting a heinous crime, and no crime was more heinous than being a Scot in England. "I am Broderick Maxwell, heir of Lord Magnus Maxwell, Warden of the West Marches."

"You are a son of Scotland?"

"Aye." This information didn't seem to alarm her.

"Do you hold me responsible in any way for your brother's death?"

How many held her da's profession against her? Broc certainly couldn't hold Lady Ives responsible for Aiden's ill-timed desire to philander with an English skirt. Broc stepped forward. Instead of backing down, Lady Ives raised herself up to her full height, which was relatively tall for a woman. Her gold eyes demanded his honesty. "The executioner is guided by your country's nobles. His hand is not your own."

Her flawless skin smoothed over high cheekbones, and the force of the breath she blew cooled his chest.

Her fingers released the ties at her neck. The black mantle slipped from her head. Light from behind cast fire-red highlights through glossy sable hair, cascading in soft waves to her waist. The quality and daring cut of her fawn-colored gown bespoke of wealth, nobility—temptation. His hands fisted, pulling tight the chain binding his wrists. The woman was indeed one of God's finest creations. The monks at Dryburgh would be sorely disappointed in the wayward direction of his thoughts. They'd trained him well, yet he could not draw his eyes from this angel of fire.

"If I aid your escape out of the city," she began, pulling his attention from her bodice to her face, "and see to the mending of your wounds, would you offer me escort in return?"

"Escort?" he asked, unable to hide the mocking question in his tone. "You mean you seek my protection." He must be wowf for even considering a pact with this woman. Damn the devil himself for placing her in his path. Her wide eyes reeked of desperation and he couldn't help but wonder whom she ran from. What was he supposed to do? Leave her? Whoever hunted her would most likely turn her over to her da for punishment.

She lowered her lids, releasing him from the imprisonment of her eyes, and pulled the tails of her sleeves into her hands. "I seek sanctuary."

"Whom do ye need protecting from, Lady Ives? What crime have *you* committed?"

Her eyes opened to him, glistening with unshed tears. "I have had the misfortune of being born to the Reaper of the Realm."

She probably could have confessed to killing her king, and he still would have given her aid. He would undoubtedly regret his next words. "I will escort ye."

Her lips curved slightly at the corners, and a little flutter tickled his gut.

Why did he suddenly feel like he was betraying the fair Lady Juliana?

Chapter 2

Through multiple rays of light, Lizzy watched Lord Maxwell drape her mantle around his back and fumble with the ties at his neck. The tincture already overtook his fingers. "Allow me." She leaned in and relieved him of his task. The hairs at the hollow of his neck tickled the backs of her fingers. Her gaze went from the knot bobbing in his throat to his eyes to see if he'd seen her shudder.

He closed his eyes, drew a sharp breath, and then snapped his head side to side. He pushed past her without a word of gratitude and stepped toward the exit. The man behaved like a . . . well . . . a Scot. She must have experienced a moment of madness to ask a man of his breeding to offer her aid.

"Keep your head bowed. We'll go north up Watling Street toward the Skinners. With any luck, the majority of London will already be at the cathedral." He ripped through the laced vines in two passes and crawled through the opening.

Mayhap she shouldn't follow. Father could still save her. She looked back into the black tunnel. Her stomach fell to her toes.

"Lady Ives?"

She whipped back around to find Lord Maxwell's shackled hands awaiting her acceptance.

"We must make haste."

Nodding, she took his hands. His grip was strong, his palms calloused, hot. Her fingers naturally curled over his as she inched her way through the greenery. Tucking her chin to her chest as he'd ordered, she flanked herself to him and matched his stride. His size reminded her of Kamden—tall, and thickly built, a semblance of protection. 'Twas good to feel safe again, regardless of the false illusion by which she came to feel that way.

Her downward gaze shifted slightly from her steps to his. *Mercy Mary!* The man wore no boots. They were certain to attract attention. She twisted, checking for any pursuers. No guards followed. The numbers began in her head as she counted her steps, calming, soothing, easing her angst as she kept his pace over the cobbled stones of Watling Street. Staying close to the empty merchants' stalls, she peeked through her lashes at a few finely arrayed courtiers making their way toward St. Paul's church for High Mass.

A matron craned her neck; her steeple headdress fluttered in white wisps in her haste. Her children stared—an occurrence Lizzy had built an immunity to long ago.

Lord Maxwell led her to a black stallion ensconced in crimson velvet and braids of gold outside the priory. He released the reins, stroked the beast's neck, then mounted with a grunt and a grimace. Freeing his foot from the stirrup, he extended his hands.

"Is this your mount?" She realized the foolishness of her question as soon as the words left her mouth.

"Aye. I left the auld lad tethered whilst I took a sabbatical in your dungeon." As if the mockery in his tone wasn't enough to ridicule her, he raised an all-knowing black brow.

"I will not be part of stealing another man's horse. Especially one belonging to the royal guard." She pointed at the gold crest embroidered on the blanket.

"Think ye your father will cut off your hand before or after he is ordered to remove your head?"

She left his sarcastic question unanswered and scanned the street for the horse's owner. She would repent her sin when she reached Fountains Abbey in Yorkshire. She accepted Lord Maxwell's assistance and mounted in front of him. When he encircled her with his shackled hands, the heat surrounding her burned her like an open hearth. The man was afire with fever.

"Halt, by order of the king's guard!" An enraged voice came from the entrance to the priory.

Lizzy turned in time to see one of the king's guards drop a bundle of religious vestments and unsheathe his sword.

"Hold tight, Lady Ives." Lord Maxwell kicked the stallion into motion, slamming her against his chest. The guard's bellows dissipated behind them as every pummel of hooves brought them closer to escape.

A single raven followed overhead, reminding her of Father's wooden birds. Rows of gabled houses darkened the street with their height. Bells rang out, calling the city to its many churches. She crossed herself. *Fare thee well, Father.* She would do everything within her power to return and free Father from Lord Hollister's clutches. Now that Kamden and the boys were gone, London only promised a future laden with more nightmares.

They passed through the city's gates. The road split. The path to the right led to Edlynn's cottage and was thick with mire from recent rainfall. They could be hidden from view within seconds of entering the thicket.

She grabbed the reins. "I have need to make a stop before we set out of London."

"Nay. 'Tis no time." Lord Maxwell batted her hands away and redirected the stallion to the left, the road leading around London and back to the river Thames.

The rumble of horses escalated behind them. Both turned

to check the gated entrance to the city. She didn't know if Lord Hollister's men were upon them or the king's guard. She held no desire to be captured by either. "They will expect us to travel alongside the river. We cannot outrun them."

"Our odds would increase if ye would release the reins." His hands closed over hers. Their battle over the leather straps jerked the bit in the steed's mouth side to side, sending him into a nervous prance.

She fought to gain control of the horse, but even in Lord Maxwell's weakened state, his strength surpassed hers. She ripped her hands out from beneath his and twisted around to face him.

Foolish Scot.

She had enough men dictating her life. The last thing she needed was some Scottish lord trying to dominate her. His determined scowl didn't sway her, and time didn't allow her the luxury of argument. "You will go where I ask, or I will return of my own volition once you are immobilized." Her voice didn't even sound like her own. She had never made a demand in her life. She crossed her arms and inhaled a breath of liberation.

Lord Maxwell's lips tightened; his nostrils flared. "Where is it ye wish to go?"

"That way." She pointed to the right. "If I am to mend you properly, I need my herbs and supplies."

He jerked his head side to side, snapping his neck in two places; then a burst of hot air shot down over her cheeks. "Enjoy this victory, for I will not grant ye another." He kicked the steed northeast. "And rest assured, ye will regret threatening me, *angel.*"

She clenched her teeth and spun forward. He made a mockery of the only name she'd ever been proud of. "You would do well to never call me that again."

The Scots were a miserable lot; rude, foul, heathens to be certain. Everyone in England knew it. Why, then, was she not repulsed? Agitated, yes. The Scot had already proven himself arrogant, domineering, overbearing, but the last thought flitting through her head when the man curled one hand possessively around her waist bore no similarity to repulsion at all.

As they entered the forest, she honed in on the lessening sounds of the guards, desperately trying to rid herself of the unusual heat pooling low in her belly. She'd lived a life of scorn and ridicule and developed a skill for burying her emotions and hiding her desires. She could fight this unwanted attraction.

Broc leaned heavily against the angel's back and guided the stallion through the glen. Her enticing scent and the feel of her silken hair against his cheek were enough to drive a man half wowf. His hand slipped from her petite waist to rest atop her thigh. 'Twas a nicely shaped thigh or at least he visualized a nicely shaped thigh beneath all her skirts. He couldn't escape the vision of two soft, slightly muscular thighs wrapped around his waist, hooked at the ankles. It was a fantasy he'd had often enough, but the thighs had always belonged to Lady Juliana.

His hand flexed.

Lady Ives flinched and straightened.

Regardless of impropriety, he couldn't bring himself to remove his hand from her person. Truth was, he felt . . . giddy, his body light, his head even lighter. As if he'd spent an eve with his brethren sipping Uncle Ogilvy's whisky. He was fairly certain his tongue would turn to ash at any moment. When her poison wore away from his body, he was determined to give Lady Ives a sound thrashing for misdirecting their flight from the city.

His mind's eye teased him with the scene. The executioner's daughter bent over his knee, her rounded arse poised for punishment. Of course, she was naked. His palms itched. 'Twas only by the grace of God he'd lasted two years at the monastery. Fortunately, English women were loose with their favors, else he would be a walking erection. The one or two women he'd bedded on occasion had eased his needs, but there would be no more. He would return to the mindset Brother Mel had taught him in the monastery and be faithful to Lady Juliana.

So why was practicing celibacy the furthest thing from his mind?

Thankfully, a cottage came into view, giving him reprieve from his lewd thoughts. A three-legged dog ran circles around a single sheep grazing the barren ground. Gray smoke wafted from a thatched roof in desperate need of repair. Lady Ives dressed and spoke with the same tongue as England's nobility. This humble abode couldn't possibly be her place of residence.

With a great deal of effort, he yanked on the reins. Their stolen steed stopped in front of the cottage, throwing him impossibly closer to her softness. She raised his shackled hands over her head and slipped from the horse. Broc shivered from the loss of her warmth and nearly fell off behind her, but managed to hold himself upright. He despised weakness, and at the moment he felt as frail as a newborn kitten.

Lady Ives dipped a tin cup into a barrel of water and handed it to him. With his hands gripped around the cup, he swallowed the contents in one gulp. It wasn't near enough.

She hesitated in front of the horse and stroked the beast's muzzle. Her big eyes, filled with distrust, stared at Broc. "You will wait?"

"Aye." His answer came quicker than he intended. If he had any wit at all, he would leave and return to the borderland posthaste. A new life awaited him in Scotland. He would honor his brother's death by accepting Aiden's responsibilities. The chieftainship of Clan Maxwell would belong to Broc, as would his brother's betrothed—Lady Juliana.

"I will only be a moment." Lady Ives interrupted his thoughts and bent to kiss a black-faced sheep atop its nose.

Broc scanned the area for the remaining herd, but found only broken fence covered in brush. "Is this your home?"

"Of sorts." She disappeared into the cottage leaving the small door open behind her.

An invitation? Mayhap. One his curiosity didn't decline. Dismounting, he landed hard on his feet. The ground cooled his toes, and his shoulders suddenly felt burdened by ten stones. He refilled the cup three more times in the reservoir and drank until his gut swished. Certain he would be sick, he managed to draw enough saliva to spit the coppery taste from his mouth before he walked through the door.

"Lizzy, is that ye?"

"Aye, Edlynn," Lady Ives called out to an auld woman sitting at a trestle table. Her misshapen fingers worked a pestle grinding herbs into a mortar. A mantel filled with useless carvings of round, fat birds sat over a fire heating a cauldron of stew. The smell of cooked meat made his stomach gurgle. How long had it been since he'd eaten?

"What 'ave ye brought me? I smell blood." The woman turned, and only then did Broc notice the emptiness in her light gray eyes. She stood, holding close to the table's edge. "'Tis another rabbit?" She sniffed. "Are we eating it or mending it?"

Lady Ives's head popped up from the satchel she was stuffing. The brilliant pink coloring her cheeks drew a bit of welcomed humor from him. The angel saved animals from certain death as well. The executioner's daughter certainly contradicted her breeding.

"'Tis not a rabbit exactly." Lady Ives returned his smile with a fiery glare. "It more resembles a pig. I am tending to this one myself."

"Think yerself all grown up, do ye? Give me the count, child."

"Two around the table. Five straightaway to the door."

The auld woman Lady Ives called Edlynn mapped out the given steps until her fingers connected to his chest. *Ach!* She had bony fingers like Grandmum. "Good den, matron," Broc offered in what sounded loud even in his ears.

She jumped. "Merciful Moses! Ye brought me a man. Oh, bless ye, Lizzy." Edlynn raised her chin to him and smiled. Surprisingly, the auld woman still carried all her teeth. Her white hair cloaked her shoulders and the lines at her temples bespoke of a woman who often found laughter.

The woman's hands were suddenly everywhere; over his shoulders, his arms, his stomach. "Built like a bred stallion, is he? Where did ye find him?"

"Beneath Father's whip. He is a Scot," Lady Ives commented nonchalantly while searching the contents of a wooden bowl.

"No? A Scot in London?"

"From the West Marches on the border," Broc provided, feeling a bit uncomfortable with her inspection.

The woman's fingers ran south and curved over his groin. Her empty gray eyes widened.

Heat blazed through his face when his cock responded to the gesture. "God's hooks, matron!"

"'Tis good your father allowed him to keep his pillicock. He's hung like an Englishman."

Aghast, he pushed the woman's hands aside and scowled at Lady Ives. She brought her hand out of the bowl with a grin and practically bounced toward him.

"Edlynn, remove yourself from Lord Maxwell's person. You are being rude." With the turn of a key she must have found while the auld woman groped him, Lady Ives unlocked his shackles and released his bruised wrists from the iron.

"Thank ye," he said, grateful he wouldn't have to seek out a blacksmith.

Lady Ives smiled, lowered a fan of long dark lashes, then pivoted on her heel, leaving a trail of her exotic scent behind.

"What are we going to do with him?" The auld woman clung to his forearm.

"He is escorting us north. We haven't much time. I will explain on the way."

"Us?" The shared response came from both Broc and the auld woman.

"Nay!" Broc argued. "We haven't even a second horse to carry ye, let alone a blind woman."

"There is a horse out back. Edlynn is going with us. I cannot leave her here." Lady Ives plucked through the garments of a standing wardrobe as if the conversation was over.

"Lizzy, ye are talking foolishness." The auld woman voiced the exact words Broc thought. "That old nag is lame and should've been put down years ago. What ails you, child?"

"Edlynn, please. I've no time for your questions or your stubbornness. Gather your things." Lady Ives showed no sign of conceding.

Standing before him, she untied her mantle from his neck and replaced it with a man's hair shirt. The material felt like a feather against his tingling skin, reminding him of his own timely demise. He latched onto her wrists with what strength he still possessed. "We will be captured. I agreed to escort *you* out of London. That is all."

"She is going with us." She easily broke free of his hold, then walked to a cupboard and sifted through a heap of gold coins that no more belonged in this beggar's cottage than the noble Lady Ives.

Broc watched her in disbelief. Why was he even arguing with this headstrong English woman? She was obviously touched by madness if she believed she could escape the king's guard with a blind woman in tow on a lame horse. A stallion awaited his exit. All he had to do was mount and leave. He could be to Bedford by nightfall. He might have to tie himself to the horse to get there, but at least he would be that much farther away from London.

"Take it all, Lizzy." The auld woman found a place on a cuttie stool by the fire. "I have but to ask, and your father will tend me."

"Nay. I cannot leave you. You are in as much danger as I."

Broc had already turned in the doorway, but stilled, awaiting a reason to listen to her. He closed his eyes and wished the poison prevented him from feeling her eyes burning his back. Damn the English! "Tell me the truth of your danger."

"I have reason to believe the king's ill health is not due to a pox. He is being poisoned."

Broc whirled around. The action set him off balance. Could Lady Ives provide him with the very information he and his brother had failed to discover? "Have ye proof?"

"The tinctures Edlynn prepared for His Majesty have been tampered with. I found the empty flasks in Lord Hollister's chamber. The remnants smelled of wolfsbane. 'Tis poison. Edlynn will be accused of high treason and executed."

"Let them accuse me." Edlynn stirred the stew steaming in the kettle. "I'll sharpen your father's ax before laying my head upon the block and smile whilst he delivers the blow."

"Edlynn!" Lady Ives stood in the center of the cottage, her sleeves wadded between her hands.

She looked up at him, but he gathered enough wit to look away, else he might be convinced to drag the auld woman along. Lady Ives must be desperate to trust him, a Scottish spy. "Is there no one else who can help her?"

Her head shook, sending dark red tresses swaying. For a brief moment, Broc saw his sisters, Lilian and Mattie—contrary, innocent, too young to have died such a brutal death. He hadn't been able to protect them. Mayhap God was giving him the chance to redeem himself. "There is an inn about three hours from here just outside of Hertfordshire. I know the innkeeper. I will send him back to retrieve Edlynn and see to her safety." Broc dared a glance at Lady Ives to see if his offer might appease her.

"Vow it upon your soul."

"I vow it. I will send someone."

Lady Ives nodded, releasing a stream of tears over her cheeks. "I will hold you responsible should any harm come to her."

"Ye must go, child. Fret not over my well-being. Take care of her, m'lord. She has been in need of a protector since Kamden's passing."

Kamden? Broc's scowl weighed heavy on his face. Her husband? Her lover? She was certainly old enough to have had both. What did it matter who *Kamden* was? And why did the familiar spikes of jealousy rip through his gut?

"He is not protecting me, Edlynn. He has offered me escort is all." Lady Ives knelt at the auld woman's feet. Edlynn kissed the top of her head and whispered into her hair.

"Lady Ives, we must go."

"Godspeed!" Edlynn yelled as they passed beneath the doorway.

After two attempts, Broc managed to crawl atop the stallion. What felt like a hundred thistles hidden inside his garments tormented his limbs. It was all he could do to steady himself atop the prancing steed. Lady Ives handed him her mantle, tied her satchels to the horse, and then disappeared behind the cottage.

When she reappeared with a speckled chicken in a small cage, he rolled his head on his shoulders and prayed for endurance. "Lady Ives, ye test my patience."

She tied the bird on as well, then finally mounted in front of him. "Do not even think of telling me I cannot bring her."

"I've not eaten in days. The bird is most welcome."

Lady Ives gasped, as he might have suspected. "She is not food; her name is Beatrice. And if you so much as pluck a single one of her feathers, I promise you, I will—"

"Ye will what, Lady Ives?" He leaned in close to her ear

to intimidate her. "Torture me? Beat me? Poison me? Think ye there is a threat you can hang over my head?"

"Cool your temper, Scotsman." Lady Ives clucked her tongue, which set the steed into motion.

Jilted backward with the action, Broc dropped the reins and curled his hands around her small waist, which was hardly enough to hold on to. He reached for the reins only to have his hand slapped away. His fondness for angels was beginning to dissipate.

"You should hold on, Lord Maxwell. I do not possess the strength to set you atop this horse if you should fall off."

"Had you not poisoned me, I would not be in danger of falling off."

Lady Ives sat erect and stopped the horse. "Use my mantle to tie yourself to me."

Though he didn't like the bite in her tone, her order did appeal to him. After wrapping the long material around his back, he fumbled with the ends around her waist while she braided her long hair. He couldn't feel what he was doing, nor could he see his task either.

Lady Ives sucked in a loud breath. Her shoulders snapped straight, catching him in the jaw. "Lord Maxwell! You will refrain from touching me with such intimacy."

He thought she might have growled. Face flaming, he immediately released his hold on the mantle, wishing he knew exactly where he'd touched her. Damn the poison for stealing that from him. "Forgive me. I can no longer feel my hands."

She made quick work of binding them together, then kicked the stallion into a fevered run, making conversation impossible.

A glance over his shoulder brought some sense of relief. The king's guards must have taken the road along the Thames, else they'd be upon them by now. Broc silently admitted Lady Ives had been correct in her assumptions. She was a smart angel—stubborn to be certain, but the lass didn't lack a brain beneath her thick skull by any means. He couldn't help but wonder what other secrets Lady Ives might have safely tucked away in her pretty head. Was it possible she knew who was poisoning the king? And if so, what would it take to convince her to divulge a name? With any luck, the name would belong to the same man he and Aiden had come to England to destroy. King Edward's brother, the Duke of Gloucester, would certainly have motive to kill the king.

Broc closed his eyes. He placed too much hope in accusations, uncertainties. He needed proof. Once they reached Hertfordshire, he would focus on getting Lady Ives to trust him. A task he admitted appealed to him.

He settled against her back as the numbness slowly eased through him. Unfortunately, his sense of smell did not desert him. Her essence tormented him the better part of the afternoon. What was worse, her dark red braid had fallen over her shoulder to reveal the sweetest patch of creamy skin. He desperately wanted to taste her.

How the devil was it possible for his entire body to go numb except his cock?

God's hooks, I need a woman.

Chapter 3

Dusk settled around them like a dying flame. Timberland grew tall and thick on the sides of the road, surrounding her in a suffocating blanket of gray haze. Yellow, glowing eyes peered at her from either side, testing her fear, mocking the numbers accumulating in her head until she felt certain she would quit breathing.

She pulled on the reins. The stallion nickered and trotted backward. "Lord Maxwell, we must stop. 'Twill be dark soon."

"Nay. Stay mounted, lass. Guide us through the wood." The Scot made no movement, but his breath fell over her neck in slow, even ribbons.

She could taste her heart in her throat. She swallowed and searched the black limbs overhead. For what, she did not know, but was certain it would attack her at any moment. Her sweaty palms slid over the leather straps.

"Come now, angel. Dinnae let the dark steal your courage." Lord Maxwell whispered his softly spoken words close to her ear. The rich timbre of his voice only added to the goose-flesh sprouting over her forearms.

"The dark stole my courage years ago."

"You escaped your enemies today in the dark."

She knew this game well. After Mother's death, Edlynn had spent many nights trying to tell Lizzy she was brave, trying to convince her there were no monsters in the dark. She knew otherwise.

Lord Hollister's evil, dark eyes entered her mind, intensifying her angst. "I fear your efforts are wasted, Lord Maxwell. I am not physically capable of moving forward."

Leaves rustled to her right. Her head snapped. Her nose brushed against his whiskered jaw. She wanted to scream, to cry, to bury her face in his neck and hide.

"What if I told ye the inn was on the other side of the forest?"

He lied. She was certain of it. But if perchance he spoke the truth, she could be free of the night. "Vow it upon your soul."

He laughed at her. Not aloud, but his chest bounced against her back. "I vow it. As God is my witness, no harm shall come to you as you pass through this wood."

She stroked the stallion's damp neck and nudged him forward. Why she found any comfort at all in the Scot's promise was ludicrous. He could no more protect her right now than Beatrice.

"When we reach the inn, you will refer to me as Julian. The innkeeper's name is John. He is—"

"The one who will go back for Edlynn?" she finished for him and searched the trees for movement.

"Aye."

"Do go on." She tried to focus on Lord Maxwell's instructions, but her entire world turned black beneath the cloak of trees. An owl hooted; a flock of birds took flight.

"My condition will arouse suspicion, as will the horse. A squire will most likely come to tend the stallion. Have him send for John."

"And your condition?"

"Tell them I drowned myself in the cups at our wedding celebration."

"Our wedding? You want me to pose as your wife?" *His wife?* The Scot was mad. She drew back on the steed. The horse must have sensed her anxiety for its head bobbed, fighting the pull on the reins.

Lord Maxwell's lips brushed the rim of her ear. "Aye. Ye make a bonnie fine bride, Lizbeth."

An unfamiliar tickle teased her neck.

Did he just kiss her neck?

Mercy Mary! He just kissed her neck. She quit breathing. The fear twisting her gut into knots shot up her spine and then washed over her skin like hot wax. Her legs tightened around the stallion's belly. The beast bolted through the wood like a stone from a catapult.

She held tight to the reins. *Twenty-seven, twenty-eight, twenty-nine . . .*

Why would he kiss her? No man had ever attempted to kiss her. Father's profession made guarding her virtue remarkably simple. Of course, the chastity belt aided those efforts.

"Slow down, angel, else you'll run us through John's kitchens."

Her eyes opened. How long had they been closed? The road widened and the forest spilled into a valley of spring grass. Twilight sparkled off the early evening dew. She saw the inn tucked away at the bottom of the hill alongside a brook. She exhaled her trepidation in a single breath, but even as her pulse began to slow, she could still feel the lingering tingle alongside the curve of her neck. Her fingers caressed the place where Lord Maxwell's lips had touched her skin. "Why did you kiss me?"

"'Twas hardly a kiss."

"But it was a kiss just the same. Why?"

"I needed to get ye through the forest. It worked. All will be well now."

She twisted to look at him. Blue eyes shone with mischief in the moonlight, and she didn't much care for his arrogant smile. He was certainly proud of himself. Instead of bantering with him, she left his vanity high on his shoulder and led the stallion down the hillside to the inn.

A branch hung over the doorway. The smell of ale sharpened in the breeze. Empty barrels stacked on their sides indicated this establishment was no inn at all, but a tippling house. No doubt filled to its third level with besotted drunkards. 'Twas no surprise the Scotsman was familiar with its location.

"Julian!" a robust woman squealed from the entranceway. Her breasts jiggled out of the top of her laced bodice as she bobbed down the steps toward them. A thin boy, no more than seven or eight summers, followed close behind and took the reins of their horse.

"Celeste, ye're lookin' healthy as ever. I'd like ye to meet my wife," Lord Maxwell slurred, playing the role of a wastrel with expertise.

"Your wife?" the woman gasped, her dark eyes rounded in a sea of white.

Lizzy smiled sweetly while grinding her opinion between her teeth. The woman looked shocked, appalled, mayhap even disappointed. Lizzy hardly considered herself past her years. Why was it so impossible to believe she might be the man's wife?

"When did ye go an' get yerself a wife?" The woman planted her fists on full hips, raised a thin eyebrow—which was the only thing thin about her—and continued her inspection of Lizzy's attire.

"Julian and I were married this afternoon," Lizzy lied with a surprising lack of effort. "After which, he drowned himself in the cups until the wine colored his eyes purple." Eager to free herself from the horse and the Scot she'd carried on her back for the past few hours, she untied the mantle binding them together and tossed a leg over the steed's ears. The moment her feet hit the ground, sharp pain shot up her thighs and stabbed her like a dagger in her lower back. Her gown clung to her skin, drenched with the Scotsman's sweat. His fever must have peaked hours earlier.

She turned around in time to watch Lord Maxwell slide sideways off the horse and land with a grunt on his backside.

"Lord Ma—ave mercy!" She caught herself.

"'Ods toes! Milo, fetch up John and Smitt."

The boy darted back into the tippling house as the overly dramatic woman dropped to her knees in a pool of dark green skirts at Lord Maxwell's side. Lizzy stilled at his feet. She twisted her sleeves and studied the shadows beneath his weary blue eyes. His lips were dry, his skin a reddish bronze and coated with perspiration. Curse her thoughtlessness. She should have taken more care.

Two men jogged out of the tavern, one husky, dark, and handsome as the devil, the other tall, lean, and bald.

"Piss 'n' nettles! What 'appened, Celeste?" the tall one asked.

"I daresay Julian pickled himself in the spirits," Celeste said in a scolding tone.

"Good den, John." Lord Maxwell swallowed hard and offered a strained grin to the man standing over him. "Think ye can put us up in a room? 'Tis my weddin' night."

John cocked his bald head and looked down his rather large nose at Lord Maxwell. "Ye got yourself married?" He shot a curious glance at Lizzy.

She bobbed her head and decided it was less of a sin to nod a lie than to actually speak it.

John pointed at the steed. "Milo, tend the horse. Celeste, go to the kitchens and find Sir Julian an' his new wife some sup. Take up his shoulders, Smitt."

The man issued his orders with authority—all of which were obeyed without question—then lifted Lord Maxwell's legs off the ground. Lizzy trailed behind but with growing panic watched the boy lead their horse away. Everything she valued was strapped to that horse: her gold, her herbs, Beatrice, the document she'd stolen from Lord Hollister's chamber. "Julian, what of our things?"

"John, have the boy bring the satchels to our chamber."

"Aye, sir. Milo, ye heard the man."

"And Beatrice?" Lizzy asked.

"Bring the chicken as well!" Lord Maxwell hollered as they stepped into a barroom, then coughed.

"The chicken has a name?" John questioned.

"'Tis something of a pet."

"Your new wife has a pet chicken? Wherever did ye find her?"

"Get me to a bed, and I'll tell ye all about it."

Lizzy stayed close to John while they carried Lord Maxwell through a room filled to its rafters with merriment. The hum of men's voices rumbled around female giggles. A serving girl, whose vest laced tight beneath her breasts, cast a flirtatious smile to a group of men gathered round a table. Her blousy undertunic fell off her shoulders, revealing far more skin than Lizzy was accustomed to seeing in public. The serving girl held every man's attention except one. A gent with brown hair tied back in a queue turned away from the fair-haired beauty and ran his gaze over Lizzy.

The merriment fell away from him in a flash.

She wormed her way tighter to John's back and searched her memory for the man's face. So many had passed through the dungeon. Did she know him? Had she tended him?

London would never be far enough behind her. The events in her past would forever haunt her, but she would never have to speak of them again. Kamden's face appeared behind her eyes, so alive and full of laughter. Her chest tightened.

"Maiden, ye walk any closer, an' you're going to be inside me," John tossed the comment over his shoulder.

Lizzy shrunk back. "Pray forgive me." Pulling her braid alongside her cheek, she began fingering through the wavy tresses to hide her scar while she followed the men up a stairwell and into a dimly lit room. The furnishings were simple, yet more inviting than her chamber in the Tower. A pitcher and two pewter mugs sat atop a small table beside a bed. A low-burning fire reflected onto a bench seat that looked in danger of falling apart. Perfume hid beneath the smell of wood chips and smoke and made her question the length of time the chamber sat vacant between occupants.

She pushed open the wooden shutters and inhaled the cool evening air, reveling in a view uninterrupted by iron bars. The boy caught her eye below, weighted down with her satchels. God give her strength to mend Lord Maxwell before her body collapsed into exhaustion.

She pivoted on her heel to find him sprawled atop the bed on his back. "Would you sirs be so kind as to flip Julian onto his stomach before you take your leave?"

John frowned at her.

"Works best if one o' ye is on your back." The handsome man named Smitt flashed a wicked grin and a wink.

Fire exploded in her cheeks. She opened her mouth but no words came out, so she snapped her jaw shut.

"Mayhap Celeste should have a talk with her, aye?" John offered to Lord Maxwell, his tone sincere.

"She is not my wife," Lord Maxwell said quickly.

Surprised, she questioned who the ruse had been for. Why would he feel it necessary for her to pose as his wife if not for the innkeeper?

"Nay?" Smitt perked up. "Is the lass any mon's wife?" He swaggered in her direction, his speech slipping into the slightest burr.

Surely he wasn't a Scot, too. He was far too pretty for a man, much less a Scot. One thing was for certain, he eyed her like fresh-cooked meat in the hands of a starving man. She found her voice, along with her courage. "Nay. I have no husband."

Smitt raised her chin between his thumb and forefinger. "Are ye lookin' for one?" Rich brown eyes the color of warm molasses sparkled in the candlelight. He blinked with lashes black as ink and smiled a smile that could steal a girl's senses. Regardless of the warnings going off in her head, her heart did a little pitter-patter. Aside from the prisoners, men didn't normally pay her interest, especially those so well favored.

"Move away from her, Smitt. She is not looking for a husband," Lord Maxwell supplied from the bed.

She peeked around Smitt's broad shoulders. Lord Maxwell's frown was anything but pleasant: slashed brows, lips pressed tight together. And how did he know whether or not she was looking for a husband? This man, Smitt, was certainly big enough to protect her. Mayhap she had other options besides Fountains Abbey in Yorkshire.

"Why would ye say she is your wife then?"

"'Tis highly probable the king's guard is looking for us, since we stole a steed belonging to the crown."

John scratched his wiry red beard and waited for more explanation.

"I also thought it best for propriety's sake to hide beneath the pretense of a married couple. I need the lass to keep quarters with me for the night without your wife's meddling." Lord Maxwell winced and licked his lips.

"My wife does not meddle."

Lord Maxwell rolled his eyes. "Celeste is a fine woman, but when your wife sets her sights to the matchmakin', I dinnae want to be the subject of her plotting. I'd wager my da's land she is spouting her mouth to the tavern wenches as we speak."

John linked his fingers behind his neck and pulled his

elbows forward. "Smitt, mayhap you should see if Celeste needs help in the kitchen? I have need to talk with Maxwell."

"Can I bring ye anything, lass?" Smitt curled her hair over her ear.

She snapped out of her trance. Men like Smitt were the reason fathers locked their daughters in the chastity belt. She combed her hair back in front of her ear and set her mind to her task. "Clean linens, a kettle for heating water, some broth if there is any available, and be certain the boy brings all my things posthaste, including my chicken."

"As you wish." Smitt didn't appear pleased with her list; nonetheless, he kissed her knuckles farewell before taking his leave.

She poured a cup of water from the pitcher and brought it bedside. She bent over Lord Maxwell, raised the back of his head, and pressed the pewter to his lips. He needed no coaxing. Water streamed into the black stubble covering his chin in his efforts to get fluid into his body.

He drained the cup. "More" was all he said.

"Wait for the broth. As soon as the boy comes, I will feed you."

"What is wrong with him?" John asked. "I see men too far in the cups most every nigh', but they can always lift a mug to their mouths."

"He is not drunk. His body is reacting to an herb. 'Twill be out of his blood by morning." She didn't have to press her hand to his skin to feel the heat coming from him. He had probably been feeling the effects of the monkshood for hours, though he never once complained. The herb would attack his stomach in a most unpleasant way when it began to wear off.

"He's been poisoned?" John's question sounded like a direct accusation in her head, and the smile Lord Maxwell didn't even try to hide did little to lessen a rising anger building inside her.

"'Tis not poison," she defended and then changed the subject. "M'lord, mayhap you could discuss the errand you have for John." She remained hopeful he would uphold his vow to send someone for Edlynn.

His nod, be it ever so slight, was all she needed. She moved to ready the fire for the kettle and listened to every word that passed between the two men. By the ease of their conversation, she gathered they'd known each other for quite some time.

"What of your brother?" John asked.

She twisted her head to peer over her shoulder. Lord Maxwell met her eyes. She prayed he wouldn't tell John who she was. She'd lived with many secrets, and if possible, she never intended to tell another soul she was the executioner's daughter.

"Aiden dinnae survive the Tower." His voice was soft, and his words pained her to the very center of her heart.

"I'm sorry. Aiden was a good mon." A long pause settled over the room. John cursed beneath his breath then lowered a chandelier and lit the tallows, bringing the room to light. "I suspect you'll be returning to the borderlands?"

"Aye."

"And the lass?" John studied her intently now.

"She travels north as well."

"For what purpose?"

"I am not yet privy to that information." Lord Maxwell looked at her, as did John.

Both men obviously awaited an explanation regarding her travel plans. An explanation she was not yet fully prepared to provide. She'd already divulged the conspiracy to kill King Edward, but she knew so much more. Did she dare trust these men with that information? Would she endanger the lives of the princes further if the Scots knew they were bastards? There was only one man she could trust—England's protector.

She stood and turned toward the bed. "I travel to Yorkshire."

Neither man spoke.

"I have need to gain audience with the king's brother," she continued.

"Damn," Broc said almost silently from the bed.

"The Duke of Gloucester? Are ye wowf?" John shrieked in a high-pitched tone.

She didn't know what "wowf" was, but she guessed he accused her of madness. She'd heard the whispered accusations regarding Richard of Gloucester's desire to steal the crown, but she'd met and known his compassion personally. Gloucester would see her safely into sanctuary and relieve Father of his duty when she provided him proof of a conspiracy. "London's nobles talk of Gloucester's wickedness, and 'tis all hearsay. King Edward has entrusted his sons and daughters to his brother's care. The king named the Duke of Gloucester the Protector of the Realm."

John's odd expression swayed between her and Lord Maxwell. "Will you be escorting her?"

She awaited Lord Maxwell's answer with tightly stretched nerves.

His eyes closed slowly. He inhaled, then exhaled. "Aye."

She didn't know how desperately she wanted that answer until he provided it. Her heart rapped against her breastbone at a quickening speed. She never intended to make such a journey alone, but she hadn't planned for Father's untimely incapacitation either. She smiled at Lord Maxwell and released the breath she'd been holding.

"I'm going with ye," John said. "After I fetch up the blind woman, we will head for home."

"Home?" she asked, puzzled. "Yorkshire is your home?"

"Nay. Scotland is." John puffed up his chest.

"You are a Scot, too?"

"Aye, and 'tis high time my wife knew it."

"Knew what?" Celeste asked as she and the boy entered the room. She carried a tray heaped with bread, cheese, drink, and two bowls of steaming broth, which she set on the table. The boy dropped Lizzy's belongings on the bench, including Beatrice in her little cage, then spun out of the room, no doubt escaping further instruction. Smitt ducked beneath the door frame carrying a pail of water in each hand. After carelessly dropping the containers by the fire, he reached for a chunk of cheese from the tray.

Celeste slapped his hand and pointed toward the door. "Out!"

Smitt offered the woman a pout that would have gained him favor with Lizzy, but Celeste merely drummed her fingers on her crossed arms and waited for the man to comply. Lizzy held on to her humor until Celeste winked at her.

A giggle escaped Lizzy's lips. She covered her mouth in an attempt to hide her inappropriate behavior and moved to pour water into the kettle suspended over the fire.

"Come, Celeste. We need to talk. Let Julian and his new wife have some privy time." John took his wife by the elbow.

Celeste jerked her arm from her husband's grip. "But I've yet to converse with her or ask her name."

Lizzy rounded the foot of the bed and took Celeste's hand in hers. "'Tis Lizbeth, but you may call me Lizzy if you like." Celeste smiled and her cheeks nearly pushed her dark eyes closed.

"Very well, Lizzy. We will see you and Sir Julian in the morn to break your fast."

"Thank you for your generosity." Lizzy's gratitude was lost on their backs as John ushered his wife out of the chamber.

John turned in the doorway. "Can ye manage, lass?"

"Aye," she responded quickly, but was skeptical of her own confidence. She closed the door and turned toward Lord Maxwell. He was easily the biggest man she'd ever cared for. Though his size intimidated her, she assured herself he was no different from the other men she'd tended. Of course, those men didn't make her toes tingle.

She stared at him—long, lean, and sprawled out on the bed like an awaiting lover. The tingle in her toes shot up her body and went straight into her nipples. She felt her eyes widen and crossed her arms over her breasts to hide them.

Mercy Mary! Control yourself! she scolded herself. *He is just another man.*

She repeated this lie in her head as she walked toward the bed, her heart setting a pace too fast to count.

Chapter 4

Lizzy positioned a second pillow behind Lord Maxwell's head to set him forward enough to eat. "Are you hungry, m'lord?"

"Aye." His eyes blinked opened.

She had never seen a more beautiful shade of blue than the color of Lord Maxwell's eyes. Not quite as blue as the sky, but paler with flecks of silver, reminding her of the beads on Mother's rosary.

She retrieved the kettle from the fire and set it on a bedside table, then wrung out a cloth in the water and lowered herself onto the bed's edge. Starting with his neck, she washed the filth of the dungeon from him. With every ounce of skin revealed, he became increasingly more handsome. Only the slightest hint of gaunt darkened the skin beneath his eyes, but food would remedy that problem soon enough.

She pushed a shock of black hair from his brow to wash the remnants of dried blood from his forehead. Her pale skin stood out in harsh contrast against his dark coloring, as if announcing their differences. The cut of his features was sharp—a straight nose, strong cheekbones, square jaw—the epitome of an ancient warrior. It seemed unfair God had blessed a man with such beauty.

Edlynn had once told her Scotland bred only trolls with tufts of red hair growing from their ears. The ugliest lots of humans to walk the earth. Lord Maxwell defied her fable.

She smoothed the cloth over his temple and then his ears. The man even had a fine set of ears.

"Lady Ives, as much as I am enjoying your coddling, I wonder if ye might fetch up some of that broth?"

"Pray forgive me." Lizzy stood and tucked her chin to her chest, her face flaming from embarrassment. What had she been thinking? Ogling him like a slice of sweet pie. She hurried to the trestle table, wiping her forehead on her sleeve, and then retrieved the food. After setting the tray on a cuttie stool, she positioned herself, once again, beside him on the bed. She raised the wooden spoon to his lips. His mouth opened, but his eyes never left her face. She should talk to him.

"The broth will give you something to expel." *Brilliant, Lizzy. Of all the topics to discuss with the man, you choose vomit.* She really had no business conversing with people.

"Lookin' forward to it." He smiled at her, branching the corners of his eyes with tiny lines and freeing her of unwanted tension.

She fed him another spoonful, then another. The silence alone set the numbers rushing through her head, but the way he looked at her stole her ability to count them in order. "Why do you stare at me?"

"My eyes have never been blessed to look upon an angel. I intend to take my fill."

She laughed outright. The Scot's attempt to be smooth of tongue only raised the walls guarding her naïveté. "Your flattery is wasted, m'lord. The name was falsely earned. I am no angel."

"Someone thought ye earned the name."

"His name was Bartholomew." She hadn't thought of him in years. "He wept at night for the angels to come for him.

Leprosy ate his flesh whilst he awaited execution. I prepared a poultice for him to ease his pain, but death followed me to his cell. I found him facedown in the rushes, sunlight shining on him from his tiny window. I believed him dead and entered his cell to cross him with blessed water."

"A saint and an angel. God has truly blessed me."

Lizzy stuffed the spoon in Lord Maxwell's mouth to still his tongue. "You mock me."

He swallowed and sputtered. "Forgive me." His eyes slid shut. "Do go on."

"Bartholomew was not dead. He wrapped his arms around my waist and begged me to end his life. When I refused him, he snatched the torch from my hand and set the rushes on fire. Six prisoners died that eve in the dungeon, all of them screaming for Bartholomew's angel to save them." She set the empty bowl aside and left the bed to pour Lord Maxwell a cup of water. Remembering the punishment she'd endured made her hands shake.

"How old were ye?"

"Fourteen summers."

"How did ye escape?"

"Through the tunnels." She held his head up while he drank, trying not to relive the ending. "After Lord Hollister's men contained the fire, he questioned the surviving prisoners about the incident, demanding to know who started it. They all responded in like."

"An angel of fire?" Lord Maxwell guessed.

She nodded and hoped he would cease ridiculing her now.

"Have ye cared for many others?" he asked, genuine interest touching his voice.

"I have. After my mother's death, Father and I moved from the cot-house into the Tower. I was fostered by the chief warder and his wife. Lord Hollister would have imprisoned me in my quarters, but fortunately his wife was very kind and very young, only five years my senior. She took pity on me and gave me duties in the larder. I had access to a great deal of food and provisions, as well as the ability to open any lock with my father's keys. Before I reached thirteen summers I was sneaking food to the prisoners."

"Ye could have been charged with thievery had your keeper discovered you." He frowned; his concern, though unnecessary, touched her.

She flashed him an all-knowing smile and popped a piece of cheese in his mouth. "Edlynn was the larderer before she lost her sight. She taught me how to mix herbs, and I showed her how to make fragrances from flowers." Mother and her flowers were never far from Lizzy's thoughts, nor was the grief she suffered the day God took her.

"'Tis why ye smell so good. Like sweet sauce poured over a bowl of flower petals."

Her gaze dropped. She doubted anything could have prevented the smile from peeling her lips over her teeth. "I s'pose."

When she took up the second bowl of broth his questions ceased, and his lips slammed shut. She touched his bottom lip with the edge of the spoon, but for reasons unbeknownst to her, he refused to open. How could he offer her the sweetest compliment she'd ever heard then behave like such a mule? "Lord Maxwell, you cannot possibly have taken your fill." She returned the spoon to the bowl when he did naught and said naught. "I cannot begin to imagine why you would choose now to flaunt your stubbornness. You need to eat."

"As do ye."

"I've already eaten." She didn't completely lie.

"When?"

"Father dried meat on Good Friday."

"Two days ago?" He rolled his eyes. "'Tis likely the reason ye have less flesh on your skin than your pet chicken."

Had it really been two days since she'd eaten? She focused

on the broth trying to recall her last meal. Her stomach clenched, telling her it had been far too long.

"If ye are going to be my charge, you will eat," Lord Maxwell demanded in a tone she thought pompous.

"I am not your charge."

"Eat."

She snatched a round of black bread from the tray and tore off a chunk between her teeth. A moan nearly escaped her. It was warm and soft on her tongue and surprisingly sweet. Another bite found its way into her mouth, then another. Cheeks filled, she returned the bread to the tray, ignoring Lord Maxwell's smug expression. While she chewed and swallowed, she filled the spoon with broth, and then held it in front of his lips.

He shook his head.

"You are a cud-chewing urchin," she ground out, frustrated to the point she wanted to strangle him. "Open your mouth." She waited, spoon in hand, wanting to slap the arrogance from him. "Are all Scots as pigheaded as you?"

He didn't dare open his mouth to respond else she would win this petty battle. She guessed he wouldn't accept defeat with grace. "'Tis a foolish game you play. One, I can assure you, I will win. You provoke me, Lord Maxwell, and force me to take measures you will not find to your liking. Now, open your mouth, or I will open it for you." She grinned, satisfied with her threat, and set the bowl aside.

He raised his brows and blew an exaggerated breath, indicating he had no intention of complying.

She leaned over him, pinched his nose closed, and waited. He held his breath for an impressive period of time before his mouth finally opened. She poured the spoonful of broth down his gullet the same time he sucked in air.

He choked. His upper body convulsed. She tossed the spoon aside and pulled him upright, careful not to touch his back. Why was he making this task so difficult, and whatever possessed her to gain authority over him? Mercy Mary. The man had been tortured by her father's hand and needed care.

She held him close, an embrace far too intimate for their association. Guilt pecked at her, adding to the onslaught of feelings she'd discovered since meeting Lord Maxwell. Did she feel indebted to him because her father took his brother's life? Or was her desperation to find protection the reason she felt she could trust him?

Once he regained his breath, she lowered him back to the bed. Her weight followed; her hands pinned beneath his shoulders. She was close enough to kiss him. Why she measured the distance between them by a kiss she did not know, but his eyes and his lips made her throat go dry and her heart quicken.

He licked his lips. "For every bite I take, you will take one as well, or I will drown in the broth."

"Aye, m'lord." Lizzy held no desire to argue the point further. She ate bits of cheese between the spoonfuls she fed him from the second bowl of broth. Although he didn't banter with her further, the slight lift of his lips told her he was pleased with his victory. She gave him water, set the tray aside, and then proceeded to gather her things from the bench where the boy had dumped them. On the trestle table she set out eight small satchels of herbs, her pestle and mortar, a curved needle, and silk threads.

"Have ye the provisions to make more poison?" Lord Maxwell asked from behind her.

The man truly didn't know when to quit. She had half a mind to add a pinch of aconite to numb his tongue. She studied her measurements and mulled over his insult. Once she began grinding the herbs against the mortar, she devised her own quip. "Mayhap this time my poison will succeed in killing you. 'Twill be one less Scot for my king to battle."

"Ye jest."

"Do I?" If he intended to keep referring to her medicines

as poison, then she wouldn't trouble herself to correct him. She added water to her powder to form a warm mash that she would apply to his wounds later and then pulled a small knife from its leather sheath. She stepped back into his view, offered him a devious grin, and angled the blade in front of her for effect. Most of London thought her insane. She'd mastered the role and used it to her advantage more than once. "Mayhap I will fail to balance your humors properly, and you will bleed to death. Then I will already have a poison prepared for the next stubborn, arrogant, thistle-tongued Scot who insults my generosity and talents for healing."

His eyes widened. "Lady Ives, forgive me. 'Twas not my intention to insult ye."

She played the part a bit longer simply to be mulish, then offered him a small smile that didn't nearly reflect the amount of humor she received from the look of horror pinching his brows together. "Take your ease, m'lord. I am jesting. I have no plans to gut you or poison you." Taking hold of his shirt, she made a small slit in the seam with the tip of her knife. "I assume John can provide you with other garments?"

"Aye." His eyes closed, and a breath of relief cooled her neck.

Lizzy cut through the material until his shirt fell open. She bit the inside of her lip at the sight his muscular chest presented. Even with the hint of a bruise wrapped around his ribs, he was a fine specimen of pure male. She wanted to weave her fingers through the smattering of hair drawing a line down a stomach rippled with tight muscles. Her gaze followed the path that thinned beneath his navel and disappeared into his trews. Her breasts tightened.

Curse it! She made a pathetic healer.

She cut the sleeves off then set the knife beside the kettle of water, hoping he couldn't see the slight tremble of her hand. After wringing the water from the cloth, she began to bath him again. Her hand moved over his shoulder and down his muscular arm. She studied the ancient design marking his skin with blue ink. Upon closer inspection, she made out the letters *g*, *r*, *a*, repeating uninterrupted around his arm. She might have asked him what it meant if the sight of him hadn't stolen her ability to speak.

Holding the cloth in one hand, she set her fingers free to search for broken bones, but secretly reveled in the feel of his skin. She'd never tended a man so blessed with looks. An unfamiliar flash of heat surged through her body and settled between her legs. Her pulse flittered in the most private place of her body, frightening her. A tremor of panic took hold. Her fingers curled around his ribs and made indentations in his skin.

"Ach!" He sucked in air.

Her hand jerked back. "You felt that?"

"Nay." He chuckled. "I cannae bear the silence or this curse of immobility."

She slapped his arm lightly, thankful for his ill-timed humor, and tried to regain some semblance of dignity. "Your ribs are slightly bruised, but seem to be whole. I might require Smitt's help to wrap them after I finish mending your back."

"I might require Smitt's help as well, unless ye wish to aid me with my privy needs." He snapped her a quick wink.

"M'lord, please." Her cheeks heated, and she questioned how she could possibly get any hotter. She wiped the back of her hand over her forehead. Sweat rolled off her wrist. In addition, she felt it between her breasts and down her back. She had to get out of her gown before she melted. She fanned herself. 'Twas as hot as the devil's own kitchen in the chamber.

Lizzy moved behind the bed and detached the false sleeves of her gown. In addition, she peeled away the top layer of her skirts and removed her boots. While rolling the sleeves of her overtunic to her elbows, she returned to his side. "I'm going to turn you now."

"Much luck to ye," he said simply, causing a nervous giggle to slip past her lips.

He said the oddest things.

She positioned his arms at his side and pushed on his shoulder and hip. Moving London Bridge might have been easier. After two attempts and a loud grunt, she managed to roll him over to one side of the bed. His shirt clung to his skin where the marks had bled through in bold splashes of red. She stood, stared, and damned her father's deed. "I'm truly sorry for what he did to you."

"'Tis not of your doing. Dinnae fash. I cannae feel a thing. But make haste before this miracle potion of yours wears off."

"Aye, m'lord. Find your rest. You will need all your energies come the morrow." She cut away the remainder of his shirt and inspected the lashes. Some were pink whelps while others broke the skin in fine lines, but at least three gashes split his flesh like a sword wound.

Tending to him should have been a mundane and tedious task, but working on Lord Maxwell was anything but monotonous. One of his lashes had sliced his skin below his waist. The rip in his trews was easily extended, but now exposed half his backside. She touched him, knowing he wouldn't feel her "inspection." A fine mist of hair tickled the pads of three fingers. Curse it if the man's rump wasn't as fine as the rest of him.

With a shake, she broke free of her thoughts and readied the needle. The task would be easiest performed atop him. She wouldn't twist her back in knots or stitch him crooked because of propriety. She hiked her skirts to her knees, and then crawled atop him, straddling his thighs.

He moaned.

"Is my weight too much to bear?" she asked and rose up on her knees, wishing he would sleep and leave her to work.

"Nay. I'd wager a mite weighs more than ye. Nonetheless, ye should count your blessings that I cannae turn over."

Another torrent of heat shot straight up her core. Cursing her body's reaction to his comment, she clenched and forced herself not to wiggle. "I like to count. Mayhap I will heed your suggestion." She settled back atop him and punctured his skin with the needle, closing a whelp one stitch at a time. Instead of counting blessings, she counted stitches, determined to mend Lord Maxwell to the best of her ability. Wind rustled outside, immersing the chamber in peaceful tranquility while Beatrice warbled in the corner in her cage.

"Have ye family in London, other than your father?" he asked, disturbing her concentration. Did the man never indulge in the simplicity of silence?

"Any sisters? Brothers mayhap? Bairns?" he clarified when she didn't answer immediately.

His questions reminded her how truly alone she was in this world. She considered not responding, but Lord Maxwell seemed uncomfortable with the lack of noise. The man talked more than Edlynn. Lizzy would appease his curiosity into her personal affairs, then demand he rest. "I've no other family besides Father and Edlynn."

"Are ye widowed? Ye seem a wee bit long in the tooth to have never married. The blind woman had mentioned a man who once protected—"

"Lord Maxwell." Lizzy clenched her jaw. "You really need to find your rest, and I work with more diligence in silence. If there is something you are wont to ask, please say it."

"Who is Kamden?"

Tears blurred her vision instantly. She closed her eyes and saw Kamden and his sons wrestling in the mud outside Edlynn's cottage, their laughter contagious to the point it made her smile even now. She swallowed and rubbed the heels of her palms over her eyes. "I am twenty-three summers and accepted long ago that I would never marry, nor bear children. My father's profession belonged to my grandfather, and his father before him. The blood of the executed has cursed the Ives's name for decades. 'Tis an occupation that steals a man's sanity and condemns his soul simultaneously. I cannot bring a child into this world knowing he will one day wield the executioner's ax.

"Kamden was my brother and was next in line to carry my family's curse. Now, if I have satisfied all your curiosities, I would ask you to rest . . . in silence."

"How did he die?"

Lizzy ground her teeth and held tight to the needle, wanting to stab him with it repeatedly. "Lord Maxwell, I really do not wish—"

"'Tis my last question, lass. I vow it."

Her heart punched her from the inside, her sorrow as raw as it had been six months ago when her brother left her behind in this world without him. "Kamden was executed."

Lord Maxwell held true to his vow of silence, though Lizzy guessed he wanted to know more. Most people did. Death intrigued the human mind. What person wouldn't be curious about a man whose grotesque occupation forced him to take his own son's life? She could still feel Lord Hollister's hand grasping her chin forcing her to watch the atrocity. Still smell the rotten vegetables embedded in her hair. The scene branded in her memory always became more colorful behind her closed eyes.

"I am truly sorry for your loss," Lord Maxwell finally said in a quiet voice laded with his own pain.

His sympathies meant more to her than he could possibly fathom. This man had witnessed his own brother's death this very day, yet offered her condolences for a death months old. Her hand covered her mouth, demanding her sorrow to remain inside. The need to cry made her throat ache, but she stifled her pain and buried it deep within.

With her composure intact, Lizzy hoped Lord Maxwell would cease any further questions. "Will you please rest now?"

"Aye." He closed his eyes.

Silence followed.

She began pulling the needle through his skin again, losing herself in the simplicity of her numbers. After ten stitches, Lord Maxwell's slow and steady breathing turned into a roaring snore, each one louder than the last. The man truly didn't like the quiet.

Lizzy pulled the fifty-seventh stitch through Lord Maxwell's back and crawled on stiff legs from the bed. Her fingers cramped and her back ached from the hours she'd spent bent over him. She moved to the basin to wash, then searched her belongings for the earthenware jar of leeches.

It was nowhere to be found. Standing beside the window, she stared at the stable. The boy must have left one of her satchels behind.

A partial moon cast blue light over the dewy grass, turning the ground into a sparkling sea. Trees loomed in black silhouettes like a curtain wall around the tippling house. Lizzy strained her eyes in search of a rider, all the while knowing not enough time had passed for John to return with Edlynn. She crossed herself and offered a silent prayer for her friend's safety.

The guards had not found their trail, else they would have been upon them by now. *All will be well,* she assured herself, using Lord Maxwell's words, and wrapped her mantle around her. She pulled the hood over her head, and then moved quietly from the chamber. The sour smell of ale and unwashed bodies led her down the stairwell and into the barroom, which now harbored only a few men, lost to sleep from the drink. She retrieved a lantern from the wall beside the door and made her way toward the stable. Mating insects squealed in crackling pitches, and sweet hay sharpened in her nose as she entered the covered stalls. She found the stallion and whispered honeyed words against his muzzle and stroked the underside of his chin. After rummaging through the single satchel the boy had tossed to the ground, she found her leeches.

Unexpected laughter broke behind her, followed by a moan and a grunt. Embarrassment raced beneath her skin. The last thing she needed was to be caught spying on two lovers. She snatched up her satchel and lantern, then stepped into the moonlight.

The sharp point of a dagger in her face stilled her steps. "You're his daughter, aren't ye?"

Chapter 5

Outside the stable's entrance, the man from the barroom stepped into her sight, the glow of her lantern highlighting the harsh planes of his face, the crooked bend of his nose. Lizzy inhaled sharply, drawing in the stagnant smell of alc. He moved her head side to side with the tip of his blade, inspecting her, tormenting her with wicked gray eyes.

She stepped backward. "I do not know to whom you refer, sir." Her voice cracked over her lie; her pulse beat in her ears.

As fast as a whiplash, he spun around her and pressed the sharp point against her neck. She dropped her satchel and lantern and dug her nails into his forearm. The flame doused, casting them instantly beneath a veil of moonshine.

He leaned close to her ear. "I know yer face, Lady Ives." He ran the tip of his blade from her temple to her earlobe, the same path as the old scar. "I seen ye on the scaffold, holdin' the executioner's basket. Collectin' silver for mercy. A blood lot of good it did to toss me wages in." The man held up his sleeve and pushed the stub of his arm through.

Your father's hand is not your own. She repeated Lord Maxwell's words and tried to believe they were true. She knew not what the man intended, but curse it, she didn't deserve his hatred. Her fingers curled into a tight fist, her arm reared forward, and then she jammed her elbow into his ribs.

He yelped. The blade slipped, nicking the skin below her ear. She spun around, fully intending to deliver a blow to his bollocks, when Smitt popped out of a stall wearing unlaced trews. Moonlight glistened off his sweat-covered chest and straw dappled his mussed hair. Smitt grasped the man by his neck and drove a fist into his gut.

"Are ye botherin' the lady?" Smitt punched the man in the face before he could answer. He fell to his hands and knees, spitting blood and teeth into the dirt. Smitt straddled the man's back and cradled his head between flexing fingertips. "Want me to kill him?"

"Nay," Lizzy quickly responded. Regardless of her desperation to keep her identity a secret, she would have no part in killing a man over it. "Release him."

Smitt relaxed his hold, giving him freedom. The man scurried to his feet and ran to a saddled steed, mounted, then disappeared down the path without a backward glance.

"Ye hurt, lass?" Smitt raised her chin and wiped a droplet of blood from her neck with the pad of his thumb.

The serving maid from the bar appeared at his back, wrestling with her garments and brushing straw from her pale hair. Her swollen lips and flushed face only heightened Lizzy's humiliation.

"Pray forgive the interruption." Lizzy pulled away from Smitt and collected her satchel from the ground.

"Nothin' to interrupt. We were finished." Smitt raised dark brows and grinned.

"Speak fer yerself," the maiden hissed and crossed her arms over her well-endowed chest.

Smitt gave the woman a look of dismissal, which she ignored. Lizzy's opinion of her changed instantly.

"Thank you for your assistance. I should get back before—" Lizzy paused. "—Julian notices my absence." She left the couple glaring at each other and raced back to the entrance of the tippling house. With her skirts raised, she flew up the stairwell two steps at a time, holding her breath until the solid wood of the chamber door flushed against her back. Her head fell back, her eyes pinched tight. Would there ever be a place she could reside without fear of recognition, fear of scorn and ridicule? Was she foolish to believe Fountains Abbey would provide her not only protection from Lord Hollister, but peace from her father's enemies?

A deep baritone hum vibrated through her ears. Her eyes opened, and a sleeping giant filled her vision. A dark muscled arm draped over the bed's edge. Hair, black as night, fell in short waves against the contrasting pale pillow. His parted lips sang a tune that made Lizzy smile.

She walked to the bed and brushed hair from his brow.

His mouth closed, the corners of his lips kicked up. "Oh, aye," he said in his sleep, then chuckled.

Though she hadn't the slightest idea why he laughed, Lizzy shared his humor. What did a man like him dream of? Family? Battle? Women? Mayhap only one woman danced behind Lord Maxwell's eyes. A wife? A lover? Lizzy imagined herself inside his head twirling in a field of wildflowers. Her face tilted toward Heaven, her spirit at peace. In her vision, Lord Maxwell wrapped his arms around her waist and kissed her neck. She wasn't the executioner's daughter or Lord Hollister's prisoner. She was a woman who laughed, and loved, and desired.

Lizzy wiped a tear from the side of her nose, sniffled, and then swallowed her foolishness. Whatever dreams she held on to as a girl were now gone. She would be no man's wife, no babe's mother. After she met with Gloucester, she would deliver herself into the hands of the church.

She pulled the jar from her satchel and set five leeches to work on Lord Maxwell's back, then stirred the poultice she mixed earlier. She pulled Mother's rosary from inside the folds of her skirt, knelt in front of the window where He might see her from the Heavens, and brought the first bead to her lips. She prayed for Mother and Edlynn; for Kamden and her nephews, Eli and Martin; then she begged God to save her father's soul. The last decade of her rosary she typically reserved for herself, but this night when she began the final ten prayers, she prayed for Lord Maxwell and his brother. She kissed the crucifix, crossed herself, then stood to collect the blood-filled leeches into their jar.

After patting his wounds with a mixture that might speed his recovery and keep him from pain, she doused the chamber's many candles, and curled up atop the bench seat with a small pillow. Her body was exhausted, her heart a heavy weight she could hardly bear. She wrapped her arms around her shoulders and focused on the single candle she left burning beside the bed. Her eyes begged for relief. She blinked once, twice, but her baser fear kept them open. Weariness soon lost the battle over her will.

Her eyes slid shut, and the monsters of her past emerged out of the darkest recesses of her mind.

Broc wanted to hang his angel up by her wings. How could a woman so seemingly caring and innocent know how to unleash a war inside a man's gut? Not even the ripest blend of Uncle Ogilvy's whisky had caused him as much havoc as Lady Ives's poison.

He rinsed his mouth for the fourth time and spit into the privy pot he'd hugged for nearly an hour. Though grateful to have regained control of his limbs, he now felt every cut, every bruise, every ache from the top of his skull to the pads of his toes. His flesh tingled and itched like a thousand insects had taken up residence on his back.

He stood, then paused, waiting for his head to catch up to the action before walking to the open window. Braced against the sill, he drew a cool breath of air. Dawn held a mist so thick he felt its dampness on his face. Aiden would revel in a day such as this. The promise of rain would have given his brother reason to languish in bed with some beauty without care or thought for consequence.

Broc tried to elicit some feeling of grief, but the familiar talons of jealousy picked at him. Aiden had been privy to everything—Da's title and constant praise, Mam's affection and approval, and the hand of Lady Juliana. The most desired woman on the border, and Aiden didn't even want her.

Her image filled his memory, though that memory was nigh three years old. Pale yellow hair adorned with gold and gemstones, sad green eyes surrounded by alabaster skin. She stood next to her father, her hand placed on his forearm, and suffered the attention of every man in the Great Hall of Skonóir Castle. Even his younger brother was smitten with her beauty. Broc smiled inwardly recalling how Ian had catered to her every whim during the fortnight of festivities, holding a tray of sweet cakes beneath her nose and tripping over his gangly limbs to refill her goblet of watered wine. But she had eyes for none of them.

Broc's chin fell to his chest, his fingers dug into the rotten window frame, remembering the contracts signed that day binding Lady Juliana to the future chieftain of Clan Maxwell.

Envy was a sin. One Broc knew well. He craved his brother's life, coveted Aiden's position, desired his betrothed. Now, Laird Scott's daughter belonged to Broc. He would marry her upon his return, gaining Da's approval. Their union would strengthen the border clans, and Broc would never again witness the death of another family member. He dared the English to breach their defenses when the Maxwell Clan held the support of Clan Scott.

His goals invigorated him, made him feel he could survive Mam's sorrow when he brought news of Aiden's death.

Determined to return as quickly as possible, Broc found toiletries in a basket and tended to his morning ablutions.

A whimper came from across the bed chamber as he finished shaving the last trace of stubble from his jaw. He turned toward Lady Ives. Curled into a ball, she looked as dangerous as a cherub. He coaxed his heavy legs toward the bench seat and then bent down on one knee. The exotic scent he now associated with his angel didn't catch him unguarded this day. 'Twas good he was able to build an immunity to her fragrance.

Another pitiful sound came from her throat. Her grip tightened around the rosary laced through her fingers. A dark red curl draped over her eyes. He brushed the tendril behind her ear, then allowed his finger to trace the soft curve of her lobe. His inspection led him to a thin scar beside her ear nearly hidden in her hairline. Her winged brows drew together and a tear fell down the side of her nose. He caught it with the back of his index finger and placed the drop between his lips.

What demons haunted her?

Broc wanted to get inside her head and fight her enemies, protect her the way he'd failed to protect his sisters and Aiden. The distress on her face called to his heart. "All will be well, angel," he cooed, and before he could stop himself, he leaned forward and kissed the backs of her eyes. The salt of her tears clung to his lips and made him achingly aware of how she complicated his goals. She sought protection from the same man whose life's purpose was to bring down Broc's country. The Duke of Gloucester would not offer her aid. Broc knew this, but Lady Ives's ignorance of warfare prevented her from seeing England's defender as anything but noble.

Her golden eyes opened and Broc saw a glimpse of her pain. She lay unmoving, as if she no longer possessed the strength to fight the battle warring inside her. She touched his freshly shaven jaw with warm fingertips. Her lips separated. "You are feeling well?"

"Nay. I fear death is inside me and awaits my body's surrender." He nuzzled his cheek farther into her hand, a part of him seeking her affection.

She smiled and blinked her eyes languidly. Another tear escaped the corner of her eye.

"Why do ye cry in your sleep?"

Her eyes sealed shut, hiding her secrets. "The same reason you laugh in yours, I s'pose. 'Tis the difference between the lives we have lived."

He took offense. "I dinnae laugh in my sleep."

"You do. I daresay you dreamed of someone who makes you happy. Who makes you laugh. Mayhap your wife?"

Broc watched full pink lips move around her words, noting every curve, every crevice. She danced around his question the same as she had the night before, conniving her way out of answering by asking a pointed question of her own.

"I have nay wife, 'cept ye," he jested, wanting to hear her bell-like laughter.

Her eyes fluttered open. Did she have any idea how her feline languor turned her actions into a seduction? Her hair spilled over a small yellow pillow in glossy dark waves, and her lips pouted in a way that made his blood race through his veins.

Her pink tongue darted out to lick those lips. "'Twas a ruse. I am no man's wife."

"Mayhap ye were my wife in my dream." He didn't know why he teased her, why he flirted with a temptation he had no business wanting.

The pulse in her temple kicked up a visible notch. Her fingers pressed lightly against his neck. "Dreams are for fools."

Broc inhaled.

'Twas a mistake.

Her scent intoxicated him—her lips, a baw hair from his,

were too close to resist. He leaned in and brushed his bottom lip against her cheek. "Then I am a fool, for dreams are all I have."

She sucked air between her teeth. Her fingers curved a little farther around his neck.

Why couldn't he pull away? He damned himself for giving in to his desires. He cupped her cheek, brushed his thumb over her parted lips.

The hand clasping her rosary flattened against her breast. *God's hooks!* Everything inside him warned him to resist. He leaned lower still until the side of his nose touched hers. Their breath became one.

A final glimpse into her flushed face told him she wouldn't resist if he kissed her.

Her rapid breathing ceased. She closed her eyes.

Three quick knocks rapped against the door. "Maxwell?"

Reality slapped his face like a February ice storm. He ripped himself away from Lady Ives.

She sprang into a sitting position, her cheeks stained with color, her gaze looking at anything but him.

"Maxwell? I have need to speak with ye."

Broc recognized John's voice. "Enter."

John stepped in, but his gaze remained steadfast to the floor. His hand slicked wetness off his bald head and hooked around his neck. He glanced up at Lady Ives, yet said naught.

She jumped to her feet, obviously as aware as Broc of John's hesitation. "Where is Edlynn?" Panic already took hold of her voice.

"Might I have a word with ye in private, m'lord?"

"Nay!" Lady Ives yelled. "Where is she?"

"I'm sorry, m'lady," John said.

She rushed to the window, her head shaking in denial of words not yet spoken.

"What happened?" Broc asked.

"The cot-house was burned to the ground. The barn, too."

Lady Ives cried out and caught herself on the window ledge.

Broc's hands formed fists in front of him. He selfishly left the auld woman behind, ignoring Lady Ives's pleas to take her. He didn't know what manner of enemy she attracted, but he had to find out if he had any chance of protecting her. "Ready the horses. We leave at once." Broc gave John a nod of dismissal and then waited for the door to latch before going to her.

He reached out to offer her comfort, but never found the courage to actually touch her. "I'm sorry. I should have—"

"Nay." She pivoted on her heel and tried to rush past him.

He grabbed her arm and pulled her into his chest, fully prepared for any words she might spit at him. "Forgive me."

She looked up at him, eyes overflowing with angry tears. "You vowed it upon your soul. You promised she would be safe. You lied." She had no idea how deeply her words cut him.

"I'm sorry."

Her fists made a pathetic attempt to hit him, but lost their might when she collapsed in his arms. She sobbed openmouthed against his chest. "Curse him! Curse him to Hades!" she screamed against his skin. "She was a blind, defenseless old woman."

Broc could do little more than hold her and prevent her from falling until the last of her tears dried themselves. He stroked her hair and kissed the top of her head, shushing her with empty words of comfort. The same words he'd used to console Mam when Lilian and Mattie died. He'd lived this scene before—the day he returned from Dumfriesshire.

Lady Ives sucked in a shaky breath, wiped her face, and then pulled away from him. Her transformation happened so quickly, he nearly missed it. Her trembling ceased, and her face smoothed. He could only imagine how much pain she caged behind her mask of indifference. 'Twas the same pain that made her cry in her sleep.

She hastened around the room gathering her things. "I thank you for your aid thus far, Lord Maxwell, but I feel it best if I continue to York alone. I do not wish to bring misfortune to you or your friends."

"Nay. I have promised ye protection. I will see you safely to York, with or without your permission."

She turned on her heel, her eyes golden flames of fury. "You have delivered me safely out of London. I have mended your wounds. Our association ends here."

"Nay." He denied her selfless request, angered by her rejection. He stepped toward her.

She stepped back, guarding her person with her satchels. Her bottom lip quivered. She bit it and snapped her shoulders back. "I will not endanger your life."

"But you will endanger yours. For the crown?" Her loyalty to her king, while admirable, was foolish. "What has your crown done for ye, Lizbeth? Why do ye risk so much?"

"You cannot understand. 'Tis complicated."

"Tell me, and I will protect ye." He cursed her obstinacy. "Ye have no one else."

"I have my father." Her chin tilted to a presumptuous angle.

"And where is he?" He splayed his hands wide and made a show of searching the chamber. "Where was he when Edlynn needed him?"

Her eyes narrowed; her nostrils flared. Her blind faith in her father infuriated him to the point of madness.

"My father is a servant to the king and is bound by the demands of the chief warder. 'Tis his duty to punish those who threaten the crown."

He backed her up against the wall. "And did Edlynn threaten the crown? Was it her punishment to die in that fire for poisoning your king?" He knew the answers, but wanted to goad her into telling him what she knew.

"Nay!"

He braced his hands on either side of her head, his toes touching the tips of her boots. "Then who threatens the crown, Lizbeth?" Her golden eyes revealed her fear, but damned if he would take ease with her now. "I will protect ye, but I must know who I am protecting ye from."

Her eyes twitched, searching his face.

Trust me, he begged her silently.

Her breaths escalated, yet her lips never opened.

God save him, but the woman was as stubborn as he. "Give me the name of the man who seeks the crown. Now!" He shouted so loud, birds took flight out the window.

She jumped and slammed her eyes shut. "Henry Stafford."

He pushed off the wall away from her, a little surprised she'd provided him a name. "The Duke of Buckingham?" He inhaled, unaware he'd been holding his breath. Of all the names he expected to roll off her tongue, Buckingham was not one of them. Not only did the man have his hand in half the lands in England; he held favor with King Edward. Broc had met Buckingham in Wales and he displayed a charisma that charmed the highest of aristocrats.

Broc's mind filled with questions he was certain she couldn't answer. "'Tis not a name ye should be tossing around with words like *treason,* lest you have proof."

"I do." She dashed across the room and retrieved a document from one of her many satchels. The corners were already mangled, but bits of red wax still clung to the outer edges. She gripped the parchment in her hand so tight, he feared it might crumble.

"'Tis Buckingham's signet and his signature." She shook the document at him. "And I must deliver it to King Edward's brother before 'tis too late."

His eyes flicked briefly toward the signature, then just as quickly returned to her. "Too late. Ye intend to save your king?"

"I fear King Edward will meet his maker before I can help him, but his sons will be in danger the moment their father breathes his last. Buckingham intends to name the king's sons bastards."

In nigh six months, Broc hadn't managed to gather half this much information against the English. And now here she stood holding the very evidence he needed to persuade his king to align with France. He guarded his emotions. "How?"

She growled between clenched teeth and stepped toward him. "King Edward entered into a secret marriage to a woman who was still alive when he wed the queen." She paused, obviously frustrated by his lack of response. "My king is a bigamist!" she yelled. "Which makes his marriage invalid, hence making the princes illegitimate."

God's hooks! He rubbed his eyes in an effort to ease the piercing pain stabbing the back of his eyeballs. There could only be one reason Buckingham would name the princes bastards. He was the leader of the rebellion. "Buckingham intends to seize the crown."

Lady Ives blew a gust of air that smelled oddly of mint leaves and dropped her arms to her sides. "Someone put poison in those vials, and 'twasn't me, nor Edlynn."

From beneath her lashes she looked up at him, her eyes pleading her innocence. Did she have any idea how much danger she was in? He tucked a loose tendril behind her ear and cupped her cheek. His desire to protect her felt achingly familiar. "Your knowledge alone places your life in danger. Why do ye risk so much?"

She stepped forward; her skirt brushed against his shins. Her soft hand slid over his as if to bind him to her. "In exchange for the information, I intend to plead with the king's brother to relieve my father of his duties."

He held her head while his thumb moved over her scar, already accusing her father of the deed. "Is a man of his ilk worth saving?"

"I believe everyone is worth saving."

"And who will save ye?"

Wet spiked lashes lay against her cheek. "Mayhap I am not worth saving."

Chapter 6

Lizzy pulled her mantle around her and followed Lord Maxwell to the stable through a curtain of rainfall. Sleep deprived and fraught with anxiety, she felt certain her sanity was slipping behind the deluge of emotions in her head. Grief was no stranger to her, nor was hatred. Lord Hollister took Edlynn from her, as he had her other loved ones. She felt more determined than ever to see the man brought to heel and her father released from his charge.

The cloak John provided Lord Maxwell poured over his broad form like black oil, grimly reminding her of the executioner. Her steps slowed as Father's likeness flashed through her head, his bloody ax clutched in one gloved hand.

Angst seized her.

She stopped. The rain quickly separated her and her vision.

He pivoted and took two strides back toward her. Her gaze shifted to Lord Maxwell's ungloved hands, which held no weapons of death. One arm carried her satchels, while the other held Beatrice in her cage, covered with a scrap of wool. Raindrops dripped from his spiked black lashes and ran in rivulets down his thick, corded throat. Her father and the man standing before her had no similarities. Lord

Maxwell's determination to protect her confused her as much as it comforted her.

"Come, Lizbeth," he ordered and continued in the direction of the stable.

She greedily followed. Of all the people God could have sent to deliver her into sanctuary, He chose a Scot. Lord Maxwell could have ended her life with one hand, taken the document she'd stolen from Lord Hollister's chamber, and used it to benefit his own cause. Instead, he remained surprisingly quiet while she tended his stitches and wrapped his ribs, then calmly collected her things and escorted her from the chamber like a proper Englishman.

He never even looked at the document.

She pulled the neck of her mantle together and sloshed through the mud in his wake. He led her into the stable, where she was greeted by an entourage of people on horseback. Celeste straddled a mare beside John, who sat atop a chestnut stallion. A yellowish mare with a black mane was weighted down with a mirage of leather satchels and was easily the ugliest horse Lizzy had ever seen. The nag only stood half the size of the all-white beast Smitt sat astride.

They were their own army, a mixture of Scotland and England, and their association with her placed each of their lives in peril.

She pulled back her hood. "What is this?"

"The road leading to Yorkshire is the same as the one leading to the borderlands," John answered. "'Tis nay reason we shouldnae travel together. 'Twill be safer, aye?"

"Aye," Lord Maxwell agreed.

"You mock my intelligence, Sir John. More than one road runs through England." Her words had no sooner left her mouth when Lord Maxwell wrapped his hands around her waist and hoisted her atop the king's stallion.

She glared down at him. "Have you no concern for your friends and their well-being?"

"John is my cousin, as is Smitt. They belong to my clan. I protect my brethren and honor their wishes to return to a land less riddled with hypocrisy and turmoil." He tied her belongings to the stallion and stroked its withers. "Not to mention, John sold the tippling house this morn to a blootered Englishman, which places him favorably high on my list of acquaintances."

When he readied himself to mount up behind her, Lizzy stopped him with one hand. "Wait. We will not travel as quickly doubled up. Can you not ride your own horse?" She didn't want to tell him she couldn't spend an entire day wrapped in his arms, smelling his spicy scent, wanting naught more than to curl into his embrace and allow him to protect her.

"This is my horse. I stole him myself." Lord Maxwell flashed her a brilliant grin and attempted to mount again.

She turned to John. "I have enough coin to purchase a horse. Have you any to sell?"

"Aye—"

"Nay," Lord Maxwell interrupted. "We ride together. I cannae protect ye if someone decides to ambush us."

"And who will protect her?" Lizzy pointed at Celeste.

Lord Maxwell rolled his eyes, an action that was beginning to annoy her. "*She* is not being sought by men trying to kill her. Besides, Celeste is a bit angry with John for lying to her about his heritage."

"Angry?" Celeste repeated the word with an acidic tone. "Angry is when a wife discovers her husband is bedding down with another woman." Celeste nudged her horse in the loins. "I would more describe my state of mind as bloodthirsty. A man doesn't keep secrets from his wife for two years and expect to . . ." Celeste's words became inaudible as she trotted out of the stable.

"'Tis not a wise man who lies to his woman." Lord Maxwell grinned at John, as did Smitt, obviously finding the poor man's misery entertaining. "At least I told ye I was a Scot."

Why did he speak to her as if she were *his* woman? "You lied to Celeste as well."

"Celeste is not my woman."

"Nor am I, m'lord." Lizzy jumped to her feet in front of him, filling the air with a burst of sweet-smelling hay. "And I intend to inform Celeste at the first opportunity that I am not your wife, and then you can bear her anger. Not I." She shuffled through the hay toward the yellow horse. "Is this mount available for purchase, Sir John?"

"Ye can have her. 'Tis the most ill-tempered nag I've ever owned."

Lizzy brushed noses with the mare and scratched her chin, already contemplating a name for her new friend.

"If ye insist on riding alone, then ye will at least ride at my side." Lord Maxwell mounted and waited for her to do the same, then clicked his tongue and the four of them trotted out of the stable. "'Tis going to be an unbearable day riding in this weather."

"I like the rain." Lizzy pulled back her hood and felt the drizzle on her cheeks. Rain reminded her of tears, as if someone else in the world cried besides her.

"Ye will catch an ague and die."

"I am afraid of many things, m'lord. Death is not one of them."

"Nonetheless. I'll not have ye catching the fever before I deliver ye to York." Lord Maxwell pulled her hood back over her head and popped her nose with his fingertip.

His gesture made Lizzy smile inside. The Scot's odd mannerisms were starting to grow on her.

Broc eased his stallion to a stop for the third time that afternoon, waving the others on over the knoll. The sun had hidden the majority of the day, only peeking out enough to dry them before another bout of rain soaked them again.

With his elbows raised, he twisted side to side. While Lizbeth's medicine relieved his pain, his stitches itched like day-old bug bites. Frustrated didn't begin to explain the state of mind he was in. He looked back at his angel, now fully draped over the mare's nape, sleeping soundly. Long waves of sable hair painted with red flames decorated the mare's black mane and hid her face from him. How could the woman sleep in such a position?

The yellow nag bent low to nibble a bit of spring grass at the base of a young alder tree. Lizbeth sagged forward, but clung to the beast like a tick to a mule. Having been informed by Smitt about yester eve's incident with the man in the stable, Broc was certain she'd only slept small hours the previous night. He had thought to scold her for going to the stable un-attended, but held no desire to banter with her this day. She was dealing with grief, and he doubted she needed repri-manding by the same person she held responsible for the loss of her friend. 'Twas best he let the matter rest. He needed no more guilt.

He scanned the foothill behind them covered with the signs of spring. Broc knew the English were amidst the thick green foliage. He wondered how many of the king's guards were now hunting them, and how many of those same men were loyal to Buckingham. He inventoried the number of weapons on his person: two *sgian dubhs* in his boots, two dirks at his waist, and a broadsword currently sheathed at his back. He could battle at least a dozen alone. Smitt could probably take twice that many, and John had shown no mercy on the battlefield during the border wars. Still and all, Broc preferred to cross England without having to draw his sword.

If he failed in his efforts to return home, Ian would be the only son remaining to reign when Da passed. Neither he nor his younger brother had been trained for leadership. Aiden had been the chosen one. Having lost the prime son, mayhap Da would now see the importance of educating more than one heir.

Casting his thoughts aside, he pushed his jaw side to side, popping his neck. He trotted up beside Lizbeth, pulled the reins from her relaxed hands, and tied them to his stallion, after which he grabbed hold of the back of her wet gown and hoisted her off the mare and into his lap.

She gasped and lurched backward, catching him in the jaw. "Be still, woman. Else you'll spook the horses."

"What are you doing?"

"I am trying to get us across England alive."

Her head whipped from side to side, searching her surroundings. "Where are the others?"

"Ahead of us." Broc patted the stallion's hindquarters, impressed by the beast's training. "A few more hours will put us outside of Lincolnshire."

"A few more hours?" she complained and slumped against him. "I cannot ride astride a few more hours. My legs are numb now."

"'Tis a most unpleasant feeling, aye?" He couldn't resist.

She made a noise that sounded like a humph, then twisted and stretched her spine, which brought her backside in direct contact with his cock. Blood rushed from every outer point of his body straight to his core. He squeezed his legs around the stallion's belly, setting a pace that moved her body gracefully against his with every powerful stride.

He'd heard many tales, most from Smitt and Aiden, about odd places they'd made love to women—in the river, over a barrel of mead—but never had either of them mentioned astride a horse. The image in his mind's eye made it look deliciously wicked.

God's hooks! Why did she have to smell so good? And why the devil was she so damned naked every time he thought about her? He splayed his hand wide around Lizbeth's waist and pulled her close. His desire to have her felt more like an obsession than a want and made his previous infatuation with Lady Juliana seem adolescent.

Chapter 7

The sun dipped into a speckled horizon, casting dark shadows over a small inn nestled in the hills. With the flex of two fingers, Broc motioned John to his side and gestured toward the half dozen stallions ensconced in crimson and blue velvets tethered outside the stable. "The king's guard," Broc whispered to avoid waking the sleeping angel snuggled against his chest.

"We go on?" John's question sounded more like a strong suggestion even in hushed tones.

"Celeste looks nigh ready to fall from her horse, and this lass"—he glanced down at Lizbeth—"gave into exhaustion only an hour ago." He flexed his backside, trying not to squirm. "The horses are depleted, and my arse feels as though I'm sitting on tiny dirks."

"I am a wee bit tired myself," John admitted.

Broc snorted. "A wee bit, aye?" John undoubtedly suffered the most, having traveled the entire previous night. Broc looked over his shoulder at Smitt—bright-eyed, straight back, and how had he managed to shave? He resembled a young buck about to play in the spoils. "How the devil can he look so full of piss?"

"He's younger. More stamina, I suspect. He'll be beneath

a gaggle o' wenches afore the eve blackens. If I had different parts, I'd tup the man."

A touch of jealousy made him pull Lizbeth a little closer.

"What then?" John asked.

Broc contemplated the situation. Anyone who'd stepped foot on Tower Hill knew the executioner's daughter. "I suspect the man in the stable might have recognized Lizbeth from London. If he happens upon the English who are undoubtedly pursuing us, I've no doubt he would give away our position for less than a ducat."

"Then we bunker down in the woodland for the eve," John suggested.

Broc gestured for Smitt to come forth.

"Want me to kill 'em?" Smitt curled a devious grin, making Broc thankful his cousin fought on the same side as he.

"If they pose a threat, aye. How many weapons do ye have?"

Smitt's fingers extended one by one. "Eight."

"Test the air. If ye feel it safe, secure us rooms and care for the horses, then find a back entrance where we can slip Lizbeth in unnoticed."

John handed Smitt a satchel. "Make haste, and give a single one o' my coins to any o' the drabs, and I'll tell them ye prefer a pillicock to a nock."

"Aye." Smitt disappeared over the knoll and into the inn.

Broc twisted to look at the bundle of beauty against his chest and brought a second arm around her waist. She whimpered and stitched her brows together, her fingers curling into fists beneath her chin. Broc caressed her forearm until her hands relaxed. Was she thinking of Edlynn in her dream? Trying to protect her old friend? He tried to imagine what horrors took place behind her closed eyes. Who tormented her? Was it the same man she was risking her life to save?

"Who is she?" John asked.

"Just a woman who saved me from the Tower." He traced a finger over her puckered brow, smoothing out her angst.

"Ye look at her like she is more than just a woman. Do ye feel indebted to her?"

He didn't know what he felt for her. Gratitude? Lust? Or mayhap it was something more deep-seated. Something he'd never felt for Lady Juliana. "Had she not appeared when she did, I suspect Ian would be the one accepting Da's title one day."

"If ye've any honor at all, ye will not repay her by delivering her into the hands of that bastard who nigh ravaged our clan."

"She thinks Gloucester a champion, a protector."

"Then she is a fool, but a bonnie fine one at that."

Broc pulled the hood of her mantle enough to cover her face, hiding her beauty from his cousin, then glared at John. "Think ye should go talk to your wife?"

John shook his bald head profusely. "The woman has held her tongue all day. 'Tis not like Celeste. I fear she may never forgive me."

Broc caught Celeste's eye. She turned away with a jerk and a snort. "She will cool. When she sees Scotland, her opinion will change. 'Tis a far greater land to live in than this godforsaken spoiled country."

"And what of ye? Scotland awaits ye as does your da's title. 'Tis something ye used to want."

"I still do. Protecting my family and the clan will always be my first priority."

"Then ye intend to honor your da's agreement with Clan Scott?"

"Aye." Marriage to Lady Juliana suddenly didn't hold the same appeal as it had before. Nonetheless, he was bound by a duty to protect his clan and that duty included a marriage to Laird Scott's daughter. He thought about Lizbeth's document and how it could aid his cause. If only he could convince her to give it to him. "But mayhap I have a means of protecting the clan along with all of Scotland."

"Does the lass have anything to do with that means?"

"Mayhap." Broc withheld any further information. John could peck at him all he liked, but he would be getting no straight answers.

"I suspect she knows something or has something you're wanting. 'Tis why ye are aiding her?"

Broc shrugged.

"Ye are not married to Laird Scott's daughter yet. Mayhap a tumble with the lass would get ye what you want?"

"I dinnae tumble. That was Aiden." *And his appetite for lust gained him a lethal beating,* Broc added mentally, not wanting to vilify his brother's name aloud.

John's gaze dipped back to Lizbeth. "'Tis a long way to York."

"'Tis two days. I controlled myself for two years at Dryburgh. Think ye I cannae keep my cock in my trews for two damned days?"

John shrugged back. "I trust ye will be meeting with King James upon your return then?" Again, John pecked at him.

"I hope to send Da while I meet with Laird Scott."

John ceased his interrogation, and they waited in silence until Smitt returned.

"Come. The guards are being occupied. There's a maiden awaiting us at the back entrance."

"Who is occupying the guards?" Broc worried over the ease of Smitt's plan, though it was unnecessary when women were involved.

"A few wenches I promised to please later."

Lizzy awoke in a darkened corridor and instantly panicked. She squirmed, and the arms holding her tightened.

"Shh, Lizbeth. Ye are safe." Lord Maxwell's deep, soothing

voice cast the biting fear from her body, making her feel weightless; then she realized she was being carried.

Knowing her legs wouldn't hold her if she insisted he put her down, she worked her hands around his neck in a foolish effort to aid him. A single rushlight cast the sharp edges of his face in shadows, making him appear dark, mysterious. Oddly enough, he didn't frighten her. 'Twas quite the opposite, she admitted. She hadn't felt this safe since Kamden died.

The cadence of sluggish footfalls sounded ahead of them. A rotund woman with a heavy limp led them through the corridor and opened a door.

"'Tisn't much, but the bedding is clean, and I added eiderdown to the mattress this morn." The woman entered and stood on her toes to light the only wall sconce in a room with no window.

Lizzy calculated immediately how long the tallow would last before examining the confines of the small chamber— the very small chamber—the size of the antechamber Lord Hollister had secured her in after the fire. Brown stained the walls from years of seepage and the furnishings were naught short of grim: a bed and a cuttie stool holding a cracked pitcher and bowl. Lord Maxwell would have to duck beneath the doorjamb to enter.

"There's a cistern at the end of the hall, if'n ye're in need of washin'." The woman pointed with a flick of her wrist, then shuffled down the hall.

"Thank ye for the hospitality," Lord Maxwell said to her back, then squeezed through the entranceway, kicking the door closed behind him.

Lizzy looked at the bed, then back at Lord Maxwell, whose stunned face matched her sentiments. "Tell me we are not sharing this chamber."

"If I told ye that, I'd be lying and I dinnae lie. 'Twas either the room or the stable with John and Celeste."

"And Smitt?" she asked, more out of courtesy than interest.

His brows slashed. "Dinnae fash over Smitt's well-being. He will have nay difficulty finding a bed, I assure ye."

Lord Maxwell set her on a sinfully soft mattress, then bent down on his knee in front of her. When he started unlacing her boots, she grabbed fistfuls of coarse bedding.

"What are you doing?" She stared at the top of his head.

"Ye lost a great deal of sleep yester eve because of your attentions to me. I am merely returning the favor."

"By undressing me?" A vibration curled around the leg he currently held. Shameless was the single word that came to mind.

He peeled off one boot and stocking and set them aside, then went to work on the other. "I hardly call removing your footwear *undressing you,* but if you're in need of a maid's service to assist ye with your wet gown, I'd be happy to oblige." His head raised only long enough to wink at her.

Was the man toying with her again? If he wanted to force himself on her, he wouldn't need to remove her boots to do so. "I have never been privy to a maid, nor have I ever needed one," she snapped.

She formed words to shoo him from the chamber the same time he wrapped his hot hands around her foot and started kneading. He rolled his knuckles over the arch, and all her defenses left her. Her limbs demanded her to remain perfectly still and revel in this moment of divine pleasure. She tucked the side of her lip between her teeth, stifling any sound akin to wanton. His fingers worked the aches from the pads of her foot, including each toe, and then she felt him raise the other to pay it equal attention. Her head fell back, and she closed her eyes.

Mercy Mary. The man was a deity from Heaven.

The palm of his hand cupped her calf, gliding to and fro from the back of her knee to her ankle. She inched her way closer to the edge of the bed.

Higher. Without a doubt, the devil slipped that word in her head. Warmth crawled from her toes, up her legs, and exploded into a blaze between her thighs. She sucked icy air between her teeth, startled by the unfamiliar sensation.

Reality smacked her like nine whips across her face. She had to distance herself from this man and his magic hands, else she find herself spoiled before she reached Fountains Abbey. "'Tis enough, m'lord. Thank you." She scooted back, flushing the backs of her knees to the bed's edge.

"A day astride a horse can make ye feel bruised from the inside out. Have ye other aches in need of attention before I go wash?" He cocked a wicked brow.

Her backside came to mind, but she pushed the wickedness from her tongue in time to respond with propriety. "Nay. I'm feeling quite right."

He stood, removed his cloak, and then hung it on one of the four wall pegs, after which he bent and pulled a black blade from each boot, two daggers from his sides, and a massive sword from inside the back of his doublet. He methodically placed the daggers and sword hilt up against the wall, then tucked one of the black knives beneath the pillow; the other remained in his grip. The man was a walking mercenary.

Lizzy stood on shaky legs and pressed her back against the wall. She hated weapons. She despised the sight of them and everything they represented. "Why are you so heavily armed?"

He turned to face her and wore an expression that called her stupid. "God's hooks, Lizbeth. We are being hunted. Five of the king's guards are within these walls. I have a blade for each of them should they discover who we are. How else would ye have me protect you?"

"Pray forgive my ignorance." Embarrassment pinned her chin to her chest.

"I regard your fear of me as an insult. Had I wanted to dispose of ye, I could have left your stubborn arse on that damned nag and let your precious English have you whilst I pressed toward my homelands," he spouted in a fierce tone.

The timid child in her wanted to beg his forgiveness, but the woman in her demanded more. "Why did you not?"

Fists clenched at his sides, his lips formed an indignant straight line. She searched his blue eyes for an answer he seemed unwilling to provide. "Why are you helping me?"

"Because I vowed it." He slipped a black blade in his sleeve and stepped toward the door.

He obviously had naught more to say on the subject, and she didn't dare suggest he might have ulterior motives. The document was the reason he kept her safe. No other explanation made sense.

"I dinnae know what manner of man has taught ye that you are of no worth, but I believe your life has value."

Awestruck by his words, she felt her body sag. Her mouth opened, but she could form no comment.

"I am going to wash. We depart before the cock crows, so we must find sleep quickly."

"In this bed? Together?" A vibration ripped through her body at the very thought of sharing a bed with the man who touched her heart with one statement.

"I will sleep on the floor." He checked the corridor and left.

The moment the door closed, she rushed to disassemble her wet gown. First came her false sleeves, then both her skirts. Her bodice posed an altogether separate problem. She reached behind her back twisting and turning awkwardly to untie the laces all the while keeping her eyes fixed on the door. If he returned now, she would be mortified.

She was panting by the time she hung the heavy damask garments on the wall pegs. Garbed in her threadbare tunic, she wrenched back the coverlet and slipped between remarkably soft sheets. A giggle and a moan escaped her lips at the same time. The bed made up for what the rest of the chamber lacked in size and frivolities. She took a moment to stretch out on her back and rub her legs against the sheets. Edlynn would have taken delight in a bed so fine. In truth, her old friend would have had no qualms about sharing such splendor with Lord Maxwell.

If Lizzy were being honest with herself, she would admit Lord Maxwell was a man she could share her bed with. Her body reacted to her thoughts like a fever. Her toes curled; her nipples tightened into hard, almost painful peaks; and a pulse beat within her womb. Her palm flattened low over her belly. She'd never known a man's kiss or the feel of a man's hand upon her breast, but Edlynn had explained that a woman desires as much as a man. That she yearns in secrecy to be held and caressed and sometimes she wants to be trea-sured. Lizzy had no doubt this is what desire felt like.

Footfalls whispered outside the door.

Rolling to her side, she pulled the wool to her neck and positioned herself as close to the edge as she could without falling off.

A click announced his entry. The fresh clean scent of juniper and mint flooded her senses, then came the rustle of garments. He groaned, and she thought of his wounds. His body needed rest more than hers. She should be sleeping on the floor. She looked down at the wooden slates dusted with dirt and bits of rushes and cursed her selfishness. Guilt would eat at her the entire night and neither of them would be of worth on the morrow. Mayhap she could bargain with him. He'd proven to be a man of his word.

Her stomach churned with nerves as she stared at the small yellow flame flickering atop the candle stub. "M'lord, if you sleep on top of the coverlet, I see no reason we cannot both be well rested come the morrow."

Long moments filled with only his breathing followed her offer. She could hear the nettles inside his mind forming a barb.

"Scotsmen are known to be lusty barbarians. 'Tis an unwise offer ye make without further stipulations." His voice towered above her.

She should have feigned sleep and left him to the floor. If he insisted she actually give him terms, then she would oblige him. "Vow you will not steal my virtue, and I will allow you to share the bed."

"Think ye I would have to steal it, do ye?"

She didn't have to see his face to know his eyes were alight with mischief. "I see arrogance followed you back from the cistern."

He laughed, only once, but 'twas a chuckle just the same. "I suspect ye want my word?"

"Aye."

A moment of silence prefaced his inhale. "I vow I will not take your virtue without your permission."

She scowled at the wall. She may not be a titled noble with lands and a hefty dowry, but she had every intention of entering Fountains Abbey a virgin, and she would not need the chastity belt to achieve that goal.

The mattress fell with his weight. He bounced a little. "'Tis soft."

An air of tension filled the space between them. He sprawled out his limbs, and her heart thumped against her backbone. He moaned, then turned. Not five breaths later, he rolled again. His arm knocked her shoulder. She caught herself before she fell from the bed.

"Sorry, lass. 'Tis small. Not half the size of my bed back home." He twisted again.

She wrestled with her lack of patience and controlled the urge to humph. The man liked to chatter. Mayhap if she talked to him he would settle. She turned toward him on her side and tucked her hands beneath her ear. He lay on his back with his thick arms crossed over his bare chest. The small candle flame cast crescent-shaped shadows over his muscles in an artistic design much like the symbol on his arm. "Your brother had a similar mark. Does it mean something?"

His head turned toward her on the bolster. "'Tis one of three words that holds significance in my clan. *Neart*, *Grá*, and *Onóir.* 'Tis the old language—Gaelic. My grandmum was born in the Highlands of Scotland and ingrained my kin with these words. Aiden was marked with *'neart,'* which means strength. My younger brother, Ian, bears the word *'onóir,'* which means honor."

She reached out and traced the letters with her finger. "And what does *'gra'* mean?"

He stared directly at her, took two full breaths, and said, "Love."

Her throat clenched. She didn't know why, but the intensity with which he looked at her and said that word made breathing difficult.

"My brethren live by these words, protecting their country and their home."

"Tell me of your home."

He turned back toward the ceiling and closed his eyes as if drawing forth a memory. "Picture Heaven and ye will see Scotland. I cannae think of another place I would rather live and die." He spoke of Scotland like a lover. "Six months have passed since I've seen my homelands, but I know spring is bearing her gentle hand. Wildflowers are coming to life around the rivers and lochs."

"What kind of flowers?" Lizzy wanted to smell his kingdom, make a scent that would capture the essence of Scotland. She reveled at the thought of making a new soap, a new oil.

"Purple ones, white ones, some pink." He shrugged. "Aunt Radella and Aunt Jean dry them and mix them with the floor rushes."

She smiled at the simplicity of his description. "You've a big family?"

"Aye. Everything is bigger in Scotland. The beds, the

chambers . . . the men. Hundreds live within the bailey at Skonóir Castle. We feast in the keep every Sabbath. The men argue and fight, the women cook and yell at their bairns. And chickens," he added as an afterthought. "The damned chickens are all over the place. The courtyard is riddled with them. They follow ye everywhere."

"Beatrice would like that."

"'Tis hardly a peaceful place, I admit, but one is never at a loss for company."

"'Tis why you do not like the quiet."

"I am simply unaccustomed to it." His tone softened.

She thought of how quiet and alone her life had been and part of her yearned for the life he described. "Have you a healer among your people?"

"Aye. A right mean auld crone. She hides her herbs and potions and is stingy as the devil." He gave a dramatic shiver, trying to humor her, no doubt.

"You jest. She cannot be so bad. Who is she?"

He laughed. "My grandmum. The bairns are terrified of her, as am I."

Lizzy tried to picture him cowering to his grandmother. "Tell me why."

"Every time I pay visit, she pokes me with her bony fingers and badgers me about breeding."

"Breeding?"

"Aye. I am the son of a man who sired twelve bairns. 'Tis expected of me to do the same."

Twelve? Lizzy practically drooled. She would have given anything for just one sister.

"I can say all their names in one breath."

The tickle dancing in her throat snuck out between her lips in a sort of hoot.

His head turned, popping his neck in two snaps. "Think ye I cannae do it?" He took a deep breath, held it, for extra drama, no doubt, and then . . . "Magnus—named after Da, but died in infancy; Aiden—named after my grandda; Broderick—that would be me, named after my da's brother; Muira—named after my mam; then Radella, Jean, Lindsay—named after my aunts on my mam's side; Beth, Deirdre, Lilian, Mattie—named after my aunts on my da's side; and Ian." He inhaled and beamed a wide grin.

Her giggles turned into outright laughter by the time he'd finished. "You must be proud of your skill."

"Oh, aye."

"Was Ian named after anyone in your family or did you run out of breath?"

He chuckled again, creasing his cheeks with dimples. "Da was so elated to get another male heir after eight girls he told Mam to name him whatever she liked."

"Your family sounds lovely. I can see why you would want to protect them."

His eyes closed. "'Tis a duty I fear I have failed."

Lord Maxwell undoubtedly thought of the brother he'd been unable to protect from Father's whip. "I wish my father hadn't stolen your brother from you."

He looked at her. "Ye should know that Aiden had been beaten nigh to death before we were delivered to the Tower."

"It does not change the fact that he was alive before Father delivered the lashes."

Silence followed.

"Mayhap we should find our rest now," she suggested.

"Mayhap."

Lizzy turned her back to him and curled her hands beneath her cheek. She anticipated the loud rumble of his snoring, but his breathing was soft and his movements restless. Her eyes fixed on the candle flame sputtering its last bit of life.

Only moments later, the light extinguished. Blackness engulfed her.

She sucked in an audible breath and stared into the darkness, wishing she hadn't left Mother's rosary in the pocket of her gown.

Nine, ten, eleven . . . She counted her breaths, which came louder and faster with each passing second as if she were drowning. She waited, not knowing who would enter her thoughts. She tried to think of anything but the people she loved, the people she hated—flowers, chickens, her boots, a stool. . . .

Emma.

Lord Hollister's wife flashed in brilliant colors inside her head. Black hair, olive skin, rose-colored lips stretched wide in horror as they tied her to the dunking stool by the river.

Emma gasped for air when they pulled her out.

Lizzy did the same.

Lord Maxwell rolled toward her; his arm slid beneath her neck while his other arm wrapped around her shoulders. He held her against his chest in a guarded embrace, his breath warming the back of her head. "Sleep, angel. All will be well. I will be here to protect ye should the demons sneak into your sleep." He kissed her hair and then fell against the pillow.

He couldn't know the value of the gift he offered.

"Thank you," she whispered and slowly crept her hand inside his, seeking a little more of his protection. He squeezed her fingers and rhythmically brushed her knuckles with the pad of his thumb. Behind her closed lids she pictured flowers— purple ones, white ones, some pink. A smile eased her tension as her toes stepped into a valley painted with color. A grand castle stood proud and tall in the distance: a symbol of strength, protection. In her vision, Lord Maxwell's fingers tightened around hers and led her into paradise. His paradise. His home.

Scotland.

Chapter 8

Broc awoke with a plan.

After pulling himself away from the warmth of his sleeping angel, he dressed with less pain than the day before. He secured his weapons within his garments and stepped into the empty corridor. Snoring guided him past two chamber doors. Feminine whimpers and the tattoo of a rocking bed led his ear to a third chamber. Deep moans escalated in time with the cadence of slapping flesh.

Then came a loud smack.

Silence.

A long throaty howl of pleasure wailed behind the door.

God's hooks! Broc shook his head and wished those sounds didn't have him raging hard and sweating like a swine. He had to remind himself why he'd left a soft, warm bed with a soft, warm woman curled in his arms.

He jerked his head side to side and set his tension free in two pops, then raised his knuckles and tapped the wood. A yellow light brightened beneath the door until it swayed inward. The ripe smell of sex attacked his nose the same time his eyes were greeted by a young naked woman.

"What do ye want?" she asked, making no attempt to hide her nudity.

Though it took him a moment, he tore his stare from her favors and searched the shadows of the room. "I'm looking for Smitt."

"He's occupied at the moment." The woman pulled the candle back far enough into the chamber to prove her point.

"What is it?" Smitt crawled off another woman and strutted toward the door like the proud cock he displayed. He rested his forearm against the door frame and grinned.

"Do ye ever sleep?" Broc knew his cousin to be a bit randy, but the man was going to contract diseases if he continued such continual play.

"I'll sleep when I'm dead. Are ye ready to go?"

"Soon. I was hoping to get a wee bit of assistance from your lady friends before we left."

"Your spitfire turn to ice, did she?"

Instantly piqued by the comment, Broc unsheathed a dirk from his waist and pressed the tip into Smitt's chin. "She is not my spitfire, and she damned certain is not ice. Reserve your filthy tongue for pleasuring the ladies, else you'll find it on the tip of my blade."

"Easy, cousin. 'Twas a jest." Smitt stepped back, raking his fingers through his black hair.

What was it about Lizbeth that made Broc so damned protective? He retracted his weapon and tamped his unwarranted anger. "Get dressed and find out where the guards are sleeping. Your lady friends may remain in their skin if they please."

Broc slipped out the back entrance and flattened his back against the side of a chicken shelter. If the warbling hens couldn't detect his presence, then neither could the guard relieving himself by an old oak. Anticipation sped up his heart rate. Perspiration dripped down his back, tickling his wounds.

He peeked around the corner. Between the moon's descent and the blush of dawn, Broc saw the guard stumble. He was blootered. An easy mark. Broc took two deep breaths of cool mist, sheathed his dirk, and bolted into the open.

His fist made contact with the back of the man's head before he even detected Broc's intentions. With any luck the man would awaken with a pounding headache and assume he'd dipped too far in the cups. Broc lifted the guard beneath the arms and dragged him through the muck and into the stable.

The horses pranced. Their tales swished in agitation. He gently lowered the guard into a pile of hay, wanting him to sleep peacefully. He scaled a ladder to the loft, where he found John snoring beneath a wool next to Celeste. He nudged John's shoulder. "'Tis time."

John sat up straight, pulling the blanket off Celeste's bare back with the action, and scratched his chest. His eyes remained closed. "I'm ready."

Broc didn't trust his response. "John, wake up. I need ye, my friend."

His eyes popped open. "What do ye want me to do?"

"Ready the guards' horses with England's colors and tie all our belongings to them. Tether the other mounts and have Celeste help ye walk them to the top of the knoll."

"Ten horses? Are ye wowf?" John spouted, fully awake now.

Celeste raised up, tucking the wool beneath her arms. "Don't be such a milksop, Scotsman. What can I do?"

Broc pulled a cobweb from her dusty brown hair and offered her a smile for her eagerness. "There's an unconscious man below. Strip him of his garments and pack his clothes with our things." Broc started back down the ladder, then popped back up. "Dinnae forget Lizbeth's chicken."

Celeste bobbed her head, making him proud to call her kin. The timing wasn't appropriate for an apology, but Celeste seemed to be in reasonable humor. "I lied to ye, Celeste. My name is not Sir Julian Ascott. It's Broc Maxwell. I am the son of Lord Magnus Maxwell, and I live in the West Marches of Scotland. I would like to welcome ye to my clan and beg your forgiveness."

Her head fell bashfully; her dark lashes batted. "Thank ye, m'lord. Ye are forgiven."

"Am I?" John asked.

"Nay," she returned sharply.

Broc dropped back down the ladder, leaving her scowling at John, and located Lizbeth's satchels. Confident his orders would be followed, he returned to the inn and back to the chamber he'd shared with Lizbeth.

Thinking the dark might steal her senses when she awoke, he replaced the candle in the wall sconce with a tallow he lit in the corridor. The small chamber filled with light, casting a glow over his angel, who looked seductively disheveled. Dark red waves fell over the pillow, and her pursed lips resembled the look of a satisfied woman. One long leg had wormed its way out from beneath the coverlet and her pale undertunic had crawled clear to her hip.

Broc's eyes drank in every curve from her ankle, alongside her calf, and locked on the top of her thigh. He angled his body to get a peek at her sweetly rounded backside. His already stiff cock gave a little kick. He jerked upright, stepped to her side of the bed, and shook her shoulder. "Lizbeth, wake up."

Her hands rose out of the covers and stretched high above her head. With feline grace, she arched her back and moaned. The laces of her undertunic had loosened in her sleep and now rode low enough to expose the soft outer ring of her nipple.

Devil take it! He wanted to taste her. He wanted to slide his tongue over the velvety texture until her nipple hardened between his teeth. His heart pounded against his tender ribs. Saliva thickened around his tongue. He licked his lips and swallowed. He had to physically and mentally stop himself from bending down and taking her into his mouth. Why did everyone have to be so damned naked? Not trusting himself to even touch her shoulder again, he bent over her and blew in her face. "Lizbeth, wake up. I need ye."

"Ohhh . . . Broc, I need you, too." She wrapped her arms around his neck and pulled him to her mouth. She suckled his bottom lip between her teeth and whimpered.

He braced himself overtop her with two fists on either side of her waist. His mind yelled at him to pull away, but his mouth completely disregarded the command. He nibbled her lips, tasting the sweet nectar she unknowingly offered and knew in that moment he would always crave more.

She'd used his given name. The fact she'd even been dreaming about him made her lips all the more difficult to leave. His conscience pushed to the forefront. He wasn't the type of man who wanted stolen kisses. He peeled her arms from his neck and raised the hem of her undertunic with his thumb and forefinger, then waited for her to ground herself in her surroundings.

Her eyes fluttered open. She looked confused and out of sorts, but not afraid. "Did you just kiss me?"

"Nay. Ye just kissed me."

Her fingers touched her wet lips; her gaze dropped to his mouth. "Why?"

"I suspect ye were having a right fine dream about your lover," Broc teased, trying to save her from embarrassment.

"I have no lover."

"Mayhap ye should take one. 'Tis a shame to waste all that passion in a cloister. I lived in a religious community for two years and nigh lost half my senses."

Lizbeth cocked her head, obviously stupefied by his suggestion. "Did you wake me to talk about entering the church?"

"Nay. I have your satchels, and I need your help."

"Do ye want me to check the stitching?"

"I want ye to mix up a potion." He grabbed her hand and pulled her from the bed, but her legs wouldn't cooperate. She wavered. He gripped her around the waist, supporting her weight from behind until she could manage the task on her own. Every second he held her was another second he held his breath. *Two days,* he reminded himself and wondered if he could hold his breath all the way to Yorkshire.

"I fear I cannot walk."

"Work the kinks from your legs, angel. We've work to do." He left her side and retrieved her damp garments from the peg. He tossed the stiff bodice on the bed, pulled her skirts apart, and widened the opening of the waist of her underskirt. He bent on one knee and waited for her.

She didn't move.

He glanced up at her. "Step in."

"What are you doing?"

"I'm dressing ye."

"I can dress myself."

"Think ye I have time for this argument again? Step in. 'Twill be quicker if I assist ye."

With one hand on his shoulder for support, she dipped her toes into the opening. He pulled the skirt over her hips and tied it with remarkable speed. He focused on his mission and damned the nervous boy inside him for allowing his hands to tremble. He snatched up her bodice and experienced a brief moment of relief when she willingly punched her fists through the openings.

"Is there something amiss, m'lord?" She stood stock-still while he tied the laces.

He didn't respond immediately. The sooner he got the lass dressed, the sooner he could quit ogling her tempting curves beneath her thin undertunic. "Not yet. Do ye have the herbs to make the tincture ye put on your father's whip? The one that steals a man's legs?"

Her gaze shifted to the bed, where her satchels lay. "I do. But the mixture can be lethal if mixed improperly. I would know who you intend to use it on before I agree to assist you."

"The guards." Invigorated by his plan, Broc rubbed his hands together.

Lizbeth agreed with one nod and set to work. He watched her mix the herbs with the utmost respect for her skill and intelligence. Grandmum had spent her life dabbling in medicines, most of which never helped. He knew firsthand Lizbeth's potions worked. 'Twas a shame her talents were wasted in the Tower.

Her fingers worked the pestle around the mortar until she achieved a fine powder. "Your attention is setting my nerves on edge. Mayhap you could fetch that pitcher of water."

While she poured the powder in the pitcher, he held his breath, not taking the chance of inhaling the dust.

"'Tis done. Enough for five men."

"Gather your things and finish dressing. Dinnae leave this chamber until I return."

"Aye, m'lord."

Broc repeated his earlier steps to Smitt's chamber, fully prepared this time for the naked beauty who answered his knock. He flashed her a flirtatious smile. "Want to earn a few extra coins, lass?"

Her eyes lit up and the black rotten grin she gave Broc made him take a step backward to regroup.

Smitt came to the door dressed and alert. "Who are we killing?"

"No one." Broc entered the chamber, far too small for four people, and set the pitcher on the cuttie stool. He pulled seven coins from his doublet and tossed them on the bed. Focusing his attention on the other girl, who thankfully wore a thin wrapper, he pointed at the coins. "There is a ducat for each guard ye manage to get a cup of this drink down, one of whom is in the stable. The two groats are for the delivery of two guards' garments. Are ye interested?"

The girl nodded her head. "'Twill be my pleasure."

Broc and Smitt followed the two girls down the corridor

and waited outside the guards' chambers. The door Smitt stood beside opened first. A hand popped out delivering the first pile of garments. Not long after, the woman Broc had followed mimicked the action.

The girl stepped out. "The drink. 'Tis a poison?"

Broc couldn't prevent the memory her question solicited. "Nay. 'Tis not a poison, but a product of mercy. Divide the drink five ways. Can ye count?"

"Aye, sir." She flashed him another ugly smile. "Five coins, five drinks, five guards. I'll tend the man in the stable myself and have Ulna deliver the other four. Thank ye, sir. Your coin is most appreciated."

Broc gave Smitt orders to head for the knoll while he fetched Lizbeth from her chamber. He opened the door and found her sitting on the bed, holding her satchels. She looked up at him, her golden eyes filled with a trust he couldn't begin to understand. But he wouldn't fail her.

Not her.

He extended his hand, palm up. "Come, Lizbeth."

She stood and placed her hand in his as if they'd known each other a lifetime and allowed him to lead her out of the inn. When he pulled her toward the knoll instead of the stable, she hesitated, but didn't release his hand. Truth was, her hold tightened. "Where are we going?"

He motioned toward the crest of the hill where the silhouettes of ten awaiting horses blackened in front of a pink dawn.

"What are you about, m'lord?"

He pulled her in front of him and raised her knuckles to his lips. "I believe ye are worth saving, Lizbeth Ives. I am escorting ye to Middleham Castle in Yorkshire as Sir Julian Ascott, guard and noble servant to the King of England. I haven't the same faith as ye regarding the Duke of Gloucester's benevolence, and I've no intention of sending ye into his domain alone."

Chapter 9

Lizzy's legs spread wide around the belly of her steed. She didn't know why Lord Maxwell put her on the largest of the stolen horses, but the strained muscles in her thighs already burned, and they'd only been astride a few hours. She watched him trade their original mounts to a tenant landlord for food and coin, then divided the fare among John, Smitt, and Celeste.

He swaggered toward her, possessing a noble air which had naught to do with the stolen garments he wore. A crimson satin doublet embroidered with golden suns stretched around his broad shoulders and tight black trews emphasized every angle in his muscular thighs. For reasons unbeknownst to her, all the man had to do was breathe in her direction and her breasts stood at attention.

"Ye will eat whilst we ride." He handed Lizzy a chunk of demain bread, dried mutton, and a flask of watered mead.

"Aye, m'lord," she agreed, knowing he would force her otherwise.

After a quick check of the horse's hooves, he stood at the beast's nose and stroked its muzzle. He peeked at her through inky lashes with the shy look of a boy, but his wandering eyes belonged to a man, for his gaze sent jolts of heat up her spine.

"He is a powerful steed. Think ye can ride him the remainder of the day?"

Nay. She redirected his question with one of her own so she wouldn't have to lie. "Why am I astride the biggest horse?"

"He is the fastest. In the event of an attack, I want ye to be able to escape," he explained and mounted a horse four hands shorter than hers.

I would prefer to ride with you, she admitted silently, but forced the valiant smile he undoubtedly searched for and picked at the bread.

"If we ride all day, we will be outside Yorkshire by nightfall." He spurred his steed forward. "I will take ye to your duke on the morrow."

Her heart fell a little. His vow to protect her would be served once she settled things with the king's brother. There would be no reason for Lord Maxwell to remain behind. Living out her days at Fountains Abbey may have once sounded glorious, but now seemed as lonely as her life in London.

John and Smitt, outfitted the same as Lord Maxwell, followed atop two black steeds on blankets decorated with gold cart wheels. They guarded her like noble knights of the throne, and Celeste played the role of her lady's maid. They were a small cavalcade traveling in disguise to Middleham Castle.

A flock of blackbirds passed in the east in a ribbon that swooped over the valley. A raven broke free of the medley and followed their progress for hours beneath a sun far hotter than April was accustomed. No breeze passed through the air, and the weight of her gown was just another suffocating burden for her to bear.

Determined to prove her vitality, Lizzy refused to show signs of fatigue this day. They traveled little on the open road, staying mainly to the riverbanks and timberland. Every village they approached gave Lord Maxwell the opportunity to inquire about her well-being. He watched her with a predator's eye, circling her like the alpha of their pack.

Late afternoon, he cantered up beside her. "Do ye wish to stop, Lizbeth?"

"Do not stop on my account, m'lord. I'm quite right," she lied. Not that it mattered. If he decided to rein in, she wouldn't be able to get off the horse. The aches in her thighs and lower back had turned to numbness hours before. This was her punishment for putting the tincture on Father's whip.

"Are ye certain? Even Smitt is starting to fade. We can press on to another village, but I dinnae think Celeste can last that long."

"Tell me you do not suggest we rein in for the night. Outside?" She searched overhead for a glimpse of an early moon. The silver arc hanging low would provide little light. "Have you tents?"

He shot her the look he used when her remarks were less than intelligent. "Nay, Your Majesty. We have no tents."

He knew her fears, yet he mocked her. She raised her chin a notch, strengthening her resolve. "Have you a particular place in mind?"

"There is a loch at the bottom of the next foothill." He leaned forward, bending awkwardly to see her face.

"As you wish, m'lord." She trotted forward, giving him no time to see the sting of tears his mockery produced.

A valley hidden by woodland came into view. A small brook bled into a dark lake surrounded by the most beautiful array of flowers to grace her eyes. Thousands of floral species: roses, lilies, wood violets, and some she didn't recognize at this distance. Excitement gave her stamina. The click of her tongue and a pat on her horse's backside set the stallion racing down the side of the knoll.

She could pick one of each, mayhap more, and take them

to the abbey. She inhaled their powerful scent and decided to mix a unique fragrance for the prioress.

The stallion came to a sudden halt at the water's edge, pulling Lizzy from her frivolous thoughts and sending her heart into her throat. Its front hooves rose off the ground and then splashed in unison. She eased him backward, not daring to look at the dark water. His tail thrashed side to side in agitation, slapping her like little whips.

More than anxious to get off the beast, Lizzy rose up in the stirrups, but her muscles quivered and pain raced up her spine. She plopped back atop the horse's back with a thud and wiggled her toes inside her boots, then rotated her ankles. She flexed the muscles in her aching thighs and rocked side to side to get the blood flowing in her hips. Obviously unconcerned about the situation, the horse dipped low to drink and threw her slightly off balance. While managing to slip one boot from the stirrup, the rumble of hooves hummed behind her.

"God's hooks, woman! Are ye touched in the head? Ye could have ran your mount straight into the damned loch. These animals are trained to follow instructions. They are warhorses. Your gown would have pulled you under. Foolish, insufferable woman. What were ye thinking? Lizbeth, answer me! Why are ye not speaking?"

Though startled by the intensity of his tone, his concern touched her. "Because you have yet to stop yelling long enough for me to speak. Pray forgive me for stealing your years. I wanted to pick a few flowers before dark settled in." She sounded like a pathetic little girl.

He slapped his hand over his eyes and rubbed his temples. "If ye were in such a haste, why are ye still astride your mount?"

"I'm taking in the view. 'Tis lovely," she lied.

He snorted. "Ye cannae get off your horse, can ye?"

She shook her head, embarrassed by her frailty. Holding the reins, she focused on the moss bordering the lake. A frog winked at her with both eyes, then disappeared into the blackness.

Lord Maxwell snapped his neck, then dismounted with a grunt and flipped the leather straps over the ears of his horse. The beast immediately bent to drink. A slight limp troubled Lord Maxwell's right leg as he approached her and eased her stallion's hooves from the edge of the water. Encircling her waist with his hands, he pulled her from the horse and set her on the ground.

She grabbed hold of his forearms and stared at his chest. "Please do not let go yet."

"Ye gave me a fright." His pale shirt, loosely laced, rose and fell with his heavy breathing.

"'Twas not my intention."

He lessened his hold. "Think ye can walk?"

She sagged. "I s'pose I will eventually."

In one swift motion, he plucked her off the ground, one arm behind her back, the other beneath her knees. The movement caused a flutter in her stomach.

"Where are the others?"

He turned back toward the lake and squinted. "Looks like they are getting Celeste off her horse."

Lizzy studied the scene, feeling only slightly frail now. "Why are they way over there?"

"The water is shallow on the other side." He set her down on a bed of silky grasses beneath the canopy of a white willow. "I will get your legs working; then ye can pick your flowers, aye?"

"Thank you." She laid back, not caring that her knees weren't touching, and thinking they probably never would again. Nor did she protest when he removed her boots and stockings. He worked the same magic as he had the night before, rolling her muscles until the aches thawed and the tingles ceased; then she let him continue simply for enjoyment. She draped her arm over her eyes and hoped he couldn't see how much he stirred her, how much her heart did a little dance when he looked at her, and how her skin pebbled when she thought of him.

'Twas a shame she would never know a man's touch. There was so much inside her she wanted to share. Before she could wallow in self-pity, a little voice inside her suggested she let Lord Maxwell touch her. She smiled, knowing that voice belonged to Edlynn.

"Why are ye smiling?" He sprawled out beside her and propped up on one arm.

"Edlynn is talking to me." She stared up at the weeping branches and inhaled the beauty of this place, curiously aware of the heat of his body beside her.

"And what is Edlynn saying to ye?" He plucked a foxtail and drew it across her collarbone.

She swished the tickle weed away, eager to play his game. "She is a lewd old woman. Your ears would turn to ash if you heard the things Edlynn says to me."

"Now ye have my interests. What did she say?" The backs of his fingers hovered beside her face.

She wanted him to touch her. She near ached for it. Did she dare share her thoughts, her desires? Would he reject her? "Edlynn told me to laugh more. Play more."

"Play? Mayhap your auld friend has a suggestion?"

Lizzy pulled her brows together, acting like there was someone in her head telling her secrets. She purposely widened her eyes and made an O shape with her mouth, overdramatizing the scene in her head. "Oh, Edlynn. You are a very wicked woman. You should not say such things."

He laughed at her theatrics. A booming belly laugh accompanied his comely smile and emphasized his dimples. "Ye are wowf."

Lizzy crossed her eyes and made a funny face at him, enjoying his company more than his seduction. "I am. And you would be half mad, too, if there was an old woman in your head telling you to—"

"Telling ye to what, Lizbeth?" He leaned closer, and his fingers finally touched her cheek.

The tingle that teased her when he was near shot up her spine. She reached up to take his hand. He met her halfway and pinned it above her shoulder, bringing his weight along with him. Positioned over her, he propped his knee between her thighs.

She gasped and curled her fingers in his, waiting, wanting, desiring anything he might give her.

He bent to her ear. "Does Edlynn tell ye to laugh, and to feel, and to want? Or is the voice in your head your own? The same voice that yelled out my name in your dream." He brushed his lips over hers. "The same voice that wants to ask me to kiss ye, but is afraid, as she is afraid of everything."

Lizzy took offense. Her eyes snapped open and met his. "I am not afraid of you."

"Care to wager, angel? If you're not afraid, tell me what the voice inside your head wants me to do."

He was goading her. She didn't care. She would win either way. "I want you to kiss me, and touch me, and tell me I'm desirable."

He descended on her mouth in one bold action. His tongue swept over hers and demanded she play with him.

She did.

She mimicked his actions, chasing his tongue, twirling in an erotic dance inside her mouth. When he sucked her top lip, she latched onto his bottom, nipping, biting, tasting. She was afraid to move, to breathe, terrified he would draw back and leave her wanting. Trapped within her was a caged desire demanding to be unleashed. Demanding more.

Her hand curled around his neck. Her fingertips pulled him closer.

Then as fiercely as he had descended, he pulled away.

"Ach!" He jumped off her like a man escaping a fire, and being on fire was exactly how she felt.

A hot, carnal inferno.

"I think it best if we keep Edlynn out of your head. She does not play fair."

Play fair? It may have started as a game, one she admitted to instigating, but certainly 'twas not how it ended. "How can you jest about what just happened?"

"I kissed ye. This is all. And ye kissed me back." He sat up, wiping a fine mist of sweat from his thick neck, then scowled at her. "Dinnae look at me as if I stole your virtue. 'Tis hardly the matter at all."

Lizzy closed her mouth, wondering how long she'd sat there with it gaping open, and crawled to her feet. She ignored the pain shooting up her back, determined to distance herself from his rejection. Humiliation was no stranger to her, but never had it felt more like a poison than it did right now.

She stuffed her stockings in her boots, then picked them up and stomped through the grasses toward her mount.

"I thought ye were going to pick flowers!" he yelled from behind her.

"I changed my mind," she spit back.

"Would that be your mind or Edlynn's?"

"Arrogant, toad-sucking Scot," she grumbled one of Edlynn's favored insults, not really caring if he heard her.

The woman was no angel.

If her kiss didn't prove it, the fire of Hell and damnation burning in her eyes did. Rage was one of many emotions Broc suspected Lizbeth kept hidden. Desire slipped past her guarded walls, and he'd been fool enough to mock her for setting it free.

He scratched the travel dust on his forearms and watched her thrash through the knee-high grasses toward her mount.

She lifted the reins and led the stallion by the nose alongside the loch's edge, not noticing that his horse followed her lead. Her movements were sharp, angry, her hand waving this way and that, slicing the air as she spoke to the horse and shook her head. She ranted continually until he could no longer make out her features.

Poor beast. Broc intended to reward the horse for taking his punishment. He rubbed the back of his neck, still aware of the soft press of her fingers. A tickle blew across his skin.

He was an ass with no skill for wooing like Smitt. Charm hadn't been part of Brother Mel's lessons, but discipline had. Two years he'd spent learning how to overcome his desires, how to suppress the want for Da's title and Aiden's betrothed.

He should be rejoicing, drinking Uncle Ogilvy's whisky, and telling lies with his brethren. Honoring Aiden's life by celebrating a new beginning. 'Twas the way of his clan. Too many died, and far too often for the kinsfolk to mourn day and night. He hoped Da would trust him to reign in Aiden's stead. To lead and preserve the clan—to protect.

But protecting Lizbeth had become a duty to him as well. Her goals were foolish, but he suspected they were all she had. She considered herself responsible for her father's sins and the sins of her country. On the morrow he would deliver her into sanctuary, where she would practice celibacy, learn to be submissive, and hide her tongue behind her teeth. The fire inside her would die, along with her passion, her desire.

A desire he touched, and then rejected like a fool.

Broc scratched his neck. The woman had him fidgeting, itching, tingling beneath his skin. He scratched his palms, his forearms. Then he held his hands out in front of him.

Splotches. Red splotches dotted his arms and the backs of his hands. He checked the ground and recognized the light green plants.

Damned itching weed!

He jumped to his feet and stripped to his skin, leaving a

trail of garments and weapons toward the loch. He gave no thought to the temperature before he dove headlong into cool, soothing water.

"Ye look a mite bit piqued, lass."

Lizzy pulled her gaze away from her bare toes and greeted John with a frown he didn't deserve. "This is how I look, sir. But I thank you for noticing."

"My wife has the same look." He graciously took the reins of Lizzy's horse and stroked its neck.

"I fear your wife is a little more than a wee bit piqued." She played with their burr, gaining a chuckle from John. She knew better than most not to hold one man's sins against another. The anger and hurt clutching her chest was no fault of John's.

"Mayhap ye could talk to her. Soften her up a wee bit, aye?" His eye's pleaded "save me."

Lizzy could save a man from bleeding to death, but she had no experience in softening wives, especially wives as angry as Celeste. Nonetheless, Lizzy welcomed the challenge and the distraction. Anything to keep her from thinking of *him*. "A wee bit might be all I can promise. Where is she?"

John bobbed his head toward an opening in the woodland while he removed Beatrice's cage from the horse and handed it to Lizzy. "I would be indebted to ye."

John intended to escort her into Middleham Castle on Lord Maxwell's orders. He risked his life to obey that order. At the very least, she could talk to his wife. "I will do it."

"Take care, lass. Celeste is a lot of woman."

Lizzy raised her skirts and walked through a bed of lavender bellflowers bordering the woodland, making a mental reminder to return for at least two sprigs. Stockings and a stained tunic hung over a low branch where Celeste spread wool blankets on the ground. An evening breeze pushed strands of hair across her face and the yellow remains of sunset shone on her like fairy dust. She displayed curves the great artists would fight to paint and wore a smile that made Lizzy feel welcome and wanted.

Celeste rushed to relieve her of her boots and stockings. "We've yet to have us a right fine chat, m'lady."

"Lizzy. I wish for you to call me Lizzy."

"As ye wish." Celeste hung Lizzy's stockings and set her boots in the fading sun. "How are ye and your new husband fairing?"

Lizzy's face fell. For two days they'd traveled in each other's company. Why had no one bothered to tell Celeste the marriage was a ruse? If Lizzy intended to befriend this woman, the truth needed to be spoken. "He is not my husband. Lord Maxwell thought it best we act the part for safety reasons."

"Damned lying Scots."

"Aye," Lizzy agreed before she realized what she agreed to.

"My mum told me never to bed down with one if I could prevent it; then I find out I been beddin' one for two years. Two years, Lizzy. Can ye even conceive such a notion? Now I'm to live with a whole herd of them." Celeste carried on while she spread out two more wools.

"I'm certain they are not all damned lying Scots." Lizzy released Beatrice, stroked her soft speckled feathers, and gathered the egg rolling in the bottom of the cage. She set it aside and took a place on the wool next to Celeste.

"I know three Scots: John, Smitt, and Jul . . . Lord Maxwell." Celeste plucked off their names with her fingers. "My John's a liar, your Maxwell is a liar, and I know for certain that drabber, Smitt, is a liar. He promises marriage to every woman who comes into the tavern."

Lizzy mulled over her words. Lord Maxwell hadn't lied to her in the short time she'd known him. Nonetheless, he did lie to Celeste. "How long have you known Lord Maxwell?"

"He and his brother came to the inn with John and Smitt two summers past. They left for months at a time. Holding court, John said. Another damned lie to be certain," she spouted and handed Lizzy a leather flask. "Spying for their Scottish king 'tis more the way of it."

The document, Lizzy thought. Buckingham's words of malice so eloquently written. Such proof of intent would hold a great deal of worth to a man who spent his days searching for a way to destroy his enemy. She battled a possibility she didn't want to accept. Was Lord Maxwell protecting her or the document? She didn't want to believe his kiss was part of a plan to gain her trust.

"The whole lot of 'em are barbarians." Celeste tossed the empty words into the air.

"As wanted as a vat of toad slime and fish guts," Lizzy added and then took a long draw on the flask while Celeste's mirth turned to hiccoughs. This couldn't be helping John.

Celeste's dark eyes searched for an insult equally clever. "As vile as maggots in meat pie."

Lizzy covered her mouth and wrinkled her nose while her stomach churned around the mead in her belly. She held up one finger, knowing she had one better. "As disgusting as the drippings from their livestock." That one had belonged to Edlynn, but her old friend would be happy for someone to voice it.

Celeste hooted and held her belly. "'Tis a wonder they find women to breed, cursed with looks as they all are."

They fell into a fit of laughter—gut-wrenching, tear-watering, unladylike guffawing. Lizzy couldn't remember a time she'd laughed harder. Even Beatrice danced with merriment, flapping her wings and bobbing to and fro.

"Good den, ladies." Smitt offered a casual greeting as he walked past.

Lizzy choked on a mouthful of mead. *Mercy Mary!* He was completely naked. Next to Lord Maxwell, Smitt had the finest backside she'd ever seen. He flaunted flexing cheeks with every stride toward the water. She gawked. What woman wouldn't?

He stepped up on a flat rock, peeked over his shoulder to see if they were watching—which they were—and then dove gracefully into the water.

"Mayhap one or two Scots have been spared such foul wretchedness." Lizzy turned toward Celeste; then Celeste's eyes eventually followed the movement.

Celeste licked her lips. "A woman wouldn't need a spoon to feast on that one."

Nodding agreement, Lizzy thought of one other Scot whose lips tasted of sin and spice.

A caterwaul sounded before she managed to gain her wits. John sprinted from behind them—naked and jumped high off the rock, wrapping his arms around his knees. Water sprayed high and soaked the stockings hanging from the tree branch.

Like frolicking boys, the men splashed in the water, dunking and fighting and performing. Through it all, John watched his wife with utter adoration.

Celeste's smile was sad, but a smile just the same. "'Tis no jest that I love my John. He makes me laugh and looks at me like I'm the most beautiful woman in all of England. I daresay I would follow the man into Hell, even if that Hell bears the name of Scotland."

Lizzy didn't know if she'd helped John, but the look in Celeste's eyes was indeed a little softer. "God save me from my king for saying so, but I think Scotland might be a little more like Heaven than you think. Mayhap you should consider forgiving your husband."

"Mayhap I will." Celeste flashed an all-knowing smile, then plucked off her outer garments. She skipped to the rock in naught but her pale tunic, pinched her nose, and jumped in. John immediately swam toward her, circled her, tested her, let her tease him with wayward glances.

Lizzy studied them, trying not to envy their play while wondering what it might feel like to have her own Scot look at her with so much fire.

Lord Maxwell popped out of the water among them, no doubt equally as naked as his brethren. She sat up straighter and checked the bank for his garments. Curse it! How had she missed his entry? Her lips pursed into a little pout.

Twilight glistened off his fine muscled chest. Water slicked his raven black hair and dripped in highlights over his strong face. He floated on his back with grace and beauty before he disappeared back beneath the water.

Completely unaware of anything but him, Lizzy propped her chin on her knees and simply watched. Something about him made her forget who she was, and what she traveled so far to accomplish. He was strength, power, and brawn, all in one beautiful man.

He glanced up at her.

She turned away before he caught her staring.

"Come in, Lizbeth. We were sitting in the itching weed." He pushed the water back and forth, stirring black circles around him.

"Itching weed? This is your ploy to get me in water far too cold for swimming? 'Tis clever."

"Think ye I lie? I've the spots on my arms." He started to rise out of the water.

She jumped to her feet with her hands up, palms flat. "Please. 'Tis not necessary. I believe you, m'lord. I have some gypsyweed in my satchels. I will mix you a poultice to stop the itching when I tend to your stitches."

Thankfully, he settled back. "Are ye not itching?"

"Nay. Some people get the spots, some do not. I am one that does not. Father can look at it and break out in a rash."

"Who is your father?" Celeste asked.

Lizzy took a step backward. Her gaze never left Lord Maxwell, pleading for his help, though she didn't know what she expected him to do. She didn't want to lie to Celeste, not now.

"He serves King Edward in the Tower," Broc explained.

His answer certainly put a new perspective on Father's duty. Curiosity satisfied, Celeste returned to taunting her husband. Lizzy quickly switched the discussion. "'Twill be dark soon. Do you want me to fetch up kindling?"

"Nay. I want ye to come swimming." He arched one dark brow.

"Pray forgive me, m'lord, but I do not swim." Still bruised by his earlier rebuff, she declined the temptation all the while knowing he would never get her in the water, regardless of how delicious he looked wet.

"Everyone swims!" Smitt hollered. "What kind o' woman does not swim?"

"The kind who is afraid of water." Lord Maxwell exposed yet another of her secrets.

Everyone feared something, be it death or spiders or storms. She was not so different, but the energy to argue the point with him deserted her. She turned and shuffled Beatrice into her cage, set her atop a soft patch of grass for the night, then bent to gather bits of dry sticks and bark.

"Gather your flowers, lass. Dinnae waste time on the sticks. We'll not have a fire this night."

No fire! Was he jesting? She whirled around, hands full of kindling. She counted to ten in one breath, determined to remain calm. The rising moon was but a sliver, and dusk already pushed mist over the lake like a low-hanging cloud.

"A fire would alight our position. We are too close to your goal to be caught now," Lord Maxwell explained, obviously sensing her anxiety.

"We should've traveled on to an inn. You should've told

me there would be no fire," she scolded, now crushing bits of debris between her fingers.

"I just did." His intention to humor her failed miserably.

She shook her hands free and plodded through the clearing. She had to find sleep quickly. After tending her ablutions, she took two long draws of mead before settling atop the blanket. Father drank heavily at night, else his thoughts tormented him and prevented any hope of rest.

Behind closed lids, she counted to one hundred twice, but their catcalls screamed in her ear like tortured prisoners. Angered by their continued play, she sat upright. Celeste and John were inching their way out of the water, while Smitt spun in circles, poised to attack Lord Maxwell when he emerged. What purpose did their foolish game accomplish?

Smitt's search took in a wider area. His head cocked, determination slipped to curiosity. He whirled, then dove below the water. Long moments passed before he broke through the water's surface, coughing. "John, come back in the water," Smitt ordered between gulps of air.

If the sound of concern in his voice hadn't alerted Lizzy, then the expediency with which John obeyed did. They talked in a hushed tone, searching, craning their necks, and narrowing their eyes.

Both disappeared into the black depths.

The sickly feeling of dread quickened Lizzy's pulse. She shot to her feet and rushed to the water's edge, her hands already wrapping around her long sleeves.

"Damned idiot." John surfaced first. "Broderick," he bellowed into the mist, then stood perfectly still, listening.

With eyes stretched wide, Lizzy refused to give pause to what their actions implied.

John looked at her. "He will come up."

"What do you mean, he will come up?! He's been under for full minutes! Find him!" she screamed and took another step forward. Her toes touched the water. She held her breath, searching for the slightest ripple. In her mind's eye, Emma's face flashed, upside down, suspended over the river, her mouth gasping for air. *They lowered her below the surface.*

"Broderick!" John yelled again.

Lizzy hugged herself and paced along the bank, waiting, feeling helpless.

They pulled Emma up, tormenting her, tormenting Lizzy. She pressed her hands against her eyes, hiding from her memory. Sickness churned her stomach. A sour taste thickened in her throat.

She was going to be ill.

John and Smitt made no movement, but Lizzy read their faces, eyes disbelieving, heads shaking in shock.

Tears grabbed hold of her heart and squeezed. Her mind shouted, *Find him!* but the only sounds echoing into the woodland were her empty cries.

Chapter 10

Broc emerged from the water gasping for air, driven by the race in his head. Five breaths had been all he needed to swim to the other side. Even Aiden would have lost this race.

Pushing the water behind him in broad strokes, he kicked his feet, searching the curtain of mist for the bank. The willow peeked through the haze, guiding him to where he'd entered until his toes stuck in thick silt. Weeds scratched his bare legs as he walked from the loch and searched for his garments. With his legs gloved in his trews, he heard the baritone drone of his Christian name.

A scream ripped through the fog.

Lizbeth!

"They've been found." He voiced his fear in a whisper, then wrapped his fingers around the hilt of his broadsword and sprinted into action. One word repeated in his head—protect.

He raced along the water's edge, nearly blinded by darkness. Bare feet crushed the ground, urging him forward—harder, faster. He would not fail.

Not her.

The warrior in him cast emotion aside and prepared for battle. Lungs burning, his skin stretched around his knuckles gripping the hilt.

Her screams repeated, knifing through his ears. Why had he left her?

Then he saw her, standing at the water's edge, draped in shadows. She was alive, and he would kill to keep her that way.

Her hands pressed flat against her ears as if her own cries were more than she could bear. Broc searched the bank for the guards, but there was no one, save for Celeste staring at John and Smitt in water to their waist.

Confusion lowered his broadsword to his hip. "What's amiss?!" he yelled when only feet separated them. Their attention turned toward him.

"Piss 'n' nettles!" The worried frown left John's face first.

Lizbeth's entire person fell a little. She stumbled back. The relief he might have noticed in those actions quickly disappeared, replaced by anger. Her brows slanted, one eye narrowed a bit farther than the other, and he would wager her teeth were suffering severely beneath the intensity of her bite. The woman was wowf.

As if she'd heard his insult, she marched toward him, all Hell and fury combined in one wee angel. She pushed him hard.

He faltered a step back, trying to understand what had transpired.

"You are an ass!" She swiped tears from her eyes and pushed him again. She sniffled, then stepped around him toward the knoll.

From the corner of his eye, Broc saw Smitt emerge like a rabid beast. "I'm going to kill ye." He drew back an iron fist.

Broc ducked the blow but heard the air swish above his head. "When I want a fight I will order it, cousin. Stand down and pull on your trews." Broc used his status, but oddly enough didn't wallow in the power.

John stepped from the water, accepting a tunic from Celeste. "Ye should not be playin' such games."

"'Twas no game. I went to retrieve my garments and heard

her screaming." Broc glanced over his shoulder. Lizbeth became smaller with each stride.

"Ye swam across the loch?" Smitt sneered. "'Tis a wide loch, cousin. I think ye jest."

"Are ye naming me a liar?" The intensity of the race still pumped through his veins, encouraging him to let Smitt take another swing at him.

John stepped between them. "'Tis over. There will be nay fight here. Your lady needs ye. She thought you'd drowned and was nigh mad with terror."

Your lady.

Broc spent no time correcting John's statement. Truth was, he rather liked the sound of it. He spun and trudged after her, stopping only long enough to light a candlebox with a flint he located in her satchel.

A hollow pocket darkened a field of bell-shaped blue flowers. Their smell so intense, he could taste them on the back of his tongue. He walked in the knee-deep blooms guided by the hymn of her numbers until he stood directly over her. Lying on her side beneath a pile of dusky skirts with her hands wrapped in her rosary beneath her head, she looked young, innocent, alone.

Stomping down an area to accommodate his size, he settled on his side in front of her and mimicked her position— bare toe to bare toe, knee to knee, eye to eye. He set the candlebox between them, casting a small glow only for them. No words were spoken, but he felt her through her watery gaze. The flame turned her eyes to gold, the treasure behind far greater than coin.

"I do not like you at the moment." She swept dark lashes low.

He smiled, but only a little, then broke off one small flower and placed it between them. "Forgive me. I swam back to the willow. 'Twas not my intention to scare ye."

She looked at the flower, then back at him. "I admit I am

easily frightened, but mayhap you could have announced your departure before you decided to disappear into a body of water the size of England."

His angel's protectiveness kindled a small fire inside him. The lass had definitely been fashing over him. A man of his size and strength rarely knew the tickling warmth of having someone worry over his well-being. 'Twas foolish, but he liked having a guardian angel. "I am skilled at holding my breath. Ye know this." He tried to humor her.

She shot air out of her nose and humphed. "Could you not have walked?"

"I was naked. I swam back to the willow to collect my garments."

Her gaze fell to his chest, and her foot moved enough to touch his toe. "I daresay you forgot most of them."

He worked his toes over hers, playing, tickling, until her taut lips softened; then he pushed the flower toward her with the tip of his finger. "My Aunt Radella says the blue flowers help ease the bad dreams."

"Mother said bluebells are unlucky. According to myth, if you walk through a patch, they ring and alert the fairies to cast spells. She told me many things when I was a child, but my mother and father truly believed the spirits followed them." Her gaze never left him as her hand slipped out to tuck her rosary into her skirt. She gathered the flower in her palm, curled her fingers around it, then tucked her fist back beneath her cheek. "Do you want to know why I like flowers so much?"

"Aye." He held his teeth together, determined to give her the time she needed to speak.

"Because my mother did. She dried them and sprinkled their dust everywhere, protecting our cottage from evil spirits. We snuck away to a market fair once and sold vials of scented oils and small soaps. We even sold a few of Father's carved birds. 'Twas the only time I ever left London. She contracted the fever when I was eleven summers." A tear slipped over the bridge of her nose. "The day God took her from me, she set her rosary in my hand and told me to place lilies upon her grave."

"Lizbeth, ye dinnae have to—"

"You want to know, do you not? You want to know why I'm so afraid."

He suspected being her father's daughter was reason enough, but he would listen to her tell him more. Mayhap 'twould set her free. "Only if ye want to tell me."

Lizbeth inhaled a shaky breath and fixed her eyes on the candlebox. "After Mother passed, my father sent me to the chief warder's new wife for fostering. Her name was Emma. She was sixteen summers and terrified of her husband. My brother had already been apprenticing under Lord Hollister for a year when I took up quarters in the Tower."

"Ye lived there?"

"Aye. In a chamber smaller than the nobles imprisoned there."

"With nay window?" he guessed, picturing a young Lizbeth curled into a ball in a dark corner.

"There was no window, but 'twas not as you think. I was free at the time to leave my quarters, to help in the kitchens and the gardens. I showed Emma how to mix fragrances and it became a passion for both of us, a release from reality. The Tower was not a horrible place to live as most might think. I had a few friends and Kamden close at hand before he left."

"And your father?"

"He did his duty," she said, as if the man she spoke of was the baker or brewer.

He wouldn't argue this point with her while her spirit was so fragile. He held his tongue, which was difficult given the number of questions he wanted to ask her.

"Emma gave birth to a son only a year after I came. Another son followed three summers later. Years passed before the bruises started showing up on her skin, most of them hidden. Her eyes lost their vitality, and she kept mostly to the keep. Lord Hollister beat Emma and used her at his leisure. I was too young to understand why and too afraid to try and prevent it."

"Could no one help her?"

Lizbeth's eyes pooled instantly. Broc wanted to drag her into his arms and chase the demons away she had buried inside her.

"Kamden would have, had he known, but he left the Tower the day he turned four and twenty to escape Lord Hollister and the family occupation. He fought four years for England."

"Against us?"

She nodded. "He returned to the Tower last fall and nigh went mad when he saw Emma. Her skin clung to her bones, and I suspect he discovered bruises and mayhap even scars hidden beneath her garments."

"Your brother was in love with her?" Broc wished he could have met the man Lizbeth put above all others.

"Aye. Had been since the day Emma came to the Tower. Lord Hollister found them in bed only because Kamden wanted to be caught. My brother intended to kill the man, but Lord Hollister had him arrested on false allegation of treason. As the chief warder, he had enough nobles in his pocket to see the lie through. The king himself signed Kamden's death sentence. He was beheaded the following day."

"By your father's hand?"

Lizbeth started shaking, her tears coming fast and furious now. Broc's muscles tightened, holding him in place. He wanted to be her savior, her protector, her champion. He wanted to touch her, to push the hair from her eyes, but he did naught, save for watch her spend her tears.

"Lord Hollister forced Emma and I to the gallows to watch. Father manned his position while he waited for his attendants to bring his only son to the chopping block. Kamden was proud and placed his chin in the divot without force."

He'd heard enough. "Ye dinnae have to finish."

"Please." She wiped her eyes with the back of her hands. "I want you to understand, if you will listen."

Broc nodded once.

"After the execution, Emma told Lord Hollister his sons belonged to Kamden. She was mad with grief and wanted some kind of retribution. She couldn't have known what he would do to Eli and Martin. Lord Hollister publicly named her an adulteress. She was tied to the dunking stool and immersed eight times in the river before death took her."

"And the boys? Did Kamden know they were his?"

"He did. 'Twas part of the reason he left, I s'pose. While Lord Hollister paid the boys little heed, they were being raised according to their station. Emma was free to take them to festival and to mass and they spent a great deal of time at Edlynn's. Kamden kept Emma's secret, knowing the boys would have a better life as sons to the chief warder."

"And not grandsons of the executioner."

"They were happy and safe from Father's curse. Had Emma kept her secret, all might have been different."

Broc waited, knowing there was more. He watched her tears dry up as she stared into his eyes. All her pain, her sorrow, her longing passed through her gaze and settled deep inside him.

"Lord Hollister murdered my nephews," she finally said, "and promised me I would pay for my brother's sins every day for the rest of my life."

Broc's heart ached. Is that what he felt for her? Pity? Or was it something greater? Did he see something no one else had because of who she was?

"I played Lord Hollister for six months. I catered to him, fed him. I did everything but lay with him, but he promised that would come. He intended to take another wife and make me his mistress to punish my family for what he believed my brother had stolen from him. So I stole the document from him, knowing his association with Buckingham would gain him a trip to the gallows."

Regardless of how badly Broc wanted to deliver her document to his king, he wouldn't take it from her now. She'd earned it, but damned if he would leave her in Gloucester's hands. Mayhap the bastard would leave the north to engage in a new battle. "Ye are a strong lass to have survived such a life."

Her eyes flashed with anger. "I did not tell you because I want your pity."

"Then why did ye tell me?"

She sat up. He followed, ready to grab her if she ran.

"Because I wanted you to know that I am a person who has fears and reasons for those fears. I am not just the executioner's daughter. I am Lizbeth Ives." She reached for his hand and pressed his palm over her heart. "I am a woman. I feel and breathe and hate and . . ."

"And desire?" he asked, wanting it to be true. Her pulse pounded against his hand. His own beat twice as fast, reminding him he, too, was a man who could feel and breathe and hate . . .

"And desire." She finished his thought and answered his question at the same time.

Even the great Achilles couldn't have stopped him from touching her. The backs of his knuckles caressed her collarbone while the swell of her breast rose to touch the tips of his fingers. What control he may have possessed deserted him when she cupped her hand over his and gently pressed.

Blood shot straight to his groin, filling him with need, hard and fast. He pulled her onto his lap, fingers tangled through her hair, drawing her head back. She searched his face with an intensity that burned his flesh.

Her eyes, beautiful, golden, trusting, would haunt him for the rest of his days. "Lizbeth," he whispered, and intended to say more, but her fingers slipped between them to still his lips.

She couldn't know that her simple caress stole the last of his resistance.

He lowered his head and pressed his lips to hers, knowing he would never leave her behind.

Lizzy returned his kiss with fervor, determined to hide her lack of expertise. She opened her jaw wide and teased his tongue with quick, creative movements. The freedom she felt for having shared her secrets opened a place in her heart—a place she wanted to fill with memories of him. Though her intentions were selfish, he seemed more than willing to give her what she desired.

Her fingers gripped his thick arm, nails piercing skin, holding on while he yanked at the ribbed edging of her bodice. Excitement tightened her nipples, sharpening them to sensitive points. A moan of frustration vibrated in her throat. The heavy embroidered damask bound her like an iron breastplate. She'd known imprisonment, known the hollow feeling of loneliness within stone walls, but never had she felt more trapped than she did at this moment in her garments. She wiggled her backside, squirming inside her own skin, her body desperate for him to find a way to free her from her armor.

He conceded and raised her skirts to her thighs.

She gasped and her head fell back, filling her vision with winking stars. She memorized the sky, the smell of bluebells, the feel of his lips on her neck. He gave her a gift she would cherish forever—a dream to champion her nightmares.

Teeth nibbled her earlobe as cool air blew between her knees. His strong hand curved along the inside of her calf, behind her knee, up her thigh. Gooseflesh broke out over her chest along with a contradicting coating of perspiration. A quickening flitted in her mons, causing her knees to fall wider.

Touch me. . . . She was insane with want. "Broc, give me a memory," she whispered.

His movements stilled, then left her all at once, stealing her air. She peeked at him through languid eyes. His dark features blended with the sky. Blue eyes rimmed with silver bore straight into her soul.

"'Tis wrong of me to want ye," he said in a voice filled with tension.

Curse him and his chatter! Her skin burned everywhere, her breasts ached, and the throbbing between her legs had become painful. "'Tis not wrong for a man and a woman to be together."

"What ye offer belongs to your husband, 'Tis not mine to take." He smoothed her skirts back over her knees with trembling hands.

"I belong to no husband, nor do I ever intend to take one. What I offer is mine to give." Lizzy cursed his honor, but caught a glimpse of the burden weighing him down. Why did he have to be tormented by chivalry now?

"Ye will marry someday and have bairns to coddle." He kissed her brow and set her on legs still weak from their tryst.

"I can never bear children as long as I reside in England."

He got to his feet, scratched his arms, and snuffed out the candlebox. "Then 'tis fortunate I am taking ye to Scotland."

"What?" Lizzy's defenses erected. "You lied to me. I must go to York. 'Tis imperative, not only for my father, but for England."

"Your father doesnae deserve your loyalty. Nonetheless, I am still taking ye to York, so quit glaring at me." He took her hand. "Ye will deliver your document and make your requests of your country's defender. If Gloucester is the man ye think him to be, then he will honor your efforts by setting your father free of his duty. What Lord Ives chooses to do with that freedom will be entirely up to him. Without the document, howbeit, your life will hold no value and your knowledge of your country's treachery places ye in danger, which is why I'm taking you across the border."

Dumbfounded by his words, Lizzy couldn't decide her mood. Of course, anger set close to the edge of her sanity. He was arrogant to act as her ward and make decisions about her well-being. He held no reign over her person. The only thing keeping her anger in check was the picture he'd painted of Scotland. 'Twas a magical place in her mind.

She had thought little about her future. Freeing her father and seeing Lord Hollister pay for his crimes had consumed her life, but after her meeting with Gloucester, she would be free to enjoy the splendor of such a place. She wasn't fool to believe Lord Maxwell offered her marriage, but a chance to live among his kin. A chance to know the love and friendship of those who might know her the way he did. He must surely understand the importance of her remaining unwed.

Her foot sank into mud. They were almost at the water's edge before she even realized they'd been walking. Though the moon was thin, it had risen high enough to cast the landscape in silver edges. The woods sounded like festival, and it was only then that she realized Lord Maxwell was quiet.

She glanced up at him. The corners of his mouth lifted into a presumptuous smile. "Why are you smiling?"

"Because ye are not sparring with me."

"I'm preparing my words in my head." In truth, she thought of all the people she would meet—his mother and brother, his aunts and sisters, and his grandmum. Lizzy would like her most of all. She doubted the woman was quite the old crone he claimed her to be. She squeezed his hand, near bursting with anticipation.

"Save your argument. My mind is made up." He released her hand and scratched his forearms. "Now mayhap ye can find this gypsyweed and relieve my itch."

"Aye, m'lord." She smiled, not certain how to thank him. "Do you think I will be happy there?"

"As happy as one can be in a cloister. Dryburgh will not be much different from Fountains Abbey. I know and trust the clergy. Mayhap after a time I will take ye to court in Edinburgh to find a husband. Until then, ye will be safe with Brother Mel. Ye will like him. He is always jesting and playing games. And there is a garden. . . ." He droned on, but she no longer heard his words.

Her chin lowered; her eyes watched the movement of her feet. Her assumptions embarrassed her. Beneath the stars he might see her as a woman, but society only knew her as one person—the executioner's daughter. 'Twould be no different in Scotland. This curse she carried would always prevent her from being accepted. While Lord Maxwell's decision to take her to Scotland proved him honorable, his intentions to tuck her away in a monastery made him just like everyone else.

Chapter 11

A sharp point poked Broc in the hollow of his neck.

His lids snapped open. Three scrawny Englishmen stood over him in the silver light of dawn, garbed in black skull-caps and doublets of crimson satin. He reached for Lizbeth. The wool beside him was empty. His fist clenched. "Ye will find it in your best interests not to hurt the girl." *Or I will kill each one of ye slowly.*

The one holding the sword cocked his head and glanced at Broc's fist, then looked at the ancient symbol marking his arm. "And ye hold what rank to threaten the guards of Yorkshire?"

God's hooks! They were Gloucester's men. "I serve Gloucester's brother. Mayhap ye have heard of him. He answers to the name 'His Majesty.' Now, remove your weapon from my person, else ye'll know the lack of mercy with which he reigns."

His words inspired instant wide-eyed fear. The Yorkist removed his sword. "Forgive us. Ye display no colors and the mark on your arm is not one I've seen before."

Broc shot to his feet, mindful to hide his back, and offered thanks for the idiocy of the English mind. While sharpening his wit to the situation, he scanned the area around the loch.

His eye caught Lizbeth's slender figure and a cool wave washed through him. Her steps were high over the grasses as she approached, her eyes focused on her footing around the heap of flowers filling her skirt.

"My colors are on the bank, and the mark is symbolic of my Christian faith." Broc decided it best to befriend the Yorkists, but mentally prepared to strike them down should they question his lies. "I am Sir Julian Ascott, guard and noble knight of our country's great sovereign leader. I am one of three guards escorting a woman and her maid to Middleham Castle on orders of our dying king." He tightened the clip of his speech, delivering his words with eloquence.

"Dying? His Majesty is ill?" The obvious leader of the threesome scratched the back of his neck and spit. With no respect for his weapon, the Yorkist stuck his sword in the marshy ground and supported himself on the hilt. He displayed the judgment of a nit.

"Aye. 'Tis rumored King Edward contracted the fever on a fishing expedition." Broc considered gutting them where they stood with the *sgian dubh* now hidden in his palm, but if Lizbeth happened to glance up, he suspected she would severely disapprove. He looked over the Yorkist's shoulder to find her frozen and staring at him. Recognizing the panic in her stance, he gestured her toward him.

All three men foolishly turned their heads. Instead of killing them, Broc snatched the opportunity to locate the others. Celeste and John no longer occupied their wool, but Smitt lay on his stomach, arms and legs spread wide, and his white arse beaming. When his cousin slept, he slept hard.

"Is the woman your charge?" The man rubbed his cullions, revealing the true nature of his thoughts.

Broc wanted to gut the pig. The hilt of his *sgian dubh* slid against his palm. "She is Lady Lizbeth Ives and has within her possession a missive sealed by the Duke of Buckingham.

'Tis my duty to see her safely to Middleham to deliver this missive to the king's brother."

"Is she of royal blood?"

"Has she caught your eye, sir?" Broc played his game.

The louse grinned through a mouth full of crooked yellow teeth and nudged the man to his right. "I wouldn't kick 'er from my bed."

"Nay? Her father might, howbeit. She is daughter to the Lord High Executioner." Broc was quite pleased with the look of repugnance on all three of their faces. The bulges in their hose shrank with astounding speed. "A bit of advice, good sirs. Lady Ives is touched in the head." He tapped his temple.

"She is mad?"

On closer inspection, Broc noticed the hilt of his broadsword over her shoulder and his dirks pinched beneath her underarms. The garments he'd left on the bank were draped over her shoulders. He laughed inwardly, then used her appearance to further his efforts. "Aye. 'Tis a difficult duty to protect a woman who keeps company with so many weapons. I am forever removing them from her person."

All three Yorkists took a cautionary step back when Lizbeth entered their circle. She was a contradiction to herself in so many ways. Femininity at its finest in bare toes, pursed lips, and exotic scents, yet she shielded her secrets and desires inside walls of iron.

He reached through her silky tresses and then withdrew, revealing the *sgian dubh* he'd already been holding to the gawking trio. He tucked the black knife into his trews and removed the dirks from beneath her arms. "Lady Ives, we have discussed repeatedly that it is not necessary for you to be armed."

Her brow gathered in the middle as she studied his words and his company. "Aye, sir."

The lass was smart and kept to her tongue. He snatched his

tunic and crimson doublet from her shoulder. "Lady Ives, these fine gents are guards of Yorkshire," he introduced and slipped into his garments. "Forgive me"—he looked at their leader—"I do not believe you gave me your name."

While the men stumbled over introductions, Broc spun Lizbeth around and removed his sword from her back. "Run along, m'lady. Find Beatrice and make preparations to leave."

"As ye wish, sir." She rushed into an open patch in the woodland.

"Is Beatrice her maid?" The guard who'd introduced himself as Oliver watched her with keen interest.

"Nay. Beatrice is her pet chicken." He ignored their sidelong glances and decided they might serve a purpose. Gaining entrance inside the guarded walls of Middleham Castle would be greatly simplified with their aid. "Mayhap you gents would escort us the remainder of our journey?"

"I s'pose we might be persuaded." Oliver sheathed his sword and crossed his arms over his chest.

"How does fifteen ducats of His Majesty's fine coin sound?"

Oliver gained a nod from the other two Yorkists. "Happy to be at your service, fine sir. Might we ready your horses?"

"Aye." Broc readily agreed, hoping to keep them occupied while he informed the others of his plans.

Lizbeth awaited him, her flowers dumped at her feet. The speed of her pacing gave away her angst. She turned toward him, one eye narrower than the other. "You converse with them like you battle for the same king. They are English."

"As are ye. Odd that ye should fear them more than I."

"I've no patience for your wit this morn." She popped her fists on her hips, making him want to laugh at her.

Mayhap she was a wee bit mad. The woman was filled with fire. Her temper lay on the surface untamed. She must have left the "aye, m'lords" and "nay, m'lords" in the patch of flowers yester eve. Submission served her well as a front, but every day she revealed more of what she kept buried inside her. At the moment, anger crawled to the surface. "Do ye not trust me by now?"

"Nay. Your vow to protect me has gone far beyond seeing me safely from London. What do you gain by escorting me to York?"

He grabbed the front of her bodice and yanked her to him. "Mayhap what I seek to gain is ye."

She wiggled free of him. "'Tis a lie. You could have had your way with me, be it with my permission or by force. But you refused me."

The lass had certainly been thinking. She spoke like a woman scorned. "I refused ye because I am honorable."

"To Hades with your honor. If you had any honor, you would have already returned home."

Broc backed away from her and rotated his neck until it popped on both sides. His fists tightened into iron balls. He escorted her halfway across England, stood by a vow to protect her, offered to take her to his homelands, and she insults his honor. Her words cut deeper than a battle wound. Brother Mel had taught him to respect the sacraments. He refused her because he wouldn't take her innocence without marriage and a marriage to her didn't protect his clan or his country.

Lizbeth's gaze shifted; then she leaned to see around him.

He glanced over his shoulder. The Englishmen gawked at her as if she'd suddenly sprouted wings and a tail.

"Why are they looking at me like that?"

"Because they think ye are mad."

"Why would they think that?"

"Because I told them ye were. Sharpen your wit, lass. We are about to enter the realm of the defender of England, and they are taking us there."

To a man she trusted . . . and a man he despised.

* * *

Lizzy followed Lord Maxwell, or rather Sir Julian Ascott, through the crowded byways of the city of York. Another day astride should have had her aching, but her body seemed to be taking the ride better this day. The sounds of the city reminded her of London: the clang of church bells, the gaiety of courtiers layered in rich colors of fine silks and brocades, the trill voice of the merchant haggling his wares, be it carpets and tapestries or gold and silver cups.

She admitted to a certain measure of excitement, but as the stone towers of Middleham Castle grew before her, the greater her foreboding became. In London, the Duke of Gloucester had been a man who'd offered her aid with a gentle hand. He'd wiped the rotted fruit from her face with his own cloth the day of Kamden's execution. But in the north, he was a king among his people, guarded and honored as heavily as King Edward himself.

For reasons she did not yet know, Lord Maxwell disliked the man immensely. Of course, her Scottish protector held no love for any English. He, however, had gained the trust of three Englishmen who were presently making preparations for them to enter the stronghold.

As they crossed the northern drawbridge and passed beneath the iron portcullis, Lord Maxwell narrowed his eyes on the castle, and a slow smile spread across his lips. He snuck her a wink. A chill of unease made her draw back on the reins a bit. She brought a Scotsman into a city whose leader prided himself on breaking their northern neighbors. Lord Maxwell could have easily sent her into Middleham Castle with the Englishmen and been on his way to the border. Instead he seemed determined to be at her side, as if he relished the moment she would inform Gloucester of Buckingham's treachery.

They met with the city's aldermen and were assigned quarters within the castle. Lord Maxwell conferred with a scheduler and secured an audience with the duke for the following morn. She had been a fool to believe she could walk into Gloucester's home and make demands for the information she provided.

Lord Maxwell, John, and Smitt accepted an invitation to gallivant among the noble knights of Yorkshire, while she and Celeste were offered resting quarters for the eve. Though the attendants treated them with reverence, she was wary of being separated from her protector.

A maidservant escorted them up a tower stairwell and through a carpeted hallway alight with rushlights spewing smoke and flame. The lanky woman opened a door. "If you've need for anything, send your maid to the servant's quarters at ground level outside the kitchens. I will order a bath be brought to you straightaway." The maidservant bowed, backed away, and then paused.

Lizzy stared at her, then realized the woman waited for dismissal. "Thank you. That will be all."

The maid scurried away without making eye contact. Though well spoken, the attendants reminded Lizzy of abused animals—compliant to a fault.

"'Ods toes, m'lady. 'Ave ye ever seen a more extravagant room?" Celeste spun a circle atop a carpet designed with fruit, while Lizzy hid the single satchel she'd brought with her beneath a bed big enough to sleep three, mayhap four people. The bed was only one of many pieces of furniture decorating the guest quarters. Gold rope tied back scarlet drapes on the bed and windows. A wooden tray filled with red and green grapes sat atop a bedside table. Wall sconces and two candelabrums filled the chamber with comforting light, and the smell was divine—a hint of mint sweetened with what she guessed to be clover. 'Twas indeed a magnificent room, more suited for a princess than someone of her position in society.

"Come, let me prepare ye for your bath, m'lady." Celeste grabbed Lizzy's hips and spun her toward the bed.

"Celeste, you really need not attend me. You are only *acting* as my maid." Lizzy held on to a mahogany bedpost carved with delicate flowers while Celeste untied her laces.

"'Tis nay trouble, m'lady."

"You most certainly do not need to address me with such reverence." Lizzy hated her title. She didn't feel she deserved to be prefaced the same as a wife of an earl or a marquess.

"'Tis a bit overwhelming to me."

"To me as well," Lizzy admitted and pulled her bodice from her arms with the false sleeves still attached. Celeste worked the ties at her waist until Lizzy was able to step from her skirts and free her of the heavy burden she'd carried for days. The weightlessness made her lightheaded. She set Mother's rosary on a bedside table as Celeste located a robe from a standing wardrobe.

"'Tis as soft as a spun web." Celeste held the sheer wrapper up by the shoulders and awaited the removal of Lizzy's tunic.

She turned, a hint of modesty causing her skin to warm, and pulled her underclothes over her head.

Celeste gasped.

Curse it! Lizzy stiffened. She should have taken care to hide the scars. She slipped her arms through the sleeves and wrapped the thin robe tightly around her, pulling the tie at her waist to an uncomfortable crunch. Celeste held her tongue, though Lizzy suspected a multitude of questions were on the forefront.

A knock at the door saved her from Celeste's curiosity. Three maidservants carried two buckets each into the chamber and filled a wooden tub halfway with steaming water. Feeling naked in the flimsy wrapper, Lizzy kept her eyes fixed out a window overlooking a river. The wet smell of steam filled the chamber, and then came the soothing scent of primrose. She waited for the quiet click of the door before turning.

"Your bath awaits ye, m'lady." Celeste giggled, snatched

up a small branch of grapes, and bounced onto the bed. "'Tis the right amount of spring." She wiggled her brows and ran her fingers over the silk bedding just before she plopped onto her back.

Lizzy ignored her wicked comment, removed the wrapper while Celeste was occupied, and stepped into the tub. Hot water seeped around her body and eased her muscles. Her head fell back against the rim, and she moaned.

Heaven. No other word could describe it.

"How old are ye?"

Lizzy rolled her eyes beneath her lids. Why did everyone seem to want to converse with her as of late? 'Twould be rude to ignore Celeste, regardless of how much Lizzy wanted to. "Three and twenty."

"I wonder why a woman of your age and beauty isn't being escorted by her husband."

Lizzy was trapped in a room with a woman who was certain to badger her with questions. "The less you know about me, the better chance we have of remaining friends."

"Friends do not keep secrets."

A burst of air expelled from Lizzy's nose. Her secrets would undoubtedly end their friendship. A small cake of soap along with creams for her hair sat on a cuttie stool beside the tub. Lizzy pulled herself upright and tended to her bath, hoping Celeste would not pursue the conversation.

"I am not one to judge a woman based on her discrepancies," Celeste said.

A laugh escaped Lizzy at the likelihood of any man wanting her in his bed. "You think I'm a courtesan? Mayhap a mistress to some noble in London?"

"Your secrets will not lessen my opinion of ye. We all have them."

"Mayhap you should tell me one of your secrets then." Lizzy had mastered the skill of redirecting conversations.

"My mum was unfaithful to her husband a fortnight after

they spoke their marriage vows. Ye will never guess what breed of man she laid with."

Lizzy gave her a sideways glance. "A Scot?"

Celeste nodded and popped another grape between her grin. "Ironic, aye?"

"Your father was a Scot?"

"Mayhap." Celeste shrugged. "I know not who he was, nor did Mum, I suspect. She was a drab. She contracted cupid's disease and died when I was young. 'Tis what's going to happen to Smitt if he doesn't keep his twanger in his trews."

"Oh, aye," Lizzy agreed wholeheartedly and ran the scented soap around her toes.

Celeste positioned herself at the bed's edge and fidgeted with the hem of her threadbare kirtle. "I've another secret. 'Tis a big one. Not even John knows."

"Do tell," Lizzy prompted, though she doubted it was necessary.

Celeste looked ready to burst with excitement. "I am carrying."

"A child?"

Celeste nodded so hard the bed shook. "John and I feared I was barren. We've been married two years and last month was the first time I've ever missed my menses."

"'Tis wonderful news." Worry had Lizzy frowning. Celeste had to take care. The travel alone could cause complications. "You must tell John."

"I had intended to tell him; then ye and Lord Maxwell arrived. John and I are still bickering, and I'd rather wait til happier times."

Happier times. Lizzy had been waiting for those days her entire life. "Regardless of the times, John will be overjoyed. He will make a good father and you a good mother."

"Thank ye." A pink blush blossomed over Celeste's cheeks and caused a tiny pang of envy deep inside Lizzy. She wouldn't allow herself to want for something she could never have.

Celeste pushed her hair away from her eyes and crossed her ankles. She waited, but she had little patience. "Now I shared two secrets. 'Tis your turn. Tell me, Lizzy, are ye running from a husband?"

"Nay." Lizzy turned away.

"Then mayhap *your* mother was a courtesan? Your father a Scot?" Celeste laughed, trying to prod her. "Or mayhap worse. Ye were sired by the devil himself," she jested, but had no idea how close her statement was to the truth.

Lizzy set the soap aside and eased lower into the tub. Celeste would eventually learn who she was, as all of Yorkshire would know after her meeting with Gloucester. 'Twas best Lizzy not grow too attached to her friend anyway. She closed her eyes and prepared for Celeste's rejection. "Have you ever been to London, Celeste?"

"Used to go with me mum to Cheapside."

"Have you ever witnessed an execution?"

"'Ods toes, no."

Lizzy couldn't see her, but the look on her face was as familiar to Lizzy as her own. "The keeper of London's criminals assigns men to erect a scaffold like a stage for some tragic play. Men, and sometimes even women, are escorted to this platform from the Tower or Newgate Prison to pay for their crimes." Lizzy kept her eyes closed, painting the picture in her head. "The person's place in society, or mayhap the extent of their crime, determines their punishment. A wooden arm might be erected for hanging or a block positioned at the right angle for an audience to best witness a beheading."

"Why are ye telling me this?" Celeste whined, the tone of her voice already changing.

"You want to know who I am, do you not?"

"I do."

"One man rises above all on the scaffold. He solicits silence and fear with his presence alone. He is the man in the black hooded cloak, the one who wields the ax or pulls the cord."

"The executioner?"

Lizzy drew a breath and felt every leer she'd ever received crush her heart. "He is my father."

Silence was what she expected and what she received. There was no shuffle of clothes, nor were there soft footsteps retreating. Just silence. She didn't have to open her eyes to feel Celeste's revulsion.

"Damn," Celeste finally said after long moments of emptiness. "'Tis good Lord Maxwell freed ye from London."

"Freed *me* from London?" Her eyes snapped open. "I freed him, and somehow the arrogant Scot thinks I'm his charge. The fool announced yester eve he intends to take me to Scotland."

Celeste shot to her knees beside the tub, her full face leaning over the rim. "He is taking ye to wife?"

"Nay. He is taking me to a house of God so I might live the remainder of my days in solitude." Her own tone shocked her. Her goals used to be simple: seek Lord Hollister's punishment; free her father of his duty; and the most pathetic of all, find a quiet apothecary where she could secretly mix fragrances. Lord Maxwell complicated her goals the moment he held her in a dark tunnel. She yearned for so much more now.

"The bastard steals your virtue and ruins ye for another man, then intends to tuck ye away? Hide ye from society? He must take ye to wife."

Lizzy snorted. If every man possessed Lord Maxwell's control, then women all over the world could toss their chastity belts into the closest body of water. "Relax, Celeste. My maidenhead is still in place."

"Well mayhap it shouldn't be." Celeste's statement was wicked, as was the spark twinkling in her dark eyes. The woman plotted. Lizzy could see it brewing. Celeste twirled her finger in the water, causing ringlets of small waves to push suds over Lizzy's shoulders.

"What do you suggest? A seduction?" The word tickled Lizzy's tongue. "I will not seduce the man to gain a marriage I do not desire. I cannot marry, Celeste. 'Tis a complication I would rather not discuss."

"As ye wish." Celeste bounced across the chamber with a lift in her gait. She gathered up Lizzy's garments and started for the door. "I am going to take these to the laundry and see about acquiring clean bed garments for us. Have ye need for anything else, m'lady?" Celeste stepped back into character with a bow.

Lizzy didn't trust her. Celeste's actions were abrupt, sneaky. She was bound to find trouble if she started conversing with the servants. "Do be cautious about whom you speak with. Remember who your husband is and the danger he is in by simply being here. Trust no one."

"I can hold my tongue. Ye relax and enjoy your bath. I'll be back a ten, and we will discuss all the ways you can seduce Lord Maxwell." The door latched behind her, and Lizzy settled into the first bit of privacy she'd known in days.

There would be no talk of seduction. Lord Maxwell's control was stronger than the Tower walls, and she held no desire to feel his rejection again.

After removing three days' worth of dust from her hair and skin, she allowed herself to take Celeste's advice and relax.

A mistake.

Lord Maxwell surfaced in her head. She heard his voice, smelled his musky scent, felt his lips against hers.

"Leave me be," she said foolishly to no one.

Her eyes slid shut. He reappeared—naked and glorious. *Curse the man's persistence!*

She tried to solicit the numbers, but only ended up counting the times his lips touched hers in her head. She tried thinking of inanimate objects. A door—he walked through it. A chair—he draped his garments over it. A bed—he made love to her on it over and over until the burning inside her was finally doused.

She conceded, thinking herself quite insane. She toyed with the soap, pushing suds over breasts that suddenly felt fuller, more tender. Her fingers skimmed over a hard, aching nipple. She pinched it and felt the string of heat connecting her breast to her womb.

In her mind's eye her fingers belonged to Lord Maxwell. She fantasized about his mouth on her breast, his hands on her bare flesh, caressing, stroking, giving her pleasure beyond anything she'd ever known. A throbbing pounded at her woman's core, begging for his touch. Her cheeks burned with heat as the woman inside her became fully aroused with thoughts of him.

"Mercy Mary!" she scolded herself aloud. She had never touched herself. She never needed to, but as her hand slipped down her thigh, she battled an untapped desire for fulfillment.

Banners of crimson and gold hung from the second-floor balcony, which was lined with lute players, jugglers, and jesters. A scantily clad woman draped in purple veils and gold rings danced before Broc on the dais. Her arms curled above her head, and her exposed belly moved seductively with the rhythm of swaying hips. She reminded him of Lizbeth, except for her black hair, brown eyes, and thin lips.

Who was he fooling? She didn't resemble his angel at all. She didn't have Lizbeth's silky full lips or her dark red tresses or the determined tilt of her chin. He looked at the dancer's eyes and thought of how dull in comparison they were to the fire in Lizbeth's.

Yet his angel was who he saw when he looked at each of the women performing before a group of gluttonous knights. He wanted no drab, regardless of the dark-eyed gypsy's efforts to gain his attention.

He, John, and Smitt had been brought to the Great Hall, where women danced, courtiers feasted, and every man savored both delicacies to his heart's content.

"I have died and gone to paradise." Smitt stood to Broc's right and squeezed the ample backsides of two wenches draped in gold rings and sheer silks fawning over him.

Mayhap his cousin wanted a third for the eve. He could rescue Broc from the dancing woman's bold advances.

"Mayhap if ye give her a coin, she will leave ye," John suggested in a low voice to avoid offending the English.

"And mayhap she would work harder to gain more." Broc kept his coin in his pocket and poured the remainder of his mead down his gullet. The whole room sickened him. 'Twas a wasteful display of debauchery.

"Forgive me, m'lord, for the interruption." Celeste appeared at his side, wringing her hands.

Broc immediately searched for Lizbeth, but Celeste stood alone, and the worried pinch in her brow had him reaching for his weapon. "What's amiss?"

"'Tis Lizzy. Two men came to the chamber and—"

"Where is she?" The English bastards would die for touching her.

"Southwest tower, second floor, sixth door on the right," Celeste provided and pushed John back to his seat when he stood to follow.

Broc ran from the hall, uncaring that his actions might expose his identity. He sprinted up the tower stairwell alight with golden rushlights. Coming here had been a mistake. His desire to drive Gloucester out of the north endangered himself and Lizbeth. He should have taken her to Scotland.

With a dirk in hand, he entered the corridor, listening for her screams over the pulse beating in his throat. He counted until he reached the sixth chamber, then kicked the door wide with the flat of his foot, knocking it back against the interior wall with a bang. A whoosh of damp flowers filled his lungs.

A gasp preceded a slosh of water.

Lizbeth's head whipped around, sending wet ropes of dark hair swinging. A scan of the chamber found it void of danger.

Ach! He'd been duped. No English threatened her life. This was the simple plotting of one woman. Celeste. He sheathed his dirk at his waist and tried to decide if he would scold Celeste or thank her upon their next meeting.

"Are you mad? Where is Celeste?"

A shoulder popped above the rim and tempted him in ways he no longer wished to battle. "I fear your maid has gone below stairs." He searched the room for a towel, but found naught. Not a stitch of garments in sight, except for a thin pale wrapper draped over the bed's edge. He laughed inwardly. Celeste was true to her cause. "It seems Celeste has abandoned ye."

"Then go get her," Lizbeth demanded and slunk deeper into the water.

"Nay." Broc didn't even attempt to leave. He didn't want to. He was damned tired of ignoring his desire for this woman. She'd been all too eager to have him give her memories. Mayhap he should and damn the consequences.

He shut the door and approached the tub. Lizbeth's hands scurried beneath the water to hide her breasts. Pink tinted her cheeks, mist glistened her fair skin, and her bottom lip looked even fuller than he'd remembered. His angel had the oddest look of an unsatisfied woman. Albeit, he'd known few women to be unsatisfied in his bed.

He bent to one knee and braced his elbows on the rim.

"What do you mean, nay?" She stared at him with darkening eyes.

Heavy breathing pushed the water to and fro over the curve of her collarbone. His eyes shifted to the middle of the water. Her hand followed the path, leaving her one hand short of covering all three of her treasures. Her knees peeked out of the top of the water, slightly spread and trembling. She slammed them shut.

If he didn't know better, he would say she was fully aroused. "I mean nay. Ye want your maid, then go fetch her yourself." He cast her a broad grin.

A burst of air shot out of her nose in a fury, popping tiny bubbles atop the surface. His gaze locked on a perfectly shaped breast, sweetly curved with an upturned nipple crinkled into a tight bud. His cullions thickened to hard stones beneath a rigid erection he couldn't control. A team of oxen couldn't pull him from the room.

"Hand me a towel and stop gawking at me."

"I cannae."

"Why?"

"Because ye are naked." He dipped his index finger in the water to his knuckle and twirled. "'Tis hot." He studied her nipple surrounded by water. It should be a soft, round, rose-colored circle, but it was as hard as his cock. "Ye are aroused."

"What?!" she yelled, obviously mortified by his statement.

"Ye are alone, naked in a tub, with only your thoughts, and ye are fully aroused. Deny it."

She growled at him in comment.

"Tell me, Lizbeth, is Edlynn talking to ye again?" One finger drew a path down her throat and into the water. He stopped between her breasts and then repeated the action.

"I will not play your game." She bit her bottom lip.

"'Tis no game. Tell me what ye were thinking before I came into the chamber." He wouldn't have thought it possible, but her cheeks turned a darker shade of crimson. The water rippled around her quivering knees. Sharp breaths brought her breast closer to the surface, temptation a hand's reach away.

He tweaked her nipple.

She cried out and grabbed his wrist, but made no resistance when he rolled the tiny nubbin between his thumb and forefinger. Her head lolled in pleasure, and her eyes twitched behind closed lids. "Oh, God."

"Tell me"—he watched her knees slowly separate—"did I enter your thoughts or is there another man who makes ye burn?"

Her eyes snapped open, fire leaping in their depths. "There is no other man, and you well know it. Now remove yourself from my person and step back."

Obediently, he did as she asked, but couldn't look away. He felt intoxicated and the weightlessness in his head had naught to do with the drink.

She scowled at him. "Hand me the wrapper on the bed."

He raised the fine linen up in front of him by the shoulders and shook it. She would have to take at least three steps to get to him. To his astonishment, she stood straight up in the tub; water trickled over her shoulders, down her breasts, and straight into the dark triangle of curls at the apex of her legs. She was probably glaring at him, but he didn't notice, nor did he care. His gaze remained fixed on luscious legs and creamy skin. The kind of skin a man could dine on for hours searching for all the places that would make her gasp and moan. He licked his lips and swallowed.

She yanked the wrapper from his hands and gloved herself inside it. She may as well still be naked for all the more it hid. In an instant, her wet skin soaked the material, outlining the curve of her hips, the lines of her thighs, and the shadowed circles of her nipples. She tied the strip of silk tight around her petite waist and lowered her head. Hiding.

"Thank ye for your assistance, m'lord. You may go," she said softly and turned toward the darkest corner in the room, combing her hair against the side of her face.

Nay! He wanted to shake her. The desirable woman disappeared and in her place returned shy, timid Lady Ives. He stepped up behind her and curled one hand around her shoulder. Gathering her thick wet locks, he pulled them aside and kissed the back of her neck. He felt the tremors rack her body. "Where is she?" he whispered against the rim of her ear.

"Who?"

"The woman who breathes fire inside ye. I want her back." He nipped her earlobe.

"You rejected her."

"'Twas a mistake. Bring her back. I'll not reject her again."

Her head fell against his chest. The hands clutching the edges of her wrapper loosened. "You will kill her if you do."

He peeled the material over her shoulder to expose a perfect brown beauty mark. He kissed it, nibbled at it, and then grazed his teeth over it. There was no going back. She wanted him, and he wouldn't deny her. He would deal with the complications of his actions when he returned to Scotland. "I will not reject ye."

"Vow it upon your soul."

"I vow it." He surrendered, turned her in his arms, and raised her chin. "All will be well. Bring her back," he whispered and drew her bottom lip into his mouth.

She suckled his top lip, but not with the passion he knew she possessed. He opened her mouth with the press of his thumb and inhaled her air. "I want my angel."

He awaited her kiss. Searched for it. Craved it. Then finally she was there, moistening his lips with her own. She caressed his mouth with exquisite tenderness, then dove in with a vengeance. Her mouth slanted over his. Once, twice, increasing her demand each time.

Their tongues mated with a born instinct, chasing one another with fervent speed. He spread his jaw wide to deepen the kiss, and she unleashed a tiny mew—the sound like bells in his ears.

He picked her up and laid her on the bed, her eyes moist, her lips pinked by his kiss. The edge of her wrapper fell away at her hips when she rubbed her legs together—her magnificently long legs. The head of his cock broke from the waistband of his trews. He was going to explode if he didn't take her. After tossing his weapons to the floor with a clang, he removed his boots and shed his surcoat and tunic in one pull. The tiniest of voices inside his head told him to consider his actions, but his desire to have her deafened his conscience.

He planted a knee between her thighs, and the intensity of her stare set his heart pounding against his spine. Her lips parted. He kissed her to silence her words and slid a hand up her thigh beneath her wrapper to squeeze her backside. Her fingers played over his chest, his arms, his stomach, tickling the skin below his navel. He had to control himself, had to reign in the beast that wanted to devour her whole.

She whimpered and ground herself against his knee.

"Lizbeth, I should warn you. There will be pain at first, but I—"

She released the tie of her wrapper and stole his words. "I am not afraid of you or of what's about to happen. I might be an innocent, but—"

"Edlynn?" he supplied, saving her an explanation he had no desire to hear.

"Aye."

He traced a finger from her chin all the way down to her patch of sable curls. She sucked in air at the contact.

"I will not deny ye or myself anymore." He bent and flicked her taut nipple with his tongue—teasing, biting, titillating—before taking her breast into the haven of his mouth while kneading her other forgotten breast inside the nest of his hand.

She grasped handfuls of his hair and pressed him harder against her. "Broc," she whispered and widened her knees. She knew what she wanted, and he wouldn't make her say it.

Braced atop her, he kissed her again and slowly slid one finger into the tight, silken flesh between her legs. She cried out, but he showed her no mercy. His thumb danced around her untouched bud until he felt her swell for him. Adding a second finger, he teased her until her toes curled, and her body shuddered; then her panting turned into mewling screams. Her hands seized clumps of bedding as she grasped for something to hold on to.

Her reaction was fast and fierce.

"Mercy Mary!" Her back arched.

A surge of liquid heat washed over his hand, shocking him. He'd never had a woman react so quickly. The next time she reached fulfillment, he would be inside her.

He stood above her, fumbling with his trews in a mad rush to free his arousal. He knelt between her parted knees, the smell of her climax driving him insane with need. Sweat rolled down his back as he positioned himself at her entrance. "Pledge your troth to me."

Her eyes fluttered open. Confusion and satisfaction combined lowered her delicate brow. "What?" she questioned between heaving breaths.

The tip of his cock slipped between her nether lips. A throaty groan vibrated through his throat. One stroke and he would be finished, but he would make love to her again and again. "I will not take your virtue until we are husband and wife. Pledge your troth and make me your husband."

"Nay. I want no husband."

Her words sent him reeling. Fury erupted beneath his skull and stabbed the backs of his eyeballs. In the last four days he'd gained everything he'd ever wanted—the future of Clan Maxwell, Lady Juliana, the chance to protect his clan and his country. He was willing to give it all up for her, and she denied him.

He bolted off her, raking his hands through his hair. For once, he had no words. He pulled on his trews and collected his garments from the floor.

"I cannot marry you. Are you mad?" She sat up and jumped from the bed, pulling the wrapper over her flushed skin.

He knew her fears, he knew what prevented her from

accepting, and she was a fool to doubt his protection. He reached for the door lever.

The soft patter of her footsteps stilled behind him. "Broc, please."

"I have been true to my vow to protect ye. I wield as much power in my clan as your precious Gloucester. I protect the borders of an entire country. Think ye I would allow our sons to be cursed with your father's profession?" He opened the door and walked into the corridor, damning her father for instilling such fear in her.

Chapter 12

Women! They would be the death of Scotland. 'Tis fortunate for Scotland *that* particular woman denied him. Broc couldn't marry Lizbeth. 'Twould be a disgrace to his clan. He was bound to Lady Juliana. Da would disinherit him if he brought home another bride.

Broc paused in the corridor to reposition his weapons, his hands shaking with a rage he should be able to control. How had he become so infatuated with her? Aiden would have never offered a woman marriage. His brother at least had the wit to spend himself inside a woman without promises. Hell, Ian probably knew this by now, and he was barely twenty summers.

The moment Broc was certain Gloucester had the information Lizbeth provided he was going home. For now, he was determined to scratch his itch the same as any lusty Scotsman.

Whisky and women.

The sharp smell of wine and lust led him down the curved stairwell and back to the festivities. John, Celeste, and Smitt had apparently retired, but the dark-haired seductress still danced for garland in the center of a band of drunkards. She teased them with her movements, bending in all the right positions to allow their imaginations to strip her bare.

He swiped two mugs of mead from the tray of a passing maidservant. The liquid amber didn't even touch his tongue as he poured it down his throat. He scoured his lips with the back of his hand and watched the entertainment. Lizbeth's face rushed behind his eyes.

He swilled the second mug of mead. He should be thinking of Lady Juliana, not Lizbeth, and he damned sure shouldn't be ogling the drab dancing with herself like a woman in the throws of passion. She caught his eye and smiled over her shoulder, flirting with him through half-closed eyes. Her pink tongue darted out to lick her top lip, and her fingers cupped her breasts and squeezed.

Broc's teeth clenched until he felt certain they would crumble into bits. His pulse throbbed in his groin. Every muscle in his body wanted to let the beauty play with him.

To hell with honor.

Two flicks of his finger was all the girl needed. She bounced through the crowd on bare toes, then rubbed herself against his side. She was just the itch he needed to scratch. Her long fingers moved over his stomach, then dipped low to stroke the hard length of his cock. "Oh, *mon dieu.*" Her eyes lit up, and her smile widened. "Ye want me?"

"How much?"

"Three ducats."

He grabbed the girl by the wrist and dragged her from the hall. Music and merriment dissipated behind them, but her grating voice replaced the hollow void of an empty hallway.

"Have ye a name ye want me to use?"

"Julian," he provided without thought.

The wench prattled on, some words in English, some in French, but he couldn't decipher any of it over the pounding in his chest. She took three steps for every one of his angry strides, desperate to rid himself of the stronghold. He felt more imprisoned here than he had in the Tower.

Six archways led them into the castle garden. Rushlights burned around a fishpond alighting alabaster sculptures of naked people. The mixed aromas of fruit trees and plots of herbs called his attention to an abundance of flowers. They were everywhere. Exotic scents slapped him in the face and nearly stopped his footing. Behind his eyes he saw Lizbeth lying in a field of blue flowers.

God's hooks! He refused to think about her and tugged the beauty behind him down a series of stone steps. The entrance to a maze presented two options, left or right. He turned right and stalked through two walls of green hedge until darkness surrounded him. He stopped, released the girl's hand, and held his aching chest. She panted, bent at the waist, hands on her knees, no longer badgering him with trivial questions.

Broc braced his legs. His head fell back. The sky above spun, turning stars into flickering circles. What was he doing? This was not his way. He didn't pay for pleasure. Village maids served him well in his youth, but after his time in the monastery, he became more selective about the company he shared.

"Ye want me naked?" The girl reached for the gold clasp on the small garment holding her breasts in place.

"Nay." He didn't want this. He didn't want her. He wanted Lizbeth.

The girl shrugged one shoulder and dropped to her knees in front of him. She looked up at him, her big doe eyes glittering in the starlight, while one hand massaged his sac and the other reached for the string of his trews.

"Ach!" He pulled her to her feet. "Forgive me, maiden. I've had a change of mind."

"Do I displease ye?" Black brows slashed at sharp angles.

"Nay." Broc pulled five ducats from his surcoat and pressed them in her palm, eager to be rid of her. "Go."

She ran out of the maze, leaving him with the misery of his thoughts. He closed his eyes, popped his neck, and inhaled through his nose. Touching the tips of his fingers together in front of him, he cleared his mind of unwanted lust as Brother Mel had taught him to do. Two years of meditation and solitude nearly drove him mad, but through Brother Mel's guidance, he learned how to control his physical state of being. He had to rein in his emotions and come to terms with his position and his responsibilities. He clasped his hands behind his back and started walking.

Clan Maxwell needed a leader, a warrior, a defender. A man willing to give up his life to protect his brethren. Not a man willing to give up everything for the protection of one woman. England's crown would be passed into the hands of a twelve-year-old sovereign. Its government would suffer duress during the transition. Scotland would be wise to take advantage of this time to build defenses throughout the lowlands and form alliances with each other along with France. With any luck, Gloucester would place great importance in his position as Protector of the Realm and leave the north to see to his nephew's coronation. The boy would need council, guidance, and the nobles would battle for these political positions. If only there was a way to take Lizbeth's document to his king as evidence of the strife that was sure to fall over England. Without proof, he had only his word, which would hold little merit with King James.

Da and the council would know what to do.

He listed the Scottish nobles he and Da would meet upon his return and deliberated on which tactics they would use to sway their king. Mayhap he should be considering ways to maintain peace with England instead of seeking alliances to battle against them. He paused and looked to his front and then his back. Two walls of shrubbery boxed him in. He backtracked, counting his steps, clipping a small branch from every corner, searching for a way out of the labyrinth. Each twist looked the same as the last until he'd memorized every damned turn.

He deserved this punishment for leaving one woman and seeking out another. A crescent moon worked its way over the stars, telling him how much time he'd wasted. He stopped and studied the map in his head.

The sound of a twig snapped like a fallen tree in his ears. Whispers followed.

"You trust the source of this information?"

"Aye. 'Tis my own brother. He's fostered by an alderman in the king's court. Said the bishop delivered the sacraments and King Edward breathed his last on the eve of Wednesday."

Broc strained his ear. The voices were two, mayhap three walls to the east.

"Have you located the girl?"

"She's inside the keep tupping with that filthy Scot she freed from the Tower. Shall I find her and dispose of her, m'lord?"

Only one woman matched that description: Lizbeth.

Broc's jaw flexed. His muscles tensed. He strangled the hilt of his dirk with a lethal grip.

"Find her, but I want her alive. Bring her and the document to me before she exposes my association with the leader of the rebellion. Inform her that her charge is here to collect her and take her back to the Tower. When she refuses you, and the little bitch will, tell her if she does not act accordingly, I will train her eldest nephew to wield her father's ax."

The man lied. Lizbeth said her nephews were dead.

A man spit. "What of the Scot and his friends?"

"Feed them to Gloucester. I've no use for any of them."

God's hooks! Broc held his breath until the sound of their footsteps faded beyond the hedge. He had to get Lizbeth and the others and get out. Tonight.

* * *

Father has amber eyes—a similar color to hers, only darker. He used to carve things, mostly those foolish birds. And he has large hands. Lizzy punched the bolster beneath her head, attempting to lessen its thickness, while trying to recall Father's good qualities and the reasons she was trying to save him. After what seemed like hours of thought, all she could summon from her childhood was that the man had carved things with large hands—hands that he sharpened his ax with, hands that he wielded his whip with, and hands that held his pewter cup when he drank himself into a stupor every eve.

Broc wanted to marry her, and she denied him, as she denied herself the chance to be a wife, a mother, a lover, all for Father's hands.

She growled and tossed and turned until her wrapper completely tied her in knots. The weight of the heavy bedding nearly crushed her. She kicked the coverlet and sheets to the foot of the bed and bucked until the thin wrapper no longer bound her. Air blew over her damp skin, sending a ripple up her spine. The sensation reminded her of what Broc's touch had done to her. While Edlynn explained many things—all in vivid detail—Lizzy's old friend failed to mention the intensity, the craving one felt until all at once there was a blinding, almost unbearable moment of pure bliss.

Mercy Mary! Sleep was never going to find her. Not to mention she was sweating like a woman ill with the death fever. She stared at the mahogany dome of the giant bed, alight with the many candles she left burning, and prayed for piety. She must make wise decisions not only for herself, but for her loved ones—both living and passed.

Since arriving at Middleham, her courage seemed to crawl farther inside her. Anticipation of her scheduled meeting with the Duke of Gloucester had her nerves taut like a new bowstring. The people of York believed him a fair and just man. He would see her efforts as noble and reward her accordingly. Then Lord Hollister would walk to where he'd sent so many before him—to the gallows. A touch of insanity tickled her mind, for the image of Lord Hollister's head atop the chopping block made her feel wickedly happy.

Click.

She sat upright in bed and pulled the coverlet around her neck. "Celeste?"

The door swung wide. The tip of a blade made her heart kick, but the arm attached to it belonged to the man who quelled her fears with a simple look. A soothing sense of security made her lips turn up at the corners.

Then he looked at her.

The determined scowl drawing his face into harsh angles made her sag into the bed.

"Get up. We're leaving." Broc closed the door and took a quick scan of the chamber with his warrior eyes.

"What do you mean we're leaving? And why must you always enter with a weapon?"

"Because there are always people trying to kill us." He sheathed the dagger and strode to the bed without even looking at her. A sheen of sweat slicked his face and neck, his raven hair was tousled, and the glint in his eye bespoke of fear. He grabbed her upper arm and pulled her from the bed. "We must go."

The man had completely lost his wit. She wrenched away, pulling the seams of her wrapper tight with both hands. "Nay. I cannot go anywhere. I have no clothes. What are you about?"

"'Tis nay time to explain." Erratic blue eyes shifted from her face and swept over her body. "I have to find the others and leave, and ye are going with me." He grabbed for her again.

"Why? What has happened?" One skill she did possess was the ability to slip from someone's grip. She bolted in front of the window and passed the empty hearth only to circle back again. The chamber didn't seem quite as big with him in it.

"Stop running from me, ye foolish woman!" The muscles flexed in his thighs under his tight black trews.

She managed to put the bed between them. When he moved right, so did she, rounding a full circle before they stopped. "Why did you even come here if you are going to leave before I give Gloucester the document?"

"I no longer care about the document or Gloucester. I care about getting you out of here alive."

"No longer?" She knew he had ulterior motives for coming here. "Tell me why you came? And do not lie to me."

He rubbed his temples. "We seek the same goal, angel. To protect kin and country. I admit what ye hold in your possession once tempted me."

"The document?" she asked, trying to keep the hurt from surfacing but failed. She'd been foolish for believing otherwise. Had the document been important enough to him that he would propose marriage? "I was never more than a means to aid your country?"

"Nay! Ye are more than that, and ye well know it."

But she didn't know it. She didn't know who to trust anymore. "Tell me how the document benefits you."

Broc glanced at the door and then the window. "Your document is the proof I need to convince the King of Scotland to align with France."

"Then why did you not take it?"

"Because it is yours."

She shook her head, not wanting to accept his words. "And Gloucester? I trust you only brought me here to give Gloucester the document. Does this benefit you as well?"

"The Duke of Gloucester led an army across the border into Dumfriesshire two years past. They burned the village, raped the women, and left naught, save for a black ash of destruction. Many of my kin died in that battle, including Lilian and Mattie. My sisters were new brides. 'Twas my intention to drive your duke out of the north."

Her stance softened; her brow smoothed. Regardless of how much his words pained her, she sympathized with him. "I'm sorry for your losses."

"'Tis an old wound, but not one worth opening if it is going to get me killed. I have to leave. They know I'm a Scot, and they know I travel with John, Celeste, and Smitt. I cannae fight all of York alone."

"I cannot just leave. I've worked too hard to get here. I've lurked in stairwells, hid in cells, played the submissive servant to Lord Hollister's demands. He stole everyone dear to me and 'tis time he served his sentence." She realized the desire to avenge her loved ones was as strong as her determination to save Father.

"Lord Hollister is here . . . at Middleham."

Her knees gave way. She clung to the bedpost, staring at the green vine design in the floor covering, certain she would swoon.

"The chief warder and his men most likely arrived in York before we did."

"How do ye know this?"

"I happened upon them talking."

She regained her feet and narrowed her eyes. "Lord Hollister knows your face. How is it he did not summon the English on you?"

He rolled his eyes heavenward. "I am a spy, Lizbeth. I am capable of lurking without being seen. 'Tis Hollister's intention to get the document before ye meet with Gloucester and take ye back to the Tower."

Her stomach turned. Fingers wrapped tighter around the bedpost while a suffocating fear clutched her chest. "I cannot go back," she whispered more to herself than to him.

"Please, Lizbeth." Broc held out a strong hand, palm up. "Come with me and trust me to keep ye safe."

She felt weak for wanting to take his hand. She failed Kamden and Emma, Edlynn and her nephews, her king and country . . . her father. She looked up at Broc wanting to cry, scream, anything to release the pressure building in her chest. "He wins then. Hollister wins. Gloucester will never know he conspired with Buckingham to assassinate the king."

"Your king is dead." Broc stepped to the window and scanned the courtyard.

News of her sovereign's death didn't shock her. She knew the man's days were few.

"I cannae wait for ye to decide. Trust me or Gloucester, but ye must choose now."

Her choice was simple. While Gloucester had shown her compassion, 'twas only once. Broc had shown her so much more. He'd given her reasons to want to save herself. Now, she needed to save him. She wouldn't let Lord Hollister take Broc away from her. While Broc was a far more superior warrior, Lord Hollister had strength in numbers. Softly, she walked up behind him and touched the back of his arm. "I trust you."

He spun, pulled her against his chest, and kissed her hair. "Come with me, Lizbeth. To Scotland."

"As your wife?" she asked, hopeful.

"As my friend." His sad smile strummed up regrets abound, but the time for that discussion would have to wait.

She nodded. "We must find the others."

Broc led her toward the door. "Celeste is most likely with John in the knight's quarters. Smitt, howbeit, may be difficult to locate."

"Lord Hollister will kill them if he suspects they mean anything to me. 'Tis his way. To dangle a person's loved ones in front of them until they yield to his demands." A twinge of guilt for not being strong enough to save her father still pecked at her conscience.

"Aye. The man is ruthless." Broc pulled his dagger out of his waistband, opened the door, and checked the corridor. "'Twas his intention to dangle your nephew beneath your nose to get his hands on that document."

Lizzy stopped beneath the door frame. The connection between their hands broke. "My nephews are dead. He locked them in the Tower after Emma told him they were Kamden's sons. He killed them." Her hands balled in front of her. Cold seeped through her, turning her insides to ice. Her mind became a whirl of memories. "I saw their blood-soaked tunics. Lord Hollister told me they were dead." She took a step backward.

"He would say anything to get the document."

"If there is even the slightest chance Eli and Martin are still alive, I have to do something to protect them. Lord Hollister's hatred for them runs deeper than any desire to punish me. The boys are a constant reminder of everything Kamden took from him. I have no choice." She looked away from him, unable to bear his pleading eyes. The press of her heart was excruciating. "I have to go back. You have to protect your kin as I have to protect mine."

He cursed beneath his breath and lowered his dagger. All his vitality seemed to fall away to the floor. "I'll not leave ye here. I will go back for your nephews after ye are safe in Scotland."

She choked on her tears, refusing to let her wants put him or anyone else in danger. He searched for a way to help her. She could see the plan brewing behind his light blue eyes, but it was imperative she meet with Gloucester now, before Lord Hollister found her. Convincing Broc of this plan would be about as easy as convincing him to pledge fealty to an English sovereign. She would have to lie.

A single step put her back in his embrace. She pulled his head to hers and kissed him with the passion he'd found inside her. She suckled his bottom lip, gaining strength to accomplish her task.

She nodded her agreement and felt the relief slump his body. Now what? A quick glance down reminded her of appearance. "I have no clothes. I cannot walk out of Middleham dressed in a robe as thin as a veil. I will draw attention to us, and we are sure to be caught. The maid told Celeste the laundry was below stairs. I will fetch something to wear whilst you get the others out of Middleham."

He shook his head. "Nay. Ye will go with me."

He wasn't going to leave; she was certain of it. Lord Hollister would kill him to torture her. Her stomach churned with anxiety. She hated this deceit, but he left her no choice. "You must. 'Tis your duty to protect them. Celeste is carrying."

"A child?"

She looked at him as though his question was stupid, even though she'd responded in like. "Aye. You must see them safely out of Middleham and then meet me outside the gates. Just tell me where."

"I am not leaving without ye." He sighed, no doubt stricken with responsibility. "You will go to the laundry, fetch a garment, and this is all. Do not come back to this chamber." He threaded his fingers through her hair and cupped her nape. "Meet me in the courtyard. In the heart of the labyrinth." With a firm grip on her chin, he demanded she focus. "Count: two rights, four lefts, one right, five lefts."

"Two, four, one, five," she repeated, easily committing the steps to memory.

Broc kissed her again, this time with an aggression that made her wanton, and then disappeared into the corridor.

His absence left her stricken with a moment of panic, but she inhaled deeply, swiveled, and searched beneath the bed for the satchel containing the document she almost wished she didn't possess. She tied it beneath her wrapper along with Mother's rosary and rushed out of the chamber. A rushlight next to the cistern lit her descent down a small spiral stairwell. Not until her toes touched the cool stone at the base did she realize she hadn't counted a single step. Not one. Fear did not drive her this day, but sheer determination. If Eli and Martin were alive, she would see them raised in Scotland—a place touched by God's hand and protected by mortal warriors. They would be free, as would she.

Two sets of double doors led her to the servants' entrance. A stinging scent of caustic soda burned her nose, and steam dampened her face before she even entered the laundry. Though the hours small, and the guests of Middleham no doubt in slumber, the activities of the laundry room were bustling with organized chaos. Maids of every age scurried about their duties, soaking sheets and tablecloths and dying robes of various colors.

A portly woman whose hair hid beneath a white wimple stood over a young girl dipping a vestment into a wooden vat of purple dye. The woman turned toward Lizzy, her face bunched into a glower. "Ye must be Adel's cousin. Ye're late."

The woman had to be either the head laundress or the Mistress Taylor. Regardless of her position, she exuded authority. She made a straight line toward Lizzy, eyeing her attire with an accusing glare. "What ye do with your time outside the laundry is of no concern to me. I know there is extra coin to be made in Middleham right now, but if those knights cause ye to be late again, do not bother coming back."

Lizzy accepted the scolding, but only because the laundress posed less of a threat than Lord Hollister.

"A fine of two pence will be deducted from your wages for your tardiness. Now, fetch up a smock." She pointed toward a pegged wall draped with garments.

"Aye, mistress." Lizzy didn't debate. She needed clothes, any clothes at this point. Eagerly, she pulled a pristine white smock over her head, leaving her wrapper beneath as her only means of undergarments. She tied on pockets and then slipped into a gray apron. After stuffing her uncombed hair under a white wimple, Lizzy's nerves loosened within her disguise.

"'Ave ye a name?" the laundress asked and rubbed her red nose.

"Emma." Lizzy spouted the first name that came to her mind besides her own. Not that it was necessary. No one knew her here.

"Help Penny prepare toweling for His Lordship." The laundress used her eyes to point Lizzy in Penny's direction. "Do not dawdle. His Lordship is early to rise and prefers his linens warm."

"Aye, mistress."

The laundress went about her bustling, freeing Lizzy from a disapproving frown and providing her a means to get to Gloucester. Lizzy positioned herself next to Penny and mimicked her dunking actions. Menial labor at Middleham wasn't performed with the same docility as in the Tower. While Lizzy tucked her chin to her chest, the other maids performed their duties in high spirits around four wooden vats of steaming water.

"Sybil, ye are grinnin' like a woman whose pockets are heavy. Did ye earn a bit of extra coin yester eve?" Penny asked.

Lizzy peeked up, curious to see what that grin might look like. Of the four maids scrubbing sheets, *she* stood out above the rest—glossy black hair, dark eyes, and heart-shaped lips tilted up at the corners around smooth teeth. Curves to envy flared her maid's smock out at the hips, and the dip of her swooping neckline revealed the shadowed cleft between her breasts.

"Five ducats he paid me," the woman named Sybil boasted, the lilt of an accent highlighting her words, "and I only asked for three." She slipped a hand beneath her apron and then flashed the number of said coins as proof of her wages. "A fine lookin' Englishman he was. Hair black as my own. I'd have serviced him for less, but he was eager to pay." Light reflected off the black orbs in her eyes as she altered her gaze between the other maids.

"Was he a big man?" another maid asked with a naughty giggle.

"*Ouais.*" Sybil's eyes rounded dramatically. "Two heads taller than I, big hands, big chest, and . . ." She pulled her hand from the vat, water dripping from her elbow, and formed a C shape with curved fingers and thumb. ". . . a cock as thick as my wrist. *C'est magnifique!*"

Though shocked by her vulgarity, Lizzy formed an image of the man Sybil described while the other maids squealed. Smitt would be happy to know the maids were gushing over his cock in the laundry.

"Sybil, ye clamp that filthy mouth shut or I'll wash yer tongue in the ashes," the laundress bellowed over their cackling. "Get back to work, all of ye, or I'll dock yer wages."

The maids ducked their heads low with the threat, but all eyes remained on Sybil, awaiting the continuation of her story.

"The man dragged me through the bowels of Middleham," she began again in a hushed tone, "and into the labyrinth. I daresay his mistress denied him, for he was insane with want."

That description didn't sound like Smitt at all.

"Did he give ye a name to holler out?"

"*Ouais.* Julian."

Lizzy's pulse jumped into a triple beat; her hands wrenched the sheets under the water. While she was not Broc's mistress, she had denied him in more ways than one. He'd fled the chamber unsatisfied only to return hours later with a detailed map of the maze in his head. She hadn't even questioned how he'd become so familiar with its layout.

Penny peeked over her shoulder at the laundress, then bent in low. "Did *Julian* pleasure ye, or did ye just earn your coin?"

Lizzy felt the cloth tear beneath the water.

One of Sybil's thin brows arched, and her dark eyes blinked repeatedly. "I always earn my coin, but I admit the man had me on my knees begging."

Lizzy had never known jealousy, but was certain this is what it felt like—a raw, aching desire to lash out. She wrapped her fingers around the wadded sheet and squeezed, wishing it was Broc's throat. She shouldn't care. The man was not her husband or even her lover. Neither of these facts prevented the bruise from spreading over her heart. She trusted him, shared her desires with him. He'd touched her in places no man had ever touched and then left her bed to rut with this harlot.

Unable to stop herself, Lizzy stared at Sybil's lips. "Did he kiss you?"

The woman stiffened her spine and shot Lizzy a challenging glare. "Julian didn't pay me to kiss him."

Lizzy bit down on her lip and returned her gaze into the water, grateful to hear the heavy breathing of the laundress behind her.

"Ye four. Fetch up your pails and take hot water to the family solar."

Grateful to detach herself from the discussion, Lizzy fell into step, mimicking their actions. She pushed thoughts of Broc and Sybil to the back of her mind and focused on her mission.

With a pail of water in each hand, she followed the maids up the eastern side of the keep. Two knights guarded the family solar. The Duchess of York sat calmly in a velvet-covered settee, her ankles crossed, her hands clasped in her lap. Lizzy couldn't stop herself from staring. She was beautiful, young, with alabaster skin that nigh glowed beneath the hint of dawn rising outside her window. A lady's maid stood behind the duchess's shoulder holding a bowl of toiletries, her eyes unblinking and fixed on nothingness.

The maids emptied their pails into a wooden tub in the center of the solar, bowed deep before the duchess, and obediently disappeared once excused. Lizzy set her empty pails on the floor and stayed behind, her heart drumming a tattoo in her chest. She folded her hands in front of her and stepped before the duchess. "Pray forgive me, m'lady. May I have permission to speak?"

The duchess nodded, her expression void of emotion.

"I am not a maid. I have traveled from London to speak with your husband about a matter of the utmost—" Before the last word left her mouth, steel hissed behind her the same time two knights seized her upper arms in a menacing grip and then crossed their swords in front of her.

The duchess never blinked, nor did her maid.

"Please. My intentions are noble. I am in desperate need of an audience with your husband," Lizzy begged as the guards' hold raised her off the floor. "I have proof of a conspiracy against the crown."

The duchess raised a hand. "Lessen your hold."

Lizzy's toes regained their position on the floor. "Pray forgive me for disturbing your morning ablutions, but my life is in danger."

Hurried footsteps sounded to her right, and the Duke of Gloucester himself walked through the double doors of the lady's solar. Why she felt any relief at all was preposterous, but she did just the same. He was a comely man, as she'd remembered—tall, slight of build, but what jarred her the most was the distant look in his tired eyes.

"What is this? Release her," he commanded. "Does she look like a threat to either of you?"

The guards' release caused a tingling in her arms as the blood returned back into her fingertips. Her lips pursed and the glare she intended for the guards was wasted on the delicate design of a crimson and gold carpet beneath her feet.

"What is your name?" Gloucester approached her, sandaled feet poking out beneath his purple robe.

"I am Lady Lizbeth Ives."

Lizzy jerked back when he raised her chin and pulled the wimple from her hair. "I know you."

"Aye." She gathered her apron in her hand and prayed she would quit trembling. "We met in London last year, just before Christmastide. I am the executioner's daughter." This information gained her a bit more personal space from the guards. As if being Osborn Ives's daughter meant she was plagued by an infectious disease. The mention of Father reminded her of all the reasons she was here.

"I have proof of a conspiracy," Lizzy blurted out. The guards were back on her like cattle to a salt lick.

Gloucester stopped them with a nonchalant gesture; his expression yielded little reaction to her statement. "Lady Ives, mayhap you would join me in the chapel for morning mass and then we can see to your proof whilst we break our fast."

How could the man be so calm about what she'd just said? "But 'tis a matter of the utmost importance."

He chuckled slightly beneath his breath. "My every day is met with matters of the utmost importance. If I pay heed to all of them without pause, my soul would suffer, and I would most certainly starve to death."

Lizzy agreed, feeling foolish for interrupting the man's morning ablutions. "Aye, Your Lordship."

The duchess rose behind him. "Joan, see Lady Ives to a privy chamber. Have the Mistress Taylor bring garments more suitable to our guest's station, and then have her accompanied to the chapel."

Escorted from the family solar by the two guards, Lizzy followed the duchess's maid to a dressing chamber. Underclothes and water soon arrived and Lizzy was provided a brief period of privacy. Stripped of her servant's attire, she was garbed in a low-necked gown of dark blue damask, almost black, with a full train trailing the floor behind her. Two braids at her temples tied together with ribbon secured her hair beneath the sheer white veil of a hennin.

Once the duchess's maid approved her attire, Lizzy reflected the guard's footsteps to the chapel. The buckram corset bit into her ribs, forcing her to take small, shallow breaths. The bitter scent of myrrh might have calmed her apprehensions had the guard not directed her into the back pew of the chapel. While she'd been strapped in a gown suited to her lady's rank, her placement in the chapel told her exactly how the duke felt about her station.

Gloucester entered in a doublet of blue velvet full of sleeve wrought with trimmings of pine-apples. He led a procession of burgesses, prelates, and household attendants richly clad in bright-colored gowns down the aisle. Shunned by his bias of her, she raised her chin and smoothed her dark skirt over the document. She retrieved Mother's rosary and watched him, studied his every movement. Would he help her? Or would he take the document she'd protected with her life and see her silenced forever. She obviously held no rank among these people of York, just as her life had held little worth thus far.

She knelt and followed along the movements of mass thinking of the only person who'd ever told her she was worth saving. The same man who probably awaited her in the labyrinth, but also the same man who spent himself only hours earlier inside another woman. Broc admitted his purpose for coming to Middleham benefited his goals, but since had abandoned his intentions. She understood his dislike for Gloucester, but warfare made enemies. Living in the Tower was no different. The battlefield was just smaller.

The rosary draped over her wrist. *Guide me, Mother. Tell me what to do.* Her fingers slid over the cool blue beads until Gloucester received the sacrament of communion. The congregation followed suit. She stood, but Gloucester's man guarded her exit and wagged his finger. She knelt and crossed herself with temper. She trusted no one.

She followed Gloucester's attendants past the labyrinth. *Two, four, one, five.* Keeping her eyes downcast, she recited Broc's directions. She considered breaking free of the procession and running to him now, but her wit guided her footing and fear for his life as well. She wouldn't lead them straight to him. If Lord Hollister was in Middleham, Gloucester would find him, and her nephews would be safe from his cruelty.

Inside the castle, she was directed into a chamber laden with tables of meat, cheese, various fruits, and rounds of milk loaves. Six guards dipped their hands in the viands before taking posts along the rounded stone walls. She accepted an appointed seat at the corner of a trestle table, where she nibbled on a milk loaf and awaited her time with the duke.

When at last Gloucester stood, she filled her hands with her sleeves and tried to inhale deeply, but the contraption binding her breasts shortened her efforts. He bid the duchess and her attendants farewell, then positioned himself on the bench opposite her. She had his attention. After six months of preparing for this moment, she finally had his attention, and curse it, she was afraid to speak.

"Now what is this talk about a conspiracy?"

She patted the parchment beneath her heavy damask skirt, deciding to keep it safe a little longer. "The chief warder in the Tower of London conspired with the Duke of Buckingham to assassinate the king. He was poisoned by my ward, Lord Hollister. I am told your brother died this Wednesday past."

Gloucester's face weighed heavy with emotion—closed lids, lips bowed downward, what resembled grief furrowing his brow. From his initial reaction, she guessed he had no knowledge of the king's death. "I am sorry to be the one to inform you of such a grievance, but I felt it my duty to my sovereign liege to expose the traitors plotting against him."

He looked up at her and whatever compassion she believed she saw in his eyes the day of Kamden's execution was no longer there. "Is anyone else privy to this information?"

"Nay," she lied. A sense of apprehension caused her to question his every action.

"You have done England a service by coming here. I trust you do not make such accusations without proof."

Again, she pressed her hand to her skirt. His questions sharpened her internal defenses. If she gave him the document, her life would hold no value. She now doubted he would offer her sanctuary, like she once foolishly believed, but she hadn't come all this way to cower to him. "I do have proof in the form of a written document. 'Tis here at Middleham, but I would ask for something in return for my act of loyalty."

"What would you ask of me?" His eyes shifted toward his guard.

Lizzy sat up straight. His demeanor caused a frigid chill to travel up her spine. The voice in her head told her to get away from him, but he awaited her demands. She swallowed. "The chief warder holds my nephews prisoner in the Tower. I want your word that they will be released into my care. Also, I want my father released of his duties."

Gloucester stared at her, then stole a bite of cheese from her trough. "Ye want me to free the executioner during a time when I will need him the most?"

"'Tis a small request for such an important piece of parchment." She grabbed hold of the bench. Sweat broke out over her scalp and instantly fell over her temples. She could no longer draw enough air.

"I trust you have made arrangements for your nephews and your father should I agree to your terms."

"'Twas my intention to seek sanctuary at Fountains Abbey. My father's soul is in need of repair."

Gloucester sat back and crossed his arms. One finger tapped lightly at his elbow. He contemplated heavily, then waved in three guards, each of whom wore a sword. "Did you travel here unescorted, Lady Ives?"

"I did." She didn't dare put Broc in danger.

His head dipped subtly to the tallest of the three guards. A slow smile spread over the guard's lips, and the ease with which he caressed the hilt of his sword made her toes crinkle. Had she not been evaluating Gloucester's every move, she might have missed the unspoken command. Broc had been right about Gloucester. He wouldn't offer her aid.

Curse it! She didn't want to put Broc or the others in danger, but her choices were growing sparse. She quickly evaluated the three guards. They each wore one visible weapon and one of the men was no bigger than she.

"Where is this proof?" Gloucester demanded in a harsh tone.

"In the labyrinth." She prayed Broc would be armed with his usual arsenal of blades. "But I will provide you the document only if you agree to my terms."

He leaned in, eyes narrowed. "I have been charged by His Majesty to protect his sons and the realm of England. Your *terms* do not benefit my obligation to fulfill that duty. As a servant to England, you are bound by the same loyalties as I. If you choose not to deliver this document, your decision will be seen as a treasonous act against your king and country. As the daughter of the Lord High Executioner, I do not feel it necessary to tell you the punishment for such a grievance." The upward movement of his eyes brought the guard at her back. "Take Lady Ives into the labyrinth and bring me this document."

Chapter 13

"Where the devil is she?" Broc paced the tiny path between the hedges. He'd spent more time than he should have locating Smitt and getting the others through the gates of Middleham, but he expected to find Lizbeth in the labyrinth when he arrived. He'd already gone back to check the guest chamber and pay visit to the laundry, but the Mistress Taylor provided him no information.

Rays of heat beat down on his head from a high sun. He stilled, popped his head side to side, then strained to hear her hurried footsteps, but only nervous knickers greeted his ears. A few twists and turns away at the exit of the labyrinth he had positioned another stolen horse to await their departure.

Devil be damned! He raked his hands through his hot hair and cursed himself for leaving her. He stared at the green foliage surrounding him. Hollister had her. Broc felt it in his bones. Every breath he inhaled was one more she took in that bastard's clutches. His fingers wrapped around the dirk in his grip and itched to run the man through.

"'Tis not much farther. I vow it."

Lizbeth.

Recognizing her bell-like voice, Broc exhaled, then counted multiple footsteps, all heavy, belonging to men. She

wasn't alone. Hollister. Broc retrieved a *sgian dubh* from his
boot and readied his aim. He waited, digging his heels into
the ground, more than eager to see the man's blood on his
blade. A boot came before the guard rounded the hedge.
Broc flung the small blade into the man's throat without hesitation. He toppled forward, choking on his own blood, and
filled the grassy floor of the maze.

Lizbeth appeared, wide-eyed, face flushed, and dressed
like the damned queen.

A scrambling of caressing steel rang out through the
hedge. Broc unsheathed his broadsword from his back, and
in one plunge, he ran it through the shrubbery. He felt the
stick, the piercing of flesh as he'd known in battle. Releasing
the hilt, he lunged for Lizbeth. He grabbed hold of her low-
necked bodice and yanked her overtop the guard at her feet.
After pushing her behind him, Broc made eye contact with a
third guard.

"Fie!" The man's eyes bulged from his head. He spun and
darted into the maze.

Heart slamming, Broc raced after him, dirk in hand. As he
chased footfalls, the hedge turned to green sheets. Fortunate for Broc, the guard wasn't familiar with the labyrinth.
Broc rounded a corner to find the man trapped. "Ye should
have turned left."

The guard spun around, his body visibly trembling, and
drew his sword with a hiss of steel. He managed a few quick
jabs, but Broc ended their dance with a swift slice that
opened the man's neck.

Hands braced on his knees, Broc regained his breath and
then cleaned his blade on the man's crimson surcoat. His attire
matched the other two. They were Gloucester's men. Rage
budding, he stalked back through the maze, picturing Lizbeth
in a near-black gown trimmed in gold. A gown she didn't
stumble across in the laundry. He removed his broadsword
from the second guard's gut. The chilling sound of metal

scraping bone preceded Lizbeth's gasp on the other side of the foliage. Angered by her distrust, he rounded the hedge and collected and cleaned the last of his weapons before he finally looked at her. "Ye met with him, dinnae ye? Ye met with Gloucester after I told ye I would return to the Tower for your nephews. Do my promises mean naught to ye?"

"They are my kin. If anyone should die protecting them, it should be me. Pray forgive me, m'lord." Her eyes cast to the ground, infuriating him all the more.

He pushed past her skirts. "Dinnae 'm'lord' me." Wiping the sweat from his brow, he didn't care if she followed. He was tired of saving her. Three rows and four turns brought him to the exit and his steed. He mounted and waited.

When Lizbeth finally appeared, he could see only the white veil covering the top of her head. Her steps were small and cautious, her hands twisted in her sleeves. She stood beside the horse, unmoving, poised for his words. He wanted to slap her, or at the very least bend her over his knee and spank her. Why had she doubted him? "Have ye naught to say, *Lady Ives?*"

She looked up at him. A surprising bit of fury fired her eyes. "I want to leave."

He snorted and rolled his eyes mechanically. At least she finally thought about herself and her wants. He hoisted her up behind him. "And where would ye like to go, m'lady?"

Trustingly, she wrapped her arms around him and laid her head against his back. "To Scotland."

Ten ducats it cost him to finally be free of Middleham. The English were so easily bribed. Gloucester would eventually find his men slaughtered in the labyrinth, but he and Lizbeth would be valleys away by then. No doubt Hollister searched high and low for her. With any luck, mayhap the two of them would cross paths and kill each other.

Broc guided their steed in silence down a dirt path toward Bolton. He couldn't bring himself to ask what had transpired. Her lack of faith pained him far more than she could know, but they were safe. 'Twas all that mattered right now. God was on their side this day, guiding them from Hell, and leading them away from their enemies.

"Did you get the others out?"

He barely heard her words over the steed's hooves. "Aye. We were supposed to meet them hours ago outside the Hospitaller of St. Thomas. I gave them instructions to press on to the border if we didn't arrive by noonday. John argued, but Celeste told him about her condition and he promptly agreed. I suspect we will be on our own for the remainder of our trip."

She hugged him a little tighter. "'Twas a good decision. John needs to get Celeste to safety."

"Aye." He suspected Lizbeth tried to worm her way back into his good graces, but he wasn't quite ready for cordial conversation. He held tight to her hand while the stallion carried them over the moorland. She eventually fell into a quiet sleep against his back, her fingers flexing sporadically around his when her demons taunted her. What was he going to do with her? His kin would be awaiting his arrival in two days. The others would beat them there by a half day and inform Clan Maxwell of his coming. Introductions would be awkward at best. *Mam, Da, this is Lady Lizbeth Ives. She is English and the daughter of the man who delivered the final blow that ended Aiden's life.*

He could already see Mam's disappointment. Hell, he could already feel the guilt she would cast over him, tugging at his conscience like a weight inside his chest. Da would sidle up beside Lizbeth and voice his opinion vocally, humiliating her in front of his brethren. The man was a wretch with the manners of a goat. Lizbeth would cower to him. She would crawl inside herself and hide behind the submissive

Lady Ives, just as she probably had for years with her own father. They wouldn't see the woman he did, the woman who never thought of herself, the woman who crossed England to save her father, the woman who denied herself a future to protect sons she didn't even have. Regardless of how Lizbeth saw herself, he knew she was the bravest woman he'd ever known.

He wasn't going to let them hurt her. She didn't deserve their scorn.

Mayhap he should take her straight to Brother Mel. Broc pulled her hand to his lips and kissed her warm palm.

Who was he fooling? She would never see Dryburgh.

Somehow, he intended to keep her. As long as Da was laird, Broc wasn't bound to marry Lady Juliana.

The random caws of a raven overhead reminded him of hourly church bells until late afternoon guided them through Penrith. Still, Lizbeth slept. Though the air sharpened with a northern breeze, the sun beat down on him like molten iron. His tunic clung to him beneath his surcoat, making his stitches itch, and his body definitely felt the effects of no sleep. Dusk would cast its shadow over Lizbeth in a few hours, and he wanted to be snug inside an inn before it did. A nice inn with food, water, and a bed. A small bed.

Broc reined in his steed where the river poured over a series of natural steps. The drone of moving water drowned out the splash of his horse's hooves in the pebbled riverbed.

"Lizbeth, wake up. I'm going to rest the horse for a moment. Think ye might want to stretch your legs a wee bit?"

She didn't answer, nor did she move. He twisted, and she nearly fell off the horse. Holding her steady with one hand, he slipped from the horse with a splash and caught her when she went limp. She was soaked clear through and unresponsive. Her hair hung in wet clumps beneath the veiled hennin and sweat glistened over her crimson cheeks. The sun was literally baking her inside her gown.

"God's hooks, woman! Why the devil did you not say

something?" He eased her onto the bank, supporting her back with one hand. He palmed a handful of water, then poured it over her cracked lips, most of which trickled down her chin and neck. "Lizbeth."

Her eyes fluttered to half open. The seal broke between her lips. "I'm quite right."

Devil take her! "Think ye could complain like any normal woman?" The next palmful of water made it down her throat, but it wasn't enough. "I'm going to fetch a cup." He gently laid her back and searched their satchels. She was on her side retching when he turned around. He pulled the veil away from her head and gathered her hair behind her back.

"Mayhap you could fetch me a maid," she panted between uneven breaths.

"And mayhap ye could trust me to take care of you." He captured a loose strand, which he neatly tucked behind her ear, and dipped the cup, filling it with water. Once her breathing steadied, she grabbed for it, shaking half the water out before it reached her lips. He refilled it and helped her drink, knowing the stubborn woman wouldn't ask for more. He laid her back and sloshed through the water to remove her boots, then wrapped his hands around her stocking-clad ankles and dragged her legs into the cool water.

"Broc!"

"I'm here, angel." He looked up at her, his hands pushing hordes of heavy material up to her thighs.

"Get me away from the water."

"Ye're suffocating inside your garments."

"Then take the gown off, but get me away from the water!" She jerked her legs out of his grip, dug her heels into the bank, and pushed backward. Her entire body convulsed with tremors as she helplessly struggled to push herself back.

He picked her up and carried her to a small patch of short grasses spotted with white blooms. Thick fingers worked the buttons of her false sleeves, then untied the laces of her bodice behind her back. He pulled the stiff material from her arms only to be met with another rigid garment clamped tightly around her ribs. He managed to untie five knots. The sixth he ripped, setting her free of the contraption.

She filled her lungs with air, arching her back off the ground, while he went to work on her skirts.

He sifted through the layers. "Three skirts? Who the devil needs three damned skirts? Who dressed ye?"

"The duchess's maid," she answered behind closed lids.

Gloucester used his wife's maid to try to kill Lizbeth. Broc fought the fastenings around her waist like a clumsy boy until he managed to slip her skirts off over her feet.

"Ach!" A wool overtunic. "I know ye're in there, Lizbeth," he teased, hoping to get a rise out of her.

When at last he had her stripped to a pale undertunic, he stood over her, panting from the chore. White flowers encircled her in a garden of innocence while waves of dark cinnamon framed her angelic face. Her toes curled around silky blades of grass, and her arms splayed wide and trusting. The hot color disappeared from her skin, leaving behind the sweetest blush of happiness. What he found the most appealing of all was the look of peace smoothing her beautiful features. She couldn't possibly know how much he desired her.

An inferno blazed beneath his skin and filled his manhood into a throbbing erection.

Now he was the one who was hot. Damned hot and getting hotter as he took in the sight of her. Her thin, wet undertunic clung to her every curve, sculpting her breasts, the fall of her waist, and the hollow gap at the top of her legs. He had to have her now.

The deafening bawl of crashing water roared behind him, silencing the sounds of his eagerness. Weapons flew away to the ground as he divested himself of his surcoat and tunic. He dropped one knee between her thighs, pulling her undertunic lower at the neck. A quick pull released the tiny blue ribbon guarding her breasts.

Her eyes blinked open, and her fingertips stilled him. "'Tis enough, m'lord."

But it wasn't enough. It would never be enough until he was buried inside her. "Again with the 'm'lords.' Think ye we are past that?" He slid his hand over the valley between her breasts where her tunic gaped open. Her heart kicked his palm.

She sucked air between her teeth. "We are past naught. You are a lord in your country; therefore, I will address you according to your station."

"Submissive Lady Ives has surfaced again, hasn't she? Put her away. I want the other woman." His hand slid beneath the material and cupped the base of her breast as his thumb and forefinger rolled her nipple.

She slapped his hand away. Animosity suddenly replaced what he had mistaken for a playful glint in her eyes. "And what woman might that be? Mayhap the kind you pay to rut in the bushes?" She pushed him.

He fell to his back growling. "What are ye talking about? I dinnae rut with drabs in the bushes."

"You are a damned lying Scot." She sat up. "I met Sybil in the laundry."

"Who the devil is Sybil?"

"The woman you dragged into the labyrinth after you left my bed unsatisfied," she spat with all the venom of a scorned lover.

Understanding finally set in. The gypsy dancer. "I dinnae touch her. If the woman said I had my way with her, then she lied." He closed his eyes and raked his hands through his hair.

A moment of silence fell between them. Then Lizbeth's knee pressed firmly against his sac.

His lids snapped open.

Lizbeth bent over him, palms flat on the ground, head tilted. Fearless, righteous anger slanted her brows to the point of lunacy. "Then how is it she knew the size of your cock?"

Her breasts touched his chest with each draw of air, torturing him further. Any normal woman would have stomped away to sulk, but not Lizbeth. She was a fighter. He flipped her over, pinning her hands to the ground. "Ye denied me. I was angry and acted out of sorts. I sent her away with extra coin to leave. Had I tupped her, I would have found my sleep, instead of getting lost in the damned labyrinth half the night."

Lizbeth studied his face. The rise and fall of her chest slowed, and her fists loosened. He let her push him to his back. She needed to dominate, to be in control, in order to trust him again. She straddled his waist and leaned low into his face, so close he could see the fine lines in her lips. "Did you touch her?"

"Nay." He raised his hand to caress her cheek, but only brushed her hair with the backs of his fingers. Like a lone doe, he didn't dare show aggression. The trust was there, building. He could see it in her eyes, but Lizbeth would insist on more.

Her gaze dropped to his lips. "Did you kiss her?"

"Nay."

She brushed the side of her nose against his and tightened her thighs around his waist. "Vow it upon your soul."

"I vow it. I dinnae want her. I want no other. I want ye."

Lizzy wanted him, too. She wanted to trust him, wanted to believe he could always keep her safe and would protect her heart. She wanted the life he offered her, and she wouldn't deny herself the chance to love. He was the light in her darkness, and she was tired of hiding, tired of being afraid.

She slanted her mouth over his, binding them together in a kiss. She danced inside his mouth while her heart pounded in her ears. The flutter in her gut exploded behind her breasts, and desire, hot and raw, pooled like liquid fire over her skin. She wrenched free of his lips and pulled her tunic over her head, baring herself to him. "I am yours."

He reached up, cupped her head, and pulled her back to his mouth, then flipped her beneath him. He held her wrists above her head in one hand and kissed his way down her neck, bathing her skin with his warm tongue. Silky grasses tickled her skin and cool air played havoc behind his kisses. The same vibration flitted through her belly as the night before.

Whimpers replaced her pants. "Broc." She pulled against the vise he held on her wrists, but he wouldn't release her. Instead, his mouth continued its exquisite torture on her breasts, drawing on her nipples until they proudly pointed upright. Unable to still her movements, she rubbed her feet up the hulk of his calves, desperate for him to . . . "Touch me."

"Not this time, angel." He stood and peeled off his trews.

"Mercy Mary!" she exclaimed, wishing she'd kept her thoughts silent. His arousal stood straight and tall against his abdomen, nearly touching his navel, and his bollocks hung low in a tight sac. Her eyeballs dried, and her toes curled in anticipation, or mayhap fear.

He knelt and spread her thighs wide until her hips rotated and her feet came off the ground. Then his hand left her leg and stroked her. One finger ran over her swollen slit, making her jerk, but he quickly deserted her.

She waited for him to pledge his troth, fully prepared to return his words.

His blue gaze met hers, full of agony, debate. He licked his lips and opened his mouth, but no promises followed. Instead, he positioned himself at her entrance ready to slide inside.

He pressed against the barrier of her virginity. "I'm sorry." With one thrust, her innocence snapped.

She cried out, not expecting the sharp pain to rip through her insides. Fingers clung to his shoulders as every muscle pulsed within her.

He stilled inside her. His eyes closed, and his head bent to gently kiss the tops of her breasts. "'Twill pass. I vow it."

She waited, trusting him, while her muscles moved around him, adjusting to his size. After a moment, the white-hot flame of intensity returned. She wiggled to encourage him to do something. She didn't know what, but there had to be more. Her body needed release, craved it, demanded it. "Are you supposed to move?"

His head popped up, a shock of black hair hanging over one raised brow. He smiled wickedly, exposing his dimples, then drew back.

Her ankles wrapped around his buttocks to prevent him from pulling all the way out, but he broke free of her hold and slipped out of her. *Nay!* she yelled in her head, disappointed by the brevity of their union. She frowned at him. "Are ye done?"

He chuckled. "Nay, but I will not last long. Ye are tight."

Before she could understand his intentions, he curled his hands around the underside of her knees and pushed them up beside her breasts. Indigo eyes hid behind black, sweeping lashes. He looked intoxicated, and the way his eyes bore into her made her feel like the most desirable woman in the world.

Her fingers touched the flexing muscle in his jaw; then her palm flattened against his chest where his pulse hammered. Was he regretting his actions? "Broc?" His name rolled over her tongue.

He closed his eyes and entered her again. And again. Stroke after glorious stroke. She whimpered and mimicked his actions with her hips, seeking fulfillment. The controlled rhythm of his movements bounced the heels of her feet off the backs of her thighs. Then all at once, his control snapped. His knees lifted off the ground, his weight pressed hard against her bent legs, and he drove himself to the hilt inside her. He shook, released one of her legs, and brought his hand between them.

Deft fingers swirled around her swollen pearl of flesh. "Set yourself free, Lizbeth."

She did. Her body spiraled in ecstasy until all that surrounded her was white light.

He roared.

She screamed.

Then their worlds collided inside her womb.

Chapter 14

Pitch black. Lizzy's eyes were open, but total blindness enveloped her. The ground beneath her was solid. Rock solid. A trickle of water echoed to her right, along with a jingle of harness and a quiet neigh. The slide of a wool blanket left her skin exposed to cool, damp air; then a burst of heat warmed her neck. Broc was on top of her kneeling between her knees and nibbling his way down her ribs. The last remnants of sleep vanished, replaced by total awareness. She felt invigorated, alive, like she'd slept for days. Mayhap she had.

He teased her soft, warm breasts—one in his mouth, one in his hand—until the blood rushed beneath her skin, mimicking the hum of passing water in the distance. Lightning flashed the same time a jolt of desire shot up her spine. She shivered.

"Dinnae be afraid. I'm here." Broc wrapped strong arms around her, hugging her, ceasing his seduction to comfort her.

But terror didn't imprison her in this darkness. No faces haunted her, no monsters. "I am not afraid." She returned his embrace and kissed his neck, filling her senses with him. He tasted of spice, smelled like wood sorrel, and felt like paradise. "The dark should be stealing my breath, but 'tis not."

"Because you trust me to protect ye." He resumed his nib-bling on her collarbone and filled his palms with her backside.

"I do," she admitted freely, empowered by this strange new courage he'd found in her. She wove her fingers through his hair, keeping him close. "Where are we?"

"In a cavern by the river. I awoke in a bed of wildflowers beside a satisfied angel—a naked satisfied angel," he corrected in a silky timbre, "and I thought it best I protect her from the storm."

"Satisfied, aye?" She tested his arrogance, though he certainly sounded full of piss 'n' nettles, as John would say.

"Oh, aye. Verra satisfied. So satisfied I daresay I might have sent her into a swoon."

She tried to recollect the moments following their love-making, but the truth was, she remembered very little. He'd wrapped his arms around her, protecting her in the shelter of his embrace until she slipped into slumber. Mayhap she did swoon. She was liable to swoon again if his lips continued their course down her belly. "Did you think to collect this naked angel's garments?"

"Aye. We are lying atop them. Three thick velvet skirts make a fine bed." His tongue dipped into her navel.

She pulled his hair and sucked in air, drawing her stomach away from his teasing tongue.

"I am famished." His teeth grazed her hip bone.

"I could fix you an oatcake," she offered.

He laughed at her and popped a quick kiss straight atop her mound. She quickly realized his hunger had naught to do with food. The thought of him kissing her *there* made her ears burn.

He sat back on his heels. "I want no oatcake. I want to taste ye, but your scent is making me wowf." A strong hand clasped around her calf and brought her foot to his lips, stretching the muscle in her thigh. He kissed the arch, leaving behind a tickle, then hooked her ankle at the curve of his neck. He leaned forward, opening her wider, and stroked the side of his erection over her mons. "My control is lost when I'm with ye. I cannae think about anything but being part of you."

His swiftness startled her, as did the brazen position. Another flash of lightning outlined his broad form between her legs. There was no hiding the fact he intended to take her again, and quickly. A dull ache warned her it might be too soon, but then he supported himself on one hand and teased her with his magic fingers, turning her ache into desire. She moaned and lost herself to his touch, while her mind yearned for his promises, his pledge, and his devotion.

The musky smell of her sex wafted up between them, and the sounds of her mewling made Broc forget who he was. He pulled slick fingers from her and sheathed himself inside her, moving in long, slow strokes. "Ah, Lizbeth," he whispered above her. "Touch me."

Her hands were everywhere—over his shoulders, his chest, titillating his nipples between her fingertips, and then her nails dug into his backside.

He found the woman inside her, and he wanted to claim her for his own. He drove himself inside her, harder, faster, until his senses were overwhelmed with her and only her. Behind his closed lids all he could see were golden eyes. All he could smell was her essence. He would never get enough of her.

Her back arched. She wailed out, the sound echoing throughout the cavern. Her muscles wrapped around his cock, and her fingers dug into his backside as she reached the peak of one orgasm after another.

"Ach!" He was going to swoon. His head lolled. He planted his fists beside her hips and pressed his chest against the back of her leg. He moved in tiny, quick draws; then a flurry of starlight exploded in his vision. He shook violently and pumped his seed inside her, marking her, mating her, making her . . .

Mine.

Completely sated, he collapsed beside her, sucking air in unison with her. The hollow cavern spun in a black circle all around him, and a feeling of weightlessness made him hold tight to the floor. His other hand found Lizbeth's and he interlocked his fingers with hers, hoping to gain his bearings.

This woman somehow managed to defeat the controlled warrior inside him. He should have kept his lusts in check, been able to fight her erotic scent and the innocence in her touch. A war of conscience battled inside him. She might be carrying his child even now. He'd ruined her, taken what didn't belong to him.

Da kept mistresses. Everyone in the clan knew it, including Mam. Da's bastards lived among them as prized warriors. His seneschal was his own flesh and blood, but held no namesake. The kinfolk turned a blind eye to Magnus Maxwell's transgressions because he held the power of chieftain. He claimed to be building an army to protect all of Scotland. Aiden had set himself on a course to rule in like fashion. Their debauchery had always soured Broc's tongue, but now he faced a similar situation. While Da would have no qualms with Broc keeping Lizbeth as his mistress, the man would, no doubt, insist Broc honor the agreement with Laird Scott.

How was he supposed to explain this to her?

Lizbeth turned on her side and nuzzled her way partially on top of him. She curled a leg around his and set her fingers free to roam over his chest, his thighs, and then her curious little fingers cupped his sac and stroked his soft member until he provided her with something to hold on to. "Ah, Lizbeth. What are ye doing to me?"

He felt her smile against his neck as she released his cock to explore his body. Entwined with one another, hands and legs became an orgy of coddled flesh. The leader scolded him, told him to make ready for his journey home, but the man fought back. He wanted to stay a little longer, feel a little more, and make his time with Lizbeth last an eternity.

He was content to lie on his back and let her bath his chest with her soft sensual kisses. She became braver and bolder with each passing second. Her tongue dipped into his navel while her breasts slid over his rigid shaft.

His hands coiled through her hair. He should stop her. *As if he could.* He laughed, but the sound came out more as a moan, inspiring her actions further. She tormented his flesh until the hint of gray slowly speckled his vision. Dawn awoke and brought the pitter-patter of a gentle rain. The pelting of drops shimmered. The low rumble of thunder drummed. The melody reminded him of music.

Broc shot up, forcing her to straddle his thigh.

"What is it?" Panic touched her voice while her body tensed against him.

"'Tis raining."

She sank. "Thank you for the report."

"Ye like the rain, do you not?" He jumped up, yanking her to her feet.

"I like the rain just fine, but hardly relish the idea of riding in it all day. Pray forgive me for not sharing your enthusiasm."

Broc's eyes adjusted to the haze spilling into the cavern. Spiked stone hung down from the ceiling to join their cone-shaped counterparts on the floor. He tugged on her arm, pulling her through the damp glittering rock toward the entrance.

"Where are you going?" She tried to break free of his hold, obviously thinking him mad.

In truth, he felt a wee bit mad. His mind was certainly not his own this day. He had the oddest compulsion to dance, and he hadn't danced since Aunt Radella's third wedding. "Come, Lizbeth."

"But I am naked," she said pointing out the obvious.

"Aye, ye are naked." He smiled, not at her, but at himself for his creativity. "'Twill make this all the more enjoyable."

"Broderick Maxwell! What are you about?"

He spun around and caught her around the waist when she tried to run. "We are going to play."

"Play?" she yelled at him.

"'Tis what Edlynn would have wanted."

"Edlynn is not here."

"Mayhap she is." He laughed aloud as uncontrollable energy brought him closer to insanity. "Mayhap she is in my head this day." Broc plucked her off her feet and carried her into a small clearing surrounded by pine trees. A slow, steady rain flowed over them, soaking them instantly. He plopped her down and kissed her open mouth, stifling any further protests. Fingers tangled into her silky mane, hanging heavily down her back. He pressed her against his chest and sidestepped her in a circle. "Have ye ever danced in the rain, angel?"

"I've never danced, much less naked in the rain." She blinked up at him and followed his movements—leg over leg, thigh against thigh.

Lacing his fingers into hers, he stretched her arms straight out from her body and began the courtship dance he'd seen at so many weddings. While the press of her breasts excited him, the mental freedom he found in her arms invigorated him. "Dance with me, angel."

"You are mad," she insulted him, yet continued the sensual steps around his body.

"I am," he admitted and spun her in circles until she laughed outright. Most likely, her mirth stemmed from nervousness, but her giggle sounded like viols in his ears. Laughter found her too little—a flaw he wanted to remedy.

Wet grasses wrapped around their calves as he guided her through the dance. Broc turned and flushed his back to hers, still holding their hands away from their bodies. His feet stopped. His head fell against hers. The rain hit his face in sharp stinging pinpricks, and though the sun hid behind a sky of gray, he knew the hour of dawn was upon them. This dance was a means of procrastination. They should have left hours before, but he didn't want to face his kin. Not yet. Not when he finally had Lizbeth on the surface.

He'd challenged himself to find the woman inside her, not realizing until now she'd awoken the man inside him. A man who treasured small moments and memories, such as this one. He wanted to share that person with her, but also he needed to explain why he wasn't free to choose her. "When I was a lad, I raced my brothers to the loch outside Skonóir Castle every morn before mass. Aiden always won, but one day I beat him in a rain like this."

He turned and flanked his chest to her back, trying to focus on the point of his story and not the way his erection nestled neatly in the crevice of her backside. He restrained her movements with a hand on each of her hip bones and kissed her shoulder. "I was twelve summers and had finally gained control over my feet. Ian was much younger and always gave up before we reached the gatehouse. But I matched Aiden's footing that day, not at his heels, but at his side. Then I accelerated forward and beat him." Broc smiled, reminded of that long ago moment of victory.

"Did you drag me into the weather to tell me this story?" She tilted her head, exposing the slender column of her neck.

He kissed the skin where her pulse beat a fast-paced staccato. "I was free then. Aiden was the eldest, the one who would rule, the one who would protect the clan. Da had him trained by the strongest warriors in the *mesnie,* schooled by his stewards. I went to Dryburgh to learn how to control my desires."

"Desires for what?"

"Everything he had. And now that it is mine, I fear I no longer want his life."

"How can you say such a thing?" She started to turn, but

he pinned her shoulders in place. He couldn't bear her eyes. Guilt weighed heavy on his conscience enough.

"You have the heart of a leader. You were born to protect. Why would you not want such a privilege?"

"For the right to choose." He closed his eyes and waited for her to comprehend his words. He wanted her to understand why he couldn't take her to wife.

"We do not choose our heritage, nor can we change who we are. I did not *choose* to be sired by the executioner. You are the laird's son and hold the power to protect your people. You are selfish to wish otherwise."

"You do. Tell me ye dinnae wish for a different sire."

"I wish for it every day, but my father is a murderer," she snapped as she stiffened her spine.

'Twas not his aim to anger her. She completely misdirected his intentions to tell her about Lady Juliana. The courage to do so failed him now.

In an effort to cool her temper, Broc pushed her hair over her shoulder and bent to kiss the back of her neck, but she stepped out of his arms. His gaze followed the curve of her spine and what he saw there ignited a rage in him that made his jaw ache. He clamped his fingers around her arms and held her in place.

Two white scars paralleled her shoulder blades—one straight, the other curved and kicked into her spine.

"God's hooks, Lizbeth!" His voice cracked, raw with emotion. "Were ye whipped?" His breathing spiraled. Bloodlust soured his tongue. His eyes fixed on the marks ripped through her flawless skin. The tip of his index finger traced the path.

She flinched.

"Who did this to ye?" he asked, already condemning her father.

The downward tilt of her head preceded her silence. Devil

be damned if he would allow her to sink inside herself before he obtained a name.

"Answer me," he demanded and shook her.

"Lord Hollister." Lizbeth freed herself from his grip and ran into the mouth of the cavern.

He didn't go after her. Instead, he stared at his shaking hands, imagining all the ways he could use them to kill the bastard. Broc finally understood why she'd been so desperate to escape the Tower. She might have believed she was saving her father's soul, but, in fact, she was saving her own.

The rain turned to a drizzle before he calmed enough to enter the cavern. Dressed in her undertunic with her hair plaited in a thick rope, Lizbeth fumbled with the ties of her stockings. He pulled on his trews and stared at her. The desire to vindicate her intensified with every passing breath.

"It happened a long time ago. After the fire in the Tower, Lord Hollister eventually discovered I'd been involved in the incident that took the lives of six men. Then he connected me to the prisoner's savior."

"The angel of fire?"

She swiped her eyes with her knuckles and sifted through her wrinkled garments. "He thought having me marked was a clever punishment. 'Twas symbolic of cutting off my wings."

Clever, indeed. Broc could be clever, too. "And the scar by your ear?"

"An accident." Eyes downcast, she turned her back to him a little more, and then pulled on the overtunic. "After Mother died Lord Hollister made me hold the basket on the gallows to collect the mercy coin. One day the guards brought a woman accused of adultery onto the scaffold. She was wide with child and the crowd pitied her and filled the basket so Father would show her mercy." Lizbeth stuffed her toes in her boots. "Her husband, I suspect, snatched the basket from my hand and tossed the crowd's coin back at them. Lord Hollister decided I was to blame and positioned me on the scaffold directly behind Father's whip. The woman received ten lashes for her crime. I caught the tail of the eighth one." She finished tying the laces, but her stare never left her toes. "'Twas the only time I ever saw Father sweat."

"When I return for your nephews, I'm going to kill Lord Hollister."

She pivoted on her heel; her gaze finally found him. "Some men are worth saving. Lord Hollister is not one of them."

Though arguing would have done her no good, he was nonetheless thankful she didn't spar with him. "'Tis done. Once you are safe in Scotland, I will make arrangements for the journey back."

She nodded and picked up the contraption that nearly suffocated her the day before. She held the stiff material against her chest, backed up to him, and waited for him to oblige her.

"You're wowf if ye think I'm going to help ye with that. Leave it. And leave one of the skirts. I'll not have ye swooning before we get to the border this eve."

"Agreed." She tossed the garment aside and let him assist her with the laces on her bodice.

"I daresay I prefer undressing ye to dressing ye," he teased, but she kept her lids lowered. He suspected her head was full of regret. He'd made her no promises other than to return for her nephews. He shook a skirt loose from the pile on the cavern floor. Her rosary fell from the masses along with the crushed document. Broc unfolded the parchment and stared at Buckingham's signature. "Ye dinnae give this to Gloucester?"

"Nay. I did not trust him, but he knows. 'Tis enough."

And the document will be enough for King James as well, Broc thought.

Chapter 15

The steed's hooves slowed and then stopped at the top of a ridge. Lizzy's head eased forward when Broc gathered air into his lungs.

"'Tis Skonóir," he announced, his voice laden with pride.

Pushing away from the heat of his body, she followed the direction of his gaze. Her heart did a little pitter-patter. The crenellated top of a tower rose above a landscape of valleys and groves tinted blue beneath the moon. They'd reached his homeland.

Broc dismounted, and assisted her to the ground. "Think ye can stand?"

A smile pulled her lips upward. "My body has grown accustomed to being astride for days at a time." As well, her body had grown to enjoy being held by this strong warrior.

The connection between their eyes broke the same time he released her waist; then he bent to kiss the ground. He crossed himself, bowed his head, and prayed in Latin for long minutes. Unwilling to interrupt his litany, she watched him in wonder while tranquility filled her soul.

He sat back on his heels and crystal blue eyes glowing with moonshine looked up at her. "All will be well now, angel. Ye are safe."

"Thank you." A wave of relief made her eyes slide shut. She felt light, dizzy . . . free. God bestowed unto her a champion to see her to safety, and while she thanked Him for putting Broderick Maxwell in her path, she selfishly wished to prolong their time together. An ache pressed against her heart.

"Ye can almost hear the stars twinkle, they are so close."

She knelt beside him and gathered his hand in hers. "Scotland is as beautiful as you described it."

"Wait til ye see the flowers. Ye will be forever picking them to make your scents." His thumb caressed her palm in circles. "Aunt Radella and Aunt Jean will be eager to learn your secrets."

Tears pooled behind her eyes. She looked down trying to hold them at bay. He couldn't know how desperately she wanted to be a part of his life, a part of his family. "Do you still intend to take me to Dryburgh?"

"Nay." He sounded appalled. "I'm taking ye to Grandmum."

While that wasn't the answer she expected, she nodded and followed him back astride the steed. The final leg of their journey was short—very short. In fact, the horse hadn't even reached a trot before Broc pulled back the reins at the base of the knoll and dismounted.

"Why are you stopping again?"

"'Tis Grandmum's estate." He gestured toward a clearing encircled by forest on three sides.

Lizzy squinted at the oddity that could only be described as a small castle. A walkway led to a square two-story tower with three windows, only one alight. Behind the little fortress was a barn with a sagging roof, a cart shed, and two other outbuildings.

"She lives this far away from your stronghold?" 'Twas an atrocity of disrespect to tuck away their elders.

"I told ye she was mean." He pulled her from the horse. "Da

moved her out of the keep when he married Mam. Claims she meddled too much in his affairs." Broc unsheathed a dagger and guided her up stone steps to a side entrance.

"You enter your grandmum's house armed?" Lizzy doubted she wanted to meet a woman whose grandson felt the need to protect himself upon his arrival.

"I enter everywhere armed. Ye are in Scotland now."

"But you said I was safe here." Her footing stuck, and his hold on her hand grew tight.

"Safe from your enemies. Not mine." A swift yank slammed her against his chest. He winked, popped a quick kiss on her lips, and gave her a not-so-gentle pat on the backside. The man's moods were a mystery.

The hinges of a heavy wooden door whined upon their entry, raising the small hairs at her nape. This was not a place she wanted to stay. A cobweb brushed her face in the dark entranceway. Hysteria seized her. She jerked back and swiped her face.

Broc swiveled. "Tell me ye dinnae fear the little creatures as well."

"I do not fear them. I'm just not particularly fond of them." She checked her garments for silky threads.

"Grandmum!" he shouted.

Lizzy jumped.

"Sorry, angel. I dinnae mean to startle ye." He returned his weapon to his waist and swiveled toward her.

"Broc, I—"

"Who's there?" A candle flame rounded the corner and with it came Broc's grandmum. She brought an ill-furnished great room to light via two wall sconces, then turned toward them.

She was easily the oldest woman Lizzy had ever seen. Wrinkles covered every bit of exposed skin, and her hair, white as a full moon, only added to her eerie countenance. She wore a crossbarred wool tunic and shuffled with the aid of a walking stick through the floor rushes. On closer inspection, Lizzy realized her walking stick was actually a sword.

"'Tis Broderick." With an arm bent behind his back, he pulled Lizzy closer.

"I used to 'ave a grandson by that name, but the liver-bellied jack quit visitin' long ago." The woman reached out a crooked finger and poked him in the breastbone.

"Ow!" He rubbed his chest and then bent to kiss her cheek. "Forgive me, I've been in London."

"Aye, I thought I smelled English on ye." She leaned a bit to get a better view of Lizzy. "Who ye got with ye?"

Broc drew a breath and switched places with Lizzy, bringing her in front of him. "Grandmum, this is Lizbeth."

Lizzy bobbed her head once and demanded her fidgeting to cease. "'Tis good to meet you."

The woman extended a gnarled hand toward Lizzy's face, causing Lizzy to blink rapidly, then curled a tendril of Lizzy's dark red hair around her finger. "She's a Scot?"

"Nay," Broc answered.

"English?" Her face puckered, deepening her wrinkles.

"Aye, but she is learning to dislike them."

Grandmum inspected Lizzy's dark gown, making her feel like an object and not a person. "Is she in mourning?"

"Nay." Lizzy beat Broc this time. She didn't travel all this way to be treated with the same abuse as she'd endured in the Tower. She didn't need someone speaking for her, telling her how to act and what to do.

"Are ye breedin' her?"

"Mayhap."

Mayhap? What kind of answer was "mayhap"? Did he intend to take her to wife or not? Of course, she didn't voice this question. Instead, she squeezed his pinkie finger with all her might.

"If'n you're plannin' to birth Maxwell bairns, then we best

get some meat on your bones." She poked Lizzy in the arm.
"Come, I've stew in the hearth."

Rubbing her tender skin, Lizzy stepped to follow and felt
the release of her hand. She turned.

Broc took a step backward. "I need to return to Skonóir."

"You're leaving me here?"

"Nay, lass," Grandmum answered behind her. "He's hiding
ye here."

Lizzy noticed the woman held the same stiff pose as she.
Fists punched into her hips and one eye squinted near shut
on Broc.

"The council will be awaiting my arrival and I need to see
to preparations for my return to London. Be nice to her,
Grandmum. She frightens easily. I will return on the morrow."
The moment his words ended, he left.

Infuriated by his abrupt departure, Lizzy humphed. Why
would he not take her with him? Was he embarrassed of her?

"Come along, lass," Broc's grandmum said from behind.

Lizzy humphed again, but conceded to follow her through
an archway. "Have you a name?" she asked, not certain how
to address the woman.

She shrugged. "Grandmum. 'Tis what the kin have always
called me." Then she added, "Or witch," and cackled all the
way through a narrow passageway. She jested. Like Broc,
Grandmum probably found her own wit far more humorous
than anyone else did.

A salty scent danced beneath Lizzy's nose when they entered the next open room. Grandmum filled two troughs and
waddled her way onto a bench seat. Lizzy wouldn't dare
insult her, so she squirmed into the seat across from her and
picked a bite of meat from her stew. 'Twas good. Salty, but
better than oatcakes.

"Ye are English, aye. A peasant?"

"Nay."

"Then ye are titled? The daughter of an earl mayhap?"

Lizzy sighed and stopped herself from rolling her eyes. Parentage. 'Twas always the first question. Another bite filled her mouth so she wouldn't have to answer, but Grandmum waited. She slurped three spoonfuls of stew through the handful of teeth still remaining in her mouth, staring at Lizzy between each bite.

"The stew is good. What's in it?"

"Mutton and turnips. Is your father a baron?"

Curse it! "Did you know if you add primrose petals to your stew, it takes the bitterness out of the turnip?"

"A duke?"

There would be no sidestepping with this woman. "I am labeled a lady among the courtiers in London because my father is the Lord High Executioner."

"*Ah chac!*" Grandmum's skin rose where there should have been eyebrows. "Weel, that should make for interesting chatter. Tell me o' your da."

Lizzy sighed. "He is responsible for upholding England's law by punishing its criminals."

"How does he punish them?"

The woman was obviously senile if she wanted to talk about Father's profession over sup. "The same way executioners have punished criminals for centuries: beheadings, hangings, the rack."

"Do they still draw and quarter a mon, like they did our great Wallace?"

"Fortunately, that 'tis one punishment I've never witnessed." To be hung, drawn, and quartered was a penalty reserved for the most heinous of crimes. Mayhap Buckingham would see that fate with Lord Hollister at his side.

"I once saw a mon confined in the stocks in the Highlands. Do they have those in your London?"

"Oh, aye." Lizzy took another bite. "I'd rather my wrists and head be bound in the pillory then have the bottoms of my feet exposed to the mob and their feathers. Some of us in the

Tower call the stocks 'the tickle bench.'" Emma had made that one up.

Grandmum chuckled and slurped her stew. The topic became sterile for Lizzy, but Grandmum displayed no revulsion throughout the remainder of their meal.

The old woman stood and rocked a few times before she gained control of her right leg, then finally took a step forward. "My Ogilvy's whisky is in the larder." She pointed at an ante-chamber with her sword. "We'll have a few quaffs before retiring."

More than eager to find a bed, Lizzy didn't argue. She located the flagon and trailed behind Broc's grandmum to a sitting area in front of a hearth. The moon speckled colored light through a stained-glass window set into the stone. Though night saturated the outer edges, Lizzy could make out the image of a woman brandishing a sword, small hands grasped at her skirts. *Neart, Grá agus Onóir* arched in bold black letters above the rendering. "Strength, love, and honor," Lizzy said aloud, remembering the blue mark on Broc's arm.

Grandmum fell into the only chair in the room. "My husband had the window commissioned for me years ago from Spain."

"Ye are the woman?" Lizzy asked, intrigued by the details.

"Aye. The hands tryin' to stop me belong to my bairns. 'Twas my husband's way of telling me to lay down my sword." Grandmum tossed back a quaff of whisky, her sword now propped against her leg.

"Ye went to war?"

"Aye. More than once."

Lizzy's gaze dropped to the windowsill. What she previously thought to be scraps of material and dried kindling was actually an assortment of dolls made of folded grasses. Twine held them together and distinguished the girls from the boys, but all were dressed in a red and green crossbarred cloth. Oddly enough, the dolls drew up an old memory she had long forgotten. "My father used to carve things. Mostly birds, but he made me a doll once."

"My dolls represent my offspring. Eighty-four of them. I bred half the kin living inside the bailey wall of Skonóir Castle."

And Broc's father tucks her away like a leper. Lizzy decided to dislike the man regardless of his status as their chieftain. Grandmum started plucking off names and the status of said bairn, be they dead or alive, which determined the placement of the doll. Those still living stood in an upright position on the sill; those deceased lay in a pile. Half her kin were dead.

"Which one is Broc?"

"Aiden, Broderick, and Ian are those three." Though the tip of her finger curved into the corridor when she pointed, Lizzy managed to follow her direction to three dolls leaning against the wall, each boy taller than the next Lizzy blew dust from the middle one.

"Nay, the big one is my Broderick. I made him stronger than Aiden. Taught the lad to wield a sword myself, I did. Same as I did wee Ian."

Lizzy smiled inwardly, picturing a young Broc in swordplay with this woman. A sense of admiration touched her heart as she reached for Broc's doll.

Grandmum poured herself another quaff of whisky. "He is more honorable than Aiden. Am I wrong?"

"I was not privileged to know Aiden before he passed."

"Passed?"

Immediately regretting her words, Lizzy explained. "I'm sorry to be the one to bring you such news, but Aiden died in London only days ago."

Grandmum pushed herself out of the chair and waddled to the window beside Lizzy. "Bluidy English." She snatched up Aiden's doll and laid it on its back atop the pile representing her deceased kin. The woman was obviously accustomed to death, for she shed no tears. Instead, she spun, swayed, and then gestured for Lizzy to follow. "'Tis late. There is a guest chamber at the top o' the steps. Best get ye some rest. We work before the cock crows."

"When did he die?" Elbows resting on his knees, Broc bowed his head and stared at the stone floor of the council chamber.

"Magnus passed in March of an apoplexy." Mam's voice caught.

Broc looked up, wanting to comfort the woman who'd given birth to him, but she held her back to him and gazed out the window, letting the slightest breeze push her silver-streaked hair around her neck. Rigid fingers gripped his scalp. "I should have been here during your grieving period."

"I would have sent word of your da's death had I known where to locate ye. Mayhap then ye could have brought Aiden home to me." Her words turned cold, accusing.

Did she blame herself or him? "Ye cannae punish yourself for Aiden's death."

"Tell me who I should punish then." She spun, her striped *arisaid* rippled around her in wavy lines of crimson and black. Hazel eyes void of tears reaped vindication. "I will bring him to heel before me and Clan Maxwell." Fists balled atop the council table, she awaited his answer, but Broc didn't have the words she sought.

The man who actually stole Aiden's last breath was not necessarily the man who killed him. Or mayhap Broc wanted to find truth in that theory since the same man was Lizbeth's father. He readied himself, hoping he possessed the strength to withstand Mam's wrath. "Aiden died in interrogation. If ye seek to place blame, then direct your fury toward England."

The tempest spiraling behind her eyes was directed straight at Broc. "'Tis easy for ye to condemn an entire country for your inadequacy. Ye accompanied him on a mission with a single purpose. To protect him. Ye failed." She bent low. "The same as ye failed Lilian and Mattie."

Broc rose from the cuttie stool and gripped the hilt of his broadsword, now hanging at his hip. He didn't deserve Mam's accusations. "I am only one man."

"The chieftain has to be more than a mon," she snapped back. "He must possess skills and strengths beyond that of a mortal. He must be a champion, a defender of people. Aiden was all of this and more. 'Twas his destiny to rule, his birthright to protect the clan." Her condescending tone twisted the knife deeper in his heart.

Her every word, her every look, made him feel miniscule. The boy inside him sought her acceptance, but the man stared at the Maxwell targes lining the walls of the council chamber—the shields that protected his kinsmen in battle. His brethren would give their lives for him, and he would not disappoint them. "I will make Clan Maxwell a proud leader."

"Aye. The clan's losses are your gain. Ye are laird now. 'Tis what you have always craved. Think ye can protect the borders when ye could not even bring your brother home to me?"

Broc rolled his neck until it popped. *God give me strength. Three, four, five* . . . he counted. "Aiden was my brother. I loved him. I watched Da shape him into a warrior, a leader, but he was only flesh and blood. He craved as well. 'Twas what got us captured and him killed. Ye gave him everything, and he abandoned his responsibilities to tup an English skirt."

"Dinnae slander your brother's name with words of debauchery!" Mam yelled, rippling the mead in their goblets.

If she sought the truth, then he would provide it. "We ended up in the Tower because the Earl of Kressdale caught his wife abed with your son. I suspect Aiden flaunted his heritage in her bed, which is why Lady Kressdale was quick to name us Scottish spies to save her own skin from lashes."

Broc had half a mind to rip his shirt off and show Mam what he'd endured for the favored son, but doubted the act would benefit his cause. "Had Aiden been faithful to his betrothed, mayhap the Earl of Kressdale would not have beaten him nigh to death. Then he would be here for ye to kiss his feet."

A growl ripped through her throat. One eye curved into a crescent shape. She snatched up a goblet and hurled it at him.

He ducked.

The goblet crashed behind him and bled rose-colored wine down the wall. Mam rounded the table. For a moment he thought she might take up a sword, as the women in his family were wont to do. He wiped his sweaty palms over his trews, preparing to defend himself should their heated words drive her to such extremes.

Her shoulders drew back; her spine grew tall. "And this angered ye, because ye felt Aiden should be loyal to your Lady Juliana."

"She is not *my* Lady Juliana."

Mam laughed—a wicked chortle. "Broderick Maxwell, ye have lusted after Laird Scott's daughter since the day she grew into her curves. 'Tis nay reason to hide your desires now."

"I admit a marriage to Lady Juliana did once appeal to me."

"'Tis no matter if she appeals to ye or nay. Lady Juliana belongs to ye, along with her properties and her title."

"I no longer wish to marry Laird Scott's daughter."

"We need the support of Clan Scott. 'Tis your duty to see that we are provided for. Ye will set the banns on the Sabbath, and in three sennights Lady Juliana will pledge her vows to ye and to Clan Maxwell."

He wished she had half the faith in him she'd had in Aiden. "I will not need to marry Lady Juliana to align the border clans if I have France behind me."

"France?" Her brows stitched together.

Mam's duty within the clan was to mandate the servants and tend to the needs of the womenfolk. She had not been privy to months of council meetings with Da and the elders. "The council sent Aiden and I into England six months past to acquire information that might convince King James to align with France."

Her head tilted, and the pompous lift returned to her chin. "But you failed your mission."

"Nay," he corrected quickly. "Aiden failed. I, howbeit, did not. King Edward is dead, and I have proof that England's nobles will be engaged in a battle for the crown. 'Twas my intention to send Da to Edinburgh to provide this evidence to King James and plead with him to align with France. Ian will have to go in my stead, for I've other business to attend to."

She scoffed. "Ian cannot represent the clan before the King of Scotland. He does not hold your status, not to mention I've only seen him once since Magnus passed." Mam paced the small walkway between the council table and the wall, her finger tapping the corner of her lips. "Ye must go to Edinburgh and upon your return you will honor the agreement Magnus made with Clan Scott."

"Nay. Da made that agreement, not I."

"If ye decline marriage to Lady Juliana, ye will insult Laird Scott and start a border war."

"I will deal with Laird Scott on my own terms when I return from London." He thought of Lizbeth and a sense of calm settled beneath his skin. Mam may doubt his abilities, but Lizbeth trusted him to be her champion. He would not fail her or his clan.

"London? Are ye wowf?" Mam threw her hands in the air. "Clan Maxwell has been leaderless for nigh two months now. Ye will send your da's seneschal into London to act as arbitrator on your behalf."

"My return to London has naught to do with political negotiations." Broc clasped his hands behind his back and stood tall. "I made a promise to someone I intend to keep."

Mam gave him a sidelong glance. "Would this someone

happen to be the Englishwoman John said ye escorted
to York?"

"Aye." Broc's smile grew in volume.

Mam's lips thinned into a tight grimace. She stepped close
enough for him to smell the bitter stench of her hatred. "I
trust ye left her with Gloucester."

"Nay. I brought her here." *And your foul temper is exactly
why I left her with Grandmum.*

"Ye would ruin ties between clans for her?" The flesh beneath Mam's right eye twitched. "Ye shame Clan Maxwell by
bringing an English whore onto my soil."

If they were visible, he would rip the horns from Mam's
head. "'Tis my soil now." He had no more patience. "Ye disrespect me as your son and your laird. Ye insult me with your
accusations. The woman I returned with saved me from the
Tower. Ye owe her your gratitude, not your forked tongue."

Mam's nostrils flared. The sting of the back of her hand
across his cheek came before he realized she'd even reared
back to slap him.

This woman was his mam, and he would not allow himself
to hate her, but in the present, he didn't much care for her. He
pivoted on his heel and walked toward the door.

"Tell me, Broderick. Who will lead Clan Maxwell should
ye die in London?"

He stopped and felt her glare on his back.

"Ian?" she suggested. "He is barely twenty summers and
has only seen a battlefield once in his lifetime. He does not
train with the *mesnie*; instead he rides with a band of reivers
on the border. He is no leader."

Broc craned his head over his shoulder, but not enough to
look at her. "Ye bore twelve bairns. Ye should have trained
more than one of them to be a leader."

Mam's skirts rustled behind him. "Are ye going to her?"

He wanted to. He thought of Lizbeth's golden eyes, her
soft lips. She caused a flutter in his gut, a fire in his chest, a

yearning so strong he feared he might give up his soul to be with her. His body ached for her. He could spend the night in her arms making love to her; then he realized how utterly exhausted he was. "I have been astride a horse for nearly a sennight. I am tired, and I have much to do on the morrow to prepare."

"Ye will find your chamber is not the way ye left it. After Magnus passed I had my things moved from the north tower in order to prepare the laird's solar for—"

"For Aiden?"

"For Aiden, but 'tis yours now, son. Find your rest. I will send a maid to tend ye." Her tone softened far too fast.

"Nay." He didn't have to see Mam's face to know she was conniving. "I've nay need for a maid or mistress. Da may have kept them, but I am not Da, nor Aiden. Good den, Mam." He blew a breath the moment he crossed the threshold, leaving the guilt she instilled in him behind. He now understood why Da tucked Grandinum away. Mam wouldn't be content. She would do everything in her power to see the alliance honored with Clan Scott. He hadn't even told her who Lizbeth's father was and already Mam hated her. And where the devil was Ian?

How was he supposed to go to Edinburgh and return to London at the same time?

Chapter 16

Lord Maxwell had abandoned her in the hands of a woman so heavily touched by madness, Lizzy guessed she slept with her sword. If the dance Grandmum performed beneath an old birch tree yester eve didn't prove her senile, then the way the woman talked to her sword did.

"Two wretched days," she announced aloud as she scooped the last stall free of manure. Broc had left her on this little estate to fend for herself. He'd taken the document, her satchels, and her soap. The sour smell following her was unfortunately her own and impossible to get away from.

She set her shovel aside, wiped the sweat from her forehead, and paid heed to her accomplishments. Six stalls she'd labored over this afternoon. The barn had suffered as much negligence as the hen hutch she cleaned the morn before. How did the animals survive such neglect? And why one old woman needed so much livestock perplexed her even further—two dozen chickens, four goats, and a herd of sheep whose wool needed shearing. Grandmum obviously didn't go anywhere, so what was the purpose in keeping two horses, nags though they were?

"Think ye can fix the roof?"

She whirled. Grandmum appeared behind her like a

specter, pointing her sword at the holes in the thatch ceiling. A breath made of surprise and exasperation moved the cobweb floating in front of Lizzy. She brushed her hands on the plaid kirtle Grandmum had provided her and rallied her temper. "Nay. I cannot fix your roof. Just like I cannot fix the kiln in your apothecary or the spade on your plow."

Grandmum shrugged. "Then milk the goats, else they'll dry up. I'll see to our whisky and fluff the feather tick. Make haste, else I'll find my sleep without ye." She teetered out of the barn.

No doubt she was tired. The old woman spent the last two days spouting orders. "Milk the goats, aye?" Lizzy looked down at the poor creatures who'd followed her around all day nipping at her garments.

Big pale eyes blinked up at her with long white lashes. "*Baaa.*"

She sighed and rubbed its long droopy ears. "I'm not baa-d. She is. And how dare you side with her."

She walked past the barn opening to fetch up pails and a stool. Dusk played havoc with the sky above the timberline. Gray clouds slashed through the remains of a pink sun. Serene though it was, she wouldn't watch another sunset in Scotland, nor did she intend to spend another day under Grandmum's watchful eye.

Her backside landed hard on the short stool and one of the goats ambled up in front of her. She began pulling its teats, squirting thick yellow milk into the pail below. The monotony of her actions sent her mind wandering. The first image that formed behind her eyes was of Eli and Martin imprisoned in a small chamber. And here she sat milking a goat. She should have left at first light the day before. Her nephews needed her, and she had to find the courage to return for them, even if it meant going alone. It seemed as though half a world now separated them. She'd been selfish to come here. The fool inside her let impossible dreams taint her better judgment. Regardless of the feelings she'd developed for Broc, she knew she didn't hold a place in his life or his heart, else he wouldn't have taken the document and hidden her away with his grandmum.

Another goat stepped into place, and she mindlessly swapped pails. She was too cowardly to think about how she would free her nephews from the Tower. She would have no choice but to ask Father for assistance. Mayhap he would lay down his ax and escape with them. They could go to Westminster.

Nay, too close.

Fountains Abbey was no longer an option as it was too close to Gloucester. Mayhap they could go south to Bath Abbey? It didn't matter where they ended up as long as they were safe and free of Lord Hollister. She filled three pails before the last goat took its place in front of her. She pulled on its teat and made up her mind to cross the border before sunup. She would buy one of the horses from Grandmum and mayhap barter for a weapon or two. The woman certainly had plenty to spare. Truth was, she could sharpen a blade, but she didn't know the first thing about wielding a sword.

Dreading the days ahead, she now wished she'd never stepped out of a tunnel with a thieving Scotsman who stole her heart.

"I see Grandmum found a use for ye."

Startled, she spun on the stool, shooting a stream of milk into the dirt below. Her breath caught. Braced against the wood frame of the barn was her Scotsman, trussed up in the garb of his country. A red and green plaid draped over one shoulder and gathered around his waist with a thick leather belt. The pleated material formed a short skirt and revealed his muscular thighs. He looked deliciously handsome.

Gooseflesh broke out over her forearms. *Curse it! He left you here, you fool!* she scolded herself, but didn't posses the wit to move. He looked refreshed with a smooth jaw and silky black locks hanging boyishly over his brow, while she felt like the filthiest peasant alive. He grinned behind a piece of straw he moved back and forth over his lips. Then she saw it. Arrogance. Prime. A superior state of authority. She quickly reminded herself of every reason she needed to leave and not fall victim to his touch.

"Good den, m'lord. I trust you found these past two days free of complications." Temper surged where it didn't belong.

"I have been met with more complications than ye can possibly fathom." He swaggered toward her, an odd twist of mischief lifting his lips. "I intended to come to ye yester morn, but the elders ambushed me, as did my mam, twice, my cousins, and . . . others."

"Others, aye?" Maidens, no doubt, from the satisfied glint in his eye.

"Others," he echoed and squatted beside her. His gaze dropped to the hem of her tunic, which hung brazenly low in her current position. He licked his lips and swallowed.

Curse him for smelling like a patch of fresh clover. And why in Hades did her breasts ache when he was in her presence?

Milk sprayed the ground.

His finger traced the laces of her tunic. "Ye look good in the *plaid,* but I'd rather see ye out of it."

Lord, prime, or otherwise, he wasn't going to strut in here and have his way with her, nor would she sit by and let him gawk at her like some drab. Wrapping her fingers around the goat's teat, she shot a stream of milk straight into his eye.

"Ach!" His hand splayed out in front of him.

One shot wasn't enough to appease her. She leaned to the side and sprayed him until pale yellow dripped down his neck and seeped into his pristine white shirt. She felt oddly happy with her outburst. She giggled.

His eyes blinked open, sending yellow rivulets over his cheeks. "Ye are a wench," he snapped the insult and then licked milk from his lips. "I should bend ye over my knee and spank your arse."

"Mayhap," she admitted, knowing she'd acted childishly and thinking his threat didn't sound like punishment at all.

His eyes shifted to the full pail beside her leg.

She managed to rise up off the stool, but wasn't fast enough to escape the downpour over her head. She gritted her teeth while the warm substance flattened her hair to her scalp and gushed down her tunic. "You horned beast!"

"*Baaa-a.*" The goat voiced its encouragement.

Without a moment's thought, she snatched up the second pail and threw it at his chest, her aim spot on.

"God's hooks, woman!"

Their gazes locked. Hers diverted first to the third pail.

They reached for it in unison and banged heads.

"Ow," she complained.

Broc kicked the pail over and rubbed his forehead. "Enough."

She swayed side to side trying to regain her footing until the spots cleared from her vision. "Grandmum is not going to be pleased. Our behavior is wasteful."

"We cannae be wasteful, now can we." He pulled her to him and bent to suckle the milk from her neck. His tongue lapped her upper breasts and sent a jolt of pleasure up her core.

"Cease." She pushed out of his arms and fought to regain her anger. "I'm not some maiden you keep hidden in the timber to ease your needs when the temptation strikes you."

He leaned into her. "Had I wanted to ease my needs, I would have done so with the two maids Mam sent to my solar this morn."

Those were not words Lizzy expected to hear or images she cared to have painted in her head. What kind of mother sends women to her son's bed? She flung the milk from her hands and started toward the barn door. "I'm leaving."

He chuckled, infuriating her further. "And where, pray tell, are ye going?"

"You have no reign over me. I will not be a prisoner here whilst my nephews wither away in London. I'm going back to the Tower."

"Nay," he bellowed behind her, his tone sharp and jagged. He wrenched her off her feet by her kirtle and pinned her inside his arms. "I will not allow it."

Shaken by his fierceness, she stiffened. He'd never given her reason to fear him. He'd been gentle, caring, controlled.

Until now.

His hold on the back of her garment tightened the material around her waist. Her fists balled beneath her chin against his chest. Her rapid breathing came in short draws through her nose. *One, two, three . . .*

Not him.

He released her and took a step backward, staring at his shaking hands. "Forgive me. I lost my senses."

Long moments passed in silence before his hand slowly extended toward her. His movement steady, cautious, like she was a frightened animal shaking in the bushes, which is exactly how she felt.

His hand remained between them, waiting for her acceptance. "Please, Lizbeth. I would never hurt ye."

She combed her dirty hair over her cheek and kept her eyes downcast. She was not a stranger to abuse. While Father never raised a hand to her, Lord Hollister had flaunted his power with the back of his hand more than once. *He is not Lord Hollister. Do not cower before him.* She needed to be strong now and in the days to come. "Never raise your voice to me again."

"I will not. Never. I vow it upon my soul."

Her eyes moved into the corners.

He still waited for her.

Trust him. Without turning her body, she extended her arm

and placed her fingertips in his palm. He curled his fingers over hers and one step closed the gap between them. Why did it hurt so much to touch him?

"We need to talk." Calm returned to his countenance. He guided her out the back of the barn, where a peach-colored moon seeped through the timberline to alight their footsteps.

Her fingers now stuck to his, her hair clung to her cheek, and the underside of her breasts felt glued to her ribs. "I need to wash."

"I suspect ye would not agree to a dip in the loch."

"Nay." She doubted he would ever make her that strong.

"I can heat water in the apothecary and fetch a tub."

His offer sounded divine, and she might have accepted had she not recalled what happened in York. She wouldn't lay with him again. She couldn't be that person. Fortunate for her, she had an excuse. "There is a cracked brick in the kiln. 'Twill not hold a flame."

"I fixed it."

"When?" She studied him and his wry smile. What was he about?

"Before I came to the barn."

"You leave me here for two days, then when you finally return, you fix the kiln before coming to see me?" She peeled her hand away from his and stomped off. "The well will do fine."

"It needed to be done. Grandmum has been after someone to fix it for ages," he said behind her, his tone far too merry.

If he was jesting, his humor was not welcomed.

He followed her to the well, leaned over the round stone wall, and drew up a bucket of cool water. "I'll fetch ye some toiletries." He slipped away and disappeared into the apothecary.

There were no toiletries in the apothecary. She'd cleaned the building the day before and had there been soap, she would have found it. She stared at the door, waiting for him to come back. He was up to mischief. He acted like a man with a secret.

She splashed water over her face, hoping to cool her temper. Broc stood beside her with a towel when her eyes opened. She stepped back, startled by the stealth with which he'd returned. Her gaze shifted from him to the apothecary and then back. In his hands was a small square pile—a cake of soap and a comb sat atop a white silk robe and a wool blanket.

He set them atop the well wall and looked down at her. "I'm going to wash inside and see that Grandmum is content for the eve with Uncle Ogilvy's whisky. Meet me in the apothecary when ye are finished. We need to settle a few things before the morrow." He cupped her jaw and brushed his thumb over her cheekbone. "Then I'm going to make love to ye." He spun on his heel and left her with his words.

Words that made her want to run for the border and protect her heart, but also words she didn't deny she wanted to hear.

Shivering like she'd been plucked from a frozen loch, Lizzy held the wool tightly around her and opened the door to the apothecary. Warmth touched her face the moment she entered, along with a sharp smell she knew to be daffodils. Each table lining the walls was covered with a white tablecloth and dusted with yellow petals. Candleboxes filled the room with a soft light, and fire lapped from the belly of the open kiln, casting golden shadows over Broc's face. No smile touched his lips, nor frown. His mood hid behind the mask of indifference he wore, but the lay of the room and his attire shouted his intentions in decibels.

A wool plaid of red and green spread over a work table in the middle of the apothecary was sprinkled with the same yellow petals. In the middle sat a circular coronet of yellow flowers. Broc stood opposite her, garbed in a scarlet robe with a gold crucifix hanging around his neck. He looked like a god awaiting her offering behind his alter. His hair, still damp from bathing, shimmered like waves of black oil. No weapons graced his hip or back. He held no threat to her person, yet she felt vulnerable to even pull the door closed behind her.

"Come, Lizbeth." He gestured across the table. "Stand before me."

As if he controlled her feet, she stepped up to the table. His intense gaze made her pulse beat out of control. Breathing became a challenge. She looked away, not wanting him to see her apprehensions . . . but he would. He knew her inside and out. He knew her desires, her wants. Her emotions lay raw on her sleeve, unguarded and exposed for him to crush.

"My hands have killed men in battle, but never have I raised a fist to a woman. Brother Mel taught me to respect life, to honor and embrace it. But mostly he trained me to be in control of my emotions and responsible for my actions. I ask ye to look at me, hear my words without judgment, and dinnae fear me."

Her head rose, along with her eyes. The power between their gazes was an unbreakable force that gave her courage. "I am listening."

"My da passed while I was in London."

She felt the frown on her face before the pull on her heart. "I'm sorry."

His hand raised, palm up, to cease any further condolences. "Magnus Maxwell lived a full life, and he lived it well. He died peacefully and will be known as a fierce warrior and honorable man."

She nodded, accepting that Broc dealt with death on his own terms, in his own way.

"As his oldest living son, I am privileged to accept his fortunes and bear his title. I am the laird of my clan now, as well as Warden of the West Marches. My responsibilities are to protect the borders of Scotland and maintain peace with my neighbors." He closed his eyes, giving her a moment of calm.

"Ye will make your clan a proud leader."

"My mam might not agree with ye. She and the elders wish for me to honor an agreement Da made with Laird Scott, the chieftain of our neighboring clan, but I intend to decline their wishes."

Broc was honorable and dedicated to his clan. She knew this better than anyone. "Alliances are important during times of warfare. Even I know this. What prevents ye from honoring this agreement?"

His gaze found hers. His chest rose and fell twice before his answer came. "Ye."

"I do not understand."

"Aiden was betrothed to Laird Scott's daughter for more than two years before we left for London. He felt enslaved by the agreement and chose to live out Da's days by tasting every maiden who walked beneath his nose."

Was she just a maiden Broc wanted to taste? Or was he trying to tell her more, and she wouldn't let her heart see it? She toyed with a yellow petal atop the plaid. "And with your father's title, you also inherit everything bequeathed to Aiden?"

"Aye. His entitlements included the hand of Lady Juliana Geddies Scott."

Juliana Scott. His words revealed answers she didn't want to accept. "Is it a coincidence that the name you chose as your English identity matches your betrothed—Sir Julian Ascott?"

"'Tis nay coincidence. I once desired her and all her entitlements."

The blood rushed from her head, and she wavered on her feet. His words felt like a punishment. He belittled her. She possessed nothing superior to this Lady Juliana. She pulled the seams of her robe tighter, feeling like a fool for coming here. "Why are you telling me this? Why have you brought me here and gone to such efforts to bed me?" She gestured toward the table so eloquently strewn for seduction. "I will not be your mistress."

"I want nay mistress. I want a wife. And I want that wife to be you."

The gush of air she blew ruffled his hair. Her hand flew to her chest. He'd asked her to take him to husband once, but he'd been driven by physical desires and mad with lust, but not now. They weren't even touching. He possessed all his senses, and he wanted her to be his wife. Tears rushed over her cheeks. From happiness? Or from the weight of complications that surrounded them. "I cannot provide your clan with riches, or lands, or alliances."

"Ye provide me with faith. Ye make me proud. Ye make me believe I can protect all of Scotland. I need a woman at my side who believes in me, who trusts me."

He made it sound so simple. "And will it be enough for your kinsmen?"

"Nay. But ye have something that will protect them and earn their respect." He reached inside his robe and pulled out the document. He flattened it on the table between them. "I wish to take your document to my king."

Her heart fell. "Ye wish to marry me to get the document?"

His head shook; his eyes rolled. "I dinnae have to marry ye to get the document. I have it. If I only wanted the damned document, I would have killed ye days ago and been done with it. You are not listening. I am giving ye the chance to earn the respect of my kin, your kin, should ye choose to accept me as your husband."

"But 'tis all I have. If I give it to you, my nephews will die. You cannot ask me to choose."

"I am not asking ye to choose. I'm asking ye to trust me.

I told ye I would go back for them, and I have never broken a vow to ye. Become my wife, and I will save your nephews."

She couldn't think. He was coercing her. She pulled the wool tighter. "And if I refuse?"

His dark brows dipped low in the middle. "I am a man of my word. I will go back for Eli and Martin either way." His gaze fell to the coronet of yellow flowers. "But I could not allow ye to stay. I would take ye and your nephews to Dryburgh."

"We would not be welcome to live among your kin?"

"Nay. I need a wife to bear me sons. If ye refuse me, then I will marry Lady Juliana. I will be faithful to only one woman. I admit that I would not possess the strength to honor my marriage vows if ye were living within my walls."

His honesty, while forthright, was nonetheless painful. Mayhap she was being selfish, but she wanted him for herself. "And if I accept you as my husband, what will become of Eli and Martin?"

"'Tis not complicated. I will raise them as my own. Teach them to be warriors, leaders in their own right."

He gave her a means to gain the respect of his people. He offered to raise Kamden's sons as his own. It all sounded like a dream—a fool's dream. "Lord Hollister will not wait. He will kill them."

"He has kept them alive for six months. If he kills them, he loses all bargaining power with you."

"I do not trust him."

"Do ye trust me, Lizbeth?"

"I do."

Broc picked up the document and ripped it in half.

She gasped. "You fool!" Her hands covered her mouth.

"I'm taking the half with Buckingham's signature to my king, and the other half I will send with Smitt back to York to find Hollister. If he has already taken his men back to London, then Smitt will go there. I will inform Hollister of my da's passing and ask for a twelve-day grieving period, after which I will go back to the Tower and supply him the other half in exchange for your nephews. I have already assembled men to accompany me to Edinburgh and Smitt back into England. We leave on the morrow."

She searched for holes in his plan, but it was solid, well thought out, except for one flaw. "Lord Hollister will want me as well."

"He's not getting ye. I am." Broc put the document aside and then retrieved two gold rings from inside his robe. He crossed himself and bent to kiss the plaid covering the table, then bowed his head in prayer. When he looked up at her, his smile and his actions filled her with peace. He was every dream she'd lost as a child. He was more than her protector. He was the guardian of her soul, and she wanted him in her life. The pressure swelling in her heart was painfully beautiful, and she knew the feeling was love.

"Come to me, Lizbeth."

She walked around the corners of the table and positioned herself in front of him. He removed the wool covering her shoulders, set it aside, and then kissed her forehead. The serious lines carved in his face made her knees weak. Odd though it was, she wished for his chatter. "You came prepared. I s'pose you were confident I would agree to a marriage with you?"

"What woman in possession of her wits wouldnae want me?" he asked in a deep breathy whisper oozing with vanity.

"You forget that I'm not a woman in possession of all her wits. I am, as you say, 'wowf.'"

"Aye. Ye are wowf." He chuckled and drew the back of his finger over the seam of her robe. "Wowf about me. Ye willnae deny me. I make ye burn." He kissed the curve of her ear. "I make ye laugh." He lightly bit the lobe, then rose back above her, paralyzing her with eyes the color of Heaven. "I am the light in your darkness."

How did he know that? She stared at him, her feet pinned in place between his.

"Are ye ready then?" He held her chin between his thumb and forefinger.

"Aye."

He turned toward the table. "Aunt Radella helped me with the flowers. She said yellow flowers represent hope and happiness. They are supposed to instill courage when given as a gift." He placed the coronet of yellow flowers atop her head.

She needed no courage to accept him as her husband.

He set the larger of the two rings in her hand and then picked up the other. "With God as my witness, I pledge ye my troth, Lizbeth Ives. I vow to protect ye, honor ye, and be a faithful husband to ye." He kissed the ring and slid it over her finger. He held his hand flat in front of her—his trembling hand—and then dipped his head.

It seemed her big, strong warrior needed a little courage as well. The fact he was nervous warmed her inside. She steadied his hand in hers. "I pledge my troth to you, Broderick Maxwell. I vow to support you and honor you as a faithful wife." She kissed the ring and slipped it over his finger.

A hand to the small of her back pulled her closer. He raised her chin, closed his eyes, and pressed his lips to hers, sealing their union with his kiss. A kiss that was heat and passion combined. A kiss that was gentle, yet commanding. A kiss she returned with equal assertiveness.

His manhood grew against her thigh. "'Tis done," he breathed into her mouth.

"Done? Shall I retire then?" she teased and ran her fingers over the silky edge of his robe.

"Nay. We have to consummate the marriage. Ye must give your body to me as well." His hands ran over her hips.

She leaned in. "We've already done that."

"We are going to do *that* again," he whispered in her ear

and released the ties of her robe. His hands slipped in around her waist and hoisted her up on the table. "Dinnae move."

She couldn't move. She felt chained to the table. He seemed to have mastered his control while she was certain all her emotions had suddenly gathered together inside her and shot straight to her womb. This dominant side of him aroused her to a level she'd not yet experienced. He hadn't even touched her and already moisture gathered at the heart of her femininity. She held the seams of her robe closed and pinched her knees together.

Broc pivoted and collected two small wooden bowls, a cloth, and a glass vial from a table beside the kiln. He set the bowls at the edge of the table beside her thigh, filled one with water, and in the other, he poured a golden oil from the vial. He moistened the cloth in the water and bent to one knee to wash her hanging feet, after which he raised her leg and pressed his lips to the inside of her ankle, then her calf.

A gentle tug pulled her a little closer to the edge of the table. He looked up at her through dark lashes and spread her knees. Cool air blew over her mons, but didn't temper the fire burning below the surface. Her fingers curled around the edge of the table when the heat of his mouth suckled the flesh of her thighs.

Tingles rippled through her body. With her bottom lip held firmly between her teeth, she squirmed beneath his touch and became shamelessly aroused. His ritual made her feel like a queen, but also made her want to yank him up by his hair and make love to him.

He stood and pushed her robe off her shoulders, exposing her completely to him. "Ye belong to me now." He dipped two fingers in the oil and made a path from her jaw to her collarbone.

She flinched, not expecting the oil to be hot. "What are ye doing?"

His lips turned up at the corners as he bent to kiss her neck where her pulse beat wildly. "Your flesh is mine. I'm marking the places I intend to claim. The ancient warriors performed this ritual with blood."

She made a sour face and regretted asking.

He held out her arm and splashed oil over the blue vein on her wrist. His lips claimed that spot as well. "Your pulse signifies life. As long as ye live, ye belong to me."

She frowned. She didn't need another man taking possession of her. Lord Hollister obsessed over controlling her, dominating her, torturing her. She wanted to be Broc's partner, not his property. She dipped two fingers in his oil and ran them over his throat. "And as long as you live, you belong to me."

She altered his ritual, seeking a balance. The dip of his dark brows told her he hadn't expected such boldness. She untied his robe and sent it flowing to the floor in a pool of scarlet. He was stealth and beauty beneath bronze steel and he was hers. She lathed oil over her fingertips and marked his chest above his heart. She wanted more than his flesh. She wanted respect, love, devotion. She skimmed her lips over the oil and then flattened her palm over his heart. "I want this."

His eyes darkened to blue-black, his chest rose and fell beneath her hand, and then he gripped the sides of her face and kissed her. A hard, demanding kiss that left her breathless.

She clenched when he pushed her back on the table and raised her feet to prop themselves on the edge. He trailed his oil around her breasts and down her quivering stomach. Her knees gripped his sides as his tongue followed his fingertips, sparking a fevered ache that ebbed her on like a low tide. He rose up off her and slid oil up and down the inside of her thighs—featherlight fingertips driving her mad. Her eyes flickered behind her lids while he toyed with her skin, creeping closer to her ailment each time.

She moaned and grasped wool into her clenched fingers, desperate to end the pressure building at such a painful pace inside her. She jerked when he grazed her silken frills. A whimper escaped her throat. Her back arched. Her toes looped over the edge of the table. "Broc, please. You are going to kill me."

He dipped his fingers in the oil, then parted her folds. "Mine," he breathed, then slipped his warm tongue inside her.

"Mercy Mary," she sputtered in disoriented shock, but that disappeared and delight replaced her misgivings. Brazen with the need for more, she tightened against him as he delved his mouth deeper.

He was devouring her. His hands slid to her breasts to tweak her nipples between his thumb and forefinger. By all reasoning, that harsh act should have hurt, but strangely enough, she grew more aroused. Her fingers wove into his hair as the tension became unbearable. She cried out and felt the muscles inside her flex and throb. When he drew the most sensitive part of her between his teeth, the embodiment of her soul exploded around his mouth, her core—they were one and the same.

Broc savored her climax. Her exotic taste intoxicated him. He drew the tip of his tongue over her velvet skin, lapping up her honeyed elixir. He claimed her with his mouth and felt powerful for having done so. He'd never tasted a woman like this before. He'd never wanted to. But Lizbeth's scent enticed him beyond the limits of his restraint.

Making love to her was like experiencing everything in life for the first time. He would never take another breath without wanting it to be filled with her fragrance, never take another bite without thinking of her taste. His cock stretched to a bursting point, and he feared the beast inside him, fighting for release, was about to take control.

He stood at the edge of the table, his erection poised outside her glistening flesh. A droplet of semen pooled on the tip, and he was more than eager to plant his seed inside her. He looked down at his wife, still reveling in her own world of ecstasy, and suspected Lady Ives hid somewhere inside her—the submissive woman who'd been controlled by men her entire life—but the woman before him now was his Lizbeth. She'd stood her ground when he foolishly tried to dominate her. He felt a sense of pride for having found the woman inside her, but worried that he might have drawn her out too far.

He latched onto her wrist and pulled her into a sitting position. The plaid slid when he gripped her hips and eased her to the table's edge once more. She leaned back on one hand panting and licking the oils from her pink lips. Her eyes hid behind blinking lids.

"Lizbeth, keep your eyes open. I want ye to watch us become one."

She did. Her gaze fell between their bodies as the head of his cock disappeared inside her. She fit him perfectly, like they'd been created to be mates. She hooked her ankles around his backside and cried out as he slid in and out of her silky flesh. He wished he could spend hours in this act, but she felt too good, too hot, too tight.

Her canal gripped him in pulsing waves. "Oh, Broc!" she screamed out and worked herself against him as best she could.

He thrust himself inside her over and over until he was certain his legs would no longer hold him. His lids became heavy, but he couldn't draw his eyes away from where they connected. Then a deafening boom hollowed his ears.

Thrust.

Overpowering rapture crawled from his cullions and through his erection, but he wanted her to share this pleasure with him. He pinched her swollen nub and watched her head snap back.

She cried out, again and again, as a flood of liquid warmth flowed over him. Her head rose to him. A sheen of sweat coated the skin above her lip, and her eyes were the color of molten gold. She clutched his backside with rigid fingers and held him inside her as he filled her with life.

Her lips parted. "Mine."

Chapter 17

"Broderick Maxwell!"

Instinctively, Broc swung an arm over his little brother. His eyes snapped open, but a bright blinding light forced him to squint. Panic settled when he realized he was twenty-nine summers, not twelve, and Ian didn't lie beside him, but his sweet wife.

'Twas a silly boyhood dream. He eased back into the softness of the feather tick he'd hauled into the apothecary from the barn loft after he and Lizbeth ended their loveplay. He exhaled, ruffling a dark red tendril hanging over Lizbeth's closed eyes. His wee wife had loved him into quite a slumber. He rubbed his bare leg between her thighs and filled one palm with her soft backside, the other with her breast. His groin tightened and his cock grew up the side of her belly. If he could awake like this every morn, he would die a happy man.

A squall sounded outside the door. Actually, it sounded more like grunting, growling, almost animalistic.

"Broderick Maxwell, I ken ye are in there. Come out this moment!"

"God's hooks!" Broc shot upright, flinging Lizbeth to the edge of the feather tick.

She scrambled, arms and legs flailing to get back under their blanket. "Who is that?"

Flattening his hands over his face, he rolled his eyes beneath his lids and wished the grating sound of her voice didn't instantly fill him with guilt. How the devil did she find him here? "'Tis my mam."

"She sounds angry." Lizbeth's wide eyes fixed on the door while she pulled the wool to her chin.

He stumbled to his feet and ripped his tunic over his head. "Maxwell women dinnae get angry. They fight." Inept fingers struggled with the pleats of his plaid. "Get dressed, angel." He pointed at a stack of garments he'd collected from Grandmum yester eve. "And tie the laces of your boots tight."

Without hesitation, Lizbeth slipped into a tunic and punched her arms through a crossbarred kirtle, then fastened an *arisaid* at the neck with a broach. Her fingers clawed through her tousled hair, pulling it forward over the small scar she always tried to hide.

Damn! The worried look wrinkling her brow filled him with regrets. He shouldn't have married her in secrecy. He should have posted the banns, spent three sennights dealing with Mam, fighting the elders, arguing with his kinsmen . . . and then married her.

Sheathing his sword at his hip, Broc popped a quick kiss on her nose to give her strength, then crossed the apothecary to pull a fur back from a small window. Garbed in a dark green velvet gown trimmed in gold, Mam displayed her status to perfection. Her stance, however, presented an altogether different threat—one hand on her hip, the other holding a sword, and a deranged look of malice narrowing her eyes. "Damn, she looks a wee bit piqued."

Smitt leaned against the trunk of a tree behind her, arms and ankles crossed, awaiting the entertainment. Broc had given Smitt orders to meet him here at dawn. Not only was his cousin late, but he brought Hell with him. Broc snapped his neck in two jerks.

"Is she meaner than Grandmum?" Lizbeth slid in front of him and stood on her toes to peek at his mam.

"Oh, aye. Dinnae cower to her. She'll eat ye alive."

"She has a sword?" Lizbeth's shoulders fell a little.

"Aye. I know ye dislike the weapons, lass, but ye need to at least learn how to handle a dirk. 'Tis necessary if ye live on the border. Come." Broc curled his hand around her waist and tugged. "Ye cannae hide from her."

"I am not going out there." Lizbeth spun away. "She's your mother. She's screaming your name. You go talk to her."

"But ye are who she came to see. We cannae stay in here, angel. Smitt is here for the document, and I need to assemble my men and set out for Edinburgh."

"And where am I supposed to go?"

"To Skonóir Castle. 'Tis your home."

"With her?" Lizbeth shook her head and waved her hands in front of her, but he managed to back her up against the door. "Nay. I will stay here with your grandmum."

"You are my wife and must stay inside the stronghold." Broc reached between her arm and side for the lever and flanked her against the length of him at the same time. He leaned down and crushed her open mouth with a kiss, swallowing her refusal and hoping to give her courage at the same time. Her growl vibrated over his tongue, but she quickly eased and curled her arms around his neck. He flicked his tongue in her mouth and enjoyed her longer than he intended.

"If ye plan to live, ye best come out wielding a weapon," Mam threatened on the other side of the door.

Lizbeth's hands flattened against his chest, and she pushed him. "I do not like you at the moment." She swiped her mouth on her sleeve, erasing the evidence that she'd been thoroughly kissed.

"I would not have known." He winked, trying to humor

her. "Chin up, Lady Maxwell. All will be well. I vow it. Remember your status in the clan is higher than hers." Broc tossed the door open and spun Lizbeth around by her shoulders. He set her in front of him like a shield and gave her a little shove into the radiant light of late morn, which dimmed in comparison to the vehemence in Mam's glare.

Lizbeth raised her chin and took two bold steps, making him proud to call her wife.

With his palm over the hilt of his sword, he sidled up behind her and held Lizbeth's hand up to display her wedding band. "Mam, I'd like ye to meet my wife, Lizbeth."

"Think ye that ring makes her your wife?"

"We pledged our troth yester eve," Broc defended.

"Ye had no witnesses," Mam hissed and sliced her blade through the air.

He placed his hand at the small of Lizbeth's back and felt her flinch. "God was my witness. I need nay other."

"In order for it to be binding ye do."

Grandmum limped into view beside Smitt, who didn't even attempt to hide his enjoyment of the situation. He thought this amusing, did he?

"Ogilvy, step forward," Broc ordered.

"Ogilvy?" Lizbeth asked.

Broc knew now wasn't the time for antics, but he couldn't quite help himself. "Aye. His Christian name is Ogilvy, named after his da. He prefers Smitt because he thinks the women are smitten with him."

Smitt obliged and stepped into their circle, his smile no longer dazzling.

Broc spun Lizbeth around, holding her shoulders tight. "I, Broderick Maxwell, pledge my troth to ye, Lizbeth Ives." He nodded his head for her to repeat the words back to him. When she stammered, he shook her shoulders.

Her mouth was open, but her head slowly turned toward Mam's menacing snarl.

He caught her chin, forcing her eyes on him, and gave her a look that demanded she be brave. "Speak the words, angel."

"I, Lizbeth Ives, pledge my troth to you, Broderick Maxwell."

"There, 'tis done. With witnesses." Broc raised a brow at Mam. "Are ye appeased, or shall we reenact our consummation before ye as well?"

Mam visibly shook, then cried a guttural scream that echoed throughout the woodland.

Within the span of a single heartbeat, Smitt lunged backward, Mam reared her sword above her head, and Broc shoved Lizbeth aside. Feet braced shoulder wide, he unsheathed the weapon at his hip in time to block the blow. Scraping metal rasped as he flung Mam's blade wide. She turned a full circle, gaining momentum, and came at him from the side.

He again deflected the strike. Battling Mam's fury was much easier with swords than words.

"Cease! Cease!" Lizbeth bellowed.

Mam balanced and reared back her elbow for a direct stab. With the hilt held tight in one hand, she aimed the sharp point straight at his heart and thrust.

"Nay!" Lizbeth screamed and dove in front of his chest with her arms clasped around her head.

His heart jumped out of cadence.

The tip of Mam's blade stopped a baw hair from Lizbeth's spine.

Broc wrapped an arm around her violently shaking body and spun her to the side and out of danger. "Enough!" he yelled at Mam. "Put down your weapon."

Mam's blade lowered, and her eyes rounded beneath raised brows. "Is she wowf!"

"Mayhap. But nay more than ye."

Lizbeth pushed out of his arms and gawked at them. Her

gold eyes twitched beneath the sun's rays like flickering flames. "What manner of woman wields a sword against her own kin?"

"Think ye I was going to kill him? He is my son."

"And he is my husband." Lizbeth stepped toward Mam, and Broc prayed his bold wife didn't push her. "Whilst I am not familiar with the way you and your kin resolve your differences, where I come from, when a blade is wielded, a man dies." She filled her hands with her skirts and rushed into Grandmum's awaiting hands.

"Come." Grandmum patted Lizbeth on the back. "Let us go inside. I'll fetch us a flask o' whisky."

"Better fetch two," Smitt suggested and followed. "Da will make more."

Broc sheathed his sword at his hip and wished he didn't turn to ice when he stood next to Mam, but she'd always had that effect on him. He'd tried to gain her affections, hoped she might one day see the strong warrior he'd become and proudly call him son, but even now she stood unmoving, uncaring. How would he ever get this woman to accept his wife when she wouldn't even accept him?

Mam's mouth closed, and the point of her sword drew a crooked path in the dirt. "Think ye I intended to kill ye?"

"Nay, but she did."

"She shielded ye," Mam stated with little emotion.

'Twas a fact Broc hadn't considered. A sudden ache clutched his heart. Pride? Love? "I s'pose she did. The lass must be growing a wee bit fond of me."

"Fond of ye?" she questioned with that familiar accusatory tone. "No warrior, man nor woman, steps in front of a sword because of fondness. Had we been engaged in actual battle, she would have sacrificed her life for ye."

"Aye." Broc could no longer contain his smile. His wee wife tried to protect him.

Mam searched the ground, her head tilting this way and

that. "Think ye Lady Juliana would have thrown herself in front of ye?"

His smile fell instantly. "Lady Juliana is no longer my concern. I will meet with Laird Scott, along with the Wardens of the Marches, upon my return from Edinburgh." Broc intended to say more regarding his plans to rally the border lords, but Mam paid no attention to his words.

"S'truth." Her gaze traveled from him to the dirt path leading to Skonóir Castle, then back to him. "I'm nay certain I would have done the same for my Magnus." She crossed herself out of respect for her deceased husband. "I loved your da. Bore him a dozen bairns, I did. But . . ."

"Has she earned your respect then?" he asked when Mam's words trailed off. Hopefully, Lizbeth's act of bravery gained her Mam's acceptance.

"She's spirited. Aye?" Mam smoothed silver-laced strands of brown hair back into her braid.

"Oh, aye." *Mayhap too spirited deep down.*

"She's bonnie for English. That wee bit of red in her hair will help." Mam tapped her finger against her bottom lip. "The aunts will take to her well enough, as will your sisters. The elders might need encouragement. Is there favor to be gained with the English through your marriage? Does she come with any entitlements?"

Broc knew the path this conversation would take, and while he once intended to hide Lizbeth's secrets, he knew it best Mam knew the truth. "She comes with nay dowry. She bears the epithet of 'lady' because her father holds a lord's rank in England."

"She is the daughter of an earl? A marquess mayhap?" she asked with far too much excitement.

A step back gave him enough distance to draw his sword. "Lizbeth is the daughter of the Lord High Executioner."

"*Mo chreach,*" she whispered and stared at him, an odd

fascination smoothing her harsh features. "She is skilled with the weapons then?"

Broc dipped his head to hide his humor. Lizbeth was so much more than the executioner's daughter. "She's a healer, like Grandmum, only I suspect a wee bit more knowledgeable of the craft. She cares a great deal for her loved ones and will make a gentle mother, but she holds nay likeness for the weapons. Instead, she is fond of flowers and making scents." His efforts to convince Mam of Lizbeth's qualities made him realize how very fortunate he'd been to find her.

"Ye cannae protect Scotland with flowers. She'll have to learn how to handle a sword."

Broc snorted. "Ye go too far, too fast, Mam. Ye have only met her, and ye already have her wielding swords. Mayhap ye can start with something less intrusive. Say, instructing her on delegation of duties." He offered Mam his arm and blew air from his nose when she took it. They shared steps over the stone path toward the entrance to Grandmum's. "Can I trust ye to keep her safe inside the stronghold whilst I'm away?"

"She will be safe." Mam turned away from him and looked down at her sword.

"Heed me, Mam, or ye will find yourself living with Grandmum and milking her goats."

"Shh . . ."

Giggle.

What is that smell? Lizzy's nose awoke before the rest of her. She moaned and hugged the softly stuffed bolster of Broc's bed, her bed—a very large, very empty bed. Her legs stretched and her feet slid between the silky sheets. Oh, the things she intended to do to her husband in this bed made her ache in places still tender from their lovemaking. He might have dominated her at noontide yesterday before he'd left for Edinburgh, but she would have her way with him soon. Very soon.

Her mind wandered to all the sinful places in the laird's solar she intended to tease him. She would await him naked on the velvet bench seat beneath the arched stained-glass window and let the afternoon light pour color over her skin. They would make love atop the dark green and scarlet carpet in front of a crackling fire in the hearth. Little did he know what she had planned. He wouldn't always be the one in control.

She squirmed, rubbing her aching bare breasts over the sheets. She yawned and then sniffed. *Dirt? What is that smell?* She sniffed again. It smelled like peach jam on burnt bread.

Giggle.

"Shhh . . ."

Her eyes flew open with a start. She flipped over, dragging the heavy counterpane to her chin. Children. She smelled children, and they were layered in rows at the foot of the bed grinning and snickering. *Two, four, six, eight . . .* She counted them in pairs.

Mercy Mary! There were eighteen of them—blue eyes, green eyes, some so brown they were black, dirty boys holding wooden swords and freckle-faced girls with flowers laced through their braids. Lizzy stared at them. What else could she do? She was naked. Curse it! Broc had told her to sleep in her skin and think of him often while he was away. Why had she obeyed that order?

She s'posed she could scream, but she didn't want to frighten them.

"Good den, m'lady." A girl in the back with carrot-colored hair splayed her crossbar kirtle and dipped a quick curtsy. "We were eager to meet ye and snuck away from our morning chores to do so."

The rest of the children nodded.

"I am Lucy, Radella's daughter," the same little girl said.

"Broc's aunt?" Lizzy asked and continued to fret over the state of her undress.

The children shook their heads side to side and frowned.

"Nay, m'lord's sister. M'lord's Aunt Radella is my grandmum's sister, but not the old grandmum who lives in the little castle on the border."

Wide-eyed head shakes followed that comment. A little boy with black hair, huge dark eyes, and grime smudged from forehead to chin reached out an equally filthy hand and pinched her toe.

She jerked her foot back. She had no experience with children other than Eli and Martin. Two was a lot smaller number than eighteen. And she knew there were many more. How was she ever going to manage such a household? The little boy reached out and pinched her other toe. He covered his nose and mouth to hide his mischievous grin.

"Broderick, behave," Lucy scolded.

Broderick? "You are m'lord's nephew?" Lizzy asked, already warming to the little hellion.

He nodded, puffed his chest, and pinched her toe again. His was ornery, arrogant, and would, no doubt, grow to be as handsome as his uncle.

"Get up," he demanded, reminding her furthermore of her husband.

Lizzy's cheeks heated while they all waited for her to follow Little Broderick's order. Of course, this wasn't going to happen. "Mayhap I could have some privy time."

They all nodded, but didn't move. The girls twisted back and forth, swinging their skirts, and the boys stood and stared. Mayhap she said it wrong. They did talk differently here in Scotland. "I need to tend my morning ablutions in private."

Again came the nods, but not one of them turned to leave. She was trapped. Little Broderick hiked one knee up onto the bed, and she felt her eyes go round and dry.

"Ye are all in verra big trouble. Verra, verra big trouble."

A tall woman towered behind them, fists on her hips, with narrowed eyes and pursed lips.

The children all swiveled, giving Lizzy their backs. Little Broderick jumped from the bed and clasped his hands behind him the same as the rest.

"Ye all are going to be scrubbing the steps before noonday. Ye laddies lay down your swords. There will be no play this day. Get yer arses to the stable and finish your chores. Girls, go to the kitchens and help prepare the morning meal; then go to the gardens to help your Aunt Jean pull weeds."

The children pushed each other like a herd of sheep to get to the chamber door. Wooden swords clattered at the woman's feet as they took their leave.

"Ye, too, wee Broderick." She pointed out the doorway.

"Be nice." Little Broderick wagged a stubby finger at the woman. He then glanced back at Lizzy, squeezed both eyes together in what she thought might be a wink, and then darted out the door.

Relief made Lizzy smile, but she kept her humor silent, not knowing the temperament of this woman. At least she wasn't wearing a sword. She shared Broc's features: wavy black hair, light blue eyes, heart-shaped full lips. Lizzy guessed she was one of his many sisters and could only hope the woman didn't have her mother's disposition. Just thinking of the many sidelong looks Muira Maxwell had given her on the way to Skonóir Castle made her cringe.

The woman gathered up the little swords with a frown. "Forgive their curiosity, m'lady. I can assure ye they will be severely punished."

"Nay. Please." Lizzy's eyes pooled instantly, which was ludicrous, but what she imagined as severe punishment for those children made her nauseated. "They only wanted to meet me. 'Tis my fault. My sleep has been minimal as of late, and I fear I retired before making an appearance yester eve." In truth, after Broc left the solar, she didn't have the courage to leave the chamber and face his kin alone.

The woman smiled, displaying the same dimples as Broc. "Four of those bairns belong to me and my husband, Gregor, including the wee Broderick. I will let them know ye saved them from cleaning out the cistern. I am Deirdre, Broderick's sister."

"Pray forgive me if I do not get up." Lizzy felt foolish for continuing to hide beneath the covers.

"John's wife is in the corridor. Shall I send her in to help ye dress for morning mass or would ye prefer a maid?"

"I need no maid, but do send Celeste in."

"Aye, m'lady." Deirdre bowed.

Lizzy craned her neck, wishing she felt more deserving of Deirdre's reverence. "'Twas lovely to meet ye. I am Lizzy."

"I ken. My mam talked about ye all eve to the womenfolk. We are all eager to meet ye, but have more discipline than our bairns." She batted her lashes. "Welcome to Skonóir, m'lady. I hope ye like it here." She bowed again, arms full of swords, and swished through the door.

Lizzy was going to love it here, as would her nephews. She could already picture Martin with a wooden sword playing warrior among Broc's kin. Her happiness felt selfish. Since learning the boys were alive, she'd thought little about Father's well-being. Even if she had the courage to ask Broc to help Father, she doubted he would ever come to Scotland, much less pledge fealty to a Scottish lord. He would live and die in the Tower serving the next King of England, then likely spend eternity in Hell paying for his sins. She would continue to pray for his soul and hope that God might show him mercy.

"Lizzeeeee!" Celeste squealed as she skipped into the solar, slammed the door behind her, and then dove onto the bed.

The feather tick dipped low and bounced Lizzy sideways. "'Tis good to see you safe and well, my friend."

Celeste rolled to her side and propped her head up on her elbow. "Ye were right, Lizzy. Scotland is magnificent. John has a cottage in the bailey. 'Tis small, but all I will need to bring our child into this world."

"Pray forgive me for telling your secret to Lord Maxwell. I worried over your well-being."

"'Tis past. John is thrilled, as are all of his kin." Celeste plopped onto her back and stared at the dome ceiling of the bed. "There is so much to tell ye. Beatrice has settled nicely in the courtyard with the other hens and is holding her ground with the cock. He is a wicked, arrogant creature, much like some of the Scotsmen I've met."

"Thank you for seeing her to safety. She traveled a great distance, and I'm certain she is happy to be settled." Lizzy chuckled, but was grateful to have something to remind her of Edlynn.

Celeste rolled back onto her side. "Ye will be happy here, too. 'Tis like being at festival. The clan gathers every eve in the Great Hall. They eat and drink, sing and dance, and act like fools. Wait til ye meet Radella and Jean. They will have your gut aching with their jesting."

"Broc's aunts?" Lizzy asked, hoping she might one day get all of their names straight in her head.

"Aye. They cannot wait to meet ye. Why are ye still abed? Are ye ill?"

"I am naked."

Celeste hooted and jumped out of the bed to search an antechamber for garments. She prattled on about all the people she'd met since her arrival until Lizzy was fully dressed in a scarlet velvet gown and wrapped in a plaid *arisaid*. Her hair was pulled into a crown of braids atop her head and sprinkled with colored gemstones set in hairpins. "Ye look like a queen." Celeste stood back and admired Lizzy's attire. "Naught at all like an executioner's daughter."

Lizzy's hands instantly clutched the tails of her sleeves and started twisting. "Celeste, please tell me you have kept my secret safe." She couldn't help but fret. There had been so few people in her life and she wanted Broc's kin to accept her.

Celeste's face lost its glow. "I confess to telling John, but he is all. I did not tell the whole clan. I promise ye this. 'Twas Lady Maxwell."

"The whole clan knows?" Lizzy sank on the bed and stared unblinking at her silk-covered toes. Her fingers found the beads of Mother's rosary inside her skirt. She didn't belong here, in this gown, in this room. They would fear her at first; then they would discover she was a coward. She couldn't bear it if Eli and Martin were treated poorly because of who they were.

"Ye are fretting for no reason. Lady Maxwell has already assured the womenfolk ye do not carry an ax." Celeste giggled, pulled Lizzy back to her feet, and guided her toward the door.

Broc's mother would make it difficult for her, and she didn't know if she possessed the strength to defeat the woman. "What else did Lady Maxwell say?"

"I overhead her talking to Radella and Jean. Lady Maxwell said she intended to train ye."

"Train me? What does that mean?"

Celeste shrugged, smiled, and pushed Lizzy into the corridor.

Chapter 18

Five days in Muira Maxwell's clutches felt like an eternity.

Lizzy readjusted the heavy helmet atop her head and stared cross-eyed at Broc's mother around the metal nose-guard. Just once Lizzy wanted to put the woman down. Mayhap then she could have a moment of peace to herself.

Broc's kin lined the outer parameter of the training field whooping and bawling their support—men, women, children, all dressed in multicolored plaids. Celeste stood beside John watching through her fingers, and seemed to be the only one who showed any concern for Lizzy's well-being.

"Come now, Lizbeth. Take up your stance." Muira held her sword at a threatening angle, giving Lizzy no other choice but to poise herself for defense.

After sparring with the woman until dusk every day, Lizzy admitted she no longer cringed when her hand touched the hilt. In fact, if she wasn't forced to wear so much protective gear, she might make a worthy opponent.

Muira circled her in the dirt clearing and then delivered another strike.

Lizzy blocked. The clash of metal coiled through her ears and felt like fingernails scraping the inside of her skull. The heat of the day made her movements sluggish, and the weight of her helmet caused a pinch in her neck. Gloved in metal-linked chain mail and men's trews, her legs failed to cooperate around the awkward plate armor covering her thighs and shins.

"Your guard is pitiful this day." Muira swung her sword wide, leaving herself open for a forward thrust, then threw one hand out in disgust. "Ye miss an opportunity to attack. Think ye can kill your adversary with defenses alone?"

Blood boiling, Lizzy controlled her tongue, but in truth, she wanted to bite the witch. If her gullet wasn't filled with bread, mead, and salty fish from a midmorning meal, she might have done just that.

"Mayhap the lass needs a wee bit more energy." Aunt Radella held up a scone dripping with raspberry sweet sauce. It had become apparent the aunts had taken on the task of fattening Lizzy for breeding. If they dare tried to stuff another mutton pie or bannock or wretched kipper down her throat, she would dump their trenchers over their red heads. Although she'd been eager to gain the respect of Broc's kin, she feared her body paid the punishment for her intentions.

"Eat it yourself, Rae," Muira said and reared her sword toward the sky. "The lass is soft enough."

Clang. Lizzy blocked another blow that pulsed through her arm and into her shoulder. With her gut in turmoil, her muscles spent, and her head swimming with daily instruction, she doubted she possessed the stamina to live among these people. Even through the protective gauntlets, the calluses on her hands had already blistered, peeled, and healed into hard knots. Dressed in men's garb and smelling of leather and sweat, she no longer felt like the woman Broc married.

"Drive your sword, m'lady!" Gregor, Deirdre's husband, bellowed his opinion while little Broderick mimicked Muira's actions with his wooden sword.

"Put both hands on the hilt and thrust." Reynold, Beth's husband, suggested.

She jerked her forearm high to block another blow on her steel arm guard. "M'lady, please. 'Tis enough for today."

"'Tis not even noonday." Swapping hands with the hilt, Muira rolled the sleeves of her tunic to her elbows, did a little skip, and brought the metal edge of her sword down upon Lizzy.

Swiftly, Lizzy shifted her blade to a horizontal angle above her head. Ringing traveled up her spine when the metal connected. Curse this woman and her sword into the devil's privy pot. Mayhap Muira would break a sweat there. Lizzy threw down her sword, pulled the leather gauntlets from her hands, and stripped herself free of armor.

"Think ye are going to quit? Do ye not want your husband proud of ye when he returns from Edinburgh?"

Broc was the only reason Lizzy parried every day with this diabolical fiend. She wanted to be strong for him and make him proud, but she grew tired of being a docile toy. She raised the sword in her bare hand with ease, feeling remarkably agile without the encumbrance of all the excessive metal. "If I win, you will leave me in peace for the remainder of the day."

Muira scoffed. "Even if ye were fortunate enough to gain such solitude, ye would only spend the hours fashing over the welfare of your nephews. Your Tower warder granted Broderick his grieving period and travel time. His terms were plainly written in his missive."

Terms that nearly sent Lizzy into an apoplexy when the English page delivered Lord Hollister's missive three days prior. The bastard wanted her returned to her father's care, along with the other half of the document, else on the Sabbath he threatened to remove the boys' eating privileges. "I do not trust the man."

"He will not kill his only bargaining power. There is naught ye can do but train and wait for your husband. 'Twill keep your mind free of the fashing."

With Hollister's deadline fast approaching, Lizzy awaited Broc's return with the greatest anticipation. Not only for herself, but for Eli and Martin.

And while she waited, she battled. "Mayhap I intend to fret over the well-being of my husband this day. Or the whereabouts of Smitt and the five Maxwell warriors who have yet to return from their mission."

"They are grown lusty Scotsmen. Smitt disappears for months at a time, the same as Ian. They are most likely tupping their way across the border. Unless ye have something else to bargain for, then we shall keep your mind occupied whilst we train." Muira smiled and tilted her head.

Even if Lizzy wanted to go back to the Tower, Broc had forbid her leave of Skonóir Castle. She hadn't been allowed outside the stronghold since her arrival, and she began to feel the familiar pangs of imprisonment. If Muira wanted to bargain, then she would abide her. "If I win, I want a bath . . . in solitude. And I wish to pick flowers . . . alone. And on the morrow, ye will grant me the day to work in the apothecary."

Muira rolled her eyes heavenward, reminding Lizzy of Broc. "'Tis done."

Now Lizzy had something to fight for. Peace from all these chattering folk. She braced her legs and held her elbows tight to her side as she'd been taught. She blocked every blow Muira thrust at her, her shoulders jarring with each one.

"M'lady, m'lady." The roar around them escalated. She didn't know if Broc's kin cheered for her or Muira, nor did she care. She wanted a bath with oils—scented oils—and some of Aunt Radella's special soap. She wanted a peaceful eve in the laird's solar, regardless of how lonely she felt there. Odd that she would yearn for the very thing she'd detested the most in the Tower—solitude.

"If ye intend to win this battle, ye will have to at least thrust upon me once."

Hades wouldn't want this woman and her arrogance. Lizzy raised her sword and swung with all her might.

She missed and lost her footing.

Muira laughed at her. "Ye call that a thrust? Looks more like a dance. Wield the sword and jab, lass. Jab! Picture your enemy before ye."

Lord Hollister's face appeared behind her eyes and filled her with so much anger she was near blinded by it. She attacked, once, twice, gaining momentum. She counted each thrust.

Muira blocked, and blocked. Lizzy would never win this battle. She would never have peace. Curse Broc for leaving her in the hands of these people and their barbaric ways. She growled behind gritting teeth and wrenched her sword upward.

She struck her.

"*Mo chreach!*"

Lizzy nicked Muira on the outside of her thigh. Blood seeped through her tan-colored trews, horrifying Lizzy. "Mercy Mary! Pray forgive me, m'lady."

Winded, Muira wiped her brow on her sleeve and waved in a squire to retrieve her sword. "A warrior does not ask forgiveness in battle. Ye struck me. I bled. Ye win." She bowed her head in concession, gaining applause from the crowd encircling them. "Ye are ready."

"Ready for what?" Lizzy panted through a chafed throat.

"To defend yourself, lass, should ye be attacked."

Victory pulsed through her veins. She felt like she could march into England and up the Tower stairwell and gut Hollister down with her own blade. Her fingers gripped the hilt while she reveled in this unusual feeling of triumph.

"Come. I'll have the maids bring ye water." Muira took a step toward the keep.

"I intend to pick the flowers first." With her sword resting against her shoulder in an upright position, Lizzy brushed past Muira and started down the worn path leading to the gatehouse.

"Where are ye going?"

"Lest there is another way over the moat, then I am going that way." She pointed in the direction of the drawbridge.

John and Reynold stepped into her path, stealing the lift in her step. She didn't have to see Muira to know the woman had placed them there, and most likely with a flick of her finger.

"Ye cannae go outside the bailey. Your husband forbid it. 'Tis dangerous."

"Your borders are valleys away. Not to mention Grandmum lives outside the bailey. He left me there for two days when we first arrived."

"Ye were not wed then and no one wants Grandmum. As the laird's wife, ye are in constant danger and must be kept inside the stronghold."

This feud was no longer about picking flowers. It was about status, and Lizzy held a higher rank in the clan than Muira. "M'lady. I have been imprisoned the whole of my life. I will not be confined behind your walls when I have only recently escaped my own. I won. I'm going to the glen. As your chieftain's wife, I demand you step back and allow it." Lizzy was desperate to get away from Broc's mother, regardless of how many guards she had to take with her to do so. She spun on her heel and looked up at John and Reynold. "Would ye gentlemen care to escort me outside the bailey for the afternoon?"

They looked at Muira for permission over Lizzy's shoulder. Muira must have approved because they eagerly accepted. They separated so she could pass, and no sooner had she done so did she hear additional footsteps behind her. She turned to find an army of six warriors trailing behind her.

She growled and stomped toward the gatehouse. When Broc returned, she had every intention of strangling him.

* * *

The threat of rain left the air damp on Lizzy's face and emphasized the sugary smell of the purple heliotrope she layered in John's arms. The fragrance eased through her, calming her, while the spittle of rain reminded her of Broc. The combination lifted her spirit along with her lips.

Bending over beside a silver birch tree, she broke off another sprig and set it in the cradle of John's arms. She happened to glance at him and caught his crooked grin.

"Celeste has been fashing over ye. 'Twill be good to tell her ye are happy." John bent at the knees to catch her eye.

"What makes you think I'm happy?" Using her blade, she cut a bundle of foliage.

"Your smile. 'Tis contagious." John gestured toward the other men with a nod, sending a trickle of dew rolling off his bald head. "I dinnae know Duffy even had teeth."

She knew John, and Beth's husband, Reynold, but was uncertain which of the remaining four was Duffy. She peeked up at the five Maxwell warriors now grinning at her like shy boys. They stood as thick and strong as the old tree trunks surrounding them in the woodland. With an assortment of flowers piled to the middle of their chests, they looked odd and out of place—swords attached to their backs and hips, black hilts poking from their laced boots, and muscles rippling behind the masses of colored petals.

She returned their amused looks, thinking they were as much misplaced in this setting as she was playing the role of Lady Maxwell inside Skonóir Castle. She would never be worthy of Muira's title. The woman had held the position for more than thirty years. She carried herself like a queen holding a scepter among the womenfolk and a warrior brandishing the sword among her kinsmen. She'd gone to war for her clan. Lizzy was everything Muira was not—gentle, timid, English.

Refusing to let the woman ruin her moment, she brushed her hands on her trews and gave her attention to John. "The flowers make me happy and the rain reminds me of a dance."

"A dance mayhap ye shared with your husband?" John winked.

"He told you?" Heat crawled up her neck.

"Nay." John's trickery caused a heavy frown to pull her face downward. "'Twas a good guess, I suspect." His eyes narrowed and scanned the woodland. "We should head back to the bailey."

John had nagged her since they entered the glen to make haste and get back inside walls Lizzy had no desire to be behind. "I fear I do not belong here."

A frustrated sound vibrated in John's throat, and he shot air out of his nose. "Agreed. Ye dinnae belong here. The laird's wife belongs in there." John glanced back toward Skonóir Castle.

"Nay. I mean here in Scotland. Muira does not like me."

"The woman has not trained anyone in years. She let ye win, lass. Trust me, ye have gained her approval."

Lizzy brushed her fingers over the hilt of her sword. "She did not let me win. I drew blood. I won on my own."

"Aunt Muira let her guard down, but I can assure ye, she would not have let ye win had she known ye intended to leave the stronghold."

Lizzy scoffed at him. "We are on Maxwell soil. The draw-bridge entering Skonóir Castle is just beyond the hill. Are your borders so ill-protected you feel we are in danger?"

"*We* are not in danger. *Ye* are. Ye are a valuable commodity to our clan. The moment Maxwell took ye to wife, ye became a mark for reivers. They run the borders, stealing livestock and anything else that might bring them coin. Lord Maxwell would pay nicely for your return should ye be captured."

"Why did Muira not tell me this?"

"She is trying to appease ye."

"Appease me? Is that what she is doing? 'Tis more like humiliating me." Lizzy started back toward the stronghold. "I do not wager, but if I did, I would bet Lady Maxwell purposely let me go, hoping I might not return. Someone should have told me about these reiver men. I do not wish for my odd fancies to cost Lord Maxwell coin or men. Forgive my lack of regard toward the title I now bear. I am not accustomed to being of such worth."

John's steps quickened beside her, as did the footfalls snapping twigs behind her. "One would think a woman bearing the executioner's name would be familiar with threats against her person."

"'Tis like a disease. Most people fear me, as they do my father." Lizzy pushed her hair back so she could see John's face, curious about his opinion of her. "Do I look like the kind of person who would chop your head off while buying a silk ribbon on Watling Street?"

"Nay." He laughed at her, making her think the Scots were not half as judgmental as the English.

A gurgling noise behind her made her turn.

One of the Maxwell men fell to his knees. The buttercup poppies he'd been holding speckled the ground in front of him. His shocked light eyes stared at nothingness while blood trickled from the corner of his mouth.

Lizzy heard her own inhale interrupted by the whisper of falling blossoms. A flurry of color dabbled the area surrounding the Maxwell warriors' boots, where they had spilled her flowers to unsheathe their weapons.

The woodland came alive. Arms and legs formed out of the tree trunks. Debris fell away from rising bodies. Then from within the shadows of foliage came bold splashes of scarlet and gold.

"Get her back to Skonóir." Reynold pointed his sword at John.

"Piss 'n' nettles!" John grabbed her by the elbow and yanked her off her feet.

Her legs didn't move as quickly as John's. "Reivers?"

"Nay. They wear the colors of York."

Her heart slammed against her ribs. "Gloucester's men?" She glanced back over her shoulder. For every Maxwell ensued in battle, there were three scarlet surcoats. Lizzy stumbled, but John clutched her arm in a bruising grip and kept the pace. Survival accelerated her sprint up the knoll. Her throat burned as her boots kicked through the grasses. The bridge over the moat appeared, but the pummel of hoof-beats escalated behind her.

John jerked and disappeared beside her.

Her own scream cried out to the frightened woman inside her as John scrambled on hands and knees with a dagger buried to the hilt in his shoulder. "Run!"

She drew her sword as her vision filled with color.

Gloucester's man leapt off his moving steed in a swirl of scarlet and purple. He landed on top of her with a knee in her gut and flicked her weapon from her grip as easily as a child. His weight was suffocating. Her ribs pressed against her lungs, making breathing impossible. She struggled beneath him with the determination of a seasoned warrior. Bucking and squirming, she pushed hard against his shoulders, his neck, his chin, digging her nails into his pasty flesh, but her efforts presented no match for his strength. The English bastard captured her wrists in a viselike hold and dragged her down the knoll on her back.

At an angle on the side of the knoll, John lay facedown, unmoving. "Nay!" she screamed and lashed out, kicking her legs and digging her nails into the hand binding them, while every muscle within her pulsed with rage. "Let me go!" she bellowed uselessly, desperate to help John.

Her heels scraped across the damp earth until the contrasting mixture of blood and flowers singed her nostrils. She craned her neck awkwardly. Amid a garden of wildflowers lay all five Maxwell warriors. Crimson blood painted multi-colored petals in a rendering that would stain her eternal memory.

Saliva thickened in her mouth. The coppery taste of bile burned her throat. They were sons and husbands and fathers. Lizzy thought of Celeste and her unborn child and wanted to weep, but six of Gloucester's men appeared all around her and pinned her to the ground, two men on each of her legs and one on each arm. Her eyes fixed on a bright gold thread outlining a cloud. That thread was broken when the darkest demon of her past emerged above her—Lord Hollister.

Black hair framed his thin face in waves, and the evil look in his dark eyes sent a shudder of dread up her spine. Her limbs shook within their binds. She turned away, not wanting to see the tilt of his jaw or the lift of his arrogant smile. Broc's attempts to make her brave failed, for fear froze her.

Lord Hollister traced the tip of his sword from her chin, down her throat, between her breasts, and stopped at the apex of her rib cage. The sharp point punctured her tunic and threatened to pierce her skin.

"You always liked to count, Lizbeth. How many men do you think I had to kill to find you?" He pulled the half piece of parchment from his surcoat and threw it at her. "I want the other half."

"Do you think I'm such a fool to carry it on my person? Lord Maxwell promised he would bring it to you in exchange for my nephews."

"I trust no Scotsman's word, nor the word of his whore."

"I am not his whore. I am his wife, and you are trespassing on Maxwell soil." Empowered by Broc's image, Lizzy snarled at him, baring her teeth.

"You dare to threaten me?" He dropped to the ground, jamming one bony knee between her trew-covered thighs. "Your guards have been gutted, and your husband is not here to protect you. You of all people should know death is a blessing compared to the deeds others might thrust upon you. Tell me, Lizbeth, would your husband still want you if you'd been soiled by thirty Englishmen?"

One finger traced the scar beside her ear. His touch was more repulsive than all the evils of Hades. She spit at him in reply to his threat. "He's going to kill you."

His lips twitched at the corners, favoring her with an ugly grin. "He'll need all of Scotland to defeat me," he boasted and wiped the spittle from his black beard. "I ride with Gloucester's men. An army of nigh three hundred en route to Northampton to collect the sovereign king."

How could that be? Her insides fell in denial. "But you are conspiring against the very kingdom Gloucester has sworn to protect."

"Mayhap I act on behalf of Gloucester's orders. Who do you think is in line to hold the crown after King Edward?"

"Prince Edward," Lizzy replied without a moment's thought.

"Not if Gloucester names the king's son a bastard. 'Twould be Gloucester himself."

"Nay. 'Tis a lie." Lizzy searched for a truth she would not find in Lord Hollister's words. "If you were conspiring alongside Gloucester, then you wouldn't have followed me to York. I exposed you and Buckingham as England's traitor."

Lord Hollister snarled. "But you didn't give Gloucester the document. You provided him no proof. He was easily swayed to disregard your accusation against myself and Buckingham when I informed him you aided the escape of a Scottish spy. Gloucester hates the Scots and now assumes you are conspiring with them."

"Then Gloucester is a fool, for his enemies are right beneath his nose."

"His error is my gain."

"If you already convinced him you are not his enemy, then why are you here?"

"Buckingham sent me for the rest of the document, and I intend to thoroughly enjoy making you pay for stealing it from me."

Lizzy had no doubt he would contrive a wicked punishment. The gory images of every execution she'd ever witnessed whirled through her head and caused her mind to weaken. Kamden died with one swift blow. She would not be so fortunate. "Why do you hate me so much?" The ridiculous question left her lips before she even had time to discern it.

"Because you share blood with the bastard who stole my wife and my sons."

"They were never your sons." With the comment barely off her tongue, he raised his hand high, then slapped her. The stinging in her cheek vibrated in time with her accelerating pulse.

"Tie her to a steed."

Chapter 19

"Go to the Great Hall and announce my arrival," Broc ordered his seneschal. "I wish to speak with my wife before I'm attacked by the brethren."

"Very well, m'lord." His seneschal dismounted, gathered the reins of both steeds, and turned them over to an awaiting squire.

Eager to locate his wife, Broc quickly climbed the steps to the keep. With any luck, his kinsmen would still be lingering in the Great Hall after sup and the womenfolk too busy with their duties and their bairns to notice him sneaking up the tower stairwell. He slipped into the corridor and found it blessedly quiet.

Confident he could make it to the north tower, he took the stairs two at a time. His travels to Edinburgh had been fruitful, and Lizbeth would be pleased to hear King James already sent correspondence to ambassadors in France and even considered making peace with the English. His time away from her made him realize she was more than an infatuation, more than a body to ease his needs. She had become part of him. He could not rule Clan Maxwell without her support. She made him strong, fearless. All of which he intended to tell her, after he made love to her—twice, mayhap three times before he set out for London. Anticipating her taste, he licked his lips and swallowed the saliva pooling in his mouth.

He opened the door to his solar and found it cold and empty. Damn! 'Twas wishful thinking. Her absence, however, meant she'd settled in nicely and was most likely prattling about with his kinswomen.

He glided down the stairwell and entered the Great Hall. The trestle tables should be filled with his brethren, but the only people present were Mam and a few dawdling maids.

Something was amiss. "Where is Lizbeth?"

Mam turned, her skin sickly pale with dark shadows beneath red, swollen eyes. "She is gone."

"What do ye mean she's gone?" Broc strode through soured floor rushes.

"Yester eve your wife went outside the bailey to collect flowers. She dinnae return." Mam's eyes diverted to the empty hearth, no doubt to hide her guilt.

His breathing became uncontrolled along with his fury. His palm slid over the hilt of his sword, itching to draw. "I gave orders for her to remain inside the stronghold. Who disobeyed those orders?"

Mam closed her eyes. "I gave her permission to go."

"What?" he yelled. The maids dropped their cleaning pails and scurried away like frightened hens. He didn't want to believe Mam capable of such malice, but she'd never given him a reason to think otherwise. "Did ye raise the bridge after she left?"

"Nay. 'Tis not at all what ye imply." Mam lifted her skirts and took a step toward him. Her hazel eyes, more gray than green now, were dull, sad, pleading.

Broc sidestepped her, trying to keep a distance. His emotions were far too raw, and his control slipped deeper inside him. His hands curled into iron fists. She was his mother, yet the anger thickening his blood made him want to fight. Why wasn't she wearing her sword? "'Tis nay point in hiding your dislike of her. Ye blame her for Aiden's death."

"Why would I blame her?"

He had no patience for her games or her feigned stupidity. "Ye are a smart woman, Mam. Who do ye think interrogated Aiden and I at the Tower?"

Mam's head cocked and her eyes narrowed. "Ye said Aiden had been beaten by a jealous husband."

"Beaten, but not to death. Lizbeth's father finished what the Earl of Kressdale started, but I suspect ye already know this. 'Tis why ye sent her out there. To punish her for Aiden's death." He knew this would happen. Why had he ever trusted Mam to protect her?

She pressed her hand against her bosom and took several long breaths. "Aiden is gone. I did not blame your wife for his death before this moment, nor do I blame her now. Ye accuse me of a treachery I do not deserve. She dinnae go outside the stronghold unprotected. Six of our warriors escorted her over the knoll. I sent your Uncle Ogilvy out at dusk to locate them when they dinnae return."

"And?" Icy fingers ran up his spine.

"He found our kinsmen butchered. Gil, Lucas, and Fin were dead when Ogilvy arrived. Reynold's chest was laid open, but Deirdre managed to close him up. Duffy lost his sword arm, and John took a blade in the shoulder. They are above stairs in the north tower. I've sent for Father Salomon. John's fever has not broke since they brought him back. I fear he may not make it through the night." She drew a shaky breath. "The tracker gathered a regiment of twenty men and went back into the wood with the bloodhounds. They followed a scent to the loch, where they found Smitt and the others bound to stakes on the bank and nigh beaten to death."

"God's hooks!" Broc's mind and body erupted with a rage that sent raw heat passing through his veins. He should have been here to protect her, to protect them. "Who took her?"

"Smitt said Hollister travels with Gloucester's men. He'd been waiting for Lizbeth outside the stronghold for days."

"Nay!" With the devil on his shoulder, Broc picked up a cuttie stool and threw it across the Great Hall. Bits of wood exploded as the crash echoed alongside his roar. He wanted to rip Hollister's limbs from his body, as well as Gloucester's. His hands flexed, preparing for said moment while a burning spasm scorched the back of his neck and spilled over his skull.

An image of his sisters' mangled bodies flitted through his head. Burnt flesh, torn kirtles lying amidst the aftermath of destruction Gloucester had reaped upon Dumfriesshire. Broc swallowed and pinched his eyes tight. He could still taste the soot on his tongue, see the ash falling like snowflakes all around them. "As God is my witness, Gloucester will not take another from me."

"Your seneschal has the *mesnie* assembled on the training field. They are prepared to leave on your command." A tear escaped Mam's eye.

He turned, his chest a frozen sea of animosity. He would not offer her sympathy, nor would he ever forgive her for not protecting his wife. "Do ye weep for Lizbeth or for the daughters Gloucester stole from ye?"

"All of them. Regardless of your accusations or your feelings toward me, I am proud to call Lizbeth daughter." Mam's voice cracked.

"Ye can tell her that when I bring her home." He strode toward the exit while his heart tore deep within his chest.

The fools were going to kill their horses.

Lord Hollister had pushed their steeds hard across the border and through England's West Marches. They rode all night on the open road, guided by the moon, then continued their hurried journey throughout the following day. Every valley they crossed and every knoll they crested put more distance between her and her protector. Rope bound her ankles beneath the belly of her exhausted mare, and her fingers worked to keep blood flowing through her hands, which were tied at the wrist. While her comforts were few, she at least gained solace knowing Eli and Martin were safe from his cruelty.

Lord Hollister had lurked outside Skonóir Castle like a sinister shadow awaiting his prey. Thank God Broc hadn't been the one to enter the glen. Not only would Lord Hollister be in possession of the rest of the document, but he wouldn't have blinked while he killed her husband. Too many had already died because of her and that document. Now she feared she would pay a grave sentence for stealing it. A punishment she would accept as long as no one else suffered.

John's limp body came to the forefront of her mind. Celeste's child would enter this world without a father. There was no doubt Smitt and the five warriors who'd accompanied him across the border were dead too. And all of it because of her. She had brought naught to the clan worthy of their loyalty, but loss.

When they rode past the ancient stones, she wondered if she'd been cursed by one of her ancestors. It seemed everyone dear to her suffered a tragic death, as if her love alone had damned them. 'Twas foolish thinking, but Broc would be safer if he didn't love her.

Her eyes locked on Lord Hollister's back. He acted the arbitrator of her curse, casting judgment without justice, the same as he had with Kamden and Emma. Love had cost them everything.

Despair weighed heavy inside her as she stroked the mare's chestnut mane and wished she'd found a place in her trews for Mother's rosary. Instead, she drew up Mother's memory for comfort and watched a dying sun slip behind a black wood. At the bottom of the next valley, a cluster of tents sat alongside the river. She counted twenty-two. White puffs of smoke smoldered within their midst and the hustle of men brought the camp to life. Lord Hollister reigned in his stallion outside the setting. With the flick of his wrist, he ordered the entire Yorkist battalion to continue, all save for the one man whose horse she was tied to.

Up until this point, her enemy had paid her little heed. She was just another body on a horse, but as the army left her in his clutches, she feared his reasons for not making the final jog down the knoll had solely to do with his desire to punish her.

"Get her off the horse." He dismounted and stepped toward the river's edge to relieve himself.

Dread washed through her gut, making her near ill. The sentry stood beside and peeked up at her with pale green eyes that didn't lack compassion. He'd led her mare throughout their travels and taken her to the brook for relief on three separate occasions. Never once did he speak to her. He pulled a dagger from his waistband and cut the rope binding her ankles. When he offered her assistance, she shook her head in little movements, silently begging him not to follow orders. The coward closed his eyes, shielding himself from her pleas. Regardless of how tightly laced her fingers were in the horse's mane, he managed to tug her to the ground.

"Please do not leave me here with him," she whispered into his shoulder, but he pinned his chin to his chest and side-stepped around her.

Lord Hollister pivoted and started in her direction, tucking himself back inside his trews. "Take the horses to camp and inform Buckingham of my arrival."

"Would you not prefer to tell him yourself?" she suggested and watched the sentry mount and give his nod of understanding.

Lord Hollister made a familiar tsking sound. "I much preferred the Lizbeth who knew how to control her tongue. I daresay the Scot has done more than ruin you."

His approach made her breathing quicken. His sour scent reminded her of blood, lust, filth . . . hatred. He gathered slick inky hair back in a thong at the same time he gave the sentry a final glare that sent him scampering over the knoll.

"Come, Lizbeth. I fear you are soiled." He wrapped one hand around her bound wrists and jerked her toward the riverbank.

"Nay! Please!" Lizzy screamed until the flesh in her throat became raw. She dug her heels into the sludge as anxiety distorted her vision at odd angles. Her fear made her unnaturally strong, allowing her to slip from his grip, but merciless hands wrenched her back by her braided hair. She slid down the bank, writhing, turning, straining to escape, but he seized her calves. Her nails filled with silt while her pulse echoed out of every pore in her skin.

Lord Hollister sloshed into water up to his knees, dragging her behind him. "Do you know what I did to my wife when I found her abed with your brother?"

She barely heard his question over the pounding in her ears. Icy water crawled up her legs the same time bile inched up her throat. She didn't dare answer.

"I ordered her a hot bath." He cocked one brow and pushed her into water that reached her waist.

A strong current pulled at her ankles. She clasped onto his wrist for leverage. "Please. I do not—"

"I even helped Emma scrub the filth from her skin when the water cooled to a temperature I could tolerate." His hand curled around her neck like a sorcerer's claw and dunked her below the surface.

Painful silence hollowed her ears. Blackness enveloped her. Water filled her open mouth.

He pulled her out.

Air. Sweet, cool air. She gasped for it. Choked on it.

"I saved Emma. The day I took her to wife she was scheduled for execution on Tower Hill alongside three other women. Her crime: lascivious thoughts and lewd behavior. She was supposed to spend three days in the stocks, after which she would know the punishment of a sound flogging with a braided whip. I should have let her serve her sentence. Mayhap then she would have known whom she belonged to." A muscle twitched in his jaw. "Instead, she spread her whore's legs for your brother."

The last of his statement hummed through her ear as he pushed her under with both hands. Her knees hit the riverbed, slamming into rock. She shook violently and tore at his trews beneath the water. Screaming.

With a jerk, she resurfaced. She gagged and spit, all the while sucking in air. "Please, no more," she begged in a hoarse voice.

"I thought of Kamden as a son. I fostered him from the time he was a boy. Whilst your father taught him how to wield an ax, I taught him how to brandish a sword. And how does he repay me? He steals my wife." He twisted her head so she could look at him, but her eyes only registered the blurred edges of shadows surrounded in a sea of white light.

He shook her. "Can you imagine, Lizbeth, what it was like to discover the sons I provided for were not even my own? And they knew. Those little bastards lied to me right up until . . ." He paused and then immersed her once more.

Her struggle lessened. She couldn't fight him.

Broc's image appeared in her mind's eye. She cried out to him—a mute scream drowned out as she sucked in wet air.

Her head lifted from the surface, her lungs so filled with water she couldn't even inhale.

"What in God's name are you doing, man?"

The faraway question came out of context.

"Get her out of the water."

Lord Hollister hauled her from the river and tossed her onto the bank. Before she could experience any mental reprieve, her gut convulsed and water spewed from her lungs like a geyser.

She sucked in air in starving gulps while her eyes blinked to see past her dark hair coiled in a silky web around her face. A fair comely man sat astride an all-white mare.

Buckingham.

She'd seen him before in the crowded streets of London. He held himself high with an undeniable air of nobility. She didn't know whether to feel more angst or relief. At the moment, she was too weak to decide.

Buckingham dismounted in regal fashion, brushing the lint from full black velvet sleeves woven with silver threads. "Do ye think her husband will give us the document in exchange for her corpse?" he asked Lord Hollister, who stood at her feet in a crop of tall grasses with his head bowed. Oddly, his all-powerful countenance withered into what reminded Lizzy of a whipped dog.

"Nay," Lord Hollister answered, his pitch eyes fixed on her, oozing with contempt and evil.

"Then curb your wicked lusts and find your rest. We ride for Northampton at dawn." Buckingham bent to one knee and cleared the hair from her face.

She jerked back, not expecting his gentleness. He set her on the back of his mare, then mounted in front of her and nudged his steed into a trot. Shivering, she fell against the warmth of his dry velvet surcoat, wishing he were Broc and not the man she suspected of poisoning her king. Regardless of who he was, she felt a gratitude toward him. "Thank you."

"I am neither your friend nor your savior, Lady Ives. You should prepare your soul, for I've every intention of returning you to Lord Hollister once I have possession of that document."

Chapter 20

Hunkered in the glen outside the East Midlands, Broc awaited word from the spies he'd sent into Stony Stratford as well as Smitt's return from Northampton. After nights of following Gloucester's progress across England, the Protector of the Realm had finally collected the young sovereign from the queen's family.

The firelights of Northampton reflected off the Nene River and the moon cast its glow over an array of tents erected along its bank. Gloucester's cavalcade had set up and broke down more times than Broc could count. If the wretch's army didn't need such frillery, he could probably have been to London by now.

Broc wanted to rip through the canvas of each tent until he found her. Lizbeth was in there. His heart told him so. She'd become so much a part of him, he swore he could feel her weeping. Her fears had become his own. He clutched his chest trying to suppress the ache gripping his heart that had grown more painful every day he existed without her. "As God is my witness, I will not fail ye, Lizbeth," he whispered the reassurance to himself and kissed the gold crucifix hanging around his neck.

"I have her location." Smitt, dressed in Gloucester's colors, pointed to a tent on the east side of the river. "Fourth one from the bridge."

"How many guards?"

"Two. Both securing the entrance. Want me to kill 'em?" The bruises had mostly faded from Smitt's face, leaving him as bonnie as ever, all save for a pink line at the corner of his mouth and a slight droop in his left eye.

"Mayhap." Broc secured six weapons on his person and then removed his scarlet surcoat, leaving him in a black hair shirt, black trews, and black boots. He would become a silhouette in the night. "I'm going in by way of the river. If I dinnae return, kill them, get Lizbeth, and return home."

Broc gave him leave with a nod of his head, thankful to have his support. Though Broc had his own battalion of Maxwell warriors, their number didn't make up a tenth of Gloucester's army of 300 Yorkists. While desperation pecked at him to storm into Gloucester's retinue after Lizbeth, Broc's conscience refused to return home with news of more death. As much as he wanted to believe the Scots could win any war, he wouldn't put his men against such a large army.

With the practiced stealth of a warrior, he maneuvered through the trees until the canopy of the wood no longer shielded him. He inched his way across the clearing and down the cold dewy grass of the riverbank. The slight ripple atop the river produced only a drone hum, not even enough noise to drown out the song of mating insects. He eased one boot into frigid water, then the other, and filled his lungs. Without pause, he pushed off the bank and dropped beneath the water's surface. Golden rushlights guided him and reminded him of the fire in Lizbeth's eyes. Keeping the bank at his left, he pushed the water behind him and counted tents. *One, two, three, four.*

He resurfaced slowly, silently, easing his breathing in controlled draws, and scanned the river's edge. The area was dark and vacant behind the tents, but an orange haze re-

flected firelight glowing on the opposite side. The melody of
a minstrel plucking out a ballad to pay homage to his dead
king spiraled into a sky filled with living stars and muted
Broc's climb out of the river. His garments clung to him, wet
and heavy, as he crawled on his belly up the muddy bank to
the back of the tent.

A man cackled in a high-pitched laugh on the opposite
side of Lizbeth's tent. "I treated him right fine, I did. The
man had a set of cullions that filled my hand."

"I'faith! A virgin lad, was he?"

"Aye. His tewel was too tense to be anything but."

With the heel of his hand, Broc freed his ears of water. If
he understood correctly, he suspected Lizbeth was at least
safe from the attentions of one of her guards. Ignoring their
continued conversation, Broc nuzzled close to the canvas and
listened. Though quiet, he heard steady draws of air. If there
was another person in the tent, then they were dead, for no
one slept quieter than his angel.

She whimpered and Broc yearned to cradle her in his arms
and stand guard at the gates of her slumber. He controlled his
wants and focused on retrieving her. He prayed she wouldn't
fight the water. 'Twas the only way to get her back to safety.
Back in his arms, where she belonged.

He pulled a freshly sharpened *sgian dubh* from the top of
his boot and cut a slit in the canvas. Her scent hit him like a
rush of pleasure. Sweet, heady, his. Broc's erection was in-
stantaneous. He rolled his eyes beneath their lids, knowing
the last thing he needed was to be aroused at such an inappropriate moment. But damned if he could control it.

Pulling the canvas back, Broc's eyes adjusted to the dim
glow of Lizbeth's candlebox. She lay in a straight line directly in front of him on her back atop a pallet close enough
for him to touch her hair. A tray of food sat at her feet by the
tent's entrance.

He slunk beneath the canvas and basked only a moment in

the warm air of her tent and then cupped his wet hand over her mouth.

She jerked and knocked the candlebox on its side. Total blackness enveloped them.

"Shh. 'Tis I, angel. All will be well now," he whispered and kissed her hair beside her ear, dripping overtop her.

Her arms reached behind her and wrapped around his head, embracing him, filling him with much-needed life. Tremors attacked her, followed by a fit of silent sobs. She kissed his face through her tears while his heart punched the ground beneath him. Everything inside him rejoiced. This woman was his mate, chosen by God. He would do anything to protect her.

Unable to deny himself this small moment, he kissed the beating pulse below her earlobe at the same time his hand slid beneath her arm and pulled.

The rattle of metal sounded like the raising of a portcullis in his ear.

She stuck in place.

The guards hushed outside the entrance.

God's hooks and blood and teeth and bones! She was chained. *Chained!* He was so close to having her back. He ached to the marrow in his bones for wanting to free her. He cupped her chin and caressed her silken lips with his thumb while he waited for the guards to resume their discussion; then he pressed his unshaven cheek against hers. "Tell me ye have a key."

She shook her head and turned into his ear. "You must go, else they'll kill you. Too many have already died because of me. I will not let him take you, too."

He could only imagine the turmoil she'd been in, fashing over everyone but herself. "John survived the attack, as did Duffy and Reynold. I ride with thirty men, Smitt included, and we are here to collect ye and take ye home."

She blew an audible breath and whispered her thanks to God. "You must go to the Tower."

"I will not leave ye here. I cannae."

She hugged him tighter, her actions contradicting her brave words. "I cannot help my nephews, but you can. Did you bring the document?"

"Aye."

"Lord Hollister intends to kill Eli and Martin upon his return. He despises them and has no use for them now that he has me. As long as he knows the document is in your possession, he will keep me alive."

"Nay. I'll take ye now. We will both go to the Tower and to the devil with the damned document." He had to get her out, but now worried over the boys' fates. She wouldn't be able to prevent Hollister from killing them the second he arrived back in London.

The minstrel's song ended, forcing them into silence. At the request of one of Lizbeth's guards a more jovial tune soon followed.

"I will not let Lord Hollister win. He must be punished."

"I'll kill him." Broc intended to do so anyway.

"Then Buckingham wins." She combed her fingers through his slick hair, pushing water down his neck and easing his tension. "Go to the Tower. Find the boys and get them out. Lord Hollister once confined me to an antechamber in the Wardrobe Tower. He may have done the same with the boys. Gloucester plans to enter London on the Sabbath. Get the document to him. You have the chance to make peace between our countries. Is it not worth the risk?"

"Nay," he answered slightly louder than their whispered words. Damn her! She played on his weaknesses.

The guards' conversation cut short. Broc held his breath. The silence was interrupted only by the beat of Lizbeth's heart. A shuffling of feet stirred. A yellow slit drew a line at the tent's entrance.

"Have ye need for anything, Lady Ives?" The nasally voice came from outside.

"Thank you, Manfred. I will need the privy pot dumped in a moment. Prunes," she replied quickly.

"Very well, m'lady. Let me know when ye are finished." Only moments later, the guards settled back into their chattering.

"I am safe. Lord Hollister spends all his time worming his way into Buckingham's good graces, and Buckingham does the same with Gloucester."

"Then why are ye chained?" Broc sensed her desperation, but would she lie to gain his agreement?

"I've escaped Lord Hollister many times in the past, which mocks the very essence of his profession as chief warder. He thrives on authority, but his true love lies in degrading a person mentally. I am immune to his threats. No harm will come to me en route to London."

Broc pulled her hand to his lips and kissed her palm. She couldn't possibly know the torment he'd suffered the past few days. "Then ye have not been hurt?"

Her pause made him question her honesty.

"Nay," she finally said. "Manfred has been assigned to me for the duration, and I can assure you, I am not his sexual preference."

Broc allowed his forehead to fall against hers, thankful she hadn't been violated, yet still in turmoil over what she asked of him. "How can ye ask me to leave ye here?"

"Please, go. Please. You must get the boys out. I will meet you where the tunnel splits into a tee in two days. Midnight. Do you remember the count?"

"I remember." Broc must be touched by madness for even considering this plan, as well thought out as it might be.

"Please." She cupped her hands over the sides of his face and drew him over top of her.

His nose touched her chin as he suckled her bottom lip.

There was so much he wanted to tell her, but he was no good to her dead. "I will place men in the Tower. They will be dressed as Yorkists and have a blade of grass woven into the laces of their left boot. Go with them. They will bring ye to me." He kissed the backs of her eyes. "I will not fail ye."

"I know. Save Eli and Martin and then save me."

Broc pulled her hand with him as he slithered out from beneath the canvas, not letting go until the last possible second. If anything happened to her, he would never forgive himself. The guilt he carried for the deaths of his kin left everlasting marks on his conscience, but if he failed Lizbeth and her nephews, he would be left with a scar on his soul.

Godspeed. Terror stricken, she clamped her hands over her mouth and closed her eyes as a flood of tears washed over her temples. She was not so brave. Had she shown any signs of weakness, Broc wouldn't have left her.

If caught together, neither of them would have been able to save her nephews. She pulled herself into a sitting position, hugged her knees, and stared into the darkness. Lord Hollister had tortured her mind with threats against Eli and Martin, promising to end their lives quickly upon his return. 'Twas his sick-minded way of offering her a gift. Mercy. An end without the agony of torture.

She, however, would not be granted such mercy.

Lord Hollister had been giddy this morn when he informed her of her sentence: *peine forte et dure*—pressing to death. No doubt he would drag the process out until Broc delivered the document; then Lord Hollister would order the iron weights added to her chest until she was dead. She didn't know if she could bear the punishment, but the process would give her time to plead with Father to free her. The boys would be safe, and that was all that mattered. Gloucester would see to Lord Hollister's punishment and Buckingham as well. *All will be well.*

She reached for Mother's rosary beneath the wool skirts Buckingham's maid had dressed her in, but her pocket was empty. She clasped her hands together. *Protect my husband.* He taught her strength and endurance, gave her courage, but mostly he'd shown her what it felt like to love.

A field of orange poppies blossomed in her mind. Eli and Martin were there running with her own sons and daughters; her father watched from afar, finally at peace with his own demons. Broc held her in front of him and kissed her hair. He whispered sweet words in her ear—words she heard only in her dreams. Words of love.

In the shadows of the glen, Broc chose ten warriors to accompany him to London, leaving twenty behind to follow Lizbeth's progress. With Smitt at his side, they rode south by the light of the moon to Stony Stratford, where Gloucester had barricaded the main road with his sentinels. There was no reason to lurk in the wood. Dressed as Yorkists, they claimed to be securing the route to London for Gloucester's cavalcade.

They traveled throughout the small hours of the night, the ground vibrating beneath the hooves of their horses. While England slept, Broc purged his steed forward at a blood-rushing pace, regret pooling in his gut until he feared the hurricane inside him might swallow him whole. Villages, tippling houses, forests passed in a dark blur.

London Bridge appeared, looming on dawn's horizon. Broc slapped the flanks of his steed and forged ahead like a raving lunatic being chased by his own black soul.

Smitt pulled out ahead and turned a half circle, causing Broc to halt his steed. The squeal of its neigh preceded the rise of its front hooves.

"Halt!" Smitt held up two hands.

"God's hooks, man!" The stillness of Broc's steed emphasized the tremors attacking his limbs. He felt crazed by a fever. His sweat-drenched skin tingled; his breathing was erratic, his wits unstable.

"Think ye to fly over London's gates?" Smitt scowled, wiped his forehead with the back of his arm, and panted.

Smitt never scowled, nor did he pant. Broc twisted to find the others stripped of stamina as well. Without a doubt these men would follow him into Hell, which was exactly where he led them.

"I need to piss." Smitt trotted past Broc in a huff toward a small brook. "Think ye we've the time?"

"Aye." Broc dipped his head toward his men, granting them reprieve. When he dismounted, the weight of his body nearly buckled his knees. He needed rest, as did the other Maxwell warriors. They were worthless to Lizbeth's nephews in their current physical state.

Broc led his horse to water, then sidled up next to Smitt. "Mayhap we should rest a wee bit. Aye?"

"Mayhap." Smitt's tone lost its bite. "Forgive my disrespect, m'lord."

Broc forced his mouth to retain its grim line, though he wanted to smile. 'Twas the first time Smitt paid homage to his title. "No harm, cousin. I needed to be stopped. We close our eyes a few hours, then we will set forth a plan. Have ye ideas on how we might enter the Tower?"

"Oh, aye." Smitt nodded, his smile returning with a wicked twist. "And it involves a great deal of bloodshed."

Broc backed his steed up to face Watling Street and motioned for his warriors to do the same. Crowds filled the narrow streets, preparing for their young sovereign to arrive with his uncle. Merchants filled their stalls with wares—pitch, wax, rope, and other goods—while the city's aldermen sent criers racing throughout London to announce the coming of their king.

The Maxwell warriors blended into the bedlam of colored brocades with their scarlet surcoats and decorated horses. Two Yorkists atop speckled steeds carried flags bearing Gloucester's crest. They trotted by and offered Broc a regal greeting. He returned the gesture, all the while thinking of how much he loathed the English.

He motioned Smitt and another of his cousins toward a vine-covered door. Gregor tethered their two steeds outside the haberdashers, not far from the same location Broc and Lizbeth had stolen the king's horse sennights before.

Once the secret passageway into the dungeon sealed his men inside, Broc guided the remainder of his small force down Tower Street. Pride and guilt consumed his conscience as the rattle of harnesses clattered behind him. His kinsmen had ridden hard throughout the night without complaint. They'd obeyed his every demand, and Broc owed them his life for their loyalty.

The caw of a raven greeted them at the gates of the Tower. Its black wings spread wide overhead as the bird circled them, warning them. An eerie feeling curled around Broc's spine. Was his plan flawless? Had he considered every possible option for a successful mission? Of course he'd considered sending all his men in through the tunnel, but they needed free reign over the stronghold to search every tower and every nook for Eli and Martin's location without having to skulk about in dark corridors. He would see them safely to Scotland and they would know the love of a family, his family, but time was not a commodity he had much of.

"Halt! Declare yourself and your intent," the yeoman waiter bellowed from behind the iron gate.

Startled out of his apprehension, Broc immediately delved into his guise. "I am Sir Julian Ascott. I come with instruction to secure the Tower for the Duke of Gloucester."

The gatekeeper approached, plainly dressed in a rust-colored doublet, tan trews, a black velvet cap, and pointed shoes. "Where are your orders?"

"My orders were given verbally." Broc looked down his nose with noble arrogance. "Your chief warder sent me in his stead to make the appropriate preparations for the arrival of our sovereign king and his uncle."

The gatekeeper's brows made a straight line of distress. He leaned to the right to inspect the Maxwell warriors through the iron grid of the portcullis. "I cannot grant ye entrance, lest ye have written orders."

"Do ye think I would want to enter this vile place had I not been instructed to do so? Raise the gate and let us pass, else answer to Lord Hollister and his evil temper." Broc could only hope Hollister made more enemies than allies.

The gatekeeper's knuckles whitened around the pike he held, and his head pushed back on his shoulders, giving him two chins. "Whilst I may not care for the chief warder's character, I have strict orders not to let anyone pass."

"Very well then. Gather the yeomen and secure the Tower yourself. Have all the prisoners moved to the northwest corner of the inner ward and clean out the refuse in the dungeon. Advise the laundress and your scullions to prepare for an increased number of attendants by this eve. We will wait here." Broc crossed his arms over his chest.

"This eve?"

"This eve." Broc raised a finger. "One more thing. Have Lady Ives's chamber prepared and inform the Lord High Executioner that his daughter has been rescued from that filthy Scot and will be arriving come the morrow."

"S'truth?" The gatekeeper's eyes lit up. "Lizzy is coming home?"

Apparently not everyone thought ill of the executioner's daughter, only those who didn't know her. "Oh, aye. She is. I spoke to her yester eve at Northampton. One of my men got himself sotted on malmsey wine and Lady Ives offered him a tincture for his head pounding. She's a gentle maiden with the oddest color eyes, am I wrong?"

"Gold. Lizzy's eyes are gold." The gatekeeper waved at a porter and the clank of metal prefaced the raising of the portcullis, granting Broc and his brethren entry. "Lady Ives saved my foot, she did. Well, most of it. Lost the little toe, but ye should have seen it before she tended me. The flesh nigh fell from the bone. S'truth."

Broc should have mentioned Lizbeth's name earlier. He and his men dismounted and turned their reins over to the awaiting attendants. Broc fell into step beside the gatekeeper and feigned great interest in the man's many ailments as they crossed the grounds. At the entrance to the White Tower, Broc turned to the gatekeeper. "Thank ye for your escort, sir. Mayhap ye might aid me by seeing to the duty of preparing Lady Ives's chamber."

"Aye, sir. If ye've need of anything else, send any guard to the gate. The name's Godfrey. I do not believe I offered it." His grin pushed his cheeks into rippling wrinkles.

"Thank ye, Godfrey. Ye have been most helpful." Broc watched the gatekeeper leave, then gave his attention to the Maxwell warriors. "Search every corner of the towers I assigned ye. When ye find the boys, take them into the tunnel as we planned and Smitt will take them to safety. Failure is not an option. We search until we find them, aye?"

Each of his brethren donned a stone-faced nod of agreement before they scattered.

Broc followed his nose to the base of the Wardrobe Tower. 'Twas easy to understand why the entrance was empty. The pungent odor had the distinct smell of a privy. He struck a flint and lit a rushlight, hoping the smoke would tamp the smell now burning his throat. He didn't want to think about Eli and Martin living in such foul conditions.

The spiral stairwell offered many detours: various chambers storing ammunitions, garments, and jewels. For hours, he checked the antechambers of each, but found little evidence anyone had even been in this section, much less lived here. On the third level, he entered a chamber stacked wall to wall with coffers. A late afternoon sun poured through a small open window and silhouetted two carved wooden birds sitting on the sill.

Where had he seen those birds before? He picked one up, and then the other, trying to recall if he'd seen them at Market Cross in Leicestershire. Then it struck him. The mantel at Edlynn's cottage was riddled with them—round, fat birds. Lizzy had mentioned in passing that her Father had carved wooden birds. Broc studied the room with the utmost intensity now.

A cuttie stool sat in the corner; wood shavings lay scattered in chunks over the floor. An archway peeked out from behind three coffers. He set his torch in a wall sconce and moved the barricade to find a small door. A moment of dread mixed with anticipation raised the hair on his neck. He heard his breath catch over the crackling sound of the rushlight as he released the iron bar and pulled the door wide.

The ripe scent of death nearly gagged him.

He retrieved the torch and held it inside. Two small decaying bodies, both wearing pale gowns, embraced each other atop a straw-filled pallet on the floor. Broc held his forearm over his mouth and tried to look at anything but them. How was he going to tell Lizbeth that Hollister lied? He played on her love for her nephews to obtain her obedience.

Broc bent to one knee and crossed the boys he'd intended to raise as his sons with the sign of his religion, then spoke the words he hoped would set them free.

The torch flickered on the wall behind them. Three names roughly written into the stone drew his attention: Eli, Martin, Lizzy. Tiny white lines etched an oval around each name. Upon closer inspection, he realized the primitive pattern covered the interior of all four walls. Then he saw the numbers. Lizbeth's numbers.

The bastard locked her in here. In the dark.

"Damn him!" Broc cursed Hollister aloud, wishing the man was in front of him so he could rip out his eyes and blind him the way he'd blinded Lizbeth.

"Who are you?"

Startled by the voice, Broc drew his sword and whirled around. "I am Sir Julian Ascott. I am securing the Tower on Lord Hollister's orders." He spewed the information only moments before he recognized Lizbeth's father.

The Lord High Executioner didn't have the grim appearance Broc had seen in the dungeon. Standing before him was a simple auld man with dark hair speckled gray at the temples and a sagging pale face. Gone was his black cloak, black gloves, black whip, replaced with tan trews, a pale tunic, and a flask of drink.

"I know you." Lord Ives tilted his head and studied Broc with dull brown eyes. "You are no English. You're the Scot who took my daughter."

"I dinnae take her. She rescued me from the Tower."

"And you have returned. For what purpose?"

"To save her nephews."

Lord Ives's gaze dipped to the floor where his grandsons lay on their deathbed. "You are too late. Months, in fact." He sat heavily atop the cuttie stool and stared at the white sky through the small window. "I did not even know they were my grandsons until my son returned from war."

"Did ye kill Eli and Martin to save them from your curse?" Broc asked in an accusatory tone, but part of him wanted to know the man Lizbeth believed was worth saving.

The executioner's eyes glazed over in obvious thought, and Broc suspected the man spent a lot of his hours atop this particular cuttie stool. "I did not protect them."

That answer was not one Broc wanted to hear. Lilian and

Mattie died because he didn't protect them, as did Aiden. Did that mean Broc held the weapon that killed them?

"Put your sword down and tell me how my Lizzy is faring." He took a long draw off the flask.

The executioner's demeanor was surreal, his mind obviously not his own. Dumbfounded, Broc stepped from the antechamber, closing the door behind him. He sheathed his sword and then set his torch in the wall sconce. While he didn't trust the executioner, he certainly presented no threat. Regardless of the man's size, Broc could easily kill him with his bare hands should the need arise.

"Did she make it to sanctuary?" Lord Ives asked when Broc failed to respond quickly enough.

"In a manner of speaking."

Lord Ives looked up at him and turned his head slightly to the side. "What's that you say? Speak up."

"I said, 'in a manner of speaking,'" Broc repeated his words a little louder. Lizbeth never mentioned the man was hard of hearing.

Lord Ives's eyes slid shut. "Then she is well?"

"She cries in her sleep. She counts in the dark, and she prays for her kin. She is by far the most selfless person I have ever known, and I find it difficult to believe a man such as ye spawned her."

The executioner tipped his flask for another drink, then wiped his mouth on his sleeve. "Have you ever been to war? Ever pierce a man's flesh with your blade?"

"I've killed on the battlefield for honor." Broc's volume increased a notch. He wanted to be sure the man heard him.

"Then we are not so different, you and I. We are both murderers in our own right. You kill to protect your country. I kill to punish those who commit crimes against mine."

Broc scoffed at the comparison. "And what crime did your son commit against your country?"

Lord Ives closed his eyes, no doubt hiding his sins. "Kamden committed no crime."

"Yet ye wielded your ax against him?"

The executioner shook his head and propped his elbows on his knees. "I did not execute my son."

"Then Hollister did?" 'Twas a reasonable assumption given the man's hatred for Lizbeth's brother.

"Nay. A porter dressed in my garb took my ax on Hollister's order, whilst I was chained in the dungeon. Hollister would have done the deed himself had he the stomach, but you see, our chief warder has no gut for execution. 'Tis the blood. I've seen him vomit in the torture chamber during a simple amputation. Make no mistake, he takes great pleasure in his position. He is empowered by ordering the executions and even delivering the sentence."

Devil be damned! Broc didn't want to pity Lizbeth's father. He wanted to hate him. He wanted to hide this secret from Lizbeth so she, too, would hate him, but Broc's honor prevented him from such deception. "Why would ye let your daughter believe you killed Kamden?"

"'Tis best she hates me. She is too much like her mother. A dreamer. Always wanting for things she cannot have."

"Things like a husband, a family?"

"Lizzy can never marry." Lord Ives's brows stitched together. He gave Broc a pointed look as if to call *him* wowf, which was completely ironic.

"'Tis too late, Lord Ives. I've already married her."

"Nay." He stood. Erratic movements seized his face. His eyelids blinked fiercely. The muscle in his jaw twitched. "She cannot bear sons. They will be cursed."

Broc became anxious watching him. 'Twas obvious where Lizbeth acquired her skittish behavior. "Your profession is not a curse, but it does die with you."

The executioner threw down his flask and reached for his hip. Thick blue veins whelped out of his neck as the puffy skin beneath his right eye pulsed. His hand curled around nothingness. He poised himself to attack. His eyes narrowed as he wielded his imaginary sword with intent. Did the man actually believe he held a weapon?

Broc drew his sword, not certain if he intended to kill the executioner or protect himself from the man's hallucination.

A bell clanged and pealed the same time a clamoring of feet made its way up the stairwell. Before Lord Ives could strike, a dozen of the Tower's guards stood outside the entranceway armed with intent etched in their faces.

Godfrey stepped to the forefront of the masses and into the chamber, his pike pointed at Broc. "This man is a fraud." He addressed the executioner and shot Broc a look of disappointment.

He shared one conversation with the gatekeeper, yet suffered a bit of guilt for lying to him? "What makes ye doubt my word?"

"You claimed to be securing the Tower on behalf of the chief warder," Godfrey explained, "but Lord Hollister arrived only moments ago to secure the Tower himself."

Chapter 21

"He is the last of those who accompanied the Scot, m'lord." The yeoman pushed Gregor to his knees on the Tower green.

Unable to fight the binds at her wrists or the two guards pinning her in place, Lizzy bit her bottom lip and watched the guards secure the Maxwell warriors in iron shackles and align them shoulder to shoulder beneath the looming shadow of the elm trees. Gregor stood beside one of Aunt Jean's sons, followed by three of Aunt Radella's sons. The last three in line were Broc's cousins and had offered her tips on the training field. Through the haze of her tears, she stared at the piece of grass laced in each of their boots. Her desperation to free her nephews would cost them their lives.

"Have them stripped and prepared for execution," Lord Hollister ordered the porter.

"Nay. Please. You have me. You do not need them," she begged in a soft voice and pinched her eyes tight.

The doors of the White Tower slammed open with a boom.

Her head jerked up.

Godfrey led a group of yeomen from the entrance. Broc stood tall above them all in the center, a giant among men. Her heart beat a painful staccato in her chest. A fury as black as midnight darkened his eyes with every stride. He was her husband, her champion, her everything, and he walked within the walls of her most hated adversary.

From the corner of her eye, she saw Lord Hollister's satisfaction, thin lips turned up at the corner, a slight arch to his thick brow, arms folded over one another in an abundance of dark velvet sleeves. He already celebrated his victory. He would win. He always did. Her mind weakened. The bold woman inside her withdrew behind a veil of fear. "Let them go. I beg of you. Have you no mercy?"

"When did I ever give you a reason to think me merciful?" Lord Hollister slapped her with the back of his hand, setting her off balance.

Pain throbbed in her cheek and shot up the back of her skull.

A roar shook the ground as Broc broke free of his guards and drove his legs hard toward them. Ravens took flight from the branches above in a flutter of flapping wings and screeching caws. He bent forward, arms secured behind him, and thrust his shoulder into Lord Hollister's chest. Both of them flew to the ground. Straddling Lord Hollister's legs, Broc rose up on his knees, and then slammed his forehead into his enemy's face.

She struggled to get to him, but the guards lifted her off the ground.

"Seize him!" a familiar male voice shouted.

Lizzy turned.

"And release her," Father demanded of the two guards pinning her in place.

Four yeomen she'd known since her childhood attacked Broc. Two of them pulled him off by his elbows while another drove fists into his gut. With his arms awkwardly stretched behind his back, he could do little more than take the beating.

"Cease. Cease!" she screamed. Chaos stole her senses,

but Father appeared at her side, then cut the ties around her burning wrists. "Help him. He is my husband."

"You are a foolish girl." Father clasped her upper arm, backed her away from the scuffle, and set her beside the young man who'd assisted him since Mother died. "If he was any husband at all, he would not have let you return."

Lord Hollister found his feet and watched the spectacle with a vile grin. Lizzy loathed him. With every ounce of her being she despised the man more than the devil himself.

Just as Broc managed to break free of the guards' clutches, one of the yeomen slapped the flat of his sword against Broc's back.

He fell to his knees.

His suffering was too much to bear. Her chest hurt with a physical pain she'd never known. Stinging tears spilled out of her eyes, dripping into the ground like daggers into her heart. "Father, please. I love him." Her declaration came out in a sob.

"Enough!" Father ended the assault with that single word.

A hush of silence stilled on a breeze; it was broken only by heaving breaths. Her own? The guards'?

Broc's.

She stared down at him through her spiked lashes. Sweat plastered black hair to his temple, but gone was his rage, his anger. His light blue gaze reached out to her and touched her heart. She didn't have to be beside him to feel his caress, to know his kiss. He lived inside her.

"Lizbeth." Her name fell away from his parted lips in a whisper.

"Take them to the dungeon," Father addressed his assistant, Madoc, "until they can be moved to Newgate Prison to await a trial."

"A trial?" Lord Hollister interjected, blood now seeping into the coarse black hairs of his upper lip. "There will be no trial. I am the warder here, not you, and I give the orders.

Your daughter stole a document from me and gave it to her new husband. I need it back, and you're going to get it for me." Lord Hollister folded his hands behind his back. "The porter will ring the bell every quarter hour. When you hear it, execute two of his men until you have the document in your hands."

"Nay!" Lizzy cried out and prayed she would awaken from this nightmare. Her eyes were locked on Broc, seeking the strength and vitality etched in the lines of his face. She sucked in two deep breaths and broke free of Father's grip. Her knees sunk into the ground in front of her husband; her arms curled around his waist. The dreamer inside her thought if she held on tight enough, she could save him. "Give him the document."

"He will have us executed whether I give it to him or not. Dinnae let him into your head, angel." Broc pressed his cheek against her head and kissed her ear through her hair. "Hollister cannae take anyone else from ye. Eli and Martin are dead. He lied to ye."

His words caused a heavy weight to settle behind her ribs. She felt as if the devil's hooves were dancing over her heart. All the grief she'd suffered months before came rushing back in waves of sorrow. Spots blackened her vision on the sides and crept close to blinding her completely. Her stomach quavered and the acidic taste of illness washed over the back of her tongue; then an iron claw in her hair wrenched her off Broc. She turned toward Lord Hollister and expelled her angst over the front of his elegant surcoat.

Two double-edged swords kept Broc from rising, as did the four yeomen circling him.

"You filthy bitch." Lord Hollister held her at an arm's length and pointed at Madoc. "Bring the pressing board and iron weights to Beauchamp Tower." He peered down his nose at Broc. "Every time you hear that bell, know that I am adding two iron weights to her chest. Comply quickly and she will not suffer. When I have the document, I will grant you a swift execution."

"I hope Satan eats your soul." Broc spit on Lord Hollister's pointed shoes.

"Tie him to the rack and stretch him."

Father nodded. "You are bleeding, m'lord."

Lord Hollister wiped his nose and then stared at the blood covering his hand as if the substance might eat through his skin. His ghostly tint contrasted with his black beard. He balled his fist at his side and latched a hand around Lizzy's wrist. "You will be a widow before the sun sets, m'lady."

"Lizbeth!" Broc bellowed behind her as Lord Hollister jerked her across the Tower green.

Fear for his life settled so strong in her heart she felt her lungs collapse inside her chest while an all-consuming terror settled in her bones.

The pink light of dusk poured into the chamber through the barred window and kissed Lizzy's face with its warmth. Behind her lids, she drew Broc's handsome face out of the darkest recesses of her mind. She refused to think about his strong body being stretched at the joints. Instead, she placed him at her side in a valley filled with lilies walking hand in hand in this place she now knew could only be Heaven.

She wept for death. Only then would she be free of England and the monster torturing her on the dank stone floor of the Beauchamp Tower. Stripped to her wool undertunic with her wrists and ankles bound to four spikes, Lizzy prepared her soul for death. The hard stone floor beneath her head didn't cause her half the burden as the pebble Lord Hollister had placed beneath her back. Her breaths came in short, shallow intakes, for the pressure would not accommodate anything more. Four iron weights sat atop the board on her chest, crushing her ribs into her lungs. She was certain she couldn't bear the weight of four more.

With one leg draped casually over the arm of his high-backed chair, Lord Hollister sat too close to ignore. He poured red wine down his gullet and balanced the next weight in the palm of his hand as if it were no burden at all.

The clang of the bell resounded through her ears.

Please. No more. She pleaded with her Maker for the lives of the Maxwell men. She prayed for their souls and begged God to see them safely on their journey.

"What number is that, Lizzy?" Lord Hollister slid from his regal chair to squat at her side. Ugly black hair fell in oily waves over his cheekbones as he bent over her making a show of the fifth conc-shaped weight before he set it among the others on her chest. He picked up the sixth weight from the floor and added it as well.

Oh, God, save me. Her breastbone felt as if it touched her spine. She moistened her dry lips, wanting to spit in his face, but she didn't possess the ability or the saliva. The pebble ground deeper into her back. She didn't know how anyone could survive such persecution.

"That bell marks the sixth Scotsman dead. It seems your new husband cares little for the lives of his men or for your suffering." The backs of his nails scraped the column of her throat. "He obviously does not share your affections. Who could blame him, really? The courtiers may address you as 'm'lady,' but you are naught more than a butcher's spawn."

Dinnae let him into your head, angel.

Cool tears rushed over her temples and pooled into the hollows of her ears. Every moment seemed an eternity beneath the iron weights, and every indignity Lord Hollister spewed made Broc's words more difficult to pay heed to.

"You are thinking of him, are you not? Mayhap the way the swine rutted over you." Lord Hollister's hand rode up the front of her thigh beneath her tunic, but the pressing board prevented him from defiling her person. "If the Scot's seed takes root, mayhap I will foster his bairn. Teach him how to wield your father's ax."

"Never," she whispered, for it was all she could summon from the pressure in her chest. Her fingers curled into fists above their binds, itching to rip his vile tongue out. If he ever set her free, she would kill him and happily go to the gallows for her crime.

"I took down a king. Do you think you are any match for me?" A jackal's chuckle vibrated his throat. "You should have heeded your father's warning to protect your maidenhead." Lord Hollister repositioned himself back in the chair and filled his goblet with more drink. "'Tis a pity your father is getting on in his years. Such a faithful servant he is. I once thought Kamden might be as loyal to his king and his country as your father, but we both know how that story ended. Eli and Martin proved to be equally disappointing. Martin had your brother's sharp tongue, and Eli was a sniveling urchin just like you. I intended to let them live out your father's curse, but could no longer bear the sight of them, so I poisoned them."

Curse him to Hades! She no longer believed him insane. Father was insane. Lord Hollister was the embodiment of evil.

"None of them ever possessed your father's potential. Ah, Osborn Ives has served me well over the years, and I have every faith he will serve the new king with the same loyalty. As will I. And our rewards shall be plentiful. Buckingham has promised me one of his estates in Wales. Mayhap if you learn to control your tongue again, I will allow you serve me there." He held his goblet up in salutation to her, as if she shared his jubilation.

She would never serve Lord Hollister again. Lizzy closed her eyes and listened to the wine gurgle down his throat. He was a glutton, corrupted by greed and power. His desire to have more than his birthright granted him not only cost the king his life, but hers as well.

Lord Hollister tormented her mentally, worming his way into her brain one word at a time until the fourth bell rang. Each of the Maxwell men's faces moved slowly through her head, as if they'd come to bid her farewell before they set out on their journey. She blinked slowly and slipped into a state of numbness.

Lord Hollister slithered from his chair and retrieved the seventh and eight weights from the floor. "I fear I may have to torture you in front of your husband to get his confession. What say you? Mayhap I'll have you whipped again, or branded, or dunked like my Emma." He poised the weights over her chest.

Small breaths passed over her teeth in preparation.

He dropped them in unison. Her next inhale came in the form of a wheeze.

An explosion of white blinded her.

What sounded like flapping wings echoed in her ears. An angel soared behind her eyes, her feathers a soft white, her skin dusted with gold, her smile serene. Lizzy placed herself inside this peaceful being. Soon she would fly. Soon.

"'Tis done." Father's baritone voice broke into her world.

Her eyelids cracked open. The half piece of curled parchment rested in the palm of Father's gloved hand. Madoc stood in the entranceway wiping perspiration from his neck.

Lord Hollister stepped overtop her and snatched the document away from Father; red wax crumbled in chunks onto the floor. With the merriment of a child, Lord Hollister held it over the open flame of the rushlight. The wax seal dripped in rivulets of crimson down the stem of the wall sconce as the tinge of smoke wafted up her nose.

He won.

The last of her resolve faded with the black ash floating to the floor.

Father had already bent to one knee and removed two of the weights before she realized he was at her side. Her inhales grew with each burden he lifted from her chest, but her heart remained in misery. A droplet of Father's sweat rolled from his silver temple and splashed over her cheek when he unlocked the shackles secured around her wrists and ankles. He picked her up like a child, his arms beneath her knees and back, and stopped beneath the archway. She felt his gaze on her face, but had no desire to look at him. He was not the man she once thought him to be. He was Lord Hollister's henchman and would die wielding the ax for him and for England.

"The bells have called the city to gather at Tower Hill," Father informed Lord Hollister. "London awaits the Scot's execution around the scaffold. After I take my daughter to her chamber, shall I have the prisoner moved?"

After long moments, Lord Hollister pulled his gaze away from the red pool of wax that had formed on the floor. He turned toward them. "Put her down. She will be attending the execution. Madoc, give her your cloak. She is going to assist her father this day."

She would accept further torture, but she would not take part in her husband's execution. "I will not."

"Lizbeth, be still your tongue," Father scolded like the loyal servant he had always been and set her on her feet.

Lord Hollister grinned. "Refuse me, and I will have your husband taken apart bit by bit until his blood runs dry."

Tears burned her eyes, but she suppressed the desire to set them free. She wouldn't let them see her cry. "Will you grant me words with my husband before his execution?" Her request was not unusual, but coin typically accompanied such a show of mercy. She didn't dare get her hopes up that Lord Hollister might grant her such an indulgence.

"After you hand your father his ax, you may have the time it takes to secure your husband to the chopping block. After which, you will ride the horse that drags his headless body

through the streets of our great city. I want the Scot's head on
the spike of London Bridge to greet Gloucester when he
arrives on the morrow."

The numbers wouldn't come. Part of her searched for
them to ease her fear, but the person Broc had found wanted
to rise to the surface and annihilate anyone who dared to take
him from her. Instead, the two women inside her battled,
while her feet followed Madoc's steps toward the gallows.
Her small frame swam in his garment, the tips of her black
boots barely showing beneath the long black robe. Silver
clasps of the inner vestment fastened overtop the only garment she wore beneath, her simple tunic. Though the cloak
weighed heavy upon her shoulders, the burden she carried in
her hands made her steps sluggish over the dampening grass.

Mother had carried Father's ax to the gallows a third of her
life. How had she been such a gentle woman? So loving and
caring? Lizzy felt sinful just holding the handle.

When they reached the wooden stairway leading to the
platform, she couldn't take the step. She froze. Breathing
failed her.

One of the five yeomen accompanying her nudged her
from behind. "'Twill be over soon, m'lady."

She shook her head. The blade thumped atop the first step.
"I cannot."

"You must. The executioner awaits ye on the dais." He
pushed her, forcing her to either take the step or fall.

She felt like an actress about to perform onstage, which is
exactly what an execution was—an elaborate performance.
London's vagrants came out in droves to witness the diabolical scene, their thirst for blood more vile than that of those
who enacted the drama. Wooden planks bowed beneath her
feet until she gained the top of the platform. The thickness of
her hood did little to muffle the jeers of the gathering. From

beneath her lashes she peered into the crowd. Her eyes focused on a small child, no more than three summers, sitting atop a man's shoulders. Wheat-colored curls bobbed around her face. She clapped as though she were at festival and pointed at the two rows of horses aligned perpendicular to the scaffold.

Hidden inside hooded black cloaks, Lord Hollister's guards made this performance an impressive spectacle of authority. Their beastly stallions pranced in place, forcing the crowd to separate into two sections.

The mist of twilight formed a cloud above the assemblage. Two of Father's loyal companions flanked each side of Lord Hollister, who stood atop a raised platform directly beside a black stallion. Her stallion. The beast he expected her to ride through the city. He applauded her with an exaggerated show of mockery, a hint of triumph lifting his brow. Her humiliation raised his bearded chin a level higher and was just another of his artfully planned machinations. 'Twas what Lord Hollister thrived on.

While she shook inside to the very being of her core, she wouldn't give him the thrill of seeing her pain. She turned and her downward gaze followed the braided ropes from the stallion to the center of the dais where the twine twisted into knots around her husband's ankles. Broc knelt before the chopping block. A hood covered his face. His black tunic clung to his muscular chest with sweat, and his hands were trapped behind him. The basket had already been conveniently placed to catch his head once Father removed it.

Her heart nearly burst from her chest. She wanted to believe she could stop this. If she threw the ax, would it save him? Or would Lord Hollister order him pulled apart?

Madoc stepped to Broc's right side, Father to his left. A glimpse of the man she'd known as a child smoothed the hard lines of Father's face. She didn't want to recognize his expression. The same expression he'd worn when he looked at

Mother. He blinked. His amber eyes moved over her shoulder to where Lord Hollister was positioned in the crowd. Father stared at him for what seemed like minutes, then motioned for her to step forward.

He brushed the side of her face with his gloved hand and pressed his lips against her forehead. "You make me proud, Lizzy. Everything I loved about your mother I see in you. I do not wish for you to be afraid anymore. For generations Ives men have wielded the ax. I am the last. Pray for me, Lizzy. I cannot get to Heaven without you." He uncurled her fingers from the ax and gestured her toward Broc. "Go to your husband."

She didn't want Father's pride, nor did she want to pray for him anymore. The world spun on an axis in dull colors. She started counting the number of armed guards filling the small wooden dais. *Eight, ten, twelve* . . . Could she push them all over the edge? Was she capable of saving her husband?

She stood between Broc and the block and removed his hood. Her hand cradled the nape of his neck as he looked up at her.

Relief washed through his sweet blue eyes. "Ye are well?"

"Nay. I am afraid."

The fool smiled. "Fear not, Lizbeth. I will be with ye soon."

A piece of the chain holding his gold crucifix snuck out from beneath his tunic. He was a man of God. He'd accepted death and made peace with his Maker. Her lips parted. Her chin quivered. She wanted their last words to be meaningful. She wanted to profess her love and hear her words returned. She wanted to kneel down before him and pray with him. A sob escaped her. "Tell me what to do."

"Kiss me, Lizbeth," he demanded.

Her eyes fell shut. She pressed her lips to his, wanting time to stand still. Salty tears slid between their lips. "Wait for me," she whispered into his mouth.

"Get on the horse." His gaze left her to look into the crowd.

Madoc pulled her to the edge of the dais and caught her when her knees gave out. He set her atop the horse with the aid of the two yeomen standing beside Lord Hollister. Her fingers twisted into the horse's mane as convulsions attacked her abdomen. Her heart had never known such suffering before this moment.

Silence settled over the crowd save for an infant's cry.

"Are you not going to watch?" Lord Hollister's voice turned her stomach sour. "His chin is in the divot."

She looked at Lord Hollister from the corner of her eye. "The time we spend on this earth only prepares us for the afterlife. I will be with my husband soon . . . in Paradise. And you, sir, will know the flames of Hades for eternity."

Lord Hollister scowled, but his glare never left her.

"May God protect this man on his journey!" Father bellowed on the dais behind her.

Thwack.

Chapter 22

Lizzy's entire body jerked.

The crowd's whispers escalated to gasps.

A loud slap to her steed's rump spurred her horse into motion behind the other stallions. "Ride, Lizbeth."

Her hood fell back. Her head jerked to the left. Broc sat astride the other tethered horse, wearing an all-knowing grin.

"Seize them!" Lord Hollister bellowed behind them.

Confused, she glanced over her shoulder. Madoc and the two yeomen latched onto Lord Hollister's arms. Not one guard followed in their wake. Father stood atop the gallows, a boyish smile curling his lips. He waved.

"Dinnae look back!" Broc yelled at her over the pounding of hoofbeats.

Lizzy bent low, held tight to the reins, and kicked the beast's belly with her heels. She was free. Broc was free. One of the guards in front of her pushed back his hood and peeked over his shoulder.

Smitt winked at her.

Gregor did the same.

Another pushed back his hood, then another. They were alive! The Maxwell men were alive and leading them through the darkening city of London past merchant stalls and gabled houses. She didn't know what had transpired, nor did she care at the moment. She only wanted to leave and never return.

They approached the city's gates. Broc raised his hand high and waved at the gatekeeper. "Farewell, Godfrey."

"Godspeed!" he bellowed and then dropped the portcullis behind them with a clicking bang.

Lizzy craned her neck. *Why was Godfrey at London's gate?* He worked inside the Tower. Yet another question added to the many accumulating in her head.

Twilight speckled through the dissipating clouds as they stormed over the outskirts of London, never once easing the thunderous pace. A silver moon rose on the horizon, and living stars twinkled like magic dust overhead. Her steed plummeted over the crest of a knoll, and a pregnant pause of silence hollowed her ears. Weightlessness flowed through her belly. She must have glanced over her shoulder a hundred times, but she couldn't prevent herself from taking another peek.

The rolling grassland spread out behind them, vacant. How was it possible not one guard pursued them?

Smitt took over the lead and Broc guided his stallion beside hers, his fluid movements one with his steed. He was grace and brawn in tight black trews drawing sensual lines over muscular thighs. He was a warrior—her warrior—and she wanted to touch him and know that he was real.

He watched her; a serious expression she'd never seen before touched his face. He blinked, and one corner of his lips curved upward.

"Am I dreaming?" she asked in a voice loud enough for him to hear over the gait of their horses.

"Mayhap." A tug on the reins brought his steed beside her. "Dinnae wake up til we get to Scotland, aye." Broc inched backward on his horse, then filled his fist with the back of her cloak and snatched her off her steed. Instead of setting her astride, he placed her feet atop the horse's back and held tight to her calves. "Ye are free, angel. Spread your wings and fly."

She found her footing, letting her knees adjust to the stallion's stride. The Maxwell warriors fell back, five to her right, five to her left, like the V formation of geese in flight. Fearless, she stretched her arms out from her body and soared. Wind blew her hair away from her face and pushed tears over her temples while her black cloak billowed in whipping waves all around her. She closed her eyes and inhaled the mist, the sweet grasses, the spice of horseflesh—freedom.

She turned her face toward Heaven and bid her loved ones farewell. In her mind's eye, Mother kissed her cheek, Kamden and his sons wrapped their arms around her and squeezed, and Edlynn brushed her hair with crippled hands. Lizzy would hold them in her heart forever and let their voices make her strong. They were setting her free. "Thank you." She offered her gratitude in a whisper no one could hear but them.

Her eyes opened in time to catch the tail of a falling star the same time Broc placed a kiss on the back of each knee. Emotions surged through her breast—relief, joy, longing—but none of them as strong as love.

As Broc slowed, the Maxwell warriors purged ahead with her horse in tow. Broc's hands gripped her hips, spun her around, and then slid her down his chest. She wrapped her legs around his waist and twined her arms around his neck, wanting to absorb his strength, wanting to be part of him. She was so very grateful for his presence in her life. *I'm never letting go.*

She brushed her nose against his earlobe and inhaled the musk of his skin, waiting for him to fill the silence with his chatter, but words didn't come. His thighs hardened beneath hers, guiding the horse behind the fading rumble of the

Maxwell warriors' steeds. He embraced her, his heart beat against hers, and then at last, she felt him tremble.

"All will be well, husband," she assured him with his own words as she caressed the soft curls at his nape.

"I was so afraid I would fail ye," he confessed, his voice deep, frightened. Shielding her inside the cocoon of his chest, he tightened strong arms around her.

The pressure against her tender ribs caused her to whimper.

His hold loosened immediately. "A day will not pass that I will not regret leaving ye with him. Can ye ever forgive me?"

"'Tis over." She pulled back, cupped his coarse cheek, and stroked the worried flesh beneath his eyes. Comforting her strong, fearless warrior was an altogether new rush of emotions.

"Ye cannae know the torment I suffered while ye were in that bastard's hands." He placed tiny kisses around the bruise circling her wrist like an opaque, sapphire bracelet.

"Tell me what happened."

He eased them into a steady canter. "The moment Hollister took ye from the Tower green, I told your da about Hollister's association with Buckingham. I bargained with him. Told him I would provide the document if my men were given a fair trial and you were delivered into sanctuary."

"And you? Did you not plead for your life?"

"Nay." He caressed the sensitive skin on her forearm. "Your father asked me the same question whilst the guards escorted us into the tunnel where I had Smitt hide the document. I thought it odd your da would be concerned about my well-being." Again he kissed her wrist. "I admit I wanted to think ill of him because of his profession. I blamed him for all your fears and questioned your desire to save a man who—"

"Whose loyalty to a monster was stronger than his love for his son," she finished, embarrassed to be Lord Ives's daughter.

"Nay, Lizbeth." He tucked a loose tendril back behind her

ear. "He dinnae execute Kamden. Hollister chained your da during the execution."

Lizzy looked down at the dark grasses passing beneath the stallion's belly. She'd cursed Father after that day. Damned him to Hades, and he never once told her the truth. He accepted her anger, her hate, and distanced himself from her, leaving her all alone.

She felt the gentle lift of her chin; then Broc pulled her a little closer. "Your father's head is often not his own."

"Why would he let me believe he killed Kamden?"

"I suspect he was tormented inside and thought it best ye hate him. It does not mean he loved ye any less."

Love. She repeated the word in her head. Her fingers spread over his, their hands palm to palm. A frisson of heat built within that barest of touches. A heat she knew to be love. If Father did love her, he'd never said it. The last time she'd heard words of love was the day Mother set her rosary in Lizzy's hand. The same day Mother passed from this world. "I know not if my father ever loved anyone. He never said the words. Not even to Mother."

"Mayhap he felt his love a curse. He failed Kamden, as he did you and his grandsons. I've known his pain. I know what 'tis like to fail someone, to be incapable of helping them. It makes ye hate yourself. It makes ye want to do anything to set yourself free from that guilt."

"Do not compare yourself to my father. You are nothing like him."

"Lizbeth, the mon went mad on regrets." He laced his fingers through hers, holding tight, as if he could sense her withdrawal.

"Stop defending him. He is a coward."

"Mayhap. But he is a coward who is eager to see your efforts through. To make amends and avenge his heirs."

"My efforts failed. Without the document, there is naught to connect Lord Hollister to Buckingham."

"Ye have such little faith." He kissed her tense brow and flattened her hand against his chest.

"Faith? The document is gone. Lord Hollister won. Is it truly necessary for me to remind you of the events that transpired? You gave the document to Father. He gave it to Lord Hollister. Lord Hollister burned it." She flung her hand from his chest and plucked off the events with her fingers. "Why it took so cursed long, I do not yet know, but my breasts will likely never be the same."

He worked the silver clasps of her inner vestment until the cloak hung over her shoulders. With one hand splayed behind her back, he bent and kissed her upper breasts through her tunic. "I'm sorry ye had to suffer for so long."

The cool night and his tenderness made her shudder. "Why did it take Father four bells to get from the tunnel to Beauchamp Tower?"

Again he pressed her palm to his chest and languidly blinked his eyes. "We worked as diligently as we could to forge the document."

"Forge the document?"

"Your da ran from the dungeon to the Constable Tower to get parchment and an ink pot whilst Madoc went to the gardens for rowanberries. If Hollister had taken the time to study the document, he would have found a very poor fabrication of Buckingham's signature. The wax seal was cheap tallow mixed with red juices from the rowanberry and stamped with a ducat. Took an eternity to harden."

She should have known something was amiss when Father came in sweating. He never sweat. Very little effort was required to cut off a man's head if the blade was sharp. "Truth?" She was afraid to hope.

"Truth. I vow it upon my soul." Broc kissed the column of her neck, then dawdled across the valleys of her collarbone.

She gave a little shiver and slid her hand up his neck to play with his ear, trying to focus on the topic and not the feel of his hot lips against her skin. "Where is the document now?"

"Your da has it. I suspect he might torture the bastard a wee bit before turning him over to Gloucester."

"He deserves any punishment Father might delve out." 'Twas quite a plan Broc and her Father had developed and performed in such a short period of time. She wrestled with the events as they'd occurred. "Why stage the execution?"

"'Twas not intentional. Your father thought Hollister would release ye into his care once he provided him the document. 'Twas his intention to bring ye to me so we could escape through the tunnel, but Hollister's desire to further torment you complicated our plan. Whilst you were being escorted to the gallows by Hollister and Madoc, we were feverishly rearranging guards. 'Tis why Godfrey was at London gate and not the Tower."

Father was certainly a powerful man. Feared by most, and definitely capable of keeping the king's guards at bay, but she found it difficult to believe Father would hand her over to Broc. "Why did Father set you free? He could have easily executed you and put me in sanctuary."

Broc's head rose. His features shadowed beneath the moonlight. "When we were in the tunnel I told him I would go to the gallows to protect ye."

"Because of your vow to me?" she asked, hoping there might be another reason. Her hand fell away from his neck and twisted inside the black cloak while she waited for him to answer, desperate for him to share part of his heart with her.

"Ye are my wife. I could not bear it if I failed ye."

The way he'd failed his sisters. Part of her suspected she'd filled the hole in his heart left from his sisters' deaths, but she didn't know how long she could live as their memory. He was willing to give his life for her. If his actions were because of honor and not love, then she would accept it, and mayhap someday he would love her half as much as she loved him.

"Do ye know what I feared most?" He cradled her head in the palm of his hand.

She shook her head and met his sad eyes.

"I feared I would be left with only your memory. I feared I would never again feel your warmth or know your kiss. That I would never see ye round with our child or dance with ye again in the rain."

A spasm convulsed in her belly. She felt his pain and wanted to weep for him, to comfort him. He'd never shown weakness, and she wanted to protect him as he'd always protected her. "We will have many memories together."

He placed a gentle kiss on her nose, her chin, then found her hand buried inside the cloak and once again pressed her palm against his chest. "Touch me, Lizbeth, please."

Her hands roamed free over the hard plains of his chest. She inhaled his air seconds before he pressed his lips to hers. A storm blew through her insides when his tongue slipped in to claim hers. He dove into her mouth, raked over her tongue, again and again, until finally ending, oh so sweetly, on each lip.

"I want to make a memory now." He pulled his shirt over his head and tucked it into the harness, then pushed the cloak from her shoulders to drape around the horse's mane.

She followed the direction of his gaze over her shoulder. The moonlight showed her a glimpse of the ten Maxwell men cresting the hill of the next valley. The world was theirs. It seemed the meadow had been created for them and them alone, sprinkled with starlight and filled with the sweetest scents. Clouds dotted the sky and the moon poured over the grasses like glistening tears.

Broc loosened the laces of her tunic and gathered the material around her waist. He embraced her, pressing her skin to his, and kissed her hair. She felt a near desperation to be intimate with him. A hum escalated throughout her body as she placed featherlight kisses along his jaw, hoping they would come upon an inn soon.

He moaned, licked his lips, and pushed her tunic high over her bare thighs. The thickness of his manhood grew to pulsing proportions beneath her bottom, causing her knees to latch a little tighter around him. Clasping her fingers around his neck, she leaned back, needing to feel his caress and the warmth of his mouth. "Touch me."

Her breasts bobbed in rhythm with the steed's canter until he caught one in each hand and circled her nipples with the tips of his short nails. At last his moist tongue sprinkled her areolas with wetness one at a time until her nipples crinkled. She wiggled, growing more aroused, feeling his passion through every ounce of coddled skin. The tension became unbearable, and the muscles inside her flexed and throbbed. She gasped and tightened the clasp of her ankles behind him as a streak of fire flashed through her. "Will we be stopping soon?" *Please say aye.*

"Nay. With Smitt leading us, 'tis quite possible we will ride all the way to Scotland." Holding her hands in one of his to aid her balance, he lowered her onto the horse's nape. "Lie back. I want to see ye. I'll not let ye go."

Her breasts glistened in the moonlight, and the wind slid over her like cool satin. He gathered her tunic at her navel and played over her skin, teasing all of her curves. "Do ye know I've pictured ye like this."

Through the slits of her eyes, she recognized the hunger in his gaze, and the vixen who'd been locked away far too long wanted to play. "Ye pictured me naked atop a horse?"

"Aye." He tickled her small nest of curls, drawing heat straight to his hand. "I pictured ye naked in the tunnel the first time I ever smelled your scent," he admitted, "but I pictured ye naked atop a horse the morning after we left the inn. Ye are far more beautiful than I could have ever imagined."

His words caused a blush to further heat her burning skin. She was about to beg him to touch her when he delved two fingers between the wet folds of her womanhood and circled her sensitive ball of flesh with the tip of his thumb. Her wrists buckled inside his grip as she lifted her hips off the horse's back. "Oh, Broc." His name passed over her teeth with a sharp intake of air. "You must stop the horse."

"Nay." He urged the steed faster across the open plain, stroking her, bringing her closer to the brink of ecstasy.

Her core fluttered in anticipation. She held tight to his hand and cried out his name over and over into the night. Desire seared through her loins. The pinnacle of her climax lay on the surface.

He tore his fingers from inside her and let go of her hand. *Nay!* Her core pulsed.

He stood in the stirrups and released the laces of his trews to free his erection from its confinement. "I need ye."

"You intend to make love to me on a moving horse?" She sat forward, struggling to keep her balance without the aid of his hand.

"Oh, aye." He curled his hands around her buttocks, lifted her overtop him, and nipped her ear. "Wrap your arms around me."

She did and tucked her face in the crook of his neck as he opened her to him.

"Make love to me, Lizbeth." He slid himself into her wet canal and fell into rhythm with the stallion's rocking gait.

Her nails dug into his shoulders, holding on, as each stride filled her with his thickness. The horse controlled the pace of their lovemaking, beat after beat, pulse after pulse, until the spiraling friction escalated and sent her searching for air. The sound of wet slapping flesh heightened her desires, exciting her in ways she'd not yet experienced.

Fingers spread wide around her cheeks, teasing the crevice of her backside, circling the puckered hole until one finger snuck in to its knuckle and mimicked the to and fro movement of his hard shaft inside her. She cried out and squeezed her muscles, wanting him to stop . . . wanting him to go faster, harder.

"Ye are mine. No one will ever take ye away from me again." His groans were animalistic. Deep, throaty . . . primal. "Mine . . ." He repeated the word with each thrust.

"Mine."

"Mine."

"Mine!" he roared and crushed her pelvis to his. Digging his fingertips into her bottom, he dominated her, and she wanted to show him the same aggression.

He was her mate, her husband, her lover. Empowered by his passion, she reached between them and squeezed his tiny nipples and sunk her teeth into his shoulder. Pleasure took hold of her body in rippling waves.

Like a caged animal set free, he bellowed an instinctual growl so fierce and loud it vibrated in her ears, and then he erupted into her heat. He flooded her, surge after powerful surge, filling her with life.

The beat of his heart thundered as one with hers in the aftermath. His thighs tightened, slowing the steed up the side of the knoll until they came to a stop. His forehead rested on her shoulder, and his harsh breaths heated the space between them. "Oh, Lizbeth . . ."

She waited for him to finish, expectation making her heart gallop faster than it had moments before. He must love her; his touch told her so. He'd been willing to die for her. She nuzzled into his neck, wanting desperately to hear him profess his love.

Say the words.

The sting of tears prickled her eyes. Her lips brushed the rim of his ear. *Love me,* she begged silently, but her plea echoed throughout her heart . . . unanswered.

Chapter 23

"Is it really necessary for you to enter Grandmum's home with a dagger?" Lizbeth pursed her lips and scowled at Broc, a face she'd worn often enough over the last few days. He suspected she was weary. For nearly a sennight, they rode hard, slept little, and made love every chance they could slip away from the others. Lizbeth was at her most playful before dawn. Twice he'd awoken with her atop him wanting to play the victor. And twice he'd put her back under him. Every day that passed she became stronger, bolder, more dominant. He was eager to get her back to Skonóir Castle, but she'd insisted on paying Grandmum a visit since the sun was still high.

Standing on the stone walkway behind him, Lizbeth crossed her arms under her breasts, displaying her stubbornness, but the effect was lost on the daring cut of the deep purple gown he'd bought her at Market Cross in Leicestershire. He paid little attention to her temper as his gaze focused on the creamy swells of her breasts, currently accentuated by a thick gold hem that followed her curves down the front of her skirt where her toe drummed an impatient tune. Waiting.

"Dinnae tap your toe at me," he demanded, which only

made her glare at him with those flaming eyes and tap with more ferocity.

"Sheath your weapon."

"Grandmum will not poke me if I'm wielding a weapon."

"You are a foolish Scotsman. Step aside." She brushed past him, leaving a sweet scent in his nose reminding him of the thick garden of white and red flowers where he'd made love to her before dawn. Gillyflowers, to be more precise. Why the woman insisted on educating him on every floral species across England he didn't know, but it made her smile. 'Twas enough for him.

"Are you coming?" She offered him her hand from the threshold.

"Aye." He sheathed his weapon, took her hand, and stepped in front of her to lead her into the entranceway. The tip of a sword found the hollow of his throat the moment they entered Grandmum's great room

"'Tis about time ye returned."

For a moment Broc thought he stared at his reflection, except the man before him was younger and wore the *plaid*. He almost didn't recognize Ian in the colored light of Grandmum's stained-glass window. Truth was, nigh a year had passed since Broc had seen his younger brother. "You've grown. A lot."

"Aye." Ian slid his sword into the sheath at his hip, then clasped Broc's hand and embraced him with a slap on the back. A hearty slap. "I've been safeguarding the border whilst ye've been frolicking about England. Is this your woman?" Ian ran his gaze over Lizbeth, bringing her eyes away from Grandmum's window.

"Aye. This is Lizbeth."

"I am his wife," she corrected, "not his woman."

"'Tis one and the same," Ian remarked with a nonchalance that made Broc consider slipping from the room. The lad still had lessons to learn.

"Pray forgive me, but nay they are not. A wife is expected to be faithful to her husband. To be dutiful and support him and help him make decisions. A woman is someone a man ruts over before he finds a wife to guide him."

Broc wanted to applaud her for standing up to Ian. No doubt, she worried over her position as Lady Maxwell. Mayhap she feared being incapable of managing the household. For days he'd searched for reasons to justify her low spirits.

Ian opened his mouth, then closed it. He stared at Lizbeth for long moments before turning to Broc. "Have ye been to Skonóir?"

Lizbeth humphed and went to the sill housing Grandmum's dolls.

"Nay," Broc answered and worried over Lizbeth's mood. "Why are ye not at the keep?"

"He is hiding." Grandmum limped into the room. Thankfully, her poking fingers were occupied with a flask of whisky, four small cups, and her sword.

"I am not hiding. Think ye a mon cannae visit his grandmum without everyone accusing him of misdeed?" Ian denied Grandmum's accusation, but Broc knew something was amiss. No one visited Grandmum lest they wanted a medicine or a place of refuge.

"*Ah chac!* Ye been here a sennight, and the roof on the barn still needs to be fixed, as do the fences." Grandmum turned a blind eye to her grandsons, set the whisky and cups on the trestle table, and then hobbled toward Lizbeth, who was completely preoccupied with Grandmum's dolls.

Broc cringed. *Dinnae poke her*.

"Are ye weel, child? Ye look a wee bit peaked." Grandmum brushed Lizbeth's hair with bony fingers.

Lizbeth didn't answer. Instead, she rearranged Grandmum's dolls with a fierce frown.

"She is well," Broc answered for her and gathered he

shouldn't have when she glared at him over her shoulder and her toe started tapping, again.

"Then ye are breeding her?" The skin raised above Grandmum's eyes.

"Oh, aye," Broc said with pride. He regarded the sweet shade of pink coloring Lizbeth's cheeks as a compliment until one winged brow arched over a narrowed eye.

"Oh, aye? Oh, aye? Is that what you've been doing, *Lord Maxwell*? Breeding your woman?" Lizbeth puffed air through her nose. A heartbeat later, her chin started to quiver. A ray of sunlight flickered in her watery eyes just before she lowered her lids.

"Lizbeth, I dinnae—"

"I'm going to the barn." She started for the door.

"If'n ye've the time, the goats are in need of milking," Grandmum said.

Lizbeth disappeared in a flash of purple velvet.

The moment she was out of earshot, Ian laughed outright. "That one's got a wee bit of a temper, dear brother."

"Aye." Broc took full responsibility for sharpening Lizbeth's tongue, and he liked her that way. She wasn't the skittish doe he'd met in the tunnel who twisted her sleeves and pinned her chin to her chest. Howbeit, something definitely troubled her. Mayhap she was carrying and the moods had already taken over her senses. The thought of seeing her round with his child made his cullions harden.

"Lady Juliana would never spout off in such a way." Ian's comment jarred Broc out of his musings.

"Lady Juliana is nay longer my concern." He cared little for the comparison.

Grandmum grinned with all four of her teeth. "Mayhap she should be."

"Explain." Broc waited for Grandmum to fill them each a quaff of whisky while Ian feigned great interest in the edge of his *sgian dubh*.

"'Tis my understanding Laird Scott has been eagerly awaiting your return for little more than a sennight. He and a dozen of his kinsmen have taken up quarters at Skonóir with his daughter in tow and is demanding a wedding. Says Lady Juliana has been soiled by a Maxwell."

Broc instantly sensed Grandmum's accusation. "I dinnae steal the woman's virtue. I've not been in her presence in three years. If the mon thinks to accuse me of such, then he will have a war on his hands."

Grandmum slipped whisky between her smirk. "Ye are not the mon in question, laddie."

"Smitt?" Broc asked. The drabber had been home only three days before Broc had sent him back into England. Damn! 'Twould take a team of oxen to get his cousin before a priest.

"Nay." Ian tossed a quaff of whisky down his gullet. "'Tis I."

"Ye jest." Broc straddled the trestle bench and tipped his own bit of whisky. The spirits stung his throat and coated his belly with fire. Ian didn't look at him. His brother hung his head like the boy who once stole Aiden's sword. But Ian was apparently a boy no longer. "She must be five years your senior."

"One, brother. One year. Lady Juliana was eighteen when Laird Scott and Da betrothed her to Aiden."

Broc tried to draw up Lady Juliana's memory, but couldn't even recall the shape of her face. The only woman in his mind's eye was his Lizbeth. Grandmum poured them each another quaff. Another soon followed. No words passed as they each engulfed three hearty doses of Uncle Ogilvy's whisky.

"What are your intentions?" Broc asked.

"I wish to take her to wife."

"Then why are ye hiding at Grandmum's?"

"Lady Juliana once belonged to Aiden. Whilst he did not want her, I know ye did."

"And when ye found out I took a wife, ye rushed out and stole the lass's virtue?" Disappointment leaked into his voice without warning.

"Nay." Ian stood and splayed his palms on the table. "I've been meeting Lady Juliana where our soil meets Clan Scott for nigh a year in secrecy. 'Twas only after I heard ye took a wife did I act on my desires for her."

Broc waited for anger to take over or even a bit of jealousy, but Lady Juliana had never been the woman for him. Lizbeth had always been inside him, waiting for him to save her. "Ye should have married her first, Ian."

"I wanted your permission."

Awe could only describe the feeling slipping through Broc's chest. 'Twas either that or the whisky. He'd gained his brother's respect as he would undoubtedly gain the respect of Clan Maxwell. 'Twas good to be the leader. He poured another round of whisky and studied the warrior woman depicted in Grandmum's stained-glass window. He read the words inscribed over her head: *Neart, Grá agus Onóir.* "Strength, love, and honor, brother. May ye achieve happiness and strength through love and honor the same as I have." Broc held up the small cup and waited for Ian to join him.

"Then I have your permission?" Ian raised his cup along with his dark brows.

"I will set the banns on the morrow. Ye will wed Lady Juliana in three sennights."

Upon entering the barn, Broc kept his distance as Lizbeth's fingers were wrapped around the goat's teat. He had no desire to bath in goat's milk before returning to Skonóir. Quite a mood had settled over his wife. Albeit, she cried in her sleep less and less, she certainly carried a burden with her, and he wanted to lighten her load.

He settled against the barn frame, feeling the effects of

Uncle Ogilvy's whisky. The longer he watched her, the broader his smile became. She was ranting to the goat. He couldn't hear her words, but her sharp gestures were made of definite scorn. God, he loved this woman. He didn't know when he'd come to realize it. Mayhap when Hollister took her from him, but with each passing day, he felt her love strengthen him, empower him, make him the dominant leader he needed to be. She suited him well.

She stood after milking the fourth goat and wiped her hands down the front of the expensive velvet gown he'd bought her.

"Milking goats is hardly work for a lady."

Lizbeth lifted two pails and started past him out of the barn, making no reply to his statement.

God's hooks. What the devil was wrong with his wee wife? "Put the pails down."

She stopped abruptly, slopping creamy yellowed milk over the edge of one pail. He studied her profile, searching for her mood, but a veil of indifference hid her emotions. The longer she stood in silence, the more frustrated he became. "Ye will tell me what has you acting out of sorts."

She turned toward him. A glimpse of fury ignited her eyes into fiery suns. "Because you order it? Because you are the leader of your clan and hold power over me as your wife? I have spent the whole of my existence pacifying men of power. I have a mind. I know what plants ease stomach cramps and what plants keep the insects from biting the skin. I've eased women's labor pains whilst they brought their bairns into this world. I may not brandish a sword like the women in your clan, but I can improve the quality of life for your kinsfolk, but I cannot do this behind you."

"Ye are not behind me." He looked over his shoulder to prove his point.

"I am in their eyes. Did you not see the dolls?"

"The dolls?" Completely perplexed, he concentrated on her words.

"Grandmum made me a doll. She put me *behind* you on the sill."

Broc stared at her wishing she were less complicated. "This is not about the dolls."

"You are the leader of your clan, and I am your wife, not your woman. I must be at your side."

"Ye are at my side." The woman was wowf.

"Nay, I am not. I take a step forward, ye take two." Lizbeth set the pails down and started out of the barn.

Broc stepped in front of her. "Dinnae walk away."

"Do you see? You did not stop me from behind. You always have to be on top looking down on me with your strength and prowess."

"I am taller than ye." His hands flew out from his sides. The lass may as well be speaking in a foreign tongue for all the more sense she was making. The whisky must be clouding his ability to grasp what she wasn't saying. Did she expect him to read her mind? "Tell me what ye want, and I will provide it."

"'Tis not so simple." Her bottom lip trembled only a second before she bit it. Her downward gaze bespoke of a woman who hurt inside.

What could she possibly want? He'd protected her. Married her. Taught her how to overcome her fears. She'd always been forthright with him until this moment. He missed her smile and the way she bantered with him in play. He bent down and plucked two clover flowers from a thick bush of greenery and then handed them to her. "If you pinch the purple petals from the stem, there is a sweet milk hidden in their ends."

Instead of smiling, she frowned. "I told you this."

"I know. 'Twas a jest. I want to hear ye laugh. I want ye to be happy. If ye want to lead, then I will walk behind ye."

She nodded, swiped her eyes, and took his offering, but those were not the words she searched for. Once they were settled, he would try again. "Come, Lizbeth. We've a wedding to prepare for. The aunts will have ye drying flowers for the next three sennights."

"Who is getting married?" She looked up at him.

Tears she tried to hide still sat in her eyes and made his heart ache. "Ian and Lady Juliana."

"*Your* Lady Juliana?"

Broc rolled his eyes. "She is not *my* Lady Juliana."

"But you once wanted her, did ye not?"

"Mayhap. But now I realize I wanted the dream that came with her. Not the woman herself. Ye showed me that." He kissed her sad smile and waited for her to take the first step forward. If she wanted to be in front, he would oblige. He wanted to hear her laugh again. "After ye, m'lady." With one arm wrapped around his waist, and the other pointing toward Grandmum's steps, he bowed deeply, trying to solicit any form of merriment—a giggle, a snort—he'd settle for one of her humphs.

Not even an exasperated sigh left her. "Thank you, m'lord."

He picked up the pails of milk and watched her bounce up the stone steps, her skirts balled in her fists.

"I can assemble a mass attack on my enemy, but I havenae the wit to understand the workings of my wife's mind," he grumbled to himself.

Chapter 24

"I love this woman!"

A roar of approval prefaced the beat of drums and the whimsical twirl of the viols as a swarm of gay attendants formed a circle for the next dance in the Great Hall.

Lizzy sat at the high table—alone—and stuffed a third oatcake smothered with gooseberry jam into her mouth. She watched the scene with a jealousy that made her temples ache, or mayhap the braids pulling her hair into a regal crown were too tight. She looked for her husband to see if he'd heard his younger brother profess his love for his new wife, but found him completely preoccupied.

Laird Scott monopolized her husband's attention, but Broc appeared to be enjoying the neighboring chieftain's wit. They laughed like men who'd bathed in ten-year-old wine and were the center of entertainment for their surrounding kinsmen. Broc played the role of leader to perfection in his crossbar plaid draped over his shoulder and pleated around his waist. A crisp white hair shirt contrasted against his tanned skin and the huge sword hanging from his hip only emphasized his status in the clan. He clamped a hand on Laird Scott's shoulder, leaned in to say something, then bellowed with laughter. His brethren roared with merriment.

She humphed. If her husband would pay her no notice, then she would be content to appease Aunt Radella by eating until her belly popped.

She fiddled with the pendant Broc had given her only days before—golden wings encrusted with amber and garnet gemstones. It felt wrong to be so angry. Of course Broc loved her. He was her husband. He kept her safe. He brought her flowers every day and worked feverishly alongside his kinsmen to build her a bathhouse so he could teach her to swim. He held her at night and never found sleep before her, and he always kept a candlebox burning bedside. They danced in their solar, made love every eve and every morn, and sometimes he would sneak away from the training field for a quick moment with her at noontide. His every action said that he loved her.

So why had the fool never said the words? He had "love" inked on his arm. All he had to do was look down and read it.

Lucy skipped up to the trestle table with a small bowl of purple and yellow flowers swimming in honey. "Grandmum Rae said ye should try these."

"Did she now." Lizzy plucked one of the petals from the bowl and dripped honey on the bodice of her red-gold velvet kirtle before getting it to her mouth. The pansy slid over her tongue in a burst of tangy sweetness that made her jaw pinch and her saliva thicken. She'd never tasted anything so divine. "Tell your Grandmum Rae she is brilliant."

"Would ye like another bowl?" Lucy asked while Lizzy dipped in for another sweet treat and tried to name the unique ingredient Aunt Radella had used.

"Oh, aye. That would be splendid." If her husband wouldn't let her dine on him, then she would satisfy her cravings elsewhere. Three more flowers melted on her tongue. She felt like a glutton, but in truth, she couldn't satisfy her taste for sweets as of late. "Mayhap you should bring two more bowls."

"Aye, m'lady." Lucy bobbed away, and Celeste slid in beside Lizzy on the trestle bench.

"Why are ye not dancing with your husband?" Celeste asked and ogled Lizzy's tray of food.

"He is busy playing prime to his kinsmen." Lizzy suckled the honey from her middle finger and glanced at Broc in time to catch him staring at her. The tiny hairs on her arms stood straight up. She waited for her nipples to harden as they always did when he looked at her with his hungry eyes. Her breasts swelled, and, as predicted, her nipples sharpened to hard little stones. He winked, and she looked away. Why couldn't she stir him the way he did her?

"He looks as if he's ready to eat ye." Celeste's laughter turned quickly to hiccoughs.

"He most likely will. 'Tis what some animals do after they breed."

"Mayhap ye should eat him," Celeste suggested with a naughty glint in her eye and helped herself to Lizzy's tray of oatcakes.

"Mayhap I should." She'd tried to dominate more than once in the bedchamber, but her husband was not one to play the submissive role. She glanced back at Broc to find him squatting in front of Lucy. She handed him a wooden bowl piled high with what looked like nuts. He popped one in his mouth, licked his lips, after which his face puckered then dimpled.

"'Ods toes! These are good." Celeste sucked the tips of her fingers. "John has to try these."

"How is your husband faring?" Lizzy asked with genuine interest.

"He is a lusty Scotsman who is still using his injury to gain my sympathies. You need to quit fretting over him. You have spoiled him with your daily visits and your medicines."

"I will continue to fret over whomever I wish, and for

however long I choose." Lizzy slid another pansy from the bowl, set it on her tongue, and propped her head on her fist.

"What troubles ye, Lizzy? Do ye fret over the state of affairs in England?"

"Mayhap a little." 'Twas true she still didn't know what became of Lord Hollister and Buckingham, not to mention the princes who were now residing in the Tower. She had hoped Father would at least send a missive to let her know he was well.

"The whole clan is fretting over ye."

"'Tis naught."

"'Tis something to have ye over here and your husband over there."

Lizzy wished to tell someone of her woes. Celeste had been a good friend to her, but the woman had difficulty curbing her tongue.

"Some of the womenfolk worry ye might be having trouble in the bedchamber."

"Nay. 'Tis not that at all," Lizzy answered quickly. Broc would put her over his knee if he knew his virility was being discussed.

"Then what is it?"

Truth was, Lizzy wanted to know if she behaved foolishly. "When did you know John was in love with you?"

Celeste searched the ceiling with her lips pulled to the side. "I s'pose when he told me." Her brows stitched together. "Are ye thinking your husband does not love ye?"

"Of course he loves me," Lizzy defended and searched over both shoulders to see if anyone overheard them.

One fist went to Celeste's thick hips as her eyes rounded, and her head craned forward. "Damned mule-faced Scotsman hasn't said the words, has he?"

Lizzy shook her head and filled her mouth with one pansy after another so she wouldn't have to converse. Her protective friend glared at Broc and huffed, as if it were her sworn duty to see the matter settled.

Curse it! Why had she shared such foolishness? She panicked, swallowed, and then took a drink of watered wine. "Oh, Celeste, you mustn't say anything. Please, 'tis a personal matter. He is the chieftain. He would be humiliated. I know he loves me. He does not have to say it."

While Celeste might have agreed to hold her tongue with a slow nod, 'twas doubtful the woman wouldn't make some attempt to intervene. "I want to help. Wait here whilst I run to the cottage. I will be back a ten."

Before Lizzy could give her leave, Celeste had her skirts in her fists and was running out of the keep. If only she could help. Though mildly curious about Celeste's intentions, Lizzy dismissed any foolish notions she might have momentarily entertained. How was Celeste supposed to make Broc love her?

Before Lizzy finished the first helping of pansies, Lucy appeared with two more bowls. Lizzy plastered a smile over her brooding frown and rubbed the pinch in her jaw below her ear. "Tell your Grandmum Rae I will be seeking out her recipe."

"Aye, m'lady. I will tell her on the morrow. She has retired for the eve." Lucy joined the others in a circle dance around Lady Juliana. While the woman who once held Broc's eye possessed unequivocal beauty, Lizzy recognized Lady Juliana's timidity. With hands clasped against a rose skirt, her pale yellow curls fell over her bowed head hiding gemstone eyes that studied her surroundings. Muira would eat the girl at the noontide meal if she didn't lengthen her backbone.

Lady Juliana's gaze traveled the length of the Great Hall and met Lizzy's. Of course they'd been introduced, but Ian spoke for his new bride. Now recollecting, Lizzy realized the girl hadn't said anything this day save for her wedding vows. Lizzy's smile brought Lady Juliana's chin up.

Muira waved Lizzy in. "Come dance with your new sister, Lady Maxwell."

Sister. "Sister," Lizzy said, wanting to hear the word aloud. Warmth swelled around her heart. Bubbling emotions made her want to laugh. Lizzy resolved to guard Lady Juliana until she found a voice strong enough to protect her from the Maxwell womenfolk.

Needing an excuse to wait for Celeste, Lizzy popped two flowers in her mouth and pointed at the bowls in front of her. "I'll be about shortly."

"No rush. Eat all ye want." Broc's mother appeared wistful, as did Grandmum. They smiled the same as Broc did when he was up to mischief. No doubt the whisky made them that way. Ian swooped in and plucked his new bride off her toes, drawing the attention back to the dance and off Lizzy.

She swished a sip of wine around her teeth to lessen the celebration going on inside her mouth and fanned her warm cheeks. An intense zing spiraled through her insides. She didn't have to look at her husband to feel his eyes caress her. Laird Scott carried on, but Broc no longer paid him any heed. Instead, he matched her stare from the corner of his eye, stalking her like the powerful buck he was.

But she was a skittish doe no more. Just once, she wanted to see her husband lose his control. Mayhap then the words would slip out. *And mayhap the reason he has not said the words is that he does not love you.* Lizzy shushed the internal voice she knew belonged to Lady Ives.

"Here. 'Twas my mum's." Celeste appeared at her side, panting with a small square bundle tied with a red ribbon. "Put it on and make him beg. He will say the words."

"Put it on?" Lizzy looked at the package wrapped in black velvet. "'Tis a garment inside?"

Thick cheeks rounded with Celeste's meddlesome grin. She

shrugged with feigned innocence and eyed the pansies. "May I take a bowl to John? He is waiting for me at the cottage."

"Aye. Do take care with the man. He is in a healing process. I will be about on the morrow." Lizzy's words grew in volume as Celeste made a hasty departure. She waved and flew out of the keep like a virgin on her wedding night.

Mesmerized by the small package, Lizzy brushed her finger over the red ribbon holding the material together. *Put it on, aye?* Could she seduce her husband? Would he want to be seduced? She'd certainly thought about it often enough. A blindfold and a feather came to mind. Her toes curled inside silk slippers. A trickle of sweat fell between her breasts. Desire thrummed deep in her womb.

Mercy Mary! She tucked the bundle beneath her arm and grabbed the third bowl of pansies. She inched her way to the edge of the trestle bench and waited for Broc's attention to be pulled elsewhere, then walked briskly toward the north tower.

The race up the stairwell had her holding her chest to ease the sharp pains slicing her lungs. The moment she closed the door to the laird's solar, she laughed out loud. She was light-headed, giddy, aroused to the point she was near mad. Anticipation had her thighs sliding together beneath her skirts. She pulled the ribbon and unwrapped the black velvet cloth, crazed to see what was inside.

Her hand flew to her chest, a tickle between her legs made her twitch. "Oh, Broderick Maxwell, ye are in verra big trouble. Verra, verra, big trouble."

"The Yorkists believe him a fair and able man. Mayhap England's new king will seek peace. What think ye?" Laird Scott asked and tipped a quaff of whisky.

"Gloucester has only recently announced his intention to

claim the throne," Broc answered, eager to free himself from Laird Scott and talk of politics.

"Aye. He will claim it though. The princes have been deemed bastards by Gloucester's tongue. 'Tis rumored he locked his nephews in the Tower."

"Ach. Hearsay." Broc wanted to roll his eyes at the man's naïveté. "They are being safeguarded in the Tower. I doubt they are prisoners. Gloucester is their protector." Broc bit into another pine nut. Why was he defending his enemy?

Mayhap because Lizbeth still continued to do so. Of course, her moods swayed like a sapling in a whirlwind. He popped the last pine nut in his mouth and glanced at the high table only to find the bench vacant. Now blatantly ignoring Laird Scott, he scanned the Great Hall. "If ye would excuse me, I need to find my wife." He swallowed, set the empty bowl on the closest trestle table, and made a hasty escape, leaving Laird Scott in the able hands of his brethren.

Mam stepped into his path and offered him another bowl of pine nuts slathered in syrup. "Have ye tried Radella's newest recipe?"

Ach! He popped his neck on both sides and clasped his hands in front of him. "I've already eaten two bowls." He knew Mam's interest didn't lie with a bowl of pine nuts. Why she chose now to be docile, he didn't know. "I've set a meeting with Laird Scott and his council to discuss—"

Mam stuffed a pine nut in his mouth. "I'm confident whatever ye and Laird Scott have planned will be in the best interests of the clan. Now, mayhap ye should dance with your wife."

Broc chewed, swallowed, and gave his mam a look of distrust. "My wife appears to have retired early."

"Oh?" Mam's lips maintained the innocent O shape as she made a show of searching the high table where Lizbeth had been sitting the better part of the eve.

"Ye are meddling."

Mam brought her hand to her chest and widened hazel

eyes. Her dramatics were so overly done Broc laughed out loud. The women in his clan were wowf, his wife included. If they would say what was on their minds, life would be so much simpler.

Mam pushed up on her toes and kissed his cheek. "Mayhap I am meddling, but I have your best interests at heart, son," she admitted in a soft voice he'd never heard. She set the pine nuts in his hand and then blended into the dance with the other kinsfolk.

Mam had been good to Lizbeth since their return, as had the aunts and all his sisters. His wife was surrounded by people who loved her. Mayhap she missed her own kin. He hoped he might one day fill the void her past left in her heart, but his efforts to make her happy had only failed, and failure was not an option.

Determined to set his wife down and flesh out the mystery behind her dour mood, he set the nuts on a side table and strode out of the Great Hall. He was the chieftain, a fearless warrior, and he refused to live another day walking behind her. If she wouldn't open up to him, then he would demand her honesty.

As he climbed the stairs to his solar, his skin began to tingle as it had the first time he met Lizbeth. Her exotic scent lingered in the corridor, reminding him of their first encounter in the tunnel. His memories spiked his senses. Gooseflesh raised on his scalp. Excess saliva pooled in his mouth. His pulse echoed through his veins and sent blood rushing into the head of his cock. He stopped outside the solar and rested his forehead against the cool wood.

God's hooks! He did not possess the wit for conversation. He closed his eyes and initiated the calming technique Brother Mel had taught him, but all he could see were Lizbeth's gold eyes looking back at him. *Talk to me. Tell me what pains ye.*

He opened the door . . . and whimpered. Any comment he might have prepared upon his entry was lost to him.

Lizbeth stood in the moonlight in what could only be described as a robe of gold ribbons. The remnants of braids spiraled in dark red curls down her back and pointed to her heart-shaped backside seductively hidden behind a veil of gold dust.

She turned.

He backed beneath the archway and crossed himself. *Oh, God* repeated in his head three times until he could form words. "Where did ye get that?"

"A friend." She drew the back of her nail over the hem following the curve of her breast. Her nipples shadowed the silk of a short gold undergarment falling just below her hips, and it swished when she took a step toward him.

He swallowed repeatedly and cupped his groin. *Devil take her! You are the chieftain. You are a warrior. You are a lusty Scotsman. Act like it!* he scolded himself mentally, yet took another step backward.

"Come back inside, husband, and close the door."

His wee wife was trying to be bold, but the quiver in her chin gave away her angst. Broc drew air into his lungs and reentered his solar.

She walked around him trailing two fingers across his chest, his shoulder, his back until she completed her circle. Her robe billowed like shimmering smoke, making her look like an angel, a queen . . . a goddess.

"Disrobe," she demanded.

He blinked and only then did he see the dirk in her hand. In his mind's eye he saw himself following her orders, but he couldn't move, couldn't speak. He held his breath and had no idea how long he'd been doing so.

She pressed her blade into the dip of his neck. While her hand trembled, her voice did not. "Obey."

He didn't recognize her tone. "Is Edlynn in your head?"

"Nay. I am in complete control of my senses."

He, however, was not. He set his broadsword and dirk on the trestle table, then removed the leather belt around his waist and pulled the pin fastening his *plaid* around his shoulder. With one tug, he divested himself of his ensemble, never once taking his eyes from her.

She looked him up and down, caressing him with her gaze. "Remove your boots and kneel before me."

He didn't know who this woman was, but she was wowf. He tilted his head. "I kneel before my God and my king."

"And your wife." Her nostrils flared, her eyes blazed, and all traces of anxiety fled her.

"What are your intentions, wife?"

"I intend to teach you how to make me happy."

That he wanted. He would demean himself, if need be, to learn this secret. He did as she asked and got to his knees on a carpet at the foot of the bed. His aching cock stood away from his body and gave a little jerk when she stepped over his legs behind him. When the hem of her gown brushed the backs of his calves, his eyes rolled upward. He felt the press of her breasts against his back as she bent over him. The pendant he'd given her felt like ice against his hot skin.

She pulled his chin toward her. "There are six places a woman wants to be touched."

"I trust I've touched all of them," he jested, but his Lizbeth was in no laughing mood.

"All of them, but one," she whispered; then her teeth found his earlobe and tugged a little before she released his chin.

"Tell me where the last is, and I will touch this mysterious place," he demanded, though his tone was not sharp.

She crawled out from behind him, leaving a trail of silk over his backside. "I cannot do this. You must discover this place on your own." She drew a line with the tip of her blade from his jaw, over the knot in his throat, and down to his navel.

He swallowed. Untrusting of her weaponry skills, he held

his cock with both hands, protecting it from the game she played with her dirk. "Think ye it might be simpler if ye just told me?"

"Mayhap. But I'm not going to." She tossed the blade on the bed, not nearly far enough away given her state of mind, and set a bowl of honey flowers atop a cuttie stool beside them. She placed a purple and yellow petal over a small blue vein on the inside of her wrist and held it to his mouth. "A woman wants to be touched in all the places her pulse beats."

He studied her expression and searched for a hint of playfulness, but this was no game to her. Broc licked the petal from her wrist and recognized the same tangy syrup that had coated the pine nuts.

She pulled his hand from his cock and placed a petal on his wrist as well, then mimicked his action. "I have put my life in your hands, and I trust you to always protect my body and soul." She uncurled his fist to kiss his palm.

She was trying to tell him something, he suspected. He focused, determined to not let his craving for her hinder his wit.

"When you look at me, my heart beats in my neck, and I hear it inside my ears." She gathered her hair to one side and stuck a petal to her neck.

Reaching up, he wove his fingers through her tresses and pulled her closer. His eyes closed in an attempt to control himself while he suckled the petal from her velvety skin. His nose brushed over her neck, inhaling her essence. Did she want more?

She pressed a cool petal beneath his ear, then held his nape as she kissed the petal away. She placed tiny kisses along his jawline and then blew in the whorl of his ear. "You are my champion. You are my king of kings, my savior, my husband."

Why hadn't he said something like that? Something meaningful, creative? Before he could contrive sweet words for her, she set a petal on his lip.

"Of course, a woman wants to be kissed. Sometimes gently . . ." She suckled his bottom lip and slid the tip of her tongue between the seams of his lips. ". . . and sometimes hard." She slanted his head, then kissed him with a passion he felt in his heart. A passion he would never find with another.

Pulling back, she set a petal on her own lips and waited.

He mimicked her kiss and the taste of her drugged him. The cool silk of her gown beneath his hands did little to temper the fever engulfing his body. He fought the burning of his arousal, certain he would die from the physical pain of it. His calves hardened, as did his cullions. "I cannae bear this."

"You must." She removed her robe, which left her in the tiny gown. With a languor that made him whimper, she pushed the straps from her shoulders and exposed her breasts. After setting a petal atop each nipple, she held his head between her hands and forced him to look up at her. "When I'm in your presence, I feel desirable. You do not even have to touch me for my breasts to ache."

A tiny burst of his seed spilled out of his erection when she guided his head to one breast. How could he think under such duress? His hands slipped beneath her miniature gown and cupped the backs of her thighs as he drew on her nipple. She cried out and quickly set him on her other breast, but not nearly long enough for him to feast. She pulled him off her with a breathy grunt. Her knees rubbed together, and he could smell the musky scent of arousal wafting out from beneath her skirt.

This was madness. She was torturing both of them. "I need ye."

"Not yet—" Her words caught. She cleared her throat, returned her straps to her shoulders, and knelt in front of him. She then placed the petals on his flat nipples and drew the flowers inside her mouth along with his nipples. She bit one, then the other, and tickled his stomach below his navel, sending a bolt of white-hot rapture through his body.

He would never make it inside her. "Oh God, Lizbeth. What number are we on?"

"Four," she squeaked and rose back up on her feet. "We are nearly there. I vow it. Howbeit, number five will undoubtedly be a test for both of us. Think of shearing sheep or some such." She wiped her forehead with the back of her hand, held her bottom lip between her teeth, and retrieved another petal.

He wanted to laugh aloud and tell her she was wowf, but he would not insult her. He was certain he should be learning something, but she'd robbed him of reasoning. He snapped his head side to side, gaining six cracks total, preparing for the next lesson.

Feet braced slightly wider than before, her hand disappeared beneath her skirt for a brief moment before she raised the silk, showing him her glistening curls. "A woman wants to be tasted . . ."

Eager to oblige, he wrapped his fingers around her hips and spread her swollen lips with his thumbs, then leaned forward and feathered his tongue over her loins. He found the flower the same time he located the spot he knew would send her screaming.

Her hands shook, causing her garment to ripple. "Oh, Broc." She jerked. Her knees bent and snapped back. A flutter tickled his tongue the same time she yanked him back by his hair.

Again she knelt in front of him. The dots in her eyes grew, pushing her irises into gold rings. ". . . and she wants to taste in return."

She placed a petal on the head of his cock and stared at it. He held his breath. When she flattened her hands beside his knees, he was certain he would either explode or be rendered unconscious. He grabbed a fistful of her hair and shook his head, knowing what she intended to do. No woman had ever pleasured him with her mouth. "Nay. I can no longer control it."

Fighting the vise he held on her hair, she angled her face up to him. "I've yet to see you lose control, husband. You are a warrior. The prime of your clan." Dragging his hand down with her, she lapped up the flower and then dipped the tip of her tongue into his tiny hole, swirling, teasing, tormenting him until she wrapped her lips around his cock and sucked.

"Ach!" He opened his mouth so he could breathe and distanced his mind from the scene before him. He thought of Brother Mel, of battle, of anything to keep himself from spilling his seed inside her delicate mouth. Her breasts bobbed against his thighs. The movement caused the gold silk of her gown to inch away from the creamy curves of her backside. What the devil was he supposed to be learning from this?

The muscles in his arms burned as he fought the desire to control her downward thrusts. He felt the scrape of her teeth, the twirl of her tongue. When the tip touched the back of her throat, a growl vibrated through his gullet as fire crawled through his erection. He grasped her hair and ripped her off him. "Tell me where to touch ye."

She stood, straddled his thighs, and placed her trembling hands on his shoulders. He steadied her around the waist as she lowered herself overtop him until her eyes met his. Only then did he see her sorrow, her yearning.

Her arms curled around his neck. "'Tis not a place ye can touch with your hands."

"I dinnae understand."

"I want ye to touch my heart," she whispered against his cheek and filled her womb with his manhood. She moved in one long draw up and down the length of him and cried out.

He couldn't take it. Pearls of sweat dripped down his temple. The muscles in his thighs cramped. "God's hooks!"

he bellowed, settled back on his heels, and wrapped his arms around her, stilling her movements. His release whipped through his body like an inferno in an ice storm.

He came instantly, as did she, again and again.

Long moments passed before the intensity subsided. Still, he cherished the feel of being one with her. Though confident he'd satisfied her physically, he knew he failed her test. He kissed her hair and held her trembling body against him. There was no doubt he would die for this woman in this life and the next, but he still struggled with the right words that would bring the smile back to her face. "Lizzy, angel, I love ye, but I have no idea how to touch your heart."

Trembles turned to tremors as she cried against his shoulder and hugged him tighter. "You just did."

He stared at nothingness, picking over his words. How could she have doubted his love for her? He pulled her head out of the crook of his neck and held her chin between his thumb and finger. Pure bliss shone bright in her damp eyes. He stroked one gold wing on the pendant he gave her. "Ye are my angel. The guardian of my heart. Ye know I love you."

"I do. I just needed to hear you say it."

His breath of relief ruffled her hair. "Then I will say it every day." He could spend a hundred lifetimes kissing her smile. He pressed a gentle kiss to her cheek, her nose, her fluttering wet lashes. "I love ye, Lady Lizbeth Maxwell, now and forever."

Her fingers slid into the hair at his nape. "I love you, too." She pulled him into her mouth and kissed him slowly, binding their souls together for eternity. Salty tears and sweet sauce from the petals made an elixir in her mouth that could never be imitated; her unique scent would never be duplicated. Even if he died tomorrow, he would never be this close to Heaven. In her embrace, he was transported into a world built only for them—a divine providence, Eden's garden. He pulled back . . .

"Paradise . . ." they said in unison.

Her smile parted, and he felt a shiver sweep through her. She twitched and rotated her hips beneath his grasp. Pink flushed through her cheeks as her eyelids slid shut. "I know 'tis too soon, but I fear I need you again." She chewed on the side of her lip and mewed.

"Ach, ye are a lusty woman," he teased and pressed his fingers into her soft backside. Even as he doubted his own virility, he felt himself growing inside her. The blood inflated him to a pulsating heat that filled her hollows.

Her eyes snapped open. "Can you do it again so quickly?"

He never had. His skin prickled, turning each hair follicle into a sensitive pulse point, the same as it had before he'd entered the chamber, the same as it had when he'd been in the tunnel. Something's amiss. Bewildered, he glanced at the bowl beside his leg. "Where did ye get the flower petals?"

"Aunt Radella made them. Why?" She rocked her hips, slicking her damp breasts over his chest.

"I think mayhap we have been poisoned."

She swiped a fingerful of sweet sauce and stuck it between her lips. Her gaze drew up to the ceiling as she studied the taste. "Saffron. Aunt Radella added saffron to the honey. 'Tis a passion flower, used to stimulate the senses."

"Damned meddling women! Oh, they will be punished. I'm going to hang them up by their toes. All of them. As if I needed a poison to battle this nigh, too."

Her giggle turned into a purr as she shifted her hips and began the slow lunges again. "'Tis not a poison, but a product of mercy."

He felt the raw stamina of desire ignite, but the urgency was gone, allowing him to frolic in the sensual feel of her. "I have no intention of being merciful, m'lady."

"Nor do I, Lord Maxwell. Nor do I." She swiveled her hips in a circular motion, adding her own spice of creativity to this ancient dance.

He held her arms above her head and watched her perform atop him. Now that he knew the secret to her smile, he had every intention of keeping her lips curved upright. "Ye are indeed one of God's finest creations." He trailed a finger around the swell of her breast. "Ye should be draped in the finest silks and decorated with gemstones. Mayhap I'll commission one of the great Italian artists to capture your beauty. I intend to spoil ye and give ye anything your heart desires."

"I have only one desire. 'Tis you."

Epilogue

Hesitant to even shift her weight, Lizzy stood firmly in place on the third step and narrowed one eye on her husband. "I do not like you at the moment."

"Come now, angel. Ye've been in water to your waist for the past fortnight. 'Tis time you take the last step," Broc pleaded from across the large stone bath. Of course, it helped that he was naked. Fire glowed from three hearths and glistened off his wet skin. He looked tastier than a slice of blaeberry pie.

That thought made her stomach growl, as she'd missed the midmorning meal. She crossed her arms. "I have no idea why you and your kinsmen built this bathhouse."

"My brethren agreed the women would like it."

"Then let them enjoy it. 'Tis selfish for us to horde such a luxury."

"Not til ye go under."

She humphed. Stubborn mule. She scooped a handful of tepid water into her palm, then poured it down the front of her tunic. The bathhouse was hotter than Hades. Bursts of snowflakes floated in through the tiny windows up high, but vanished into the heat of the room.

His determination to eliminate her fear of water had been the ultimate test of her love for him. She wanted to find the courage to step down and make him proud, but there was still the slightest hesitation. He couldn't possibly know how difficult this was for her. "If I take the step, what would you reward me with this day?"

He considered his answer while he leisurely pushed water back and forth around his waist. "I'll have Aunt Radella fix ye some raspberries and whipped milk poured over a sweet bannock."

Tempting. She'd been craving that dish since the Sabbath. "Have you anything new, Scotsman?"

Broc splayed his arms wide and beamed his most devilish grin. "I'll let ye have your way with me."

Tempting, again. She laughed at him. She always laughed at him. He made her smile with his wit and his crooked grins. "I've already had my way with you this day."

He clasped his hands behind his neck and flexed the bulging muscles in his arms and chest, purposely making a show of his physique. "What woman wouldnae want this twice in one day?" He gave her a sidelong glance, no doubt testing the effects of his offer. "I'll let ye use the feather."

Giggling, she shook her head and splashed him. "You'll not use the feather to bargain. 'Tis my toy and I will use it whenever I like."

"Ach! What then?"

"Will you let me go visit Grandmum?"

"Nay." He frowned and dropped his arms back into the water with a plop. "Ye know I cannae let ye leave the stronghold. Ye are carrying my son."

"Or mayhap your daughter." Her toe tapped beneath the water.

"'Tis not safe yet. 'Twas only August that King James sent your Gloucester a proposal for peace."

"He is not *my* Gloucester. He is England's new king, and he will see the right in signing this peace treaty your James has offered."

"And when he does, I will take ye to see Grandmum."

Lizzy had tried repeatedly to get Grandmum to accept Broc's offer to move back to the keep, but she was a stubborn old woman who liked her peace.

Broc dove beneath the water and resurfaced in front of her. "'Tis one step, Lizzy. Trust me to protect you." He extended his hand.

She inhaled deeply, grumbled, and focused all her energies on her footing. *Do it. Take the step.*

Curse it! Her stomach became aflutter with nerves. She took his hand for support, knowing he wouldn't pull her in. Her gaze lowered. Long moments passed in silence while she stared at her toes. *Take the step. This day. Now.*

The rough stone slid beneath her foot.

Her knee bent.

She took the step. Her feet flattened on the bottom as water rose to her breast. She sucked in air, but her vision remained clear, as did her senses. Worry lines etched Broc's face. "Are you breathing?" she asked, concerned about the red tinting his bronze skin.

He shook his head.

"Breathe and get me."

Without hesitation, he pulled her into his protective arms and filled his lungs with an audible gasp. "I'm proud of ye, Lizzy."

In truth, she was proud of herself, but going under would have to wait another day. "Do not let go."

"Never." He kissed her hair and curved his hand over the bump in her belly. "Mayhap someday we will get ye into the loch to swim with our children."

"Mayhap." She wrapped her arms and legs around him and kissed him. Naught seemed impossible anymore. As long as she was with him, in his embrace, feeling his love, the world belonged to her.

A tap came at the door, followed by a click. "M'lord, may I enter?"

"Nay!" she shrieked and tightened her thighs around Broc's waist. She was practically naked. While everyone in the clan respected their privacy, Smitt was a lecher.

"'Tis important," Smitt said and opened the door a little wider.

Broc turned his back to the doorway, hiding her, and craned his neck over his shoulder. "What is it?"

Smitt's head popped through the cracked doorway. "John and Ian came across an Englishmon riding on Maxwell soil."

"A messenger?"

"I know not for certain. He claims he was invited and is demanding entry. He is detained in the gatehouse. Ian sent a squire to retrieve ye."

"Give us a moment," Broc said and waited for the door to click.

Lizzy held tight as he carried her from the water, his brows pinched slightly and a grim line tightening his lips. He had immense responsibilities that weighed heavily on his mind daily. "Do not fret, husband. 'Tis only one man."

He nodded as he helped her into a heavy robe, then vested himself in the *plaid*. He laced his boots and sheathed the sword that was never far from his person at his hip.

When the rustle of clothes settled, Smitt poked his head in again. "Did she go under? Can the rest of us use the bath-house yet?"

Lizzy shot him a warning glare. "You are not going anywhere near my bath until the little beasties have moved out of your forest. Are you using the medicine I gave you?"

"Aye, m'lady." Smitt frowned like a scolded boy and

redirected his attention toward Broc. "Want me to kill the Englishmon?"

"Nay. I will tend to the matter. Go to the kitchens and have Aunt Radella prepare our guest a warm meal and fetch a flask of your da's whisky."

Smitt dipped his head and exited.

Broc raised her hand to his lips and kissed her palm. "Go dress in something suitable to your station and meet us in the Great Hall."

"Why?" she questioned as unease sent her fretting.

"I invited only one Englishman onto my soil. In truth, I dinnae think he would come."

"Who?"

"Your father."

Four, five, six. Cease! You are no longer that person. Lizzy chided herself for her nervousness.

She released the tails of her sleeves and smoothed her garnet-colored skirt, determined not to fidget. Instead, she paced in front of the crackling hearth of the Great Hall and rubbed the gemstones encrusted in the pendant hanging around her neck. She was wife to the chieftain. She carried the heir who would lead Clan Maxwell. Lady Ives was dead and gone. So why was she counting?

Father was her only kin. She didn't know if she feared him, his curse, or the news he might bring with him from the Tower. To her knowledge, he'd never once left London. She was hard-pressed to believe he'd traveled all this way in such treacherous weather to pay visit.

Completely lost in her worries, she stared at the fire, unblinking.

"Lizzy."

She spun around, her heart beating out of cadence, and looked at her father. A heavy fur speckled white with flurries made him look even bigger than she remembered him. His hands balled at his sides, one fist larger than the other, and his red nose shone above a full dark beard crusted with white chunks of snow.

Father never wore a beard. Her head tilted as she studied him. He looked cold, but his amber eyes were warm, glassy . . . sane. The silence became unnerving as he waited for her greeting.

Broc leaned a little to the side behind her father and mouthed the words, "Say something."

"You look cold."

"'Tis cold in Scotland." Father nodded once and mayhap even smiled behind his beard. His eyes lowered. "You look well."

Her hands immediately went to protect her unborn child. "We are." Her chin rose and she curled her hair behind her ear. "Lord Maxwell's aunt is forever fattening me. She warmed mutton mawmenny boiled in red wine for you." She gestured toward a trestle table where a trencher piled high with food sat alongside a goblet of wine and a flask of whisky. "'Tis sprinkled with almonds. You like almonds, do you not?"

"I do." Father didn't move, nor did he take his gaze from her. "Your husband most graciously invited me, but I will not stay if I distress you in any way. I only wanted to bring you news."

"Could you not have sent a missive?" she blurted out, wishing she could quit staring at him. He was the man she remembered from her childhood. The father who carved things and held Mother's hand when she was dying. He was not the executioner this day, but a man who looked as frightened as she to speak. A knot swelled in her throat.

"I wanted to see you." Father's hand flexed around the object he held.

A too familiar pang erupted in her chest. She swallowed

and blinked the tear from her eye. "Please, warm yourself and eat," she said, her voice soft, but not afraid.

Father raised bushy brows and turned his head slightly, giving her his better ear.

Broc slipped out from behind Father and into his vision. "She said, 'Warm yourself and eat.'" Her husband splayed a hand toward the hearth.

Father nodded finally, removed his fur, and shuffled through the floor rushes to her side. He held his hands to the fire's warmth, the one still fisted now piquing her curiosity. Father was never a man of many words, nor was she. Of course, a hundred questions whirled through her mind, but not one formed on her tongue. Instead, the two of them stood arm to arm in silence.

Heat melted the snow in Father's beard before Broc finally pulled up behind her and wrapped his arm around her waist. She held on to his hand and blew air so forcefully the flame tips ruffled. He would save her from this awkward silence with his chatter.

"While my wife forms her words, mayhap ye can tell me how Gloucester is faring?"

"King Richard is causing quite a stir along the countryside. He finally had Buckingham executed in Wiltshire a fortnight ago."

The skin around her eyes stretched wide. "You jest."

"I do not jest, child."

Broc kissed her hair and squeezed her, giving her strength to ask the question that had her most troubled. "And what of Lord Hollister?"

"I arranged to have him moved to Newgate Prison to await a trial. I confess I held on to your document longer than I should have, but I wanted Hollister to agonize over his fate. I gave him time to remember all those he'd condemned without a trial, and then I assured him I would show him no mercy." Father's hands fell to his sides, and he looked up at the broadsword hanging over the hearth. "Even after I gave King Richard the document, he wanted a full confession. I was most willing to provide it."

Father's pause lasted longer than her patience. "Lord Hollister confessed to poisoning King Edward?"

"Nay, but he confessed to being involved in a conspiracy to expose the princes' illegitimacy. He was quick to name Buckingham as the leader of the rebellion." Father turned slowly toward her. "King Richard sentenced Hollister to a private execution, and I hope the bastard is carrying his head in Hell as we speak."

Lizzy lessened the grip she held on Broc's hand and stared at the tiny arcs her fingernails left behind in his skin. She inhaled deeply and freed the last bit of fear Lord Hollister would ever hold over her. "'Tis done then."

"'Tis done." Father raised his hand to her cheek and caught the tear she didn't even know was there.

She wanted Father here with her at Skonóir Castle. She wanted to see him at peace, but Muira would have difficulties with such an arrangement. Regardless of how badly beaten Broc's brother had been when he'd entered the Tower, the truth was Father delivered the final lashes that took Aiden's life.

"If ye've naught pressing, Lord Ives, mayhap ye could spend Christmastide with us," Broc suggested and then leaned low to her ear. "He is your father, and ye have the right to see him. I will help Mam see the right of it," he whispered as if reading her thoughts. "All will be well, Lizzy angel."

All *would* be well, and for the first time she actually believed him. She near turned in his arms to hug him; instead, she looked up and mouthed, "Thank you."

"I s'pose I can return to Lincolnshire after the season."

"Lincolnshire?" she asked.

"Aye. My loyalty to England has brought me recent rewards. The sheriff of Lincolnshire offered me a position as constable." An odd look she'd never seen before lifted the hair above his lip. Pride.

"Will your services no longer be needed in the Tower?"

"King Richard will undoubtedly need a henchman, but 'twill not be I. He has only begun what I suspect will be a long and bloody battle to protect his position on the throne. There are nobles awaiting trial in the Tower even now."

"Including the princes," Broc stated matter-of-factly. "Mayhap ye could settle a dispute between my wife and I. 'Tis rumored your noble king had his nephews murdered in the Tower."

"'Tis hearsay, and you well know it." She scowled up at Broc for even broaching the subject. "Gloucester was sworn to protect his nephews."

"Protect them, aye. 'Tis why he declared the princes bastards to parliament and claimed the throne for himself," Broc pointed out, as he'd done repeatedly over the past months.

"Things are not always as they seem." Father cocked a brow and drew his beard into a point. "Rumors can evolve out of the simplest interpretation."

"Can you explain?" she asked in a tone that demanded more information.

"As a servant to King Richard, I am not at liberty to discuss the happenings within the Tower walls. I can, howbeit, tell you that a maidservant stumbled upon Madoc and I whilst we collected Eli and Martin's bodies for burial. 'Twasn't long before the minstrels started singing woeful tunes about tragic death throughout the streets of London."

Glad to be the victor over their quarrel, she swiveled and looked up at Broc. "'Tis hearsay. The makings of one woman's imaginative mind."

"Then ye have seen the princes in the Tower?" Broc asked Father, obviously still not willing to dispel the rumors.

"The last two boys I saw in the Tower were ghosts. I am sworn to secrecy to say anything further."

"Ghosts?" Broc questioned, and she was prepared to stomp his toe should he mock her father.

"Aye." Father inhaled and stared at his fisted hand. "I am a deeply disturbed man haunted by so very many souls."

'Tis to be expected, she thought, but kept her comment silent.

"Do you know why I carve the birds?"

Lizzy thought Father's question odd and out of context, but she would listen to him. "I suspect to ease your mind."

"'Tis one reason, but also 'twas my way of setting the souls free of those lives I took. Your grandfather planted a tree after every execution to symbolize the life after. I carved two birds for Eli and Martin to see them on their journey, though I fear they have not yet left. I saw them playing behind the Garden Tower just before I departed for Lincolnshire." Father's eyes became distant again.

Broc leaned into her hair. "He is wowf."

Her elbow found his ribs. Fortunately, Father's poor hearing saved him from Broc's insult. Father may not possess all his wits, but she had never seen him so at ease, so calm and free. Nor had he ever spoken so openly about his profession or his grandsons.

"I know I do not deserve your love or your prayers," Father continued. "But I want you to know Lord Hollister was the last." Father opened his fisted hand before her. A carved bird sat in the middle of his palm.

She pushed back into Broc's embrace. "If that is Lord Hollister's soul, I do not want it."

"Nay, Lizzy. This one is mine, and I want you to have it because you set me free."

Emotions surged through her once again and thickened in her mouth. Father fought his demons and broke his curse. She didn't know if her prayers would save him; nonetheless, she would reserve him a place on her rosary. She wrapped her hand around his gift and held it tight against her breast.

"I will protect your soul in this life and the next." She looked up at her husband and found his dimples curved around his smile.

Father released air through his nose and said nothing more.

"Please, eat, Lord Ives." Broc stepped to Lizzy's side and gestured toward the trestle table.

Father sat heavily upon the bench and engulfed the full goblet of wine, then poured himself a quaff of whisky.

Broc spun her around in his arms and kissed her forehead. "'Tis a big duty ye have accepted . . . to protect your father's soul. I trust ye will not falter on the obligation I have entrusted to ye."

Broc toyed with her, but she would play his game. "What obligation might that be?"

"To guard your husband's heart."

She flattened her hand over his chest. "I will guard what is mine with the strength of a thousand warriors."

"Vow it." He gently kissed her lips.

"I vow it upon my soul."

Author's Note

The human mind is not easily swayed against convention.

Form a mental picture of the Lord High Executioner. Who do you see? A man in a black cloak with an ax who mercilessly takes the lives of both the guilty and innocent. While most of us might picture this man as grotesque, he was not a vigilante, but an officer of the court. The executioner was, no doubt, tormented by a profession that might have left him soulless, but it is also possible that he might have been a gentle man who loved his wife and his children.

Though most of the characters in this book are fictitious, some are based on historical figures. While it has been suggested that King Edward IV might have been poisoned, there is no evidence to support this theory, nor is it known who might have committed such a heinous act. As research will show, some historians believe King Edward's brother, the Duke of Gloucester, was a hideous villain who was disfigured, as depicted by William Shakespeare. Then there are those who carefully examine factual documentation to form judgment.

Another mystery that has baffled historians for centuries is the disappearance of the princes in the Tower. It is believed by some that the two young sons of King Edward IV were smothered in their beds in the summer of 1483 in the Garden Tower, now known as the Bloody Tower. Again, no factual evidence proves that these murders ever took place. It is, however, a fact that two skeletons were discovered in the White Tower under the stairs leading to the chapel nearly 200 years later, in 1674.

There are those who believe two boys in white gowns haunt the Bloody Tower. One might form an imaginative judgment that those bones and those spirits belong to King Edward IV's sons, but it is possible that those spirits, if they even exist, belong to two *other* boys. The very walls of the Tower contain secrets that have never been documented and therefore must be questioned.

Who would have given the order for such a crime? The boys' uncle, the Duke of Gloucester? Or the king's cousin, the Duke of Buckingham? Or, did the crime even occur?

It is possible that the Duke of Gloucester, who was loved by those in York, was not an evil demon. Perhaps he was viewed by his people as a king of kings. Is it then possible that the Duke of Gloucester, King Richard III, loved his nephews and saw them to safety for their own protection? And is it possible that the princes grew to be men who found love during an era of violence and treachery?

While historians might discredit this notion as idealistic, a lover of romance might sit back and say, "Mayhap."

Glossary

HISTORIC TERMS

ACONITE: A most formidable poison. It comes from all parts of the plant belonging to the family Ranunculaceae, but especially the root. The smallest portion of either root or leaves when first put into the mouth occasions burning and tingling, and a sense of numbness immediately follows its continuance. Also referred to as monkshood or wolfsbane.

CUTTIE STOOL: A type of three-legged chair used in Scotland. It was a short stool, often having a round seat on the top, but the term also designates a larger piece of furniture associated with public penance in church.

KNOUT: A wooden-handled whip with braided thongs used to whip a prisoner. Whipping was recognized as a death penalty, with the executioner skilled at dislocating the victim's neck.

MAWMENNY: A dish composed of meat, usually ground chicken or capon, in a spiced sauce.

PEINE FORTE ET DURE: Pressing to death. A form of torture delivered upon a cell floor and used on a prisoner who refused to plead. A board was placed across the prisoner's chest and stomach and heavy iron weights were added to the board until submission or death. For 366 years pressing to death was a standard punishment in England until 1772.

PLAID: A crossbarred or checkered cloth associated with Celtic countries, especially Scotland, and often worn as a garment.

SGIAN DUBH: A Scottish knife that is worn on the calf of the leg (tucked into the sock). The name comes from the Gaelic meaning "black knife," where "black" may refer to the usual color of the handle of the knife. It is also suggested that "black" means secret, or hidden, as in the word *blackmail*.

EXPLETIVES AND SLANG

AH CHAC: Oh, shit!

BACK A TEN: Back in ten minutes

BAW HAIR: Hair's breadth

BLOOTERED: Drunk

CULLIONS: Testicles

DRAB: A woman of low character or a prostitute

DRABBER: Someone who spends too much time with drabs

GOD'S HOOKS: Derived from the hooks (or nails) used to fasten Christ to the cross. Later evolved into "Gadzooks." Many of these "God's" expressions were reduced to "'od's" or "odds," as in "'ods toes."

MO CHREACH: Literally "My ruin!"; equal to "Goddamnit!"

NOCK: Vagina

PILLICOCK: Penis

TEWEL: Anus

TUPPING: To have sexual relations

TWANGER: Penis

WOWF: Insane, crazy, mentally ill or deranged

Discover the Romances of
Hannah Howell

My Valiant Knight	0-8217-5186-7	**$5.50**US/**$7.00**CAN
Only for You	0-8217-5943-4	**$5.99**US/**$7.50**CAN
A Taste of Fire	0-8217-7133-7	**$5.99**US/**$7.50**CAN
A Stockingful of Joy	0-8217-6754-2	**$5.99**US/**$7.50**CAN
Highland Destiny	0-8217-5921-3	**$5.99**US/**$7.50**CAN
Highland Honor	0-8217-6095-5	**$5.99**US/**$7.50**CAN
Highland Promise	0-8217-6254-0	**$5.99**US/**$7.50**CAN
Highland Vow	0-8217-6614-7	**$5.99**US/**$7.50**CAN
Highland Knight	0-8217-6817-4	**$5.99**US/**$7.50**CAN
Highland Hearts	0-8217-6925-1	**$5.99**US/**$7.50**CAN
Highland Bride	0-8217-7397-6	**$6.50**US/**$8.99**CAN
Highland Angel	0-8217-7426-3	**$6.50**US/**$8.99**CAN
Highland Groom	0-8217-7427-1	**$6.50**US/**$8.99**CAN
Highland Warrior	0-8217-7428-X	**$6.50**US/**$8.99**CAN
Reckless	0-8217-6917-0	**$6.50**US/**$8.99**CAN

Available Wherever Books Are Sold!

Visit our website at **www.kensingtonbooks.com**

More Historical Romance From
Jo Ann Ferguson